TWO

Vivien Kelly was born in York. Her first novel, *Take One Young Man*, was published by Arrow in 2000 to wide acclaim and won a Betty Trask award.

Acclaim for Vivien Kelly:

'Spectacularly sensitive and accomplished . . . we need more stuff like this!' Lisa Jewell

'Kelly adeptly draws the reader into Sam's world which is populated by engaging figures, realistic in their struggles and ambitions . . . written with panache and subtlety'
The Times

'An incredibly ambitious and assured first novel . . . Quite an achievement' Esther Freud

'Clever, witty and well written' *Express*

'This novel is so brilliant that it's hard to believe the author is only 25. Moving and hilariously funny'
Woman's Own

Also by Vivien Kelly

Take One Young Man

TWO RED SHOES

Vivien Kelly

ARROW

Published by Arrow Books in 2002

1 3 5 7 9 10 8 6 4 2

First published in the United Kingdom in 2002 by Century

Arrow Books
20 Vauxhall Bridge Road, London, SW1V 2SA

Random House Australia (Pty) Limited
20 Alfred Street, Milsons Point, Sydney,
New South Wales 2061, Australia

Random House New Zealand Limited
18 Poland Road, Glenfield
Auckland 10, New Zealand

Random House (Pty) Limited
Endulini, 5a Jubilee Road, Parktown 2193, South Africa

The Random House Group Limited Reg. No. 954009

A CIP catalogue record for this book
is available from the British Library

Papers used by Random House UK Limited
are natural, recyclable products made from wood grown in
sustainable forests. The manufacturing processes conform to
the environmental regulations of the country of origin

ISBN 0 09 940985 2

Typeset by SX Composing DTP, Rayleigh, Essex
Printed and bound in Great Britain by
Bookmarque Ltd, Croydon, Surrey

ACKNOWLEDGEMENTS

With thanks to Patrick Walsh and to Kate Elton

The poem 'Don't Wed' by Taras Shevchenko was translated by John Weir. It is reproduced courtesy of the Taras Shevchenko Museum of Canada from: www.infoukes.com/shevchenkomuseum/

ONE

When Kalyna Beimuk married Ray Stevenson on the fourth of October 1976 she hoped she was committing bigamy. They walked together down Godwin Street, towards Bradford City Hall, and the wind blew in from Huddersfield, chafing Kalyna's cheeks so that by the time she stood before the registrar she looked quite the blushing bride. She had borrowed a blue suit for the event, with mother of pearl buttons which slipped too easily from their holes and made her glance down every so often to check that her jacket was not gaping open. Her shoes too were borrowed, brown suede affairs which gave her an extra inch in height and blisters on the backs of her heels. She had tied her hair back for her wedding into a thick brown bun which nestled against her neck, tilting slightly whenever she dropped her eyes to check her jacket.

Kalyna saw her marriage to Ray as the beginning of a new life for her and her son. As she stumbled her way through the unfamiliar words of the ceremony she told herself over and over again that she was doing the right thing. When the time came for her to sign her name in the large book she could not help but think of Stefan, her first husband. Her hand trembled and her throat tightened. Once she had signed she laid the fountain pen down as quickly as she could and looked over her shoulder to glance at her six-year-old son.

Kalyna had wide, load-bearing hips and broad shoulders. She found her hips useful – they were an ideal place to rest her hands or an overflowing bag of shopping. Whenever she picked up Nicholas that was where she held him: just above one hip, his legs dangling by her thighs, his arms tight and grasping round her neck, his mouth just by hers. Her breasts were large and their drooping curves mirrored the plumpness of her cheeks and the roundness of her eyes. Her breasts, as a teenager, had irritated her because they were too large and purposeless; now, at thirty-one, she had finally got used to them. She was an attractive woman: she cared less about the size of her thighs and more about what she could do and what she knew. She had straight, dark hair and simplicity in her features. A gap between her front teeth and a firm attentiveness in her eyes snared many admirers.

Kalyna forgot to kiss Ray once the ceremony was over. She turned on the spot and bent down in the direction of her son, holding out her arms and tossing her head briefly backwards as a smile parted her lips. Nicholas was shy. The shirt in which Kalyna had dressed him itched him around his neck and wrists, the women who stood beside him fussed over and poked at him. He did not understand what was happening, why they had all dressed up smartly to come to a small, stuffy room on a cold afternoon where his mother and a man spoke a funny language to each other. He knew that he was the only one there who didn't understand but he felt, as he stood a few feet away, that his mother was being separated from him. When she turned to him and stretched out her arms he hesitated for a moment and then ran to her, too fast and too suddenly, catching the toe of his shoe on the strip of metal which separated lino from carpet and falling, with a loud slap, flat on his face. For a moment everything in the room seemed to stop. Nicholas looked at the pale pink lino in front of him in a confused silence. Then he raised his head and, with a face that moved from dazed surprise to sulky humiliation in a few seconds, he began to cry.

Ray watched as Kalyna dashed to her son and hoisted him in the air, positioning him on her hip and pressing her wide lips onto the top of his head as he wailed into her shoulder. What an extraordinary child, Ray thought, who found Nicholas headstrong and passionate, too intense for a six-year-old. He looked over to Kalyna and smiled politely at her, not wishing to intrude on a mother comforting her son. Kalyna saw his smile and thought it pained. He thinks my child is difficult, she thought, but she lacked the language to tell him otherwise.

Kalyna married Ray so that she could remain in Britain; he married her out of the kindness of his heart. Refugees should be treated well, he maintained, embarrassed and angered by his government's policy on the matter. He did what he could in his own small way to make up for it, working one day a week for a charity which concerned itself with housing and assimilation. Ray was a filthy man with a kind heart and strong political beliefs. Kalyna thought he was a good person who would have been improved beyond belief by a bath.

When they walked out of the registry office and into the street the wind was still howling and Ray offered Kalyna his coat — a black wool roadworker's jacket with an orange panel across the shoulders — which he wrapped around her because Nicholas had refused to get down. Ray, Kalyna, Nicholas and the two women who had come as witnesses and translators, decided to go to a pub to celebrate the union.

Ray sat opposite Kalyna with a pint of beer which seemed, as he put his hand up to the glass, suddenly too cold to drink late on an October afternoon. He eyed his new wife timidly, daring himself to look at just her lips, catching a glance from her dark, round eyes as he raised his own. The two other women translated for them: Kalyna asked Ray what he liked to eat; he asked her what she missed from her homeland.

The rules of the marriage had been laid down before the ceremony, on Ray's insistence as much as Kalyna's. They were written in English and Ukrainian in a lined pad, dated, signed and witnessed: the two of them were to remain financially independent, Kalyna was to be solely responsible for Nicholas and she would file for divorce after eighteen months of marriage on the grounds of adultery. There was to be no physical involvement. Ray, however, could not help but be attracted by Kalyna. He liked the way she had dropped her eyes throughout the ceremony and took it as a sign of an innate humility. Sitting across from her, he sipped his beer and imagined running a finger around the edge of her lips. Kalyna looked at his hand gripping his pint glass and wondered whether she would ever know him well enough to tell him that he really ought to scrub his fingernails.

Ray looked from Kalyna to her son and thought that perhaps he should befriend Nicholas before embarking on anything with Kalyna. Nicholas sat close to his mother and fidgeted, running a short index finger around his collar and scratching impatiently at his wrists. He was tall for his age and had the face of a doll: dark hair and dark eyes with thick, curled eyelashes. Ray sensed that the child would be easy to befriend: he clung too much to his mother, but his broad face and fiercely vulnerable eyes showed a curiosity which would win out in the end. Ray also saw that the boy was frightened. He watched Nicholas lift his head every few minutes and look up at his mother, checking her expression for fear or pain. Ray did not think any less of the boy for this almost compulsive behaviour. I do not know what he has been through, he thought to himself, I do not know what he has seen.

Ray thought of himself as a subversive and worked in a

large bookshop where Kalyna and Nicholas would go to see him sometimes. Nicholas would play on the staircase which had been built to look like a pile of books with pastel covers and textured spines. Behind the till Ray would scratch his stubble and judge his customers by their purchases. Though Nicholas wouldn't remember it, Ray was responsible for developing Nicholas's liberal attitude towards shoplifting.

'Some people should be allowed to steal from time to time,' he said to Kalyna after she had seen someone slip a copy of *Crime and Punishment* into their coat.

'They could go to the library,' Kalyna objected. She had a strong sense of civic duty in her new country.

'You can't take your time with library books,' Ray replied. 'Metered reading,' he sniffed and carried on unpacking and sorting greeting cards. Ray educated Nicholas in the politics of subversion and taught him to look for connections. 'Everything isn't necessarily a conspiracy,' he'd say, 'but look for connections – you'll quite often find them.' Since he was a women's-libber he did not expect Kalyna to clean the neat, yellow circles of urine that he left on the loo seat or extricate the coffee cups, complete with dog-end croutons, which were to be found underneath his dirty clothes. He expected no-one to clean up after him, not even himself. He was so dirty that Kalyna often wondered how he could see out of his eyes.

'Shall I be like Ray?' a young Nicholas used to ask Kalyna, meaning not *should* he but *would* he. Ray was essentially a good person. Beneath the layers – and layers – of dead skin, grime and grease, beat a good heart.

'If you want to,' she would reply. 'But cleaner.' One day Ray's tooth fell out mid-conversation – an upper left incisor – and Kalyna took it as a sign that he was in a general state of decay. When he finally moved out, she scoured the flat from top to bottom.

As a child Nicholas was considered by some to be soft. His brown eyes watered too easily. He loved his mother too much and told her everything that happened in his life, gabbling away noisily once he'd come in the door from school. Kalyna had raised – how could she not? – a mother's boy. He was honest, impulsive and liked to laugh. At primary school he preferred the company of the girls to the boys, hanging around with them at breaktimes joking and chatting while the boys screamed around the playground chasing balls. He was good at English, liked writing long, involved stories in his curly handwriting and excelled at music.

At the start of his final year at primary school he arrived to find that his new form teacher had decided to seat his class alphabetically. Such a system placed Nicholas next to Lee Barton, a ratty kid with short ginger hair and a pinched mouth who was always in trouble. Lee, as Nicholas approached his seat, leapt out of his chair and onto his desk.

'Lee Barton, get down,' Mr Norman yelled, while he searched for a red biro in his top drawer.

'No,' Lee said. Nicholas looked up at him and sat down at the desk next to where Lee was standing.

'Urgh!' yelled Lee and jumped over to the next pair of desks, landing in a crouch like a wild boy.

'Lee Barton.' Mr Norman stood up and looked Lee in the face. 'What do you think you're doing? Get back to your seat this instant!'

'No,' said Lee testily. He was standing again now and crossed his arms over his narrow chest. He was short for his years and from the age of four had been ignored by a mother who was described by her neighbours as a 'meth-head'. Lee Barton never hesitated to kick or punch. He saw no reason why he should.

'Sit in your seat!' Mr Norman yelled, raising his hands to

his hips and turning pink in the face.

'I won't sit next to *him*,' Lee replied, jerking his chin in Nicholas's direction. Nicholas was astonished to find that Lee seemed to have indicated him. He looked around at the other kids. They dropped their eyes, each hoping that Lee wouldn't pick on them. Nicholas turned his head from one side to the other, seeing only the blankness and rejection of lowered eyelids.

'Why on earth not?' Mr Norman demanded. He had approached Lee and they stood the same height as each other, eye to eye.

'Because he's a *girl*,' Lee Barton cried. 'Nicholas Beimuk is one of the girls.' Heat filled Nicholas's head and spread to his skin, bringing pink blotches to his face which he could not see himself and imagined looked much worse than they actually did. 'No I'm not,' mumbled Nicholas. He hated Lee Barton in that moment.

'Be quiet, Nicholas,' Mr Norman said. He was desperate now to get Lee Barton down off the desk. The headmistress passed each morning at the end of registration and he did not want her to peer into his classroom and see a runt of a child standing four feet taller than he should be.

'Why don't you get down, Lee, and we'll see about where you can sit?' Mr Norman suggested.

'I am not sitting with *girls*,' Lee insisted. There was, in Lee's world, little worse than girls. Indeed, as he grew older he would barely modify this belief. Girls remained scum, an intricate collection of lures and needs, sweet nothings and sharp reprimands, and he would treat them with a fearful contempt.

'I am not a girl,' Nicholas protested. He could not understand why he had been labelled as such. Talking to people was more interesting than playing football. He preferred writing stories to learning his times tables. What

7

was wrong with that? Through the window Mr Norman caught sight of the headmistress across the playground beginning her rounds.

'Okay, Lee, Okay. You don't have to sit with girls. Now get down and go and sit with Leon over there,' Mr Norman suggested. 'Altaf, you come and sit next to Nicholas here,' he said to the boy whose seat Lee had just taken.

'*Aw, sir,*' Altaf moaned but he did as he was told. Nicholas ignored Altaf as he took his seat. Nicholas had both the humility to entertain the notion that Lee Barton might be right and the strength of character to know that he liked himself as he was. Out of nowhere his deep brown eyes filled with water and a tightness took hold of his throat. Perhaps I am a girl, he thought to himself, hating himself for his weakness. He stared down at the desk in front of him and fiercely hoped that no-one was looking at him.

Kalyna encouraged the forgiving side of Nicholas's nature. She wanted a child so aware of the privileges and opportunities he enjoyed that he couldn't help but exploit them. She thought that his sympathy and consideration would turn him into a compassionate and thoughtful man. A humanist, a liberal, a philanthropist. And this would happen, eventually. But it can be difficult for a boy to live with a soft heart.

TWO

Nicholas walked across Hyde Park with a red folder tucked under his arm. His walk was brisk, too fast for the heat of the afternoon, and he noticed little of what he saw. The folder he held had turned up earlier in the day: a straightforward, cardboard folder, powdery to the touch, the colour fading to a light pink around its edges. He had held it loosely in one hand for a good five minutes while he'd chatted to Sean, his colleague, and opened a packet of sandwiches with his other hand. When he had finally opened the folder and had a look at the pieces of paper inside it his head dropped to one side and his hands began to sweat.

Nicholas was twenty-nine. He was broad and lean, with something apologetic in his walk and a tendency to dart about, as though startled by a sudden noise. His dark hair curled loosely around his face, and he wore an expression of polite amusement, an expression which he had learned to hide a vulnerability he felt inside. Though he would rather die than admit it, Nicholas still had a soft heart.

It was the hottest day of the year so far and the swell of the afternoon was beginning to be stirred by an evening breeze, blowing in from the sea along with rain clouds and a few gulls. Nicholas had removed his jacket and loosened his brown nylon tie, but he still wore his cap with its SSS badge. With every few steps it lifted in the wind, making him start and thrust his hand to his head as though struck by a great thought. The park looked like a refugee camp, with groups of people scattered here and there, sleeping, eating, laughing. As Nicholas walked a young boy with a cricket bat was urged by a crowd of children to 'run!' but just stood, bewildered by the heat, the bat hanging at his side. Further away a woman in a small kite-tail bikini caught Nicholas's eye as she pulled her ponytail through her cap and lay down on her stomach. On a normal day the thought of approaching the woman would have passed through Nicholas's head. Today he thought of nothing but the folder under his arm.

There had been no need for Nicholas to take the folder home with him. He could have easily copied out the details he wanted in his neat, looped handwriting when no-one was looking. But when the time came to leave work he had felt a urgent need to take the folder and the bits of paper back to his house, as though their presence in his bedroom could precipitate some sort of involvement. On his way out of work he had bumped into his boss, Gareth.

'Are you all right there, Nicholas? Got enough clothes on, have you?' Gareth had jovially asked, jerking his head back towards the sun in the sky behind him. In an attempt to conceal the folder Nicholas had pressed it to his chest and zipped up his jacket right to his super sternal notch.

'I've got a cold,' Nicholas replied, standing still with his hands clasped in front of him and his arms pressed tight against his stomach to keep the folder in place. He felt sweat breaking out on his forehead and nose as he stood there in the heat.

'A cold what?' Gareth asked, lifting his chin high into the air as he spoke. He eyed Nicholas suspiciously. As manager of a supermarket he saw himself as good with people.

'I don't feel well,' Nicholas explained.

'A lot of stock has been going missing lately,' Gareth said with a brief bounce of his head. He was short and slightly plump with prematurely greying hair. He thought of himself as something of a visionary.

'Really?' Nicholas already knew about the disappearing stock. Last week had been the birthday of Alexandra, the woman who usually stole tins of beans, and she had taken a bottle of Orvieto and a cake in the shape of an aeroplane instead. On top of that there had been an R&B concert in the park and so groups of students had hurried in and wandered out with cans of beer up their sleeves and packets of Rizla in the pouches of their hoodies. Nicholas had let them all go. If they have to pay for their education they should at least have free beer, he thought.

'Yes,' replied Gareth. The two of them regarded each other. 'Ah well, see you in the morning,' Gareth said finally and he walked off in the direction of the West End. Nicholas paused and pressed his lips together as he watched Gareth depart into the hazy orange air. He crossed the road slowly and headed into the park. Only when he had been walking for a good five minutes did he take off his jacket and casually tuck the folder under his arm, as though it had belonged to him all along.

Nicholas gently put his key in the lock and turned it. His landlady, Mrs Sten, had taken a shine to him as soon as he had set foot in the house and, while her heart was as soft and generous as the waves she put in her light-brown hair, there was also something in the neatness and dedication she put into her appearance that spoke of a loneliness and boredom with things as they were. She had, sadly, no interest in the decoration and running of the house, for if she had she could have found plenty of distractions for her idle hours. The toilet on the ground floor had started, about four months ago, to flush continuously; there was a stair on the first flight which had no top and gaped incredulously at the ceiling above it. In addition to these two problems was a hall light which had no switch, a cellar door with a handle on the outside only, a hole in the bathroom wall two foot from the floor and partially covered by a watercolour of a toad on a lily pad, and finally a cupboard in the kitchen which opened onto a cold brick wall.

Almost everything in the house was covered with a doily. Like decorative bacteria they multiplied and expanded, covering horizontal and not-so-horizontal surfaces, a triumphant testimony to what mankind could do with a piece of string. Nicholas hated the doilies. More than once he had knocked a couple to the floor, only to watch Mrs Sten tut a little when she noticed them and return them, with a quick shake in the air, to their rightful places.

Looking at the ground, Nicholas pushed the front door open. 'Nicholas!' Mrs Sten said with pretend surprise. She stopped in front of him in the hallway. She was carrying a tea tray. He noticed, as he took in the two cakes and two cups, a newly painted pink thumbnail, pressed into the side of the tray.

'Hello,' he said, and felt the folder under his arm and his heart beating against it, urging him on.

'I've just made tea. And I bought one cake too many. Would you like to join me?'

She asked him the same question almost every night. He looked up at her face for the first time that day and saw her carefully waved hair and blinking, neat eyes. More than on any other night, Nicholas wanted to go straight up to his room. He looked down at his feet.

'That would be very nice,' he replied and followed her through to the sitting room. It was a pale grey room, with a large cast-iron fireplace and a three-piece suite decorated with interwoven pink roses. The long curtains in the bay window were made from the same cloth, which was slowly disintegrating and tore easily as Mrs Sten pulled them open. Though the house was in a bad state of repair it was worth a lot of money and Nicholas often wondered exactly how rich Mrs Sten was. He moved her lace-making to one side and perched on the sofa. Then he placed a cushion over her needles and lace, with the hope that she might not find them again.

'Have they taken to giving you homework?' Mrs Sten asked, indicating, with an incline of her head, the pale red folder which Nicholas still clutched to his side. She did not understand why he had taken a summer job. He worked, normally, as a teacher in Thorten Hill Primary School, on the south side of Clapham Common. He taught music and gave private cello lessons to seven of the pupils – sweet children, as far as Mrs Sten could gather. When the school had broken up a couple of weeks ago, Nicholas had announced that he was to spend the summer working as a security guard in a supermarket in Queensway.

'You don't need to take a summer job, do you?' Mrs Sten had asked him, horrified by his news. The school where Nicholas taught was known for its long holidays and Mrs Sten had looked forward to having him around the house for three whole hot months.

'Well, I,' Nicholas began, fidgeting on the sofa, the fingers of his left hand spread evenly over the upholstered arm, 'all of my pupils have gone away and I thought I should do something different, you know. And the money will come in useful.'

'But you should take a holiday. Everyone needs to rest, Nicholas,' she said, a little too sternly, annoyed with him. For weeks now she had been imagining his holiday, looking forward to it.

'Well,' Nicholas shrugged and tapped his fingers. 'If I don't like it, I can give it up. It's only a temporary job,' he replied and, sensing her hostility, had reached for his tea. He was, although he was not going to tell her, about to embark

13

on the process of applying for a new job, that, if he was offered it, would mean he would leave London.

The father of one of Nicholas's pupils at school was a gangly man with too many teeth in his mouth. He smiled far too much and gave the impression of being a bit simple, which he wasn't, and goofy, which he was. He played the flute by profession. He went by the name of Gulliver and had two daughters, too young to sense their father's air of foolishness, but old enough for private music lessons: one learned cello and the other clarinet. Every Wednesday Gulliver came to pick up his elder daughter from her lesson. He would rap gently on the classroom door and then press his face into the strip of glass which ran down the centre, grinning fiendishly at the two of them. Nicholas would nod back and with a jab of his head motion for Gulliver to come in.

'Hello Christabel. Hello Nicholas,' he said on this particular Wednesday, shortly before the end of the summer term.

'Hello Daddy,' chimed Christabel. Nicholas picked up her practice book and wrote down the exercises for that week: '*The Shepherd Boy*' – *slow it down! (Your Shepherd Boy could be looking after a flock of mice!)*

'Nicholas, I've been meaning to say,' Gulliver announced, clasping his hands before him.

'Yes?' Nicholas looked up from his writing. Christabel neatly pushed her instrument into its case: a moulded plastic affair in which it could be buried.

'I've been meaning to say,' Gulliver said again. Nicholas looked at him.

'You've been meaning to say that you've been meaning to say?' Nicholas asked.

Gulliver grinned and bit his lower lip with his top teeth. 'Come and audition!' he announced, 'I think you'd be

14

awfully good,' and with a flap of his hand he indicated Nicholas's cello, safely resting between Nicholas's knees.

'Audition for what?'

'Birmingham Symphony Orchestra! Where I play! We're in need of a new desk of cellos. Auditioning over the summer. You might like it. Rehearsals during the days. Concerts at the weekends. A fair bit of touring.'

Gulliver was a Rotarian with a trust fund. Educated at a minor public school in Sunderland, he had married a woman with a dolphin tattooed on her upper arm because he liked her hair and she spoke nicely.

'What do you think? Shall I tip them off?' Gulliver asked. Nicholas scratched at his chin and regarded the man. 'Good salary, if that's what you're after.' In truth Gulliver had more of an idea of the circumference of Pluto than of what money he received from the orchestra.

'Thanks, Gulliver. Good of you to think of me. Whom do I contact for an audition?' Nicholas asked. He liked the idea of playing in an orchestra again, taking his place amongst the concentric rows of scalloped edges and shifting elbows. Gulliver gave him the details, a sloppy, bubbling grin, and was pushed from the room by his daughter who wanted to get home because her programme was going to be on the television.

'Call me when you've arranged it,' Gulliver yelled over his shoulder. 'I'll give you a few pointers.' Nicholas, in his head, saw Gulliver arriving on his doorstep with a pack of dogs late one night. I brought those pointers, he would say and grin.

Though Mrs Sten questioned Nicholas's decision to take a summer job – and a job which she thought was beneath him – she had never questioned his decision to live in her guest house. If she had, she might have come to realize that

Nicholas, for all his smiles and jokes and gentle conversation, had a terrible fear of being alone. He knew it himself but he did not acknowledge it; he arranged his life so that he was alone as little as possible, but constructed other reasons for his actions. If you asked him directly, looking straight into his smoky brown eyes, why he lived in Mrs Sten's house, he would tell you it was because he didn't need much space, because the rent was cheap, because it was fairly near his school. The truth of the matter was that the thought of sitting, even for a few moments, in a house entirely alone filled him with a dread which shortened his breath and pressed on his stomach. Nicholas hated the feeling. And he hated himself for his cowardice.

Mrs Sten had no inkling of Nicholas's disquiet, but she would have understood his feelings entirely. The only reason she climbed from her bed in the morning and peered in the mirror to apply her lipstick was because there were other people in the house. She liked to be at the centre of things. She liked to know everything about her three tenants and she liked to know it first, for it was her house and they were her tenants, after all. She saw it as the height of impudence if any of them dared speak to each other without letting her overhear. Whenever Martine knocked on Nicholas's door, Mrs Sten would sit herself firmly in front of the television, the volume increased by woodpecker hits of her index finger against the remote control, to distract her mind from the awful thought that the two of them had a life outside her. She was aware of her weakness, but awareness did nothing to ease her proprietorial expectations. She behaved towards them as she would towards figments of her own imagination.

She saw it as her responsibility, as a landlady with three tenants, to know as much about them and their whereabouts as possible. She was naturally curious, but she masked her curiosity with a sense of duty: her tenants were alone in this city and if she didn't keep an eye out for them, like a guardian angel, then no-one would. It was with this sense of duty in mind that she took her time cleaning their rooms, loitering over postcards and notice boards, emptying their bins item by item. Sometimes, in Nicholas's room, she would stop and sit down on his bed, feeling almost faint with an intimacy that she wished existed.

'No, no, I haven't got homework,' Nicholas replied, laying the folder next to him. 'It's a friend's. I'm looking something over for them,' he said and didn't meet her eyes. 'It's a beautiful day,' he went on, taking the tea she had poured for him.

'The last day of June,' Mrs Sten said dreamily. 'When does your school start again?' she asked. She enjoyed seeing Nicholas in a uniform, although in this job he came home later and she had to busy herself with her tea tray in the kitchen for longer.

'The first week of September. Still two months to go,' he replied. If I go back, he thought.

'And you still don't think you'll take a holiday? Not even a few days off?' She pushed her lips together and tilted her head to one side as she regarded him.

'No, I don't think so,' Nicholas replied with a tiny shake of his head. 'The people I work with are nice. It's good to have a break from teaching. What about you? Will you be going away?'

Mrs Sten shook her head delicately at her lodger. She would not do anything as reckless and neglectful as go on holiday. 'Besides, I still have the room to finish,' she said with a lazy shrug.

There were a total of eight bedrooms in the house but Mrs Sten rented out only three: to Nicholas, the music teacher; Martine, who worked for the local council, and

Martine's eight-year-old son, Harvey. Mrs Sten could tell them all apart by the sounds they made on the doormat outside. Nicholas, unlike Martine, spent a while fumbling for his key, and so there would be a pause between footsteps arriving at the door and any sound from within the house. Once he had his key in the lock he would barge in like an actor who'd missed his cue, letting the door slam behind him and tripping up the stairs. Like Nicholas's mother before her, Mrs Sten felt that he filled the house with life.

The other rooms in the house were in various states of repair. Mrs Sten had been redecorating one of them ever since Nicholas had moved in, eighteen months ago. She loitered in DIY shops and tinkered with paint charts but little seemed to happen to the room. Nicholas assumed that she didn't really need the money, and he was right. She had spent the afternoon waiting for the sound of his return, stirring her tea carelessly and daydreaming of a villa in the south of Spain where a pink bougainvillea would grow by the porch and the tiled floor would cool her naked feet as she passed through the house.

'But I think I'm getting there with the decorating. Not too much left to do,' she said, and leaned back against the straw-stuffed roses behind her. She looked suddenly deflated and the folds of her blouse hung lazily over the light blue cotton of her skirt.

'That's good,' said Nicholas, taking a sip of tea. 'Once it's finished you can have a rest.' He never suggested that she might mend the stair with no top or the hole in the bathroom wall, through which it was possible to see bricks and even a chink of the house next door. He thought she should do as she liked.

'I shan't be renting it to a gentleman, Nicholas, you know that. Do you mind at all? Sometimes I worry about you – a lone gentleman in a house full of women,' and she raised her well-maintained eyebrows at him.

'No, that's fine, Mrs Sten. I think I can cope by myself.' Nicholas smiled at her.

'I think one gentleman is enough for any household, don't you? As long as it's a gentleman of *calibre*.' She spoke the last word carefully and smoothed her skirt over the front of her thighs. Nicholas replaced his cup and saucer on the tea tray and clasped his hands in front of him. He felt uncomfortable in his supermarket uniform and fidgeted.

'I still have to choose the wallpaper,' she said. 'Flowers or stripes. I would, of course, say flowers, but girls these days are different, aren't they? What do you think, Nicholas? What would the girls whom you know want?'

'Stripes. That way you could always rent it to a man if you changed your mind,' Nicholas said. *The girls I know*, he thought. He had not known a girl, in the biblical sense, for the past nine months and he was getting anxious. Usually he tried to keep himself distracted with girlfriends. He did not like to wake up alone in bed. He twirled a ring on his little finger.

'You're not thinking of leaving, are you?' asked Mrs Sten, her attention focused suddenly on his thickly lashed eyes and the broad, rectangular forehead above them. Most of all Mrs Sten admired Nicholas's hands. Like an artist's figurine they were clearly jointed and often she wished just to reach out and bend one of his fingers until his knuckle protruded in a neat right angle. Nicholas's hands were constantly moving: his fingers liked to drum, his thumb liked to oppose. When he had first come to look at the room Mrs Sten had served him sandwiches in the living room: small, de-crusted triangles with flags sticking out of them: 'cheese and avocado', 'prawn and egg', 'chicken and pineapple'. He had eaten one, taking it carefully between finger and thumb and Mrs Sten had been transfixed by the neatness of the movement. It was not mannered nor overly precise. It was exquisitely graceful. His fingers were flattish, with pink nails like seashells, and two veins worked their way over the back of each hand, testimony to the work the hands did, the blood they required.

'No, I'm not thinking of leaving,' Nicholas lied. He smiled at Mrs Sten. 'Although I think I'll head off to my room to change my clothes, and I have to do some practice, so −'

'Yes, of course,' replied Mrs Sten, a bloom of relief settling on her cheeks. 'Yes, yes. Well, it was nice to see you, Nicholas.' Now she could look forward to hearing him play his cello, as he did most nights. She imagined, could almost believe some evenings, that he was playing it for her.

'Thank you for the tea,' he said. He took the folder from the sofa and quietly left the room. The cakes, as every day, remained untouched, and Nicholas, not for the first time, wondered what would become of them.

THREE

Kalyna, Nicholas and Ray rented the top half of a house in the north of Bradford. The whole house was owned by Borys Smyck, a priest from the Ukraine, who presided over his services with a steely authority and carried a small, threatening look at the back of his blue eyes. He let the top of his house to Kalyna for a reduced rent. He liked her and imagined her on her back beneath him, gasping for breath as he lay on her, eyes wide with surprise at his power. He frowned at her breasts when she came down to pay the rent and thought that one day he might own her.

Kalyna worked as a cleaner in the local secondary school. All the cleaners there were Ukrainian women, one, in fact, came from the same village as Kalyna. They were paid half what a British cleaner would accept and fewer of them were employed; Kalyna washed the corridor floors in the early mornings and emptied seventy-three bins in the evenings. Ray spent four days of the week in the bookshop, ringing up prices and helping customers with their alphabet. At the weekends he sold *Socialist Worker* on Princes Way outside the Odeon cinema, pacing backwards and forwards amongst the preoccupied shoppers. They settled down to life in Bradford like an ordinary family. Ray helped his new wife and her son with their English. Nicholas went to school.

It was not, in the end, an entirely loveless marriage. Once, after they had been living together for a month, Ray stopped Kalyna outside the bathroom with a hand on her shoulder. When she turned to him, her large brown eyes scanning his face, he put his lips to hers. She did not exactly kiss him back, nor did she push him immediately away. He kissed her immobile mouth – she might have been sleeping – until she took a small step backwards and lifted herself away from him.

'I'm sorry,' she said, consciously stopping herself from wiping his saliva off her mouth. She felt a lot of affection for the man. But he did not attract her. And besides, he was so dirty.

'No,' Ray interrupted. He looked sheepish, closed his eyes and shook his head. 'I – that didn't – it's okay,' he held up the palms of his hands to her. 'I'm sorry. That won't happen again.'

'Okay,' Kalyna said and blinked slowly at him. 'I go –' and she indicated the bathroom with a glance.

'Yes, yes. Good night,' Ray said and he returned to his room where he picked up a book and tried not to think about what had happened.

Kalyna liked Ray as a friend and nothing more, and felt that in marrying someone she did not love, she had set a bad example for her son. Nicholas was six when she married for the second time, too young to understand that her relationship was a pretence, a masquerade of domestic harmony for the bureaucrats. When she took Nicholas to school in the morning and kissed him goodbye on the top of his head she worried that he would develop peculiar ideas about relationships. The only consolation, she thought, was that she and Ray rarely argued.

Of course Kalyna doubted herself. When she slowly brushed her hair before she left for work in the morning she would look in the mirror and see the face of a woman who had done a terrible thing. When she lay in bed at night, grinding her haphazard teeth and listening to the rain hammer on Borys's patio below she would try to remember her first husband and imagine how her life might be if there and then she could roll over and press her face into his solid shoulder. The antidote to Kalyna's doubt was her son. She had come to England for Nicholas. He would have a better life than she had had, a better life than the one his brother would live. *A better life* was what it was all about. Kalyna could not see that the obligation to be successful and happy in England might be a burden to Nicholas. She was confident that he would lead a glorious life filled with opportunities.

There was a man in Kyiv at the time who went by the name of Sacha. He was a short man, twice the weight he should have been, who had an interest in home-made bombs and rocket launchers. He had never made either, but read up as much as he could about both, and kept his handwritten notes and copies of booklets in a blue cardboard box in the shed of his allotment. He liked secrets but lacked the courage and conviction to involve himself with anything significant. He worked in a postal sorting office, flinging letters into trays, lifting sacks up by their corners to empty their contents. Once the letters were piled in front of him he sorted through them quickly, putting aside those that had arrived from Britain and America. The rest he threw into their trays, often missing, often placing wrong letters in the wrong trays. The pile from Britain and America he took home with him. During the long evenings he would sit with a penknife and slit them open, one by one, removing money and cheques. The letters and photos he would throw away. In one year he had collected over $200.

Kalyna wrote four letters to her husband Stefan. Each ended up in Sacha's bin. When she received no replies she tried again. Sacha took her letters home again. After she had sent the tenth letter – a simple, pleading request for a sign of life – she gave up. Sacha, however, did not. That year he earned $450 in clean, papery bills which fluttered out of his stolen post, landing on his bare floor with barely a sound.

After eighteen months Kalyna did not file for divorce. There was no need. One evening when Ray had come home from work at the bookshop he announced that he was going to go and live in Sweden for a time, perhaps for ever. Kalyna sat down heavily at the kitchen table. She frowned.

'Why?' was all she said. Nicholas was seven. While he enjoyed a level of attention from his mother that few children would ever know (she took immense pride in his flawless English and his mathematical ability), Kalyna thought it important that he received attention from Ray. Ray shrugged off his donkey jacket and sat down to explain to her what he found attractive about Sweden.

'They have a good immigration programme,' he told her, 'and environmentally they're way ahead of most other Western countries. I want to see how the country works.'

'Do you know anyone there?' she asked.

'Did you know anyone here before you arrived?' he asked in return. Although the flat would suddenly become a lot cleaner and Kalyna would have more time to herself, she was on the whole sad to see Ray go. Nicholas, at nearly eight, just didn't understand. It seemed to him that life was full of people he liked who disappeared.

Kalyna and Nicholas saw Ray off at Bradford station, one early morning in May. Nicholas cried and Ray gave him a copy of *Peter Pan*, folded up in an article about the TUC. Kalyna embraced him and wished him well. Ray passed a can of Tizer from one hand to the other and smiled a little too broadly. When the train pulled away Nicholas clung to his mother's hand and sobbed. His eyes folded up in red creases, his mouth opened and turned down at its corners, revealing small cream teeth. Kalyna looked down at her son and felt sick with guilt. Nicholas, it seemed, had no concept of hiding his emotions. He showed what he felt. Today she would rather not have seen it.

There were others who would rather not see it as well. Mr Squirrel, Nicholas's cello teacher, often told Nicholas that he felt too much, that he played with too much emotion.

In his first music lesson at Moorside Secondary School Nicholas was told that he could learn a musical instrument for free. More to the point, the music tuition would take place during normal school hours and so would entail the missing of lessons. The news was greeted with an unprecedented silence from the first-year pupils, as each had fantasies of never attending another school lesson again. And so Nicholas found himself the proud caretaker of a Taiwanese cello, into the back of which the school, since stealing was a burgeoning problem, had scratched its initials and in so doing completely ruined any hope the instrument had ever had of producing a sonorous note.

Mr Squirrel approached the pedagogy of the cello with passion. One afternoon, while Nicholas sawed his way through his scales, Mr Squirrel held up his fat hands in the air for silence.

'Do you know how many horses *died* so that their tails could be used for bows?' he asked lightly. Nicholas was unsure whether he was joking or not. 'Do you know how many horses out there have lost their spindle-legged foals in the name of music? Well? Do you?' He stretched out a hand into the air above him. 'When you play it sounds like all those equine souls crying for their lost tails, all those horse parents mourning their children. Have you done any practice this week, Nicholas?'

Nicholas nodded slowly. Late the night before, remembering that he had his lesson today, he had hastily unpacked his instrument and tried to coax something pleasant from it.

'Well, it doesn't sound like it,' Mr Squirrel announced and he briskly rubbed his large hands together.

Nicholas stopped playing and his final note, a deep and confident C (the luxury of an open string) resounded around the empty classroom. Nicholas was missing a history lesson today and knew that at this very moment the teacher, a young man recently discharged from the army, would be pacing before the class telling them how they had scored in their exam on Henry VIII. Nicholas knew little about Henry VIII and found history, as a subject, utterly confusing. He had revised for his exam during the breaktime before it. Though he didn't know it yet, he had scored 86% and the teacher had written on his report card that Nicholas had 'a thorough and in-depth understanding of the topic'. Early in his school career Nicholas would become acquainted with the tempestuous relationship between effort and attainment.

'Do you know how to practise?' Mr Squirrel asked Nicholas as he took a seat beside him. Nicholas thought the question strange. He liked the feel of playing the cello, even if the sound at times could raise the dead. At first he played by himself in his bedroom, crossing strings with a drop of the elbow and shifting positions over and over again. The tips of his fingers had become hard and flat. 'I enjoy everything about it apart from the sound,' Nicholas declared one day to his mother. 'I don't think I have any natural talent.'

'Nothing's natural,' his mother had replied, 'least of all playing the cello. Just practise.' And so he took to practising in the bathroom, sitting on the toilet with the lid down, because the room was small and the acoustic better. That he had perfect pitch was both a blessing and a burden. For the first two years the strokes of his bow produced horror in his ears.

'You know sometimes, Nicholas, you say things you don't want to.' Mr Squirrel continued with the lesson. 'I've often found myself in that position. Something just comes right out of my mouth and I wish I could take it all back. I feel misrepresented and worry that someone might think something about me which isn't true at all.' Nicholas nodded and marvelled at just how fat Mr Squirrel's fingers were. 'That is what practice is about. When you practise an instrument you never let yourself be misrepresented: you turn back, over and over again, until everything happens exactly the way you wanted it to in the first place. If you say the wrong thing in practice, you go back to it. Practice is all about going back and clearing the air.'

Mr Squirrel was an emotional man who was often misunder-stood. He had a black sense of humour and a fiery impatience; he was known to have once locked another teacher in the music cupboard for a whole afternoon because she objected to his noisy lessons. He had taken it upon him-self, at the age of twenty-eight, to give up trying to perform on the cello and teach it instead. He had been playing in the Hong Kong Philharmonic at the time. One afternoon, in the middle of a passage from Sibelius's Second Symphony, he lifted his bow from the strings and, with a clarity of thought that would occur only a few times in his whole life, decided that he wanted to teach. He took the trans-Siberian railway home the following week and decided to start off in Yorkshire, teaching at schools in and around Bradford.

When Nicholas first met him he was fifty-four, with a shock of white hair and fingers which looked as though someone had tried to squeeze his arms into them. The fingers were not those of a cello player but he played well nonetheless, and while twenty-six years' experience of teaching children made him realize that most would never get beyond the back desk in an orchestra, a belief in the random nature of events told him that the next Robert Lindley could appear before him in his class any day.

Mr Squirrel reached up to Nicholas's music stand and flicked through his music book until he found the first page. 'Play that for me,' he said. Nicholas did as he was asked. It was an easy piece, a simple lullaby which Nicholas had learnt a few months earlier. 'Not bad,' said Mr Squirrel, 'but it could be better. Play it again.' Nicholas did as he was told. Mr Squirrel asked for it again and then again. 'Always go back, Nicholas,' Mr Squirrel sang out into the classroom. 'Practice is about returning.'

Gradually Nicholas became acquainted with his instrument. He wiped away the fine, sticky resin dust from underneath the strings with a soft cloth. His small hands learnt how to manipulate the crude clockwinder's pegs which tightened the strings. He became used to the feeling of this *thing* on his left shoulder, so much so that in later life he would often reach for his shoulder with his left hand, fingertips brushing along his collarbone, when he felt unsure of himself. At first he preferred to practise the instrument and not actually play anything. To commit himself to a finished version of a piece of music was too much for him; he did not want to admit that a single performance was the best he could do. Later on, in his late teens, he loved to play but not to practise. The tone he produced on the cello by now was quite lovely: controlled, precise, rich. At fourteen he would play one piece of music after another, racing through them, unwilling to stop and ponder a section or passage. He was young and he wanted to play.

FOUR

Nicholas called out goodbye to Mrs Sten and leapt up the stairs to his room, relieved to be free of his obligations. He shut the door to his room behind him and placed the folder on his bed. Taking off his clothes, he wondered whether he should practise first and leave the folder for later. He pulled on some tracksuit bottoms and slipped on a pair of flipflops. Curling his fingers absent-mindedly in the small patch of dark hair on his chest he stood and looked at the folder. Then he sat on his bed and opened it.

Curriculum Vitae: Faye Victoria Peters
Date of birth: 30th July 1970
Marital Status: Single
Current Address: 223 Lincoln Street, London W3 5HT
                   tel: XXXX XXX XXXX
Education:
1982–1987   Moorside Secondary School, Bradford,
                   six GCSEs, all grades A–C
1987–1989   Morgan Lodge, three A levels:
                   Geography A, English B, French B
1989–1992   Durham University, English Literature
                   and Language, 2:1
Employment History:
Assistant to Deputy Editor, *Intrinsic*
Features Writer, *Intrinsic*
Features Writer, *Bon Appétit*
Senior Features Writer, *The Decade*
Senior Features Writer, *Courrant*

Other Experience:
Duke of Edinburgh Awards Scheme, Gold (1988)
Voluntary Service Overseas – Zimbabwe and Nigeria (1989)
Lacrosse All-County Finals (1987)
City and Guilds Art Foundation Course, London College of Printing (1994)
Extensive travelling in Mexico, Guatemala, Honduras and Nicaragua (1993)
References:
Available on request

Nicholas stared at the words in front of him, almost unable to believe what he saw. Was this really her? He checked the details over and over again: the years, the school, the middle name. Then he took a London A–Z from his cupboard and looked up her current address, running his finger slowly over her street as he chewed the side of his mouth.

Nicholas had seen Faye Victoria Peters around school for a few weeks before the day that she spoke to him. They were in their first year, not in the same form, but he had noticed her playing netball in the playground one morning. When she came sauntering down Culler Avenue one evening, in cut-off trousers and a sleeveless pink top, Nicholas's throat dried: for Faye life seemed a breeze, a sweet breeze on a spring evening, in which her blonde ringlets bobbed up and down and her smooth skin gently goose-pimpled.

'Hey there Nick.' She stood, hand on one hip, on the pavement in front of him, a cigarette poised in her mouth. He looked up at her and could only think of that cigarette between her lips. He looked away.

'Hi,' Nicholas said, trying his best to be cool, to be unsurprised that she was, for the first time in his existence, talking to him. He had made a few new friends at school, but he knew no girls.

'Have you got a light?'

He took out his lighter and flicked it (he had practised this so many times that it just *had* to work), relieved when the flame leapt up and he could offer it to her.

'Cheers,' she said and took a long drag, staying where she was on the pavement, hand on hip. 'You know, you should be in the circus. I could just see it: "Nicholas Beimuk" large on a tent in red and white with stars around it.'

'It's Beamish,' he said, 'Nicholas Beamish.' His mother had recently relented and agreed to let him anglicize his surname, though his mother's friends and Borys Smyk disapproved of what they saw as the wilful abandonment of his Ukrainian heritage and culture. Tough, Nicholas thought. His mother, however, had forgotten to inform the new school of his change of name and so he was down on every register as Beimuk, a name which made teachers hesitate and the other kids sneer.

'Where's it from, anyway, Beimuk?' Faye asked, eyes narrowed. He was aware of her thigh, long, taut and aerofoil under her narrow trousers as she rotated the foot that was nearest him.

Here we go, thought Nicholas. 'It's Ukrainian,' he replied. 'It means "stud".'

'Really,' she said, blowing smoke up in the air above her. He looked at her small breasts in the little pink top and liked looking at them. She caught his stare and he flushed, glancing over to the other side of the road. Nicholas's vegetable-pale skin was from his Swedish ancestors, Scandinavian Varangians who came down from above into warmer, flatter territory which they held until they reached Byzantine Greece. His eyes must have come from marauding Mongols – the people of the felt tents, with their

31

flat, windblown cheekbones and darkly lashed, far-gazing eyes. Nicholas too had these thick lashes, which lent his eyes a drawn-round quality, like those of a china doll or a Sixties hooker. They were, in the end, women's eyes: would have mesmerized on a slender teenage starlet, would have inspired trust and admiration on a weary young mother. On Nicholas they lent his face a girlish quality.

'Yeah, well,' Faye said, and walked on by. Nicholas walked a few paces and then turned to look, to see her hips swinging on down the road, her shoes falling off her heels with each step.

The next time they spoke he was going into the youth centre at school, reluctantly carrying a cup of coffee for the teacher who was on break duty. Faye was on her way out and she stopped just outside the door.

'Hi Nick,' she said, her face straight and eyes narrowed.

'Hi,' he said. In her school uniform she looked younger than she had in the street. She had a number of bangles around one wrist and he noticed the slenderness of it and the neatness of her hand.

'That for Mrs Jackson?' she asked with a smile, looking at the plastic cup in his hand.

'No,' he said defensively. She shook her head at him because she knew he was lying and so he put the cup to his lips and casually took a mouthful. Strong, scalding coffee. He almost gagged. She watched as he steeled himself to swallow it.

She lowered her voice. 'Got any ciggies?'

'Yeah,' he said.

'By the tennis courts in five minutes?'

'Okay,' he said, feeling excitement in his chest. He took the coffee through to Mrs Jackson, hoping that she wouldn't notice the dribbles down one side of the cup. He grabbed his bag and headed for the courts.

It was a cold grey day, a fine vapour hung in the air, and she was waiting there, standing alone, leaning into the mesh that surrounded the courts. Slightly further along was another group of illegal smokers, boys mainly, and Nicholas recognized some of them as trouble-makers. He rarely came here. He didn't smoke during school hours, only occasionally in the street at night.

'Hi,' he said and took out a cigarette. He had shoplifted this packet last weekend and had only smoked two so far. He held it between his lips and lit it, before passing it to her and thrilling to see her own lips take it, just where his had been. He lit one for himself. He didn't know what to say, so he took a deep drag and blew out through the side of his mouth.

'How many brothers you got?' she said.

'None,' he replied. This wasn't strictly true.

She nodded. 'I've got two older sisters. They say nice boys don't smoke.'

'Why not?'

'It's a dirty habit. Nice boys don't smoke, don't drink — apart from communion wine — and let you keep your knickers on, that's what they say.'

Nicholas flushed, hoping that these sisters wouldn't suddenly appear. He looked at Faye, leaning into the mesh, one hand on hip, the other on her cigarette. She had soft, pinkish skin covered with blonde down and kept her eyes narrowed and her lips pouting. From where he was standing, a couple of feet away, he couldn't glance down at her body, though he longed to see how her breasts looked in her white blouse, how her hips looked in her slim grey skirt. Most of all he longed to take her knickers off.

'And what about nice girls?'

She laughed a quick laugh, 'Nice girls definitely don't smoke or drink. And nice girls don't even take their knickers off to go to bed.' A ripple of contempt passed over her face. In the distance the bell rang. Nicholas's heart sank. He didn't want this to end.

Faye took a deep drag of her cigarette. 'What have you got next?'

'Geography,' he said, with a sneer.

'I've got double science,' she said and looked off over the tennis courts. 'Let's stay here.'

He caught his breath. He wanted to stay, but he had never skipped a lesson before. His mother would kill him if she found out. His education was a privilege, she told him almost every day, though often he found it hard to believe her. 'People die to have an education like yours,' she would tell him when he moaned about school. He was taught maths by an ex-jockey with one tooth, History by a man who was said to have a masseuse tattooed around his navel and English by a Spaniard who obsessively chewed small pieces of paper, which he would tear off the top of their school books.

'Okay,' he said, trying to appear calm.

'Let's hide over there,' she said, motioning to the cricket pavilion. They strolled across and tried the door. It opened and Faye went in.

'Come on,' she said, and Nicholas followed her into the small room, stacked with nets and cricket pads, stumps and bats. There were tufts of blanched grass on the floor, cobwebs and dust on the exposed brick walls. The air in the room was sweet with sweat and earth and it caught Nicholas at the back of his nose. Faye sat down on a wooden box and looked around her.

'It's not too bad in here,' she said, 'and we can be sure that no-one will find us,' and she giggled. Nicholas's heart pounded in his chest and he sat down beside her, taking care to leave a gap between them.

'What must it be like to be here in the dead of the night?' she said, crossing and recrossing her legs. 'I'd shit myself, I reckon. What about you?'

Nicholas shook his head and blew smoke above him. 'Nah, it'd be fine. Just like the daytime, only dark.' He wanted to tell her that he preferred night to day. He felt safer in the dark and always would. But to explain why he felt that way would take too long.

'Can you do this?' she said, sucking on her cigarette, pausing for a moment, and then blowing a series of pretty rings which rose in the air above her and made him think of an angel with its halo. Nicholas couldn't really see Faye as a conventional angel, with large white wings at the gates to heaven. He took a drag on his cigarette and tried to copy what she had done, though in truth he thought it a terrible waste of smoke. His puffs billowed through the air like steam from a train. He watched them rise and turned to her. 'No,' he said and she giggled.

'What you do is gather it in the back of your mouth and then make this shape with your lips,' and she pouted at him, a small dark hole in the centre of her lips. 'Go on, try.' He gave it another go, feeling, at the same time, suddenly uncomfortable on the wooden crate. Again the smoke just floated out into the air.

'Come on, do it with me,' she said, and moved closer so that they were sitting with their sides pressed against each other. She lifted her cigarette theatrically to her mouth. He did the same. She placed it gently between her lips and inhaled. Beside him Nicholas felt her small ribcage rise. He did the same. She held the smoke in her mouth for a few seconds and then formed her mouth into a small O, and let the sweetest, neatest smoke ring rise above them. Watching her creations glide above him like fish in the sea, Nicholas tried his best and managed three quarters of a circle, which slowly unwound itself like a snake from a bag, as it escaped his mouth.

'Not bad,' she said with a smile. He glanced over at her and found himself looking at the triangular strip of pinkish skin at the top of her shirt. She saw him looking and slid her hand along her shoulder underneath her blouse, to straighten her bra strap it seemed, or perhaps just to invoke in him a deep sweet envy, which almost made him groan out loud. 'But not quite good enough,' and she laughed.

'Okay,' Nicholas replied, laughing now as well. 'What about this?' and he made his tongue into a loop, which was how he had passed his last science lesson. When he had got home he had asked his mother whether she could loop her tongue. Once she had stopped laughing and actually tried in all seriousness, it transpired that she couldn't. That meant, Nicholas told her, that his father must be able to.

'Your father could do a lot of things,' Kalyna had replied with a half-smile. 'Can,' she added. 'Your father *can* do a lot of things.'

'Urg,' Faye said, with a laugh. 'That's horrible. You look like an anteater,' and she stubbed her cigarette out on the floor with a neat twist of her foot. She turned to Nicholas, close enough that he could feel her warm, smoky breath, and stuck the tip of her tongue out, flat and pink.

'Go on then,' Nicholas said.

'I can't,' she replied with a smile, putting her hand up to try and force her tongue into position. He reached out too, placing a chewed forefinger and thumb on the side of her tongue, and laughed at her efforts. Her tongue felt almost liquid between his fingers and the side of her lip brushed his knuckle. He wanted to lean forward and kiss her.

She retracted her tongue and frowned suddenly. 'What's your brother called then?' she asked. Nicholas would make a good boyfriend, she thought. But a slightly older

Nicholas, who shaved and sweated, would be even better.

'I haven't got one,' he said, alarmed that he had perhaps missed his moment and confused by her question. I should have kissed her then, he thought. Now it was too late. Maybe she had changed her mind. She stretched out her legs and put her hands behind her head, leaning back onto some gym mats.

'Oh yeah. Would you have liked one?'

'Not really.'

'Why not?' she asked.

'I dunno,' he replied, running out of patience with the conversation. He finished his cigarette and tossed it across the room. 'Never really thought about it.'

'What about your mum and dad?'

'What about them?' he said. He ran his hand along the rough wood of the box they were sitting on, pulling off rogue splinters here and there and tossing them onto the floor.

'Which do you look like?' she asked, shutting her eyes. He looked over at her and examined her eyelashes, resting lightly on the pale skin of her cheeks, each one dark blonde and carefully curled.

'Neither,' Nicholas replied.

'Don't you look like your dad? You must do.'

He shook his head into the silence and looked at the weave of Faye's grey wool skirt, like a field which has been finely ploughed horizontally and vertically. A brief image of the geography lesson he was missing appeared in his head.

'What are all these questions for?' he asked and turned to look at her. She opened her eyes and leant forward, resting her chin in her hands, pretending to think. She glanced up at the ceiling with a smile in her eyes and pushed her lips together.

'You,' she said at last, with a pulse of her eyebrows,

'you're interesting.' Nicholas looked at her face for a beat and she stared straight back, hazel eyes which seemed to see too much inside him. He looked away.

While Nicholas had chosen to learn the cello, Faye had chosen the violin, because it was smaller and because it was impossible to wear short skirts and play the cello without showing your pants. Although the thought of showing her pants did not entirely horrify her, she had the good sense to know that she ought to be selective about who should see them.

On Monday nights after school Nicholas and Faye stayed behind to rehearse with the school orchestra. Nicholas always seated himself in the cello section so that he could see her and she, in the shuffling of chairs that went on once the conductor had chosen his spot, always seemed to need to move into Nicholas's eyeline, whether it was eight people that separated them or two. Often they would meet each other's eyes while they played. For Faye this flirting – because that was what it was – had no particular consequence. She had learnt, early in her studies of the violin, that the less her bow touched the strings the better. Nicholas, burdened with masochistic honesty, felt obliged to actually play the notes before him, and frequently fell entire lines of music behind, thanks to the tennis of glances which went on between the two of them.

Nicholas began at the top left-hand corner of the CV and moved slowly from one piece of information to the next, caressing the thick cream paper with his right hand as he read sections telling him things he would never forget: her full name, her date of birth – and others telling him things he never knew – that she had worked in South America after her A levels and that she had lived for a time in

Durham. He could see her in his mind as he sat there, aged fourteen with her shiny blonde hair and a slightly lop-sided smile. He saw in front of him the name of that terrible school where her new stepfather had sent her at the age of sixteen.

Nicholas put the CV down and crossed to open the window, letting the stealthy air creep into the room. He rested his folded arms on the window sill and leant out into the evening, the air warm on his bare skin. He could hear, below him, the sounds of Mrs Sten in the kitchen, making toast, boiling the kettle. Next door Mr Samuels, their neighbour, patrolled his garden. Nicholas did not exactly feel alone. Leaning out of the window he could convince himself that he was part of something, a member of some sort of community. When he turned back to his room it was inescapably empty.

He returned to the CV, looked at Faye's phone number and said the digits out in his head. He bit his lip as he felt an instinctive need for self-defence. The character that the page in front of him evoked seemed to bear no resemblance to the girl he had once known and he wondered how she would now look. A dizziness passed over him and he shut his eyes and lay back against the dinosaur-skin wallpaper, feeling a lust stir in him once again.

FIVE

When Nicholas became a teenager his gaze turned sour.
He looked at his mother and saw what he had learnt from
her: to give up too easily, to distract himself with
meaningless chores, to take things to heart which he
should just brush aside. He looked at himself and did not
like what he saw. He began to treat his mother and her
friends with scorn. He hated to listen to them babbling on
in Ukrainian in the kitchen, comparing the comfort of
their shoes or relaying news of their relatives back home.
Consider the collective brainpower of those exiled in
Siberia, he would think, and then listen to your chatter.
Oksana, Nadya and sometimes Irena would sit heavily on
the wooden chairs, drinking tea and talking. Kalyna could
see that Nicholas found her friends irritating. She knew
that he thought the topics of their conversations trivial and
her eyes would take on an amused gleam when he
shambled into the kitchen for some food to find her telling
Nadya about a new shop which sold plastic pegs, which,
they all agreed, were much better than wooden ones. If the
conversations that took place in Kalyna's kitchen were
taken as representative of the women it would appear that
finding a sink strainer which fitted the plughole of a
kitchen sink and didn't go rusty was the collective life goal
of the friends. The habits of a communist upbringing were
hard to break: if they had to queue for sink strainers they
would. If need be one of them would have travelled to
London for a sink strainer and returned with as many as she
had been allowed to buy.

Kalyna imagined that she could read her son's mind, but there was one thing that she missed and which, had she even suspected such a sentiment, would have hurt her deeply. Nicholas looked at these women – his mother included – and saw that their spirits had been broken. They looked upon themselves as victims, found it unsurprising if they accidentally left behind a bag of apples at the fruit stall. Irena in particular suffered what Nicholas termed in his head immigrants' luck. She would take it as a personal affront if her shoelace snapped and assumed that machines – from her radio to a cashpoint – broke just before she got to them and then mended themselves once she'd left. Kalyna and her friends would have been livid if they knew Nicholas thought this of them. Life is hard, they would have told him, that is why we complain and sigh and rest our heads in our tired hands. Nicholas left his mother to her companions and vowed that he would never become like them.

One evening, when Nicholas was fifteen, Kalyna called Ray in Stockholm. She had not spoken to him for over a year, although they exchanged greetings cards and sporadic letters. When he answered the phone he sounded far away and she had no image with which she could fill her head. She bent into the phone and listened hard to his voice.

'Ray! It's Kalyna.' She hoped he would remember who she was.

'Hello,' he replied, dragging out the word as though talking to a baby.

'Are you available for talking?' she asked. Somewhere across the ocean he laughed.

'Yeah, sure. I was just reading,' he replied. Kalyna should have guessed.

'It's Nicholas,' she said. Her voice sounded strained. She held the phone tightly in her hand and clenched her jaw into the pulses of silence and echoes which punctuated the call.

'Is he okay?' Ray asked.

'He's started smoking.' She was on the verge of tears. She had always known what to do with her son, but for the first time she felt that more than anything else he needed a father. She felt she wasn't enough.

'Did he tell you?'

'I smelt it. Last night when he got in. He admitted it to me today, but I had to ask many times. He doesn't talk to me any more, Ray.' Nicholas had smoked for many years. It was only now, at fifteen, that he decided to stop hiding his habit from his mother. He knew it would upset her.

'He's a teenager,' Ray yelled down the line, 'you have to give him some privacy.'

Ray could barely imagine what it must be like to have Kalyna as your mother. He respected Kalyna and admired her, felt her to be a more remarkable person than himself. He pushed a telephone directory off an armchair and sat down, lifting a knee to his chest and looping his index finger between his toes.

'But we always talk to each other,' Kalyna replied.

'Is he still playing the cello?' Ray asked.

'Yes,' came the response. Kalyna's grip loosened on the receiver. She breathed out and felt the exhalation judder through her.

'Okay. This is what you do. Smoking is just the start of all this, you know that, don't you? Teenagers smoke, drink, have sex, take drugs, sniff glue, carry knives, stay out all night, get arrested.' Ray paused and listened to the tail end of his voice echoing down the line. Perhaps I should stop there, he thought. 'Take an interest in his cello playing and ignore everything else,' he said. 'If he dyes his hair, ignore it. If he paints his room black, ignore it. If he grows marijuana, *ignore it*. Just make sure he does his cello practice. Be really strict about that.'

Kalyna frowned into the phone. 'What are you talking about, Ray? Where did you get that plan from?' Ray paused at the other end, lifted his finger to his nose and smelt it. Kalyna heard nothing. 'Ray? Ray?' she said, turning her back to the wall and leaning against it, glancing at the same time at the clock opposite her. Ten thirty. She didn't want Nicholas to come home while she was having this conversation.

'It's what my mother did with me,' Ray replied at last. 'One night when I was fifteen I drank fourteen pints of lager and black, vomited on a policeman and awoke the next morning on the road in front of the fire station. When I got home my mother told me off because I hadn't read Alexander Herzen's *Ends and Beginnings*.'

At the other end of the line Kalyna was speechless.

'That was all she ever cared about. Had I read this? Had I read that? Why not? I think she thought that if I was going to be a lout then I was at least going to be a well-read lout. It worked, in the end. After a few years I got bored of being a teenager. Reading hasn't bored me yet.'

You're crazy, Kalyna almost said into the receiver. She stopped herself just in time, remembering that she had rung him for advice and it was kind of him to give it. The cost of the phone call came into her head and she felt suddenly self-indulgent for having made it.

'Okay. Perhaps I'll try it,' she said. 'Thanks.' She pressed her cheek against the wall, feeling the coldness of the plaster against her skin. In a second a key turned in the lock and she was standing upright. Nicholas walked in. Eyes on the floor he walked straight to his room and kicked the door shut behind him.

'No problem,' came Ray's tiny voice from the phone.

'It's good to hear from you,' he told her. Kalyna took a deep breath. The bitter smell of smoke hit her nostrils mingled with something else – something altogether softer and sweeter.

'And you too,' she said gently, wishing, without really meaning it, that he were there, with them in their flat. Then *he* could talk to Nicholas. 'I'd better go,' she said. 'I'll write to you.' The sound of music came from Nicholas's room. It was The Smiths.

'Okay,' Ray called. 'I look forward to your letter,' he said, and then regretted sounding so formal. Once he'd replaced the receiver he pulled his other knee up to his chest and sat for twenty minutes, scratching at the hairs on his toes and remembering life with Kalyna and Nicholas.

In Bradford, as a mild night closed in on the town, Kalyna stood gazing at the phone, listening to the too-loud music coming from Nicholas's room. She banged on his door, resenting having to knock so hard to make herself heard. Seconds later the music stopped.

'Nicholas?' she called out. She felt hopeless standing there, shouting at the door, daunted by what she might find behind it. At the same time she didn't understand what had happened to her son. It seemed like yesterday that he had been a happy child who would have looked her straight in the eye.

'What?' came the response.

'Can I come in?' She waited a few moments, staring at chips in the paintwork on the door, wondering what was going on behind it. Suddenly it opened. Nicholas, her beautiful son, regarded her with an almost theatrical contempt. It stood out on his face as a fly sitting on his cheek would and, though he would hate anyone to know it, could be chased away just as easily.

'What?' he repeated. Kalyna looked into his eyes and he

44

looked away. She found that she didn't know what to say. His hair was greasy and lank. Besides, it was getting too long. A redness burned on his chin and his jeans, she noticed for the first time, had a rip over one thigh so that his bony, boyish leg could be glimpsed beneath. The smell of smoke embraced her.

'Have you done your cello practice?' she asked. A calmness fell over her face and her eyes opened wide. She was panicking.

'*What*?' Nicholas said.

'Your cello practice, have—'

'I heard you the first time.'

'Make sure you do your practice before you go to bed tonight,' she said firmly and then, feeling that she might cry, she turned briskly on her heel and walked to the kitchen with a purposefulness and determination that Nicholas knew well.

Without meaning to, Kalyna followed Ray's advice. Though it took almost all her willpower she ignored the smell of smoke that moved through the flat with Nicholas when he walked in the door. She held her tongue as he let his hair grow. And while she never exactly came to appreciate The Smiths, she became acquainted with their music in such a way that listening to it drone all over the flat was not as trying as it once had been. She insisted, during all this time, that Nicholas practise his cello. It was, in the end, largely thanks to Ray that Nicholas became a cellist.

When Nicholas was not playing his cello he spent time with Faye. He had just turned sixteen when she told him that she was leaving Bradford to go to a different school. At home Nicholas became even more unbearable for Kalyna. She shut her eyes to his behaviour, ignored his sneers and cursing and made sure he played his instrument. Nicholas saw Faye as much as he could. He looked upon her as his salvation. She was the only person with whom he did not behave badly.

Nicholas and Faye had met up for coffee, in a coffee bar with textured walls and picnic tables with benches attached, over which they had to climb to sit down. Most of the kids from their school hung out at the Paw Paw Bar and Grill in the town centre. Faye and Nicholas had deliberately chosen somewhere else. Nicholas sat opposite Faye, his arms folded on the table, precise, agile fingers tapping gently on the side of his arm. He tore the ends of two tubes of sugar and emptied them into his drink and then sipped it nervously. Faye was due to leave for her new school in two days. Nicholas wanted at least to have kissed her before she left; he wanted, as he sat there and bounced his foot up and down, to have unburdened himself of his desire.

'Nicholas, stop it,' Faye grinned at him. His fidgeting was making the whole table shake. Faye felt the tremors in her seat and they unnerved her. 'Are you sure you want that coffee? You're wired enough already,' she added. She clipped her hands onto the edge of the table and looked down at her fingernails, admiring the reflection of the fluorescent strip lighting in the sheen of her nail polish. They began to talk about school, as though nothing was going to change. Neither mentioned the quartet in which they had played together for the past two years. Nicholas talked with a gentleness, as though at any moment he might confess a secret. Faye kept a robust cheerfulness around her: she flicked her hair, she smiled and rolled her eyes.

'Are you looking forward to going?' Nicholas eventually asked her. The question didn't mean what it pretended to. Nicholas wanted to know whether she'd miss him; he wanted to hear her say that she would. Faye thought she knew what Nicholas was trying to ask her, but she didn't want to risk being wrong and look foolish. She accepted the question as it was.

'Yes,' she said, with a couple of nods. Her hair bounced around her face. Nicholas looked at her hairline, where pale, smooth skin gradually gave way to tiny blondish curls, coiled around themselves like springs from a pocket watch. There was a pause. He shifted on the bench and his knee caught hers beneath the table. He pulled it away, fidgeting more as a tremor passed through him.

'Actually, no,' Faye said suddenly. She looked down at her cup and raised her eyebrows. She felt herself weak for her admission. Keep things to yourself, she told herself. Nicholas's large dark eyes showed a vulnerability which invited confession.

'You're not looking forward to it?' he asked her, tracing the rim of his cup with finger and thumb. He imagined the cup as her lips, willed the china to yield to his touch.

'No, I'm not,' she said. She felt suddenly that she wanted to cry, a looseness behind her eyes, and she raised her cup to her lips, though it was already empty. I am sixteen, she heard in her head. Toddlers cry about their first day at school.

'Do you have to go?' Nicholas began. 'Why don't you stay? It'll be much easier staying on here, have you told your mum that?' He blurted the words, a frown puckering his brow, the fingers of his left hand pressed tightly into the wood of the table.

'Yes,' Faye replied, cleanly, 'I have to go.' She looked up at him and saw what she didn't want to see: his big eyes scrutinizing her. She wanted to take him to her, would have liked to reach out and interlink her hand with his, feeling his even fingertips close over her knuckles. Inside her head she and Nicholas were close friends who could sleep beside

47

one another, trade in secrets, share their clothes. In reality, despite the hours they had spent together, she still felt nervous in his presence. She could not look at him without being aware that he too was looking at her and worrying about what he might see.

'Are you going to carry on playing your violin?' he asked her, inadvertently letting his eyes fall to her breasts. He looked back up to her face. He had tried, on many occasions, to imagine her naked. Each time the task defeated him. Her body became lost in a collage of limbs: of body parts that he had seen – her legs, arms, neck – and that he tried to remember correctly, and those that he hadn't and couldn't, despite intense concentration, visualize. Time and time again she defeated him.

'I don't know,' she said, shaking her head. 'I'm supposed to. There's an orchestra and all the usual shit. But I never practise,' she said, and smiled. 'As you well know.'

They sat in silence for a few minutes, while Nicholas concertinaed the end of a paper tube of sugar and Faye looked over his shoulder and into the street outside. Nicholas cleared his throat and fidgeted, his knee caught hers again underneath the table. He left it there, his jeans against her bare leg, and slowly – letting them cross the surface of the table, her hands around her cup, her blue shirt – raised his eyes to hers. She looked at him and looked away. He saw in her face a flicker of fear. She did not move her leg.

Nicholas felt his body slow and stop; he seemed locked in this posture. He felt himself stiffen, he wanted to push his body towards her, so that his thigh might touch hers. His hands tingled, craving to reach below to feel the resistance of her knee give way to the soft curve of her leg. He couldn't move. Breathing became an effort. This, thought Nicholas, is desire. Like a butterfly poised for a moment, a single vibration of the string of his cello, he forced himself to confront what was inside him, mistakenly believing that his introspection might ease what it was he felt.

They sat there without talking, knee pressed against knee, like locked wrestlers, silently sweating on a mat. Nicholas had lived with this lust for four years. It seemed to his teachers that he was a bright boy with a passion for the cello. Only he knew that he played it solely for Faye. When he sat and worked out the perfect fourths in the scale of B he did it for her. He took his instrument to him when he was angry with her, when he resented her, when she confused him. He was a fool over the relationship between his cello and Faye, and he knew it. She could not possibly know that he tuned his strings for her, that each time his finger pressed a string he wondered whether she would like the note. Still, as he dropped the shiny neck of the instrument against his shoulder, he did it as his own private homage to Faye.

It was Nicholas who broke the silence.

'It's a girls' school then?' he asked. He flicked his cup and a single, high note sounded. Faye smiled. With his leg against hers she was confident enough to *interpret* his question. He did not mean what he said: he knew that it was a girls' school.

'Yes,' she said, looking at him, amusement on her face. 'No boys allowed. All the teachers are women. They probably lock us up at ten every night.' Nicholas flicked his cup again. A dimple appeared on her cheek and she slid his cup towards her so that he would have to stretch to reach it. Beneath the table their knees still rested against each other, like the knees of an old couple, married for decades. Both of them pretended that they had not noticed the position of their legs; both of them felt nothing else.

'But there'll be a boys' school, won't there? There always is. Dock leaves always grow near nettles. It's the same

49

principle.' Nicholas said, leaning in towards her. He looked at her hairline, her fingernails, a freckle just by the corner of her mouth. She did not follow, nor particularly like, his simile. She frowned and then laughed.

'Well I suppose there'll be a boys' school somewhere nearby. Not too far away. It seems likely, probably,' she replied lightly. She wanted to reassure him and laughed because she knew he had nothing to worry about. Nicholas saw her smile and heard her laugh. He took it as a demonstration of her attractiveness, a display of brightly coloured tail feathers. She was aware of her power to entice.

'There'll be boys in it,' he said. His throat was dry.

She laughed again and he looked at her dimples and wondered at their depth. Three, four millimetres perhaps? The denim of his trousers was around the same thickness. Our bare flesh is separated by the depth of your dimples, he thought.

'Of course there'll be boys in it. It's a boys' school. What do you expect, Teenage Mutant Ninja Turtles?'

Expect, no; prefer, yes, Nicholas thought. His heart hurt, it actually hurt. Perhaps I am having a heart attack, he thought. 'Well, what will we – I mean – what do you think – will you write to me?' he asked. He needed to clarify where he stood. At times he imagined himself in his own world, construing meanings and analysing signals that weren't there.

'Of course I'll write,' Faye replied, knowing as she said it that a miserable, cold piece of paper could not make up for the feeling of his leg against hers, for the sight of his agile hands, which lay before her now, still fiddling with a tube of sugar. The very idea of writing being some sort of substitute for seeing Nicholas was ludicrous; it sat in her head and mocked her. How could words hope to compete with flesh? 'Will you come and visit me?'

'Only if I can stay,' Nicholas said. He smiled, a sly, slow smile. Her question reassured him and he wanted to lean over and kiss her. A couple entered the coffee bar: an overweight man in a suit who had long forgotten how it was to have hair and a woman, wide-hipped in copper eyeshadow. They sat down opposite each other and shared a cigarette. I will kiss you before you leave, Nicholas thought to himself. I will kiss you properly.

'I should get home,' Faye announced with a pulse of her eyebrows. 'I have to pack.'

'When are you leaving again?' Nicholas asked. He knew the answer. He had circled the date in his calendar and written it repeatedly in his diary.

'The day after tomorrow,' she told him. Neither of them moved. Getting up would entail separating their legs. 'What are you doing tomorrow?'

Nicholas shrugged. 'Nothing,' he said. Practising my cello, he could have told her. Thinking of you. His school was not due to start back for another week.

'Do you want to do something tomorrow afternoon, then?' she asked.

Yeah, thought Nicholas, I want to kiss you. He nodded.

'Okay,' she said with a smile. She climbed out from her seat and stood up, brushing her skirt down around her and flicking her hair over her shoulders.

'Okay,' he smiled back. He dropped the dog-eared sugar tube in an ashtray and stood up, interweaving his fingers and clicking his knuckles. Faye looked up at him as they made their way to the door.

'Okay,' she said, smiling.

'Okay,' he replied.

They did not see each other again.

SIX

The morning after Nicholas found the folder he got up unusually early and left for work, crossing the park in the low, eastern sunlight which lent a pinkish glow to the grey stone of the Italian Gardens. The cleaners were still in the supermarket when he arrived, polishing the floors. Nicholas carefully replaced the folder in the cardboard box which he and Sean used for lost property, sliding it underneath a grey skipping rope and checking to see that it looked undisturbed. The night before, with a creeping sense of unease, Nicholas had taken a note of Faye's details, writing her telephone number and address on the back of a receipt which he folded up and slipped into his wallet. He sat down in the office he shared with Sean – a small corridor of a room with a bank of TV screens along one side – and fished out the receipt. Be careful, he said to himself.

'Good morning!' Sean came in through the door and took a deep breath, raising his hands to his hips and eyeing Nicholas. 'You're in early. Can't sleep? The pressures of life as a security guard keeping you up?' he asked with a loose grin. He sat down and began to unlace his shoes. Sean was a year older than Nicholas. He was smart and sharp and enjoyed Nicholas's company but at the same time resented him, because Nicholas, it seemed, had got himself a degree with no particular effort and Sean had never passed an exam in his life. He had dark fluttering eyes, large hands and a straightforwardness which Nicholas found reassuring. Sean thought his job was beneath him, and it was. The collection and protection of items of lost property however usually cheered him up, if only because he had long ago become convinced that this was the best way for him to meet women. One day, two years ago, a woman with feline cheekbones and jet-black hair had told him, once he'd produced her gold mobile telephone from a shabby cardboard box, that she loved him.

'I love you!' she exclaimed, a lock of hair falling over her face, 'I can't tell you!' and she threw her arms around his neck and kissed him on his jaw, large soft lips pressing into his rough skin. She then kissed her phone, over a sticker of a cat's face just by the screen.

'Thank you so much!' she cried, brushing the lock of hair off her cheek.

'Only doing my job,' said Sean with a grin. She turned to leave but he called her back. 'I think you've forgotten something,' he said. '*Again.*'

'What?'

'My phone number,' he replied.

'Oh,' she said. She met his eyes. 'Okay,' she mumbled. 'What's your name?'

'Sean.'

Her face lit up. 'It's fate!' she cried. 'This is a sign. The guy I met at the weekend. His number's in this phone. *His* name is Sean too. He's sending me a sign, I know he is,' and she bounced off, thrilled at the prospect of a whole new relationship and without Sean's phone number. She was, as Sean later explained to Nicholas, 'savoury and sweet all in one' and Sean had watched her departing rear, almost liquid in PVC trousers, with sadness and resignation.

'We're in the reunion business, Nicholas,' he had said. 'And reunions are necessarily happy. We are *the reuniters*. Some people will feel immense gratitude.' And so Sean waited for the day when the I-love-you woman would return, or another come along in her place. Next time she would mean what she said and they would live happily ever after.

The general public lost between one and three items a day in the supermarket, because it was a large store and because, with its harsh lighting and humdrum distractions, it was easy to forget who you were, let alone what you came in with. As Gareth used to tell them, 'people have a lot of things on their minds these days,' and so Sean and Nicholas had a lot of things in lost property: a glass eye, two prams, a huge wooden box almost like a coffin which they couldn't open and which was never claimed. It still lay underneath their desk, covered in monitor cabling, the powdery green paint slowly flaking off in the two patches where they rested their feet. When he'd first started the job Sean had found a camera case in which was £100,000 in £50 notes, all bundled up with elastic bands. The owner came in the next day – a female tourist from Malaysia who bowed her head when she smiled to thank him and told him that she would dream of him that evening and pray for him the following morning.

This week in lost property they had a black umbrella; a skipping rope with grey rubber handles; a beaded purse with £3.78 in it; an empty notepad with a Garfield pencil; a pair of pliers; a mobile phone; a pale red folder; two pairs of sunglasses; a guidebook to London and the back half of a novel. Sean's hopes were on the last item – he felt that it had to be reclaimed, reasoned that women read more than men and had already read it twice himself so that when the inevitably delightful woman came to collect it, he could tantalize and tease her with the rest of the story.

'I'm not so sure about your theory,' Nicholas told Sean. 'Not everyone wants everything they lose back.'

'Tell me one thing,' Sean replied, 'that you wouldn't

want back? If you've lost something of course you'd want it back.'

'My virginity,' Nicholas tried.

'We haven't had any mislaid virginities yet. Though you can't say I don't try.'

'A scarf that your grandmother had knitted for you and which you felt obliged to wear but actually hated.'

'Not convinced,' Sean shook his head.

'Your appointment card for the dentist. A bomb.'

'Maybe. Anything else?'

Nicholas paused. 'Your heart?' he said.

'Get away with you, Nicholas. I win. The reunion business is a happy business.'

'I'm going on a course today,' Sean announced to Nicholas that morning. 'Will you be all right on your own?' he asked with a sly smile. Sean had worked in the business long enough not to bother stopping everyone who shoplifted. He concerned himself mainly with the ones who took too much or stole too often. Nicholas had been in the business for such a short time that he wouldn't have been able to spot a theft even if he'd wanted to. Between the two of them most shoplifters got away with their goods.

'I'll be fine,' Nicholas told him. 'What course is it?'

'Time management,' Sean replied, slipping his feet from his shoes and sitting cross-legged in his office chair.

'When does it start?'

'In a couple of minutes. It's at some hotel up the road,' he said, scratching at a stain on the front of his trousers. Nicholas let a moment pass. On one of the screens in front of him he watched Harold, one of the staff, open the doors to the street. Gareth appeared on another screen, striding away from the potential influx of the general public.

'Hadn't you better go?' Nicholas asked at last. Sean

raised his eyebrows and slipped his feet down from his chair.

'I'll give it another five minutes yet. It's only respectable to be late for a Time Management course.'

Nicholas spent the day constructing criteria which might help him make a decision. If, when he walked into the freezer section, there was anyone standing by the oven chips, then he should get in touch with Faye. If he could walk the length of one aisle in under forty paces then he should call her. Nicholas was not good with decisions. His approach was too thorough and balanced, he saw advantages and disadvantages everywhere until the two blurred together in a whirlwind of confusion. His sympathies were too easily aroused for any kind of decisiveness.

That afternoon Nicholas spotted a theft for the very first time. An elderly woman in a flat brown raincoat pulled a tin of beans from the shelves in aisle number four and slipped it into her pocket. Nicholas got to his feet in the office and made his way out to find her.

'Did you want something, dear?' she said loudly as he approached, as though speaking to him through soup. She was an ex-nurse with a hatred of euphemism: she hoped that Nicholas wouldn't beat about the bush.

'Well, I'm sorry to bother you,' Nicholas replied and then he hesitated. The earth was slowing on its axis, the last truly wild Siberian tiger had died, the hole in the ozone layer would take over sixty years to recover and the North Pole was melting. Where did a stolen tin of green beans fit into this? 'Did you know that we have the smoked bacon on special offer this week?' he said to her, seeing that she had only one pack of it in her basket.

'It's buy two get one free,' he told her. 'And you don't even have to steal it,' he muttered.

'Pardon?' she said, and her eyes seem to bounce unseeingly before him.

'We have an offer on smoked bacon,' Nicholas said again, separating out the words, glancing down at the curtain of coat behind which the tin of beans had disappeared. He felt ashamed that he'd even entertained the notion of taking this woman back to the office and searching her.

'I'd offer you something in return,' she said quickly and quietly. He looked at her, puzzled, and could see the thinness of her skin, covered with liver spots like the bubbles in a milkshake. 'But I haven't got anything.'

''S all right,' replied Nicholas gently. 'There's a camera at the other end of this aisle, so make sure you have your back to it in future.'

'It's terribly thrilling,' she said to him, 'you should give it a whirl yourself. A friend and I have competitions to see what's the biggest thing we can get out of here. My husband was in Colditz, you know. He says I wouldn't be doing this if I'd been with him.'

'I dare say he's right,' replied Nicholas and he took her arm and led her to the back of the store. 'They're just down there,' he said, pointing with his right hand.

'What are?' she said.

'It's for the camera,' he said, 'so I look like I'm giving you directions. Good day then.' And he paced off in the opposite direction.

Nicholas had given it a whirl. He used to take sweets or cigarettes or magazines. When he was sixteen and Faye had gone away to her new school he went one grey and turgid Saturday afternoon to W.H. Smith in the centre of town, where he picked up a paperback copy of *A Tale of Two Cities*, looked through it for a few moments, noticing the dull gleam on his ridged thumbnail which hooked over a page. He shut the book and walked out of the shop with it still in his hand, only to be woken from his reverie by a low-pitched shout and a firm hand on his upper arm. He turned back readily, happy to return with the overweight shop assistant – a boy who couldn't be more than two years his senior and who after this no doubt would be angling for a promotion – and leave his fate to the management of the shop. In the end they called the police, who, tired of unruly adolescent boys, took him to the station where they searched him, just in case he had managed to sneak any ink rubbers or packets of cartridges into his pockets. He hadn't, but they did find a book token to the value of ten pounds in his back pocket. This had them stumped. Single-handedly Nicholas brought the combined brainpower of the West Yorkshire Constabulary to a standstill.

'Why did you steal the book?' a long-faced policeman asked him, a pen poised over the wide-spaced, dotted lines of a statement pad. It reminded Nicholas of the paper he had used at infant school to practise handwriting on.

'I don't know,' Nicholas replied. He had, as a teenager, an air of cockiness. The policeman looked at him down his long nose.

'I forgot to pay for it,' Nicholas tried.

'I've heard that one before,' replied the policeman.

'I've heard *that* one before,' replied Nicholas and the policeman sneered at him.

'Are you taking the piss?' he asked.

'If you have to ask—' Nicholas began but at that point they showed his mother in and the expression on her face took the words from Nicholas's mouth.

'We don't understand it, Mrs Bee –'

'Beimuk,' she said.

'He had a book token all along. We think he might be

involved with a gang. Glue, probably. That's what they normally take.'

Nicholas resisted the temptation to ask them what they thought glue-sniffers would want with a copy of *A Tale of Two Cities*. In fact he resisted all temptations and listened to his mother plead with the officers and explain that her son was actually *a good boy*. She struggled with her English and Nicholas hung his head as he listened to her unfinished sentences and mispronounced words echo around the small room. The officer regarded her suspiciously and sneered every so often when he couldn't understand what she was saying. She was adamant and wilful, unwilling to accept their verdict on her son. In the end the policeman gave up, bored by the weird kid and his jabbering mother and let them go with a caution. On his report he noted down that the child was most likely retarded and the mother was foreign.

Towards the end of the day Sean returned from his course, his hair dishevelled and his tie loosened. He came into the office and slumped down in his chair, crossing his feet on the desk.

'Hey, how was your course? Did you learn anything?' Nicholas asked him. A straw from a small carton of Ribena was wedged in the corner of his mouth. The carton he held by his mouth, as though he might be advertising the product.

'"Time is linear,"' Sean said. '"A sequence of events from birth up to the present and continuing into the future. The present and future events can be controlled, scheduled and determined by you. The past is completed."'

'They didn't tell you that,' said Nicholas.

'Oh yes. They also told me to only ever touch a piece of paper once,' Sean continued.

'Oh,' said Nicholas, and he thought – how could he not? – of the folder and the CV and the intrigue he had felt as his fingers touched the sheet over and over again.

'I threw away all the course sheets they gave me, because I'd already touched them. At the end we had to fill in a survey to say how it was. They said there were no right or wrong answers, so I wrote "Pedigree Chum" in every box and came back. Did anything happen while I was away?'

Nicholas smiled. 'No,' he said. Sean took off his cap and scratched at his head.

'Oh well, nearly hometime. What are you doing tonight?' he asked.

Nicholas opened his mouth to speak and then stopped. 'Nothing much,' he said, shrugging. 'What about you? An evening of Mediterranean passion?'

'Well, I thought I might lie on the right-hand side of the sofa. Or perhaps the left. Or possibly strew myself across the middle. Either way, by staying in I shall single-handedly unravel the dreams of London's young women and unmap into abstraction their pressing carnal desires.' Nicholas shook his head and drummed his fingers briskly on the desk in front of him. Sean continued, 'Though having said that my brother is doing his medical exams at the moment and he just sits and watches hours and hours of *ER*. He says it's revision. Perhaps I'd be better off out of the flat. Do you want to go for a drink?'

Nicholas paused. As he watched the minute hand of the clock in their office inch towards six o'clock he felt filled with a new kind of life, as though he turned from reptile to mammal in the space of a few seconds. 'I can't, actually. Thanks anyway. Another time.'

'I thought you said you weren't doing anything?'

'Well, I –' Nicholas stood up and stretched, hunching his shoulders and pushing out his arms in front of him. Sean looked at him and not for the first time decided that Nicholas was rather strange. Polite, friendly, funny even at times, but there seemed to be something else going on inside. 'I've got plans, actually.'

'Okay,' Sean replied. He watched the supermarket doors close on a monitor in front of them and then switched off the TVs. With a brief goodbye he departed. For the second time in as many nights Nicholas left work with the pale red folder concealed beneath his jacket. He was going to return it to its owner.

SEVEN

Far far away there is a broad land with black soil and a black sea, which stretches underneath a swathe of blue. It is a land of lost property: as the years have tumbled by it has been passed from one people to another, stolen, taken, surrendered, until finally, in 1991, it was returned, battered and incomplete, to its original owners, those that were left. The old ones would rather die than lose it again. The young ones are not sure that it is worth that much. It is a land of sun-blessed flowers, of red skirts and embroidered linen blouses, of corruption and cherry orchards and mass graves.

Stefan Beimuk never knew for sure whether his wife had planned her departure from the Ukraine with their youngest son, or whether she had just been caught up in the heat of the moment. Their disappearance coincided neatly with the departure of a Danish swimming team who were passing through their village on the way to Kyiv for a competition. They left no note, but Stefan did not need an explanation. He had always known that were his wife presented with a choice between freedom for one child and keeping her family together she would take the former. She was a wilful, determined woman with remarkably clear sight. He told his elder son, Bohdan, and the rest of the village that they had gone east, to Korosten, to visit a sick relation, and they might be gone some time. His colleagues on the farm tutted and shook their heads, a look of thunder in their eyes as they realized that it must have been her then, Kalyna Beimuk, who had taken that evening's bread from the kitchen.

Stefan felt, for those first few days, a searing anxiety for his lost child and wife. He pictured them – he couldn't help it – caught and locked in police cells, mown down by an errant train on a level crossing, killed by robbers, or Poles or Russians, abandoned in the middle of nowhere, starving. He prayed silently that they would make it across the border and felt, as each day passed, more relieved: no news was good news when it came to getting out. Bohdan began to stop asking where they were and Stefan, gradually, had less and less idea.

Kalyna and Nicholas did leave town on the Danish swimming team's bus, that much was true. They stowed themselves away, a mother crunched up tight beneath a minibus seat, urging her four-year-old son to silence. She breathed carbon monoxide during the day in great lungfuls as it seeped through the floor of the bus and Nicholas slept fitfully. At night they would enter out into the darkness to stretch and to steal whatever food they could find. Usually Kalyna headed for animals: dogs or perhaps cats, to see what food she could take from them.

It was four days before they were discovered by a Danish swimming coach, bright blue eyes and a small hand bending back the board beneath the seat because she thought she could smell something peculiar. *Please, help me, take me to the border, I want to leave*, Kalyna urged her in Russian. Heda looked from Kalyna to her child and nodded slowly – they had been warned of this by a diplomat from Moscow – but Heda decided to ignore his instructions and take them back with her. Why not? she thought. She brought in a small loaf of springy white bread and some salami, encrusted with peppercorns around the edge and thick with beef fat. Kalyna wept, she couldn't help it; and she thought perhaps she had reached heaven: perhaps heaven was a Swedish-made minibus filled with bright blue blinking eyes and

63

Danish food. Nicholas picked off the peppercorns and dropped them into his mother's dirty cupped hand. Heda smiled and told them that that evening she would take them into the hostel so they could wash.

At the time of leaving Kalyna had a strong instinct not to do what she did: not to break up her family, not to desert her elder child. But she had chosen Stefan for good reason. She knew that he would care for Bohdan. In the back of the bus Kalyna looked at her younger son's face, pale and pinched but with the same thickly lashed eyes as hers. This child will know freedom, she decided.

The driver of the minibus had other ideas. On the way into the Ukraine, just after crossing the border in the town of Lviv, he had met a prostitute with long limbs and hair cut to her head whom he wanted to take home with him. She had made love to him for the price of a packet of chewing gum in Denmark, and the driver had spent the trip so far dividing his salary by this figure, over and over again, until he finally managed to work out that the answer was 73,000. He could have this girl 73,000 times a year, he calculated. That's about two hundred times a day, he thought. And then he decided he would marry her. Two hundred times a day was worthy of marriage, surely. Then once he was married he could keep his money, do it 200 times a day and buy chewing gum instead. Since there was only enough space for one stowaway in the bus the driver agreed to take the woman and her child to Lviv and then exchange her for his slender beauty, despite Heda's touchy reprovals.

So Kalyna and Nicholas were dumped out of the bus at Lviv, where Heda pressed 200 kroner into their hands and her St Christopher's cross. Kalyna pushed it back to her, shaking her head, frowning, speaking, though she knew that her words were no use. Heda believed she was refusing the necklace out of embarrassment since it was a finely crafted piece of silver, which Heda had just moments before removed from her own neck. Kalyna was trying to explain that religion was forbidden – the possession of such an object meant trouble – but it did no good. In the end Heda forced it on her, putting, in her moment of triumph, her hand on her stomach, for she was three months pregnant with her first child, though her swimming team didn't know yet.

As a final parting gift, Heda pointed west for them – saying the name of her country ('Danemark') and pointing emphatically – as though scolding the field of rye, dotted with poppies, that lay directly ahead as the road curved round. Kalyna nodded and shrugged and then set off back into Lviv so that she would be able to get her bearings. Even if she had been able to understand Heda, Kalyna would not have followed her direction. She and her son were heading for Hungary.

While his wife travelled at night, between homesteads and farms, walking in what she hoped was the right direction with her son on her back or dawdling beside her, Stefan worked on the farm, deflecting Bohdan's questions and urging him to play with the other children. 'Go find another brother,' he would say when Bohdan moped around in the evenings, wondering what had happened to his mother and her bedtime stories. Stefan was not a harsh man: he was a gentle father and a good husband, but half of his family had gone and he knew there was nothing he could do. He missed Kalyna; they used to hold hands in the street when they walked home from work in the evening. And he missed his little boy terribly.

Kalyna learnt her craft quickly – her hearing had always been good and her eyesight better and at the first sign of movement or noise in the empty blackness of the night she would hide until whatever it was had passed. Sometimes she felt that they were accompanied by the benevolent ghosts of members of the Ukrainian Insurgent Army, who had refused to fight with both the Germans and Russians during the war and who had crept through the forests at night, gathering supporters and arms.

She had startled a wild boar with her young in a forest once, freezing on the spot, her heart running away inside her. *Don't move*, she had hissed at her son. *Look at the ground and don't move.* For two hours they stood as statues in the forest, a tableau of mother and son in terror as branches cracked around them and sweat ran smoothly from Kalyna's armpits down her ribcage and into the waistband of her trousers. The boar was static too, its hair erect, grunting, ready for attack. After one hour its agitation passed. After two hours it herded its young away and went off to find food, leaving Kalyna, with flickering muscles, to pick up her son and press her face against him. *Thank you*, she whispered into his ear.

It was about a week later that they met the other woman and child. They had reached the beginnings of mountains now and they filled Kalyna with both an anticipation and a dread. She was desperate to be out of the country, since she could no longer sleep in the Ukraine for fear of an unseen army of old friends and strangers tracking her down and sending her and her child away. The regional headquarters of the Soviet Secret Police was at Slavsko, not far from where she was. The dread she felt was inspired by the mountains themselves and what they held: everyone knew there were bandits there. Just as the land had ruptured and come into conflict with itself to produce these towering granite beasts, law and order broke down in their vicinity, creating a prehistoric savagery which loomed over the rocks like a rain cloud waiting to burst.

Kalyna pressed on, still walking at night, sometimes spending hours searching for tracks and paths which would take her over cols and through valleys. She told Nicholas tales, tales he knew already but still listened to: about how some storks came to be black; about how the snowball flower came to be called Kalyna; about the man who sought the magic flower of the fern. 'The history of our land is spoken,' she told him, 'and after me you must tell what you know.'

It was early one morning, as she and Nicholas were searching, shivering, for a place to make their beds, that she saw, on a path above them, what she thought for a moment was herself. A woman was coming towards them, a weary weight in her walk, a small child climbing down on her bottom behind her. Kalyna stood in the path and waited.

'Hello,' said the woman. Kalyna was twenty-nine. The woman looked of a similar age. Kalyna felt a surge of gratitude: that the woman had no man with her, that she was here, on the mountain with them, evidence that it was conquerable.

'Hello,' replied Kalyna. 'Are you on holiday?' she asked. Either of them could have been a spy. They knew not to trust each other.

'Yes,' replied the woman, dropping her eyes to the ground. 'You too?'

'Yes,' replied Kalyna. Nicholas, who had grown painfully thin and malnourished, was staring, open-mouthed at the woman's daughter, a pale-skinned girl with a head of blonde ringlets which bounced around her face as she scrambled down the mountain. Kalyna took her son's hand in her own and shook it slightly to wake him up, but still he stared, as though the earth had opened and Venus emerged. The other woman laughed at him, knowing that her daughter would captivate men one day.

'We saw the Hungarian border,' the woman said with a heavy look at Kalyna.

'How nice,' replied Kalyna, without conviction.

'Yes,' said the woman, 'it is well manned with three, perhaps four, fences. I am happy that our motherland is so thoroughly protected.' She spoke with a slant in her voice, a crushing of vowels and shortening of consonants. Kalyna thought she must be from somewhere near the seaside. They talked a little more, about their children and then decided, as a gesture of goodwill, that Nicholas and the little girl should swap shoes: Nicholas, in a pair of neat red leather lace-ups which his grandmother had acquired from a friend in Moscow, stepped into the little girl's trainers which fastened with two velcro strips and she put on the red shoes, admiring their colour amongst the autumnal bleakness of the mountains. They wished each other luck once again and went their separate ways, Kalyna having casually enquired how much further it was to the border. Nicholas watched his red shoes walk away from him, mesmerized by their bobbing up and down, in time with the gold ringlets above them.

In two days' time Kalyna and Nicholas had reached the border. They travelled alongside it for two more nights until the fenceposts stopped and all that was left was a farmer's stone wall with brambles growing over it. They crossed into Hungary, the first time either of them had ever been outside the Ukraine. The following morning the other woman and her daughter, coming down out of the Carpathians, had their throats slit by a robber who took the woman's wedding ring, their clothes and the child's shoes, which he wore on a leather thong around his neck, to show that even with four-year-old girls he had no mercy. The robber, who called himself Kozak, rode on his horse to Lviv, for he had contacts there who had sent for him.

*

In Dytyatky Stefan said to Bohdan, 'If anyone asks where your mother and brother are, you don't know.'

'But I don't know,' replied Bohdan, who had the same doll-like eyes as his mother but who hadn't grown even a centimetre since she and Nicholas had left. Stefan had noticed that his son was short, but said nothing about it. He had started, over the past few months, to feel angry towards his wife for what he now saw as a desertion. He missed her more than he could say. And he worried about both his sons.

'Exactly, good,' replied his father, and Bohdan wondered whether his father knew where his mother was. He could not forget his mother and brother, but as time passed they became blurred around the edges and he could no longer remember their voices. He had not found himself another brother, but instead four new mothers, for each of the women who lived on the farm took it upon themselves to care for this motherless boy, spitting on their broad palms to flatten his hair, inspecting his hands before he took a seat at the long communal table. Bohdan rejected their concern with a sullen shrug. At eight he thought himself a man already and, despite his lack of height, he was strong and could use a scythe just like the older boys to gather in the harvest before it was despatched.

The winter that year was a hard one. Bohdan refused to grow and at night he would huddle into a ball on the floor cursing like a soldier as the world contracted and froze around him. He dreamed of wearing a uniform and going to sea, like the pictures of the men he had seen in a newspaper once. He was a straightforward child, interested in reasons and explanations. He was sure of himself and of the rational arrangement of the world. He approached his jobs on the farm methodically and seriously. Nicholas, had he grown up beside him, would have found his older brother dishearteningly good at most things, but would have decided that he was boring. Bohdan would have found Nicholas flighty and excitable.

Stefan had started a relationship with the wife of a friend and early each morning, just before dawn, she would creep fully clothed to where he slept and climb on top of him. Her warm, pale flesh felt like pudding to Stefan and she would jiggle around until he gave her the sign, when she would prise herself off him with a sucking noise and he would spurt his juices while the day arrived. Sometimes his semen would hit the small window at the head of his bed, where it would slide lazily for a few centimetres and then freeze slowly against the icy glass. Bohdan, in idle moments while getting ready for bed, would press his finger to these whitish fossilized dribbles and wonder what they were.

Kalyna and Nicholas spent that winter in Hungary, travelling when they could, sheltering in barns and farmhouses when they couldn't. Kalyna recounted a story almost every morning to her son before they went to sleep – her voice a whisper. Nicholas frequently asked, as evening came and they set out on their way, whether they were going home.

It's a funny thing: you can just walk across Europe. There are rivers, fenced-off factories, forests, motorways but there are always ways round these obstacles. Europe is small and green and temperate: you can just walk, and walk they did. Kalyna watched as her upper arms became sinewy and her hip bones began to protrude. Nicholas was slow so she took to carrying him. Often he slept, a dead weight on her front, his bony chin digging into her shoulder, wet, muddy shoes scuffing the top of her thighs.

In Budapest, having eaten only bread and snow for the

past week, Kalyna dared to enter a bank and change some of the kroner Heda had given her. When she saw the exchange rate she knew that here, for this stretch of her life, she was a millionaire. She offered only two notes over the counter and was presented with a handful in return. In her head she thanked Heda. She did not dare think what would have happened had she not met her. Kalyna and Nicholas went to the largest department store and chose some clothes from the small selection the State saw fit to provide. Kalyna counted out her money note by note, making a show of digging in her pocket for each one, as though they were the last of her parents' savings. Nicholas had new socks and shoes (though Kalyna kept his small stiff trainers in a plastic bag), a new pair of thick cotton trousers bought too long, for, unlike his brother, he was growing. Kalyna piled her purchases for her son on the counter: a vest, a shirt, two jumpers, a thick felt coat with a fur-trimmed hood, a pair of gloves and finally a scarf. She also bought herself some new things, finding the most practical items she could in amongst the purple nylon slacks and beige pleated jackets which were supposed to represent the pinnacle of Eastern bloc fashions.

From the department store they went to a swimming baths and sat, for much longer than was healthy, in a sauna, astonished that after months of cold they could now feel so warm. Nicholas emerged from the changing rooms in his new clothes, pink-cheeked and clean-haired. For the first time in weeks he smiled at his mother. 'You will know freedom,' she whispered to him, but he didn't understand what she meant. To him it seemed that life was a long, nocturnal walk, where the need to sleep and the need to keep warm battled for his attention.

From the baths they went to a hotel and had what seemed like the first meal of their lives: strips of beef and calf's liver in a stew with beans and peas and red wine, served in white bone china on a damask tablecloth. They hardly spoke. Kalyna had little to say: she was not yet clear of the danger of her homeland and felt only fear of it. She knew nothing of where they were going. Nicholas, halfway through poppyseed cake with sour cream, burst into tears. Kalyna picked him up, stroked the back of his head and smiled, apologetically, at the waiter. She checked into a room and put him to bed.

Kalyna and Nicholas spent four months at the Hotel Pannónia in Budapest. They arrived at the start of December and did not leave until the very first signs of spring appeared towards the end of March, when the cherry trees along the Duna burst into blossom and the earth around their bases started to soften. During this time Kalyna and Nicholas thrived: they ate well and stayed warm in their hotel room, from time to time stepping out onto the balcony to breathe a few lungfuls of the sharp air. Kalyna dropped her Russian and began to speak Ukrainian to Nicholas, who at first frowned at his mother and sulked, but gradually began repeating words she used, until he spoke his own language with the simple fluency known only to a child.

Kalyna, with an admirable instinct for self-preservation and her dark, defined eyes, started up a relationship with the hotel manager, who overlooked their absent passports and visas and was happy as long as they paid for the room and the twice-weekly visits from the dark buxom woman continued. After a few weeks he gave them a discount and took them both to the circus, where Nicholas had marshmallows covered in chocolate. Igor was a bloated man with crooked teeth and a swathe of dirty blond hair, who approached his staff and guests alike with a wide-eyed placidity and the conviction that as long as the cakes and desserts were up to scratch, then the rest of the hotel would run smoothly. He was often to be found loitering in the kitchen, where he would test the puddings and noisily lick his fingers, one by one.

Kalyna explained to Nicholas that they were going to have to make one more journey through the nights: across the border to Austria, but they would stay in guest houses in Hungary as far as they could since Igor had promised to call up some friends in the trade and persuade them to let this passport-and-visa-less woman and child stay for one night. Kalyna planned to cross the border in June, to make it as easy as possible. She still had some kroner, but had no idea what they would be worth once she slipped under the curtain and entered the West.

The thought of Western Europe scared Kalyna. She had awoken one morning with a dry mouth and a hot head fresh from a dream of a man in an overcoat who had chased her along across a motorway, grinning maniacally and appearing in front of her when he should have been behind. She climbed from her bed that morning, and leaning into the bath so the high porcelain rim left a red dent across her thighs, washed her hair. Then she went to the kitchen for a pair of scissors and found Igor in his office.

'Will you cut my hair?' she asked him, taking a metal chair over to the window and seating herself with her back to the light. She had come down in her robe, a beige towelling gown which she pulled over her legs as she sat down. Heavy drops of water dripped from the ends of her hair.

'Good morning!' Igor exclaimed and hurried over to her, placing his fat wet lips on hers for a kiss.

'Will you cut my hair, Igor?' she asked him again. She held the scissors, the blades covered by her fist, in the air.

'Your hair?' he asked, reaching over gingerly and taking a few dripping strands between his fingers. 'I love your hair, Kalyna. It is . . .' Igor struggled with words.

'Please,' Kalyna said and she pressed the scissors into his hand. 'Short all over. Like a man.'

'Oh, no,' gasped Igor. 'You are not a man, you are a *woman*,' and he slipped his free hand down her robe and cupped a breast in it. 'Men come from monkeys but God created women,' he told her, running his fingers lightly along the channel between breast and ribcage. He closed his eyes and sighed. Igor liked pleasure. He would like nothing better than to run the Hotel Pannónia from his bed, in which he would keep Kalyna, some cakes, the day's newspaper, and a television.

'Not now, Igor,' Kalyna said softly, turning her face towards him. His eyes roamed hungrily over the zealous curve of her upper lip. She removed his hand and pushed her hair over her shoulders. 'Please cut it.' Igor looked down helplessly at the scissors in his hand and snipped pathetically at the air a couple of times. Under normal circumstances Kalyna would not have slept with him. She liked him a lot, found herself charmed by his crooked teeth and admired his complete lack of guile, but she did not find him wholly attractive. He shuffled around to stand behind her and rested a section of hair on his palm. As he regarded the sleek chestnut mousetails he saw something behind them which was much more interesting. From this angle he had a clear view of Kalyna's magnificent bosom and he gazed at it, thinking vaguely of the florist's accounts which needed to be completed that morning and imagining at the same time his ideal world in which he could spend the morning dozing on such a bosom. Finally, with absent-minded, half-hearted snips, Igor began to cut Kalyna's hair. He took a long time to complete the task.

When they left the hotel Igor stood in the doorway with fat tears rolling down his cheeks and landing on the green felt of his jacket, where they disappeared, like fish after a mouthful of air, into the depths of the cloth. Igor had given Kalyna a package to take with her. In it was a gun – a pistol which he had taught her how to use – a knife, a water bottle which had been his father's during the war, an old map marking with red circles the invious mountains on their journey and an inflatable pillow which had been made in England and was actually an armband, but Igor didn't know it. He was hot and flushed and his heart ached, as though he'd strained it. In his head he ran through the events of the past few months, over and over, thinking who had said what and when. God forbid, he thought, I'm in love, and he stood up a little straighter in his jacket and tried to blink the tears from his eyes.

'*Viszlát!*' Kalyna called from the taxi window and they sped away to the bus station, to spend three hours waiting for a bus to leave as the driver finished his lunch. Igor had packed them some food: pickles, tomatoes, thin ham sandwiches, a couple of shrivelled apples and a bag stuffed with pastries and cakes. Kalyna was late with her period and as she sat on the bus she wondered whether she was bringing not one, but two, children to freedom.

Nicholas was sad to leave: he liked pudgy, docile Igor and his grand hotel. He could have stayed there for ever. It was the spring of 1975. The North Vietnamese had captured Ban Me Thuot in the Central Highlands, King Faisal had been assassinated and Aristotle Onassis had died. Nicholas was to be five the following month, Kalyna thirty. Across many kilometres Bohdan had just turned nine, and Stefan, at Christmas, thirty-three.

EIGHT

223 Lincoln Street, London W3, was a redbrick Victorian house set back from the road with a front garden of dark green, sculptural foliage. Nicholas glanced in through the bay window as he climbed the steps to the red front door and saw a well-designed modern kitchen, metal and wood, a vase of peonies and a newspaper on the table. Some of the flowers' petals had fallen onto the wooden surface and lay in deep pink curls, like small boats in a sea of buttermilk.

Nicholas swallowed and tried to calm his insides. People must do this every day, he thought, but as he reached out to push the bell he became acutely aware of a fine, steam-like sweat coating the palms of his hands and he cursed his nerves. His finger – long and fine with a flattened fingertip – trembled before the porcelain doorbell. He swallowed again and dropped his hand. A flush rose in his face.

Nicholas had polished his shoes before he left work, and then had straightened his tie and tucked his shirt in. His features, though he didn't know it, stood out in his anxiety against his skin: his lips coral pink, his eyes the colour of treacle. He took a breath and, willed himself to be sure of his own value. He reached forward and pushed the doorbell. He imagined that he might walk away, hurrying down the street and back to his room where he could resume imagining a life he didn't lead. The tips of his ears were pink in the soft evening sunshine. Under his arm he held the pale red folder, its contents arranged as they had been when he'd first laid eyes on it: the CV followed by a few blank pieces of paper. Its corner, pressed up into his armpit, was hot and damp.

'Hello?' It was a woman: attractive and dark and imposing. Nicholas scanned the face for something he might recognize. In his agitated state he asked himself whether someone could change so radically: the features were too large and bold, the face broad. It took him longer than it should have to be sure that this wasn't her.

'Yes?' she said, with a contemptuously slow blink.

Nicholas opened his mouth. His tongue stuck to his teeth. A pain rose when he swallowed. 'I'm looking for Faye Peters.'

'Really?' replied the woman with a light shrug and she walked back into the house, her shoes clattering on the oiled wood floor. Nicholas stood on the doorstep and felt lightheaded. He looked down at the neat pile of the doormat beneath his creased, soft shoes and felt himself out of place. Somewhere inside the cool and the darkness it sounded as though someone had called out. She will think me quite mad, he thought.

He looked into the hallway and saw the trappings of a luxurious urban existence. The decor and furnishings looked as if they had materialized from a magazine. Nicholas seldom saw houses like this. There was nothing – not one object or picture or colour – that seemed out of place: in the pale yellow hall botanical prints hung from the picture rail above high-backed chairs. He knew that the house should not intimidate him, but it did. He knew that what his mother had taught him was true – money was not to be respected – but at the same time he felt awed by the house, by the soft clean stone of the steps. He slipped his free hand into his pocket and pressed it against the cloth of his trousers, hoping to dry it. His clothes felt too small for him.

Straight in front of him were the stairs and it was to these that his eyes were now drawn, for at the very top of them had appeared a pair of bare feet, neat and pink, with a portion of black trouser hem hanging just above them. Nicholas watched as the feet descended, taking their time down the carpeted steps. His heart, he noticed, was beating faster than the feet were walking: plod, plod, plod down the stairs as gradually more and more body was revealed. His breath came in spikes. He hoped that his hair looked okay. Something small and white shot into the hallway and came straight towards him, veering off to the left a little as it approached the threshold. Nicholas pressed the folder under one arm and bent down to grab the blur, feeling, as he did, its soft deep fur and the panic in its ribcage. You and me both, he thought. He held in his hands a small rabbit. 'Stop her!' he heard, but he already had.

As he picked her up he felt her weight and realized that she was, beneath all her fur, a rather small creature. As a student he had worked on the meat counter at Tesco in Bradford and as he lifted the animal in front of him he couldn't help bouncing her a little to gauge her size. She couldn't weigh more than 4 lbs, he thought. The rabbit, two large hands around its middle, froze, as though it could read Nicholas's thoughts and knew the history of his hands. Just then Nicholas looked up and found in front of him a friend.

'Faye,' he said.

The low sunlight caught her thick hair and her irises glinted like water. She looked exactly the same. In his ears the bell to announce the end of breaktime rang. She looked into his eyes for a few moments, as though something might be written there. The blood buzzed in Nicholas's ears. It seemed for a minute as though time had paused, as though everyone across the wide city was waiting, still and silent, unsure of what to say. Nicholas stood on the step, searching her face for signs of aging or change.

'Nicholas,' she said.

'Hello,' said Nicholas and he smiled. Something inside him started to hum. He thought of one of his cello strings, fiercely plucked and left to resonate in the soft evening air. He looked into her face for too long, searching for something he remembered. She met his eyes and he became aware of his obvious scrutiny. He flushed.

'Hello,' she said, dropping her eyes briefly to take in his uniform.

'Hi.'

She paused and looked at him, briefly catching his eyes, taking in a curl of brown hair behind his ear, a straight section of jaw, a peculiar cloth badge sewn on to the front of his shirt.

'What a surprise,' she said slowly, thinking, it seemed, of something else. Her lips remained open for a moment after she had spoken. She blinked and shut her mouth.

'Well, come in!' she said with a smile that arrived too quickly and she stood back from the door. What are you doing here? was what she wanted to say. Who are you now? What have you come for? but the questions were too blunt. She could find no way of phrasing them. 'How are you?' she said eventually, shutting the door behind him. She hoped that he was well, that he was normal, believing, as she did, that most people were mentally, emotionally and physically sound. She did not want to be embarrassed by him, would be repulsed at any sign of neediness in her old friend. If she had her way she would have kept him in a cage for a few days under intense observation. Only once she was completely satisfied that he was quite, quite normal would she let him into her life. She had, since she'd gone to university, got into the good practice of surrounding herself with normal people. People who did not scare her.

Nicholas smiled. A vertical groove formed in each cheek, matched by the straight sides of his face. A vein in his temple flickered. He thought his smile weak; Faye found it beautiful. 'I'm very well,' he replied. 'How are you?'

'I'm well too,' she said and she smiled back. In that moment Nicholas felt a swell of relief. His lungs filled with air. I am just an old friend looking her up, he heard in his head, just an old friend. The relief was swiftly followed by a slow, cool disappointment which Nicholas would barely let himself feel. I mean less to her than she does to me.

The rabbit, sensitive to the reunion, waited until this moment to kick its feet out at nothing.

'Oh,' Faye said, 'thank you for saving Jessica.' She reached out and took the rabbit from him, pausing for a few seconds while he moved his hands to give her space for hers on the tiny furry body. Their fingers overlapped for a moment. Faye moved hers away too quickly, the rabbit almost fell. Holding it to her she took it through to the back of the house.

She reappeared and invited Nicholas inside, taking him to a deep red sitting room, where the tall dark woman who had answered the door was draped across a sofa, bare feet splayed on a glass coffee table, head thrown back, eyes closed. Beside her feet stood a wine glass, a trace of red slowly slipping down the inside.

'I have a friend here,' Faye turned and said to him.

'Oh, I'm sorry, I—' Nicholas began but Faye was already introducing them.

'Nicholas, this is Beatrice. Beatrice, Nicholas.'

'Oh, you,' Beatrice said.

'Bea, you let Jessica escape again,' Faye told her.

'Oh, did I?' asked the woman from deep inside her throat. She remained in her position, oblivious to the chaos that had just taken place in the hallway and ignoring her best friend's guest.

Nicholas took a seat on the brocade sofa behind him. He looked, Faye thought, larger, fuller than she remembered

80

him. She wanted to ask him everything all at once: where he had been, what he'd known, wishing to absorb every part of what had happened to him.

'Nicholas and I were at school together,' Faye explained. 'I haven't seen him for – well – I suppose twelve, thirteen years.'

'The same school?' Beatrice asked. 'How extraordinary,' she remarked. As far as she was concerned boys and girls did not go to the same schools.

'Would you like a cup of tea?' Faye asked and she dashed off to bring in a sleek teapot and three mugs, her bare feet slapping lightly on the wooden floor.

Nicholas sat opposite her and soaked in detail like a cat in the sun. He had not been able to remember her forearms. He had supposed they were narrow and slightly freckled, with blonde hairs that would occasionally catch the light. He was able, after many years, to sit and observe them. To look and actually see them. The pleasure this act – and the examination of her fingernails, the line of her shoulders, her bare feet – gave him was hard for him to describe. As a musician he had not imagined that so much pleasure could be derived from the simple act of *looking*.

As he sat across the room from her Nicholas could easily imagine that he was sitting on the third desk of the cello section watching her. Without realizing it he straightened his back and sat closer to the edge of his seat, a ridiculous, uneasy posture, but one which came naturally to string players. A drop of tea dribbled from the spout of the teapot and Faye wiped it carelessly with the back of her hand. Deborah, the last girl Nicholas had been out with, had always kept a tissue up her sleeve for moments like that. She had also managed to break both her nose and her toe the first time they had sex, banging her nose into his chin as she moved on top of him and then, both hands clasped over her bleeding nose, walking straight into the edge of the bed.

She liked hair clips and Radio Four, and after three and a half weeks Nicholas could take no more and ended it. He wondered now what Faye was wearing beneath her clothes. He could see for himself what he felt for her: knew that it was lust which brewed inside him. Yet this knowledge did nothing to abate the feeling.

'So how did you find me?' Faye asked him. A sneaking feeling of impotence had come upon her. She did not like surprises. She wished Nicholas had not come to her home, that Beatrice would go away. The sense of loss of control tightened her cheek muscles and brought a hostility to her throat. Nicholas explained to the two of them about his job and the folder that had been handed into Lost Property. The folder lay on the coffee table between them.

'I am supposed to have given up the world of work,' Faye said, 'but I have had a few headhunters send my CV out. It must belong to one of them. I haven't seen it before, I mean this particular copy,' and she picked it up and looked through it briefly before replacing it.

'Let's have a look,' murmured Beatrice, barely stirring and revealing a lethargy that had haunted her her whole life. Beatrice could spend, and indeed on many occasions had spent, three or four days in succession fast asleep in bed. She slept at the theatre and at the cinema. She had fallen asleep at the dentist, at bus stops and on her yoga mat at the gym. She dreaded going to the doctors and being asked to lie on the couch because she knew she would be asleep in seconds. She had even been known to give in to sleep mid-sentence. She had long hair and long limbs and moved like lava. Faye handed her the folder but by the time Beatrice had it in her warm hand she couldn't really muster the energy to look at it.

Before Nicholas arrived and confusion erupted in the hallway Faye and Beatrice had been talking. And so as soon as Faye brought Nicholas into the living room Beatrice knew the role he could play. Beatrice, who was currently living with Faye, had arrived home from work early to see what Faye had achieved over the past few days – namely the clearing out, cleaning and arranging of the attic, which was going to be Faye's studio.

Faye liked to paint. She had dreams in her head of becoming a prominent painter, whose work would hang, neatly lit and delicately framed, in offices and banks, where it would be puzzled over by harassed employees. She had dreams of transforming the medium, of speaking for a generation, of making something just so beautiful that jaws would drop and doors open and those that knew a lot about art but didn't know what they liked would instinctively reach for their chequebooks. And so she had cleared out the attic. She wanted to begin, she told Beatrice, with the face. Skin interested her, she said. Eyes too. Not to mention hair and expression and age.

'Would you model for me?' she had pleaded with her best friend.

'Perhaps,' Beatrice had replied, 'as long as you paint me thin and beautiful. None of this true-to-nature rubbish.'

'Thank you, Bea,' Faye had said, and filled up their glasses with more wine. 'Now I just need a man.'

'Don't we all?' scoffed her friend, but Faye sidestepped the conversation she didn't want to have again.

'Can you think of a man who would model?' They had listed their friends, acquaintances and colleagues and then moved onto exes, neighbours and relatives. Their friends were professionals: they wouldn't have the time.

'It must be awfully boring, just sitting there. Someone strapped for cash but with some time. All the men I know are as rich as Croesus. They just won't marry me,' Bea said.

'Oh for heaven's sake,' replied Faye and she had gone upstairs to get a cardigan. At that point the doorbell had rung.

Beatrice eyed Nicholas without moving her head. She thought he'd probably be all right to paint. And besides, the evening so far bored her.

'Faye has a proposal for you, Nicholas,' she said. In the opulence of the furnishings and her own lazy confidence Beatrice decided to have some fun.

'Do I?' asked Faye, looking at her friend. Her smile coagulated and she gripped her mug.

'Yes, of course you do. Faye, you see,' Bea continued, raising her head to look at Nicholas, 'is a painter.' She said the word carefully and not, thought Nicholas, without a hint of malice.

'Beatrice,' Faye objected.

'A painter in search of models,' Bea finished.

'Ah,' said Nicholas, and he turned his gaze to Faye. 'A painter,' he said and he smiled at her. He looked down at her hands in a new light, seeing them, like his own, as tools, essential in the struggle for self-expression. Her fingernails were long, which surprised him, and her skin showed no traces of paint.

'Well, I—' Faye began.

'Well, what would you – um, what kind of model do you need?' Nicholas asked. He felt that there was a gulf between him and these women that could not be bridged. Although she sat right there opposite him Faye seemed to be distant – more distant than she had ever been in his imagination.

'Just a face model,' came Faye's reply, quick as a bullet. 'I paint portraits.'

'Ah,' said Nicholas.

'Have you done any modelling before?' Beatrice asked. She was enjoying this and Nicholas knew it.

84

'I was a *before* model once,' Nicholas said.

'A –?'

'You know, when they have those *before* and *after* photographs. I was the before one.'

'Oh,' Beatrice said, nonplussed. Faye laughed at him. He caught her eye and during the brief moment when they looked at each other, Nicholas seemed to travel in time and felt a warmth at the bottom of his stomach, a solid reassurance that Faye hadn't changed that much.

'Anyway,' Faye said. 'The thought of asking you to model for me really hadn't occurred to me,' she began. She was embarrassed by the impression Nicholas might have of her: that as soon as she had set eyes on him she had begun to think about his potential uses.

'I'd be more than happy to,' Nicholas replied. 'Honestly, I mean, it would be nice to . . .' He caught Beatrice looking at him. He felt uncomfortable.

Faye had grown up three streets away from Nicholas. She had two older sisters, two working parents and Archie, a wiry mongrel. Her family had less money than he and his mother had. She shared a boxroom with her two sisters, wore their clothes and shoes and often went without an evening meal. For her fourteenth birthday she got three bottles of nail polish: First Flush; Peach Dream; Mellow Cherry. He remembered, as clearly as if it had happened just now, how thrilled she had been with her new nails, how pretty she found them, how she walked around for days with her hands in fists in case she chipped the shiny polish. How she had to borrow some money from her grandmother to buy a bottle of nail polish remover.

When Faye was fifteen her parents got divorced and her mum married a man she had met in a bar. Of all the children only Faye was still at school, and even she was supposed to be leaving. So that he could have his new wife all to himself and because he found children tiresome, her stepfather paid for her to go away to school, and go away she did.

'Well, if you're sure,' Faye was saying to him, 'I mean, if you actually *want* to sit for me, I'd be—'

'Yeah,' Nicholas said, 'I do.'

As Nicholas jogged down the steps to the tube, turning over different scenarios in his head for his first portrait sitting with Faye at the weekend, Beatrice was laughing, her clumsy feet back on the glass table on which they had already deposited a small patch of moisture, just beneath her heels.

'I can't believe you just asked him and he said yes. That was so random. He didn't even ask to see any of your paintings. You can't even paint portraits, can you? He'll be there for hours – years probably.'

'Oh shush,' replied Faye irritably, as she rolled up the sleeves of her cardigan and felt something move, uneasily, in her stomach. She could hardly believe that the man who had just been sitting on the sofa *was* Nicholas. He did not seem that different from how she remembered him, but she was struck by the peculiarity of events. Nicholas had had a couple of days to accustom himself to the coincidence; now Faye needed to do the same.

'It will be good. He's really nice,' she said. Her voice lacked conviction.

Beatrice was silent for a moment, overcome by the plushness of her sofa and the unbridled pleasure that she derived from just lying on it, doing nothing.

'Did you think he was good-looking?' she asked, taking a cushion and putting it under her head.

'What do you mean, "did"? When I was thirteen or just now?'

'Oh of course!' shrieked Bea. 'You went out with him! How was it? Did you . . . you know . . . *do* him?' she asked, with heavy emphasis on the 'do', so that it sounded rounded and nasal and just like the response her mother would make if a visitor asked whether they could sit down.

'I didn't go out with him,' replied Faye, 'we were friends. Of course I didn't sleep with him,' and she twirled a blonde lock between finger and thumb, rubbing at the strands of hair, knowing she was tangling them. Something strange was going on in her stomach and she was annoyed with Beatrice, wishing that she would go up to her room and leave her to relive the past hour in her own mind.

'I have to make supper,' Faye said and left the room for the kitchen opposite, where she cleared the peony petals from the table and threw them, along with the newspaper, into the bin.

She opened the fridge out of habit and stared into it, seeing none of what was in there. As her eyes rested on a tub of crème fraiche she thought of the last time she had seen Nicholas, when he had sat opposite her with active fingers and alert eyes in the coffee bar. She remembered how their legs had touched. She had felt paralysed by fear and by attraction, by the unknown body of a boy.

Faye's new stepfather had told Faye that he and *her mother,* as he called her, would drive her to her new school on a Saturday so that she could spend Sunday *making herself at home,* as he put it, running his thumbs around the inside of his trouser waistband. He drove a Rover, because it was British-made and showed, he believed, that he was a person who took driving seriously. He had thinning coppery hair and a swollen stomach. He thought himself a perfectionist and prided himself on knowing the distinction between the words *uninterest* and *disinterest.* Children, he thought, were a nuisance. Pets too. He had made his money importing novelty gifts from the Far East: paper fans, rubbers shaped like melon slices, sequined silk purses, pocket calculators in rainbow colours.

Faye and Nicholas had met up on a Thursday afternoon. On Friday morning Faye's stepfather woke up and heard on the radio that the weekend was going to be a remarkably hot one for early September. He lay in bed, thinking that he and Faye's mother should go away somewhere, to the Dales perhaps, to enjoy the weather and have some time just to themselves. And then he remembered that he had said he would drive Faye to her new school on Saturday. As he lay there waiting for Faye's mother to bring him a cup of tea he decided that they should take Faye to school that very day, so as not to disrupt their weekend. He climbed hurriedly from bed and went downstairs to inform Faye's mother of the plan. He wanted to get a move on and be back before the rush-hour traffic started.

Faye had no choice in the matter. Her boxes and bags were carried to the car by her all too enthusiastic mother. Her stepfather co-ordinated the proceedings, standing by the open boot and pointing to spaces. Faye barely had time to wash before they were ready to leave. Her mother and stepfather, already sitting in the car, told her to hurry up. Her mother found the right page in the road atlas; her stepfather planned the route. Faye felt like a leech torn from skin. She pretended she had forgotten something and, with a dry mouth and churning stomach, went back into the house to call Nicholas. There was no reply from his number. She sat in the back of the car and cried. Her mother put her tears down to nerves. Her stepfather boasted of how he had been sent away to school at four and would not have dreamt of embarrassing his parents by crying. Faye pressed her hands into her face and wished, she remembers it still, that they would crash.

★

At school the new uniform made her soft, pink skin itch. The censorious teachers found her slow-witted and ignorant (she had no Latin, for goodness' sake). The other girls told her that she smelt, that she was a gypsy, that she wasn't fit to clean the school, let alone be taught there. When at first she responded to the taunts as she would have done at her old school – 'I'll set my sister on you' – she was met with uncomprehending sneers. 'What do you mean, "you'll set your sister on me"?' Victoria Saunders had replied. 'My father's a barrister so if your sister even approaches the school gates he'll see to it that she ends up in prison, which is surely where she belongs.'

To hear Faye crying in her bed in the morning, or sobbing in the toilets at night-time brought the other girls immense satisfaction. They saw it as an admission, a watery confession that, indeed, she wasn't good enough to be there. So Faye stopped crying and went for days without speaking – eating on her own at a stained yellow table, sitting in her own corner of the waxy-smelling new library, passing Sundays writing letters on lined paper to friends and relatives who didn't exist. Instead of wailing like an abandoned kitten, she began to observe like a watchful cat. She listened to how the other girls spoke, she noted what they wore, she watched how they confidently rebuffed questions to which they did not know the answers. There was no blushing or hesitating here. They smiled at the teachers and asked them how they were. And Faye resolved, as she watched and waited to ascend from her own private hell, that she would become one of these girls.

NINE

In the summer of 1975 a man called Kozak came to Dytyatky looking for Borys Markus. Borys had arranged to sell four crates of Seven-Up, three rifles and sixteen fridges to Kozak's friends in Lviv, but Borys had taken the money and not supplied the goods. In actual fact Kozak's friends had stolen the goods from Borys the night before he was due to exchange, but the man in charge of the transaction had made a mistake and let Borys get away with the money. Kozak's friends wanted their money back for the goods they said they'd never received, but first of all they had to find Borys. Kozak was chosen to find him; he was the most merciless among them.

And so Kozak rode into Dytyatky, where he invited himself to stay at one of the farms and ordered the workers around like the slaves he thought they were. He was six foot three and had a long vertical scar down the left side of his face, which ran from temple to chin, starting as a thin shiny line of scar tissue and broadening out over the flat of his cheek to a neat band. He had longish dark hair and flat, blinking eyes. He wore a dirty pair of Levis, which the young people of the village stared at, a yellow polo neck and a sheepskin coat. Around his neck he wore a pair of red children's shoes, which dangled on a leather thong, hard and dirty with grease and sweat.

Stefan was finishing ploughing a field, slowly, because the horse swayed and the machinery was blunt. One of the farm boys came to tell him that there was a visitor at the next farm along and all the men were going to see him.

'Finish this for me,' Stefan said, handing the boy the horse's tether and trudging off. Three of them went to see the stranger and find out what he wanted, walking into a fierce wind on a Thursday afternoon. As they left their farm Stefan glanced back to check on the boy he had left ploughing, but saw instead one of the storks that had made their home on the farm roof that summer, standing resolutely in its nest, face to the wind, waiting, Stefan supposed, for its partner to return with food for the young ones. It was a sign of luck to have *ciconia ciconia* nest on your rooftop and Stefan hoped that it meant they would have a good harvest. Bohdan was about a foot shorter than the other boys his age. He didn't get enough to eat. At times Stefan would lie awake all night worrying about him.

'Borys Markus': the name was buzzing in the air as they entered the farm's main room where men were striding about, questioning each other, shrugging, shaking their heads. The wind sneaked in through the cracks in the floor, around the windows and doors, stirring up a thick dust and bringing with it the smells of cooking from the next room, where the women were preparing soup. Kozak stood by the window with a group of men. One sniffed compulsively and another chewed on a piece of leaf and rubbed his hands together, as though he might actually know where the fabled Borys Markus was and was just hatching a plot to blackmail him in return for not revealing his whereabouts. Stefan and his colleagues approached and were introduced. No-one shook hands.

Kozak looked from one man to the next to the next, a wave of repulsion and contempt rising in him for these ragbag people, poor and hungry and broken. They were no better than the serfs of five hundred years ago, he thought, and drew renewed inspiration from his belief that the Ukraine, were it ever to rise as a country of power, needed him, Kozak, and not these oafs. He thought himself, of everyone in the room, far and away the best man.

'I am looking for Borys Markus. He is in debt to some of my friends,' he said slowly, moving his gaze in time with the metre of the sentence. 'I am Kozak.'

An older man in the group shook his head. 'What does he owe them?' he asked.

'His life,' Kozak replied and, as he had hoped, a hush descended on the group. The sniffer sniffed, the hand-rubber rubbed his hands. The wind whistled in and sent a shiver down Stefan's spine. He didn't move. One of the men, a young gangly creature burdened with intelligence and an uneasy social presence spotted the shoes around Kozak's neck and asked, to ease the silence, whether Kozak had children of his own. Kozak, in keeping with his bravura and brutality, was a little slow.

'I have a child in every village in this whole land,' he replied, meaning, by land, the Ukraine, and not the Soviet Republic. 'One day, my sons will come of age and replace the cowardly tripe-bellied population of today. My sons will wage a war for freedom and peace. They will die and be victorious! The blood of Turks and Muscovites and Poles and Jews will mix together and feed our fertile earth, where a hedge will grow to keep out everyone who is not pure-blooded Ukrainian. We will become famous as a nation of warriors. Fearsome and brutal, this land will no more be walked through and on and over by people who do not belong here. This land of ours that is not our own is that way because of men like you. My kin will finally make it ours. We are the true Ukrainians!'

'I was admiring your necklace,' said the gangly man. Nationalistic talk was not allowed. The group ignored it. The gangly man heard his own question repeat itself in his head and realized that the word 'necklace' sounded distinctly womanly and that he should have chosen something else.

'They belonged to a child,' Kozak said, tossing the shoes into the air with a brief flick of his wrist. 'It was with its mother in the mountains. They were thin and bedraggled – they had been walking for months. They were young and innocent. I slit their throats. First the child's, then the mother's. I wear the shoes as a symbol.' Kozak finished speaking and cleared his throat noisily and spat on the floor. 'A symbol of my power,' he growled and a sneer passed across his face.

Stefan didn't move. He was staring at Kozak's unusual pendant, knowing where he had last seen those shoes and yet unable to comprehend what he had heard. He left the room, turning his back suddenly on the visitor, brushing past the tired shoulders of farm labourers who had gathered around them. Kozak was sorry that he had paid so little attention to the man's face. He thought him rude and would like to punish him for it.

Stefan entered the kitchen of the farm and approached a thin, jowly woman chopping onions with an impatient expression. He pulled the half-chopped onion out from under her knife and she looked up at him, confused and annoyed at this interruption, at a man coming into what she considered to be *her* kitchen. He took the knife from her calloused hand and turned his back, a glint of blade in one hand, half an onion in the other, calmly retracing his steps like a butler taking tea to the drawing room, one rainy afternoon in rural England.

A sweat broke out at his temples, and between them, like a current set flowing by the arrival of moisture, ran pictures of his wife and son, patchily remembered and mixed grotesquely with newsreel footage of Jackie Kennedy and her little boy saluting at JFK's funeral. Stefan was excited now, agitated, alarmed, disengaged. He wished he had been there to protect Kalyna and Nicholas. He tried to keep the images of his wife and child with their throats slit from his mind. He walked back into the room, watching a montage in his head, seeing, from time to time, himself, far away, walking across the room.

'Those are Nicholas's shoes!' he bellowed to the men, holding what he thought was the knife high above his head. It was actually the onion. The men stopped and stared. Those near to him saw the knife glinting in his lowered hand, those far away wondered what he meant with his words and why he was holding a vegetable in the air. One, the hand-rubber, felt a throb of annoyance that their meal would be deprived, it seemed, of half an onion. Kozak turned his head a little and saw not only that these men were pathetic, but also driven to a torpid insanity by their own wretchedness.

'Those are Nicholas's shoes!' Stefan bellowed again, his lungs pumping in and out like the throat of a mating bullfrog. 'My son left this village in those shoes!' He ran at Kozak and thrust the onion into his chest, expecting it to draw forth a fountain of red and bring a peaceful vengeance to himself and his tiny son, who had once slept on his shoulder. Kozak, on the floor but unhurt, drew his own knife and lashed out at Stefan as the latter withdrew. Kozak caught him on the face, piercing the skin at the temple and drawing his knife downwards, puncturing the flesh of the cheek through to the mouth and hitting finally the chin, where the blade ran for a second along the bone before breaking contact. Blood seeped from the side of Stefan's face, frantically dripping onto his shoulder, glinting in the late sunlight of the afternoon, falling in neat, heavy drops onto the grimy wooden floor.

The gangly youth leant in and tapped Stefan's wrist. It

was the wrist of the hand that held the knife and it was all Stefan needed: with the tap came the resumption of feeling, of a consciousness of which hand held what. He lunged, this time with the knife, for Kozak's stomach. Stefan's aim was true and his thrust strong. Kozak let out a cry, a crushed exhalation and collapsed back on the floor. He fidgeted as the fluids of his body left him.

The men stood around and surveyed what had happened. There was a stream of blood, flowing and pooling endlessly like an obscene water sculpture in an art gallery. There was a dead man, and half an onion lying, an unblinking eye, on the floor. Some were exhilarated by the performance, proud to have witnessed something they would tell their grandchildren, embellished to the hilt and quietly ecstatic that they had not had to take part in any way. Others, a few, were shocked by Stefan, a caring father who was known to disapprove of beating the horses. None were shocked by Kozak's sudden transition from life to death, by the paltry few seconds it took to change the state of the man. These people were not used to having death around them, but they were used to sudden disappearances in the middle of the night, to jeering consequences coming out of the blue and taking over a life for ever.

Someone pushed Stefan and walked him out to the kitchen, where the women washed his face and then bound it tightly. They had to pour four cups of water over his head until the hand he had pressed to his wound finally became unstuck. The skin flapped around and one woman said that he needed stitches, but he shook his head a little and they carried on. There would be no point going to a hospital anyway: most were empty of doctors and nurses. The sheet strips kept the skin in place fairly well, apart from around the chin, where it was difficult for the material to stay in place.

'The shoes,' Stefan had said while a grey strip was tightened and fastened around his head. He saw, as the cloth was stretched before him, a yellowish stain on it in the shape of a kidney. 'Someone take the shoes,' and he had a vision, a sudden thought that he should bury Kozak's body under one of the farm's fields, because it would nourish the soil and perhaps bring a good harvest and that way Bohdan, his son, might finally grow. A couple of children stole the onion and ran off to eat it. It was the tall, gangly man who cut the thong around Kozak's neck and brought the shoes to Stefan. As Stefan had expected, there, in swollen ink letters, was Nicholas's name, neatly written by Stefan's mother when she had received them from a friend in Moscow.

It was on this day, when Stefan killed the man who had killed his wife and child, that his wife and child arrived in Vienna, having successfully travelled across the Alps and through the small, uncertain villages that lay between the capital city and the border. Kalyna was frightened: she squeezed her son's hand tightly as they walked through the narrow alleys and wide streets. The thought that, now that they had got this far, that she might lose Nicholas, accidentally, in a crowd of Viennese shoppers haunted her.

Almost everything she saw amazed her. She had told herself to be ready for a vast array of colourful goods, piled high and enough for everyone to enjoy. She had imagined women in fur hats with baskets bulging with steak fillets wrapped in white paper and fresh beans, peas, lettuces. She felt, as she approached the city centre, that she hadn't enough eyes, that she was being assailed from all directions by things that demanded her attention. Ignore it, she told herself, ignore it and look for a hotel sign, she said over and over in her head, but she could not stop herself from being distracted and then being distracted from being distracted, so that by the time she had managed once again to wrangle control of her attention, she had forgotten what it was she was supposed to be doing.

Part of the problem was that she had difficulty recognizing what buildings were. Some were so brightly lit with chains of tiny lights and glowing doorways that she thought they must be churches, for that was how, after years of her own religion being banned in her homeland, she would build her own church, if she had the choice. She entered with a sigh and a raised head, only to see floors and floors above her, with escalators circling up and down between them, the air thick with the smell not of incense but of scent, expensive and sweet.

She took her remaining kroner to a bank and changed them, unsure of what the notes she received in exchange meant but thrilled with their pretty pictures of musical instruments and shadowed faces. They trailed through the city looking for a hotel they could afford, but the only one they found where the woman behind the counter wrote down a reasonable nightly rate was at the end of a run-down street. Its sign – which read Pension Grillparzer – hung from one corner, like a dead man swinging. It had once been an acceptable guest house, but had had its business ruined by a bad review. Now its only guests were a group of glassy-eyed men who played cards in the hallway and drank in the bathrooms.

A few doors up the street Nicholas glanced into another hotel hallway and was sure he saw a bear, but when he turned his head again he saw that it was instead a large, black dog with teeth bared. '*Senta! Komm her!*' someone shouted from a side alley and Kalyna quickened her step as the dog retreated. They went straight to the station, where they spent the last of their money on tickets to Munich.

Stefan went from face to face in the farm requesting that no-one tell Bohdan what happened. He stopped the children, a pale lilac colour beneath their ragged farm clothes and promised to slip them his piece of pig's trotter, or an extra potato at dinnertime if they would keep their little mouths shut. He returned to his farm, his large hand cradling the small shoes, and wondered what had happened to that life of his where he had had a wife, two happy children and needed nothing more than the call of the nightingale. He hid the shoes in his pillow and said nothing to Bohdan. Stefan was not a violent man. His deed had shocked him, and he sat for many nights nursing the shock inside him. He told himself that Bohdan did not need to know of his mother's and brother's fate. In truth he lacked the courage to tell him.

In Munich Kalyna and Nicholas had no money. Kalyna could not afford to be superstitious and she sold the silver crucifix that Heda had given her and Igor's gun and inflatable pillow. No-one, it seemed, wanted the maps, and the knife and water bottle had proved their use. They ate a good meal and bought tickets to Hamburg, from where their nocturnal journey started once again as they travelled on the trains, each time hiding in the toilet or in the mail car. Kalyna knew that they had to get to Holland. She learnt to avert her gaze and blend into the background as best she could, so that many of the passengers who boarded the train with her would neglect to mention the pale woman with her thin son, were they asked to describe their departure. The pair of them drank from the taps in the toilet and ate what food they could steal from the restaurant car. They became used to sitting on dirty floors and sleeping with their eyes half-open.

It was the late summer of 1975. Faye, in Bradford, was five years old: she stood straight, with blonde curly hair, and wherever her tired mother took her, people regarded her fondly and said that she looked like a doll. In England a woman was elected leader of the Conservative party and inflation was at its highest ever. Haile Selassie and Dmitri Shostakovich were dead. In Germany some of the Baader–Meinhof gang blackmailed their way out of prison and left for the Middle East. Flower power and flares were fashionable.

Nicholas still wore his trousers from Budapest, already too short. Kalyna could barely understand how he managed to grow on the scraps they lived off. She regarded women her age with a guarded curiosity, astonished by their clothes and the carefree radiance in their eyes.

Eventually they climbed from a train one evening and saw that the sign read 'ROTTERDAM'. Kalyna had looked at a map in Munich and knew that this arrangement of letters meant they were on the coast, and if they were on the coast then it was time to try and get onto a boat. For the first few nights they did nothing but watch: memorizing what time the boats went, observing how the passengers were herded in and out. After four nights of living amongst the rats of the docks they sneaked onto a ship bound for Hull. In Hull they took a train to Bradford, where they got off and stood on the platform. Kalyna was unable to believe that they had come to the end of their journey.

'We're here,' she whispered to her son, having picked him up and rested him against her shoulder. She looked into his tired, pinched face and prayed that what she had put him through would be worth it. The journey had been entirely her decision and her responsibility. She would have to make sure that this country worked for her son. She knew nothing of Bradford, only that a woman in their village had

99

an uncle here who said that life was good and that there were some Ukrainians here. She struggled to believe it as she stood in the grey early morning and looked at the dark, rubbery surface beneath her feet, at the peculiar bright green ironwork of the bench, at the signs, in colourful plastic with letters that meant nothing to her.

It would have been possible to tell her, at this point, that Bradford was the centre of the Western world, and she would have believed it. One could have told her of the mountain range of Bradford, of its blue-green lakes and snow-capped peaks, and she would have believed every word. She thought the man in the ticket booth looked charmingly rotund and friendly (in reality he was a lazy, iracund man), the light rain flowed down drainpipes and dripped off the roof like the water of a baptism, where all, and not just the baby, were blessed by God. She felt an enormous sense of relief. Compared with what they had been through, Bradford station was nothing, and she walked confidently out into the street.

She was not naive enough to believe that she had brought her child to Eden. She had been forcibly exiled from her culture and now she had chosen to exile herself from her land. But she had achieved what she set out to achieve. She took a word of Ukrainian – *kimnaty*, meaning 'room to rent', which would often be seen at railway stations in the Ukraine – and savoured it in her mouth. She didn't speak it, but felt it sitting there like a frog waiting to jump to freedom.

TEN

Most nights when Nicholas came home from work he would have tea with Mrs Sten. When he finally got to his room he would change into his tracksuit bottoms and take out his cello, positioning its spike carefully in a knot in a floorboard and tightening the end of his bow absent-mindedly. He would flick the strings casually to listen to their tones, delaying the moment of putting bow to string. Usually he turned the television on and muted it, so that he could watch what was going on while listening to what he was playing. On many occasions he left his door slightly open. He didn't like shut doors or tidiness or solitude. He played frantically, displeased with what he heard and rushing, as though somewhere up ahead of him lay a beautiful passage and if he could only get there in time he might catch it. He played naked except for his trousers. By the end of the evening when he finally climbed into bed his feet would be black, a red crescent would run across his bare chest and the fingers of his left hand would feel numb.

Nicholas got in from Faye's house after eight o'clock and was relieved to see that Mrs Sten was not hovering with the tea tray. He let the door close behind him and headed up the stairs, thinking of the cello practice he wanted to do that evening.

'Nicholas!' Mrs Sten appeared in the hallway. She wore wide, light blue trousers which billowed about her like smoke, and a neat pink T-shirt. The heat was lasting, making skin supple and hearts cheerfully indolent. Nicholas had been convinced, as he crossed Hyde Park on his way home, that he could smell the sea.

'Hello Mrs Sten.'

'You're home late,' she said lightly and fixed her eyes on his.

'Yes,' Nicholas replied. He scratched at the banister with the side of his thumb. Mrs Sten waited. She did not move.

'Well,' said Nicholas and he climbed one more step.

'Oh,' she said suddenly. 'Mr Samuels asked whether you could go round in the next few days. I think he needs some help with his garden.'

'Okay, sure,' Nicholas replied. 'Perhaps tomorrow.' Mr Samuels was the next door neighbour, a cheerful man in his seventies who could grow, it appeared, anything he wished. He grew fruit with a passion. He also had a penchant for drama, and squeezed every last drop of histrionics from the propagation of currants and plums. Occasionally a pained cry would be heard from the bottom of his garden – either that or a plaintive wail – and the residents would know that the aphids had gained territory of a new branch. Sometimes Mr Samuels would just stand in his garden and watch – waiting for a bug to make its move. He never saw them. They came at night, perhaps, but Mr Samuels was an admirer of Rudolf Steiner's approach to land and agriculture and he was often out in his garden at night, watching the moon, sowing and tending. He never saw a bug make its move then, either.

He didn't like chemicals, least of all on something that he, or someone else, would at some point eat. So he was always experimenting with new ways of keeping the bugs from his trees. He let tasty, succulent weeds grow nearby, he hosed the bugs off with a kinked green hose, standing with his back to the house so that from Nicholas's window it appeared that he was urinating in a great, powerful arc from a bladder the size of an elephant's. And he collected lady-birds as though they were limited edition. He picked them up in the street, appealed to his neighbours to look out for them, and wandered the park coercing them to come back to his house to see his fruit collection.

Nicholas, when he had first moved into his room, had listened each night to erratic, paper-light flicks as he tried to sleep, and deduced after a few days that there was a family of ladybirds living somewhere in the room. When he mentioned it to Mrs Sten Mr Samuels was round within minutes, pushing aside the chest of drawers and peering at a crack between the wall and the skirting board.

'I suspect they're in there,' he said and they let him get on with it. Since then Mr Samuels stopped Nicholas whenever he saw him to ask whether the creatures had returned.

'Would you like to join me for some supper?' Mrs Sten asked casually and she folded her arms limply in front of her. 'Just salad, er, nothing special.'

'Thank you, but I can't,' Nicholas replied. 'I have to do some practice tonight. I have an audition at the weekend,' he said out loud, speaking as he was thinking.

'An audition? But Nicholas, you didn't say! How typical of you,' she scolded him. 'I must tell the others in the house to be especially quiet, and if you need any help or advice, or a classically trained ear,' she went on, 'I studied singing for many years, you know, Nicholas, I—'

'Really, don't worry,' Nicholas said, moving up one more step. He glanced down and counted the rest of the stairs to the top: seven. 'But thank you all the same. I should get on,' and he moved, quickly, with determination, up to his room.

He took off his clothes and sat down on the edge of his bed. There seemed too much to think about: Faye, his audition, Faye, Mr Samuels, Faye. He took out his cello and held it to him, contorting his hand around the fingerboard to find the first harmonic on his D string. He turned his head to his right shoulder to listen to the note he produced: clear, ethereal. Slipping the mute onto the bridge he began with a few arpeggios, major and minor, crossing from one string to the next and back again. Finally, sliding his bow across his knee, he opened up the music for his audition and looked it over.

At midnight Nicholas packed away his instrument and climbed into bed, the smell of resin on his fingers. He lay on his back on the sheets, staring at the fuzzy darkness of the ceiling. He could not bring himself to admit it, but he was looking for a family. He wanted a father and brothers and sisters. He would like aunts and uncles, cousins, second cousins, once, twice removed and replaced cousins. And lots of children. A daughter and a son. Another daughter and another son, each one as it came into the world gradually lessening the anxiety he had for the safety of the others.

He pictured himself living in a house scattered with toys and sports gear. He imagined himself shaking his head at the mess his daughter had made, at the plasticine she had trodden into the carpet, the cat treats she had left on the floor by her bed. Faye made him think of a family, she always had. He would never bring himself to say it – *I lay in bed one night and thought about our children* – but that was what he did. He lay in bed in the July heat and imagined his and Faye's children. They existed only as vague, pale babies, indistinct in feature and character. But it was their imagined existence which quickened Nicholas's pulse.

Gareth was standing on the bench that ran along behind the tills. It was seven thirty in the morning. Nicholas and Sean were leaning against a gondola end of special-offer crisps. Sean had toothpaste stains down his brown tie. It was the monthly management meeting.

'As you know, we have been aiming at an average rate of fourteen items per minute scanned at the checkout, and I'm sorry to say that we haven't yet made it this month. I shan't mention names, but we still have quite a few people averaging ten items per minute, a smaller number with seven and one person averaging four. *You know who you are.* On the positive side, this month's book token goes to Amul who has an average of . . .' Gareth peered at the Post-it in his hand ' . . . of eighteen items per minute.' He started to clap, slowly, scanning the heads in front of him for the mortified Amul, who was supposed to go up and collect her prize. The rest of the staff made paltry efforts to join Gareth in his applause, bringing their hands together in sporadic blows as though idly swatting flies.

'Four items per minute,' Sean murmured to Nicholas, 'that's one every fifteen seconds. If they can only scan one item every fifteen seconds they probably *don't* know who they are.'

'You've got toothpaste on your tie,' Nicholas said.

'Shoplifting last month was higher than ever. Most of you know Nicholas by now, who is here to help Sean over the summer. Please spare the two of them no effort to help them with store security. The elimination of shoplifting offers us a considerable challenge but also commensurate rewards. I shall come and talk to the pair of you later on about this problem more specifically.' Nicholas smiled around at everyone when they turned their heads and then frowned and nodded at Gareth, convincingly manufacturing a concern for rising crime levels. Sean spat on his finger and rubbed at his tie.

Gareth liked to think that he would be remembered

with a monument at the supermarket's head office with a plaque beneath it that read: Gareth Mitchell, Corporate Revolutionary. He thought long and hard about the issues that faced him as store manager, sometimes lying awake the whole night wondering how he could increase sales at the meat counter or whether, since he had a lot of office workers popping in for their lunch, he should have more than one Five Items or Fewer till. He considered these problems thoroughly until the right answer hit him, usually in a burst of white light, and he would announce his recommendations to his staff.

While Gareth had a special insight into the situations which surrounded him – he thought of himself as a natural – he always came unstuck with implementation, to the extent that he was lucky if one of his ideas was carried out for more than a day before staff, bored and disillusioned, went back to doing their jobs as they had always done them because it was easier that way. On top of this he had a brain like a filing cabinet – only one drawer of it could be open at a time – and so each new idea came to replace the last. Ultimately, Gareth's presence or absence in the supermarket made no difference. He soared through the ranks of management.

Closing up the meeting now, he looked tired and dishevelled. He had not been able to sleep the night before. He had lain awake trying to work out why he was losing unprecedented levels of stock from alcoholic drinks and beverages, and, more to the point, why Sean and Nicholas didn't spot it happening. He had started out thinking that the culprit must be a member of staff – one of the shelf-stackers who came in at night most probably – but then it occurred to him that perhaps Sean and Nicholas just weren't looking in the right places. At about ten to two in the morning it hit him and he opened his eyes wide in the darkness and stared at it accusingly: prams. Women with children were tossing cans of lager into their chaotic prams and walking right out of the supermarket, of that Gareth was sure. As he lay there he saw in his head a whole legion of mothers, sitting around slatternly in their underclothes necking from cans of lager for which they hadn't paid. It almost paralysed him with anger. When he got to work that morning he started a memo with the succinct title Prams.

'Where's that pink folder that was here the other day?' Sean asked Nicholas later on. They were sitting in their office, staring at the screens of the TVs. Both of them had their feet up on the desk, Nicholas's twitching and jiggling.

'Oh,' replied Nicholas, blinking twice and swallowing a mouthful of sandwich 'well, the thing was—'

'You haven't,' said Sean.

'Haven't what?'

'If you have pulled a woman using my technique I'll be . . .' Sean began. 'That was my folder – she looked the right age, had a nice name—'

'But I knew her,' Nicholas grinned. 'Well, I know her.'

'Get away.'

'I do, honestly. I went to school with her. I took the folder round to her house last night.'

'Did you really?' Sean didn't believe him. Nicholas nodded. Sean pulled down his feet and turned a quarter-circle in his chair to look at him. 'That was very unprofessional,' he said earnestly.

'Well, I—'

'I could get into an awful lot of trouble.'

'I think she was happy to see me,' Nicholas offered. Sean raised his eyebrows and put his feet back up on the desk. He lifted his cap from his head and began to scratch around his hairline. 'Is she pretty?' he said with a grin, stopping midway through his scratching.

'What do you mean, is she pretty?' Nicholas asked, smiling back. 'Am I going to get you in trouble or not?'

'Aw, I'll handle it. Now, is she pretty?'

'Faye?' Nicholas said and stood up.

Sean clicked his fingers. 'That was it. Faye. Pretty name.'

Nicholas paused. He had admired Faye's looks for a long time. It seemed that he'd never had long enough just to look at her. He tried to conjure up her face before him. He failed. 'Yeah,' he replied. 'I'd say she's pretty.'

'Was she really?' asked Sean, taking in the excitement and lifting his head to look at Nicholas. 'So a quite pretty woman owns a pink folder,' he said, with a knowing smile, and he tried to file away this new piece of information somewhere in the swamp of his mind. 'Are you seeing her again?' Sean asked him.

'On Sunday morning,' Nicholas blurted out with a smile. He liked Sean too much to keep anything from him. 'She's painting my portrait.'

'Jesus. Watch the canvas doesn't crack,' Sean said.

'Sean, Nicholas, I want you to stop and search every mother with a pushchair,' Gareth told them that afternoon, clicking his heels together softly as he finished his sentence.

'I think that it's more probable that it's single young women doing the stealing,' Sean said, for that was who he'd like to search.

'We can't stop mothers. And we do not have the right to search people,' Nicholas replied.

'You can and you will. Mothers with babies are working as agents for alcoholics, stealing their beer and selling it on to them for half the price. It's all because they haven't got husbands. Look!' Gareth screeched, pointing at one of the video screens where a woman in her early twenties with a pushchair and three permanently dispersing kids was standing by the fish counter, staring into space.

'Her! She's one! The kids probably do it for her! She's got them trained!' he yelled and rushed out of the room, letting the door bang shut behind him. A few moments later he too appeared on the monitor, marching down the aisle at the top of the counter and peering around the corner of it, the black and white delineations of his cheap suit making his movements all the more pronounced on the TV screen. A young man walked past and stared at him.

'Oh God, this is awful,' Sean said, as Gareth dived into the next aisle as the mother moved away. On the screen Gareth was escorting the woman to the back of the store, complete with her train of children.

'Here you are, men. Just because you're here only for the summer doesn't mean to say you don't have to do your job properly, Nicholas,' Gareth announced. 'A routine search on this young lady, if you please,' and he pressed his lips together in a zip of a smile: long and thin and easy to undo. The mother, Nicholas could see, was younger than both him and Sean, had still a soft evenness to her skin and wide, crudely made-up eyes. Her three almost white-haired kids were happy to advance from her, stumbling into the room, finding things to distract them.

'Okay,' Sean said briskly. 'Thanks Gareth. We'll follow your lead on this one,' and he showed him out.

'I'm sorry about that,' Nicholas said. The woman looked from one to the other, a restless alarm in her eyes.

'Yes,' said Sean. 'Your kids are nice.'

'Oh no,' she said. Her soft, straight accent told them that she was not a native speaker. 'I'm the au pair.'

'Oh,' said Sean, a glint appearing in his eyes.

'Pair,' said the woman, nodding. She had huge blue eyes

which gave her the appearance of a nocturnal mammal and short, spiky blonde hair.

'I see,' Sean replied, taking his cap from one of the children, who had started to chew its rim. 'Well, sorry to inconvenience you. You can go now. But, well, I had just one question . . .'

'Yes?' said the girl as she took the tiny hand of a child in hers. She wore a necklace with a turquoise feather on it which swung around as she bent down.

'Would you like to go on a date?' Sean said lightly. For a moment the woman looked at him, as though trying to assess whether he was serious or not. Then she smiled.

'Okay,' she said and she put a hand to the back of her head, playing with the short strands of hair at the nape of her neck. 'How did you dare to ask me?' she said.

'I knew you'd say yes,' Sean said with a smile.

'You must be psychotic,' she replied, without breaking eye contact.

'I'll say,' said Nicholas.

ELEVEN

26th April 1986. The country of the black soil and the Black Sea has a black day. Into the straight broad blue strip of their flag rises a cloud, dense and poisonous and stacked. Into the sunny yellow along the bottom falls cooling, toxic rain which leaves behind puddles of green. But worse is still to come: for a large section of the Ukraine that yellow will never be the same again. Corn will still spring up, but its ears will be inside out, Siamese-twinned, elephantized ears which can hear. They will listen, writhing dementedly, for an explanation.

It was almost half past one in the morning when a series of explosions destroyed the nuclear reactor and the building which had housed it at the Vladimir Ilich Lenin Automatic Power Plant. Fire broke out, but this fire had no flames and no smoke: instead a blue unearthly light glowed on the planet, bringing an iridescent radiance to the whole sky which, for the next few days, people in the nearby towns crowded onto their balconies to watch, holding their children aloft in the softening spring air.

At the plant, robots, created for research on Mars and brought in to help seal the reactor, broke, their insides burned by the high levels of radiation. Men – Ukrainians, Belarusians, Russians – in boiler suits and rubber gloves, worked on. They didn't think that it would take long to get everything sealed and safe, to show that Mother Russia could easily cope with a small accident, and they had been promised new apartments and cars as a reward for their service to the country. While they were working at

Chornobyl they were kept in high spirits by a plentiful supply of good sausages and vodka. So far only seven men had died – all of them in the explosions – and only one, a senior operator, had been so far in that they hadn't been able to retrieve his body. He had been buried beneath the sand and concrete poured onto the reactor, his very own pyramid.

Only the locals knew about the accident for the first few days, as news spread from village to village that there was a fire at the magical factory that made energy out of nothing. Alexandrov, the godfather of Russian nuclear stations, had sworn that they were so safe that one could be built in Red Square, but as it turned out the Russians built most of them far from Moscow, putting five – including Europe's largest – in the breathtaking endless expanses of the Ukraine. On the day of the accident the wind was blowing not towards Kyiv, but north-west towards Belarus, and so it was in that direction that tons of caesium, iodine, lead, zirconium, strontium, cadmium, beryllium, boron and plutonium fell down to the land. Like rain falling into the sea it left no trace.

Two days after the accident happened it was announced to the world and, along with the low-flying planes which had been regularly passing over Stefan's village, came soldiers and clean-up workers, bare-headed in their boiler suits, with bottles of vodka and a few paper lists. Also two days after the accident, the systematic removal of all books on Hiroshima and Nagasaki from public libraries was complete, much to the relief of concerned officials who did not want an alarmed public, though in this case the amount of radiation was ninety times that of Hiroshima and so its consequences, even to those familiar with the effects of radiation, were hard to project. Stefan found a dead mole in the plot of land that he tended at the back of the farm on that day and picked it up to see how it had died but its sleek fur showed no punctures. Stefan wondered, as he looked at the soft pink skin of its paws and its screwed-up eyes, how it would taste.

Their village was put on the evacuation list, but the head of the communal farm gave the soldiers a case of vodka and got a good thick line through the village name, since he disliked cities and was happy here, being the boss as he was. Men from Moscow visited the farm and told them all to wash each room from top to bottom and to wash their kindling too, before lighting a fire. No-one did either: how could this invisible danger get through glass and stone walls, and what kind of fires did they build in Moscow with wet logs?

The men visited the other farm and houses and some families decided to leave, to stay with relatives in Kyiv or Minsk or Moscow, pinning notes on their doors pleading with the clean-up workers not to shoot their dogs and cats because they would return in a few weeks. Others left a loaf of bread on the table, along with some salt and a bowl and spoon for every member of the household, since tradition told them that that way they would return some day. Later more men came and dug up the topsoil from Stefan's garden complete with his potato crop, his cabbages and beans, removing the dark earth until they hit the lighter calcareous layer. Bohdan watched and laughed as they saw the men burying the soil in a pit at the end of the village. 'They are skinning the earth,' he said with a bemused shrug of his shoulders. 'Burying earth in earth.'

'Accidents will happen,' replied Stefan. The Ukraine had not yet died.

The village, its two communal farms, its school and houses, fell apart. Some people stayed and helped the clean-up crew. Some people stayed and tended this land of theirs that was not their own. A lot of people left, learning, for the first time in their lives, to think of themselves as individuals and not part of a group. It is said that tropical birds, when disturbed in their nests, do not to fly away, but stick out their feathers and scream. Most of these people had not the brightly coloured self-belief or the voice to do such a thing: sick and irradiated they left. Some travelled east to the Dnipro river, where the silt had been contaminated by radioactive particles. They bathed and washed their hair, since the men from Moscow had told them to clean everything.

Bohdan Beimuk had stopped growing at five foot two. He was agile and sure of himself and still sought a satisfaction in reasons. He would often be seen explaining the mechanics of the old combine harvester to some of the farm kids or taking apart a meat mincer to mend it. While in England Nicholas listened with fascination to the journey stories of refugees, reading how a family of Turks arrived in the cargo of a trawler, how a family from Belarus on their way to America lost their uncle when he climbed from the boat in Hull, mistakenly believing that he'd reached Ellis Island, Bohdan sought to answer the question *why?*

He took machines apart – an old tractor engine, a coffee grinder – looking for something which was never there. Time after time he was surprised to find that these machines were made up simply of bits – a confetti of small metal parts which he rolled between finger and thumb, getting a feel for their shape and function. It seemed that machines had no heart, and he liked them for it. He had his mother's easy smile and his father's sturdy build and climbed from his bed in the morning with a chilled alacrity that surprised even himself.

Slowly, as autumn came and leaves fell from the trees and sparrows from the sky, he lost weight. He stopped working on the farm one day after he dropped an axe on his foot and couldn't muster the strength to remove it himself. He collapsed on the ground, his right leg bent out awkwardly, knowing as he lay there that the sickness was everywhere – in the sky and the air and the muddy grass pressed beneath his cheek – until someone happened to walk by and help him up.

He was one of a band of young people in the village who suffered similar things, as though some sly fashion were working its way round the whole lot of them, and they all wanted to be part of it. Each and every child left in the village became thinner. Stefan watched as they began to disappear, flickering around the edges until they were too ill to be outside and would not be seen again. Everyone knew what had happened. The Russians had poisoned them. They had put something in the air, or perhaps the water, to kill them all off so that they could come and profit from their *chernozem*, which had been coveted by all around for centuries. Some said that they were in collusion with the Poles, a rerun of 1666 and 1922, since the Poles believed that most of the Ukraine should still be theirs; but others were adamant that it was Moscow alone who could be responsible for all the sickness.

'At night I swim,' Bohdan wrote down for Stefan one day, when he could no longer talk. His skin broke off him in patches and clumps of his hair lay on the pillow. 'I fall into a deep blue lake and swim beneath, without needing to breathe. The water is clear and I see all sorts of things: brightly coloured fish, seaweed, coral and huge creatures like dinosaurs. I don't have to talk to anyone there and it seems that I breathe through my skin. I am glad I have learnt to swim. In the lake is everyone we knew – Roman, Lidia, Oryna, Hryhorij. They swim with me too.'

The list of people they had known was now longer than

this, longer than Bohdan could have guessed, but Stefan lied to his son. He told him that Lialia had got better again, that Zenon had woken up cured, that you could barely tell that Volodymyr had ever been ill. Stefan was desperate. He hated to think that his son was experiencing something which he hadn't experienced. In everything Stefan was supposed to go first, to be able to advise and help. Most of all he hid the news which shocked everyone still left in the village, despite what they had been through: Wasyl Koval, a twelve-year-old boy who had been at school with Bohdan, had hung himself two days ago with his belt from the rafters of the barn.

Stefan had been furious when his son had started to show symptoms of the illness. He would sit the boy down and steal the best food for him from the kitchen, and then stand over him as Bohdan tried his best to eat it. Once Bohdan was asleep in bed Stefan would pace out into the night, where he would run into the middle of nowhere and yell into the sky. A burst of anxiety would make him race back to the farm and for the rest of the night he would sit looking at Bohdan's even brow. He had a terrible urge to do violence to the spectre that had Bohdan in its grip. If someone could have presented him with the man responsible for his son's illness Stefan would have torn him to pieces with his bare hands. Bohdan's skin seemed to thin on him and pull white and tight around his body, as gradually the boy lost what he had had.

Stefan nursed him, watching himself intensely for the same symptoms, which he willed himself to develop as each day passed. When he looked at his son he tried to forget how he had held him when he was a child, how on many occasions Bohdan had fallen asleep in Stefan's lap, straight stocky legs sticking out over his knees, his mouth hanging open like the lowered drawbridge of a fairy castle, eyes swivelling furiously beneath almost transparent eyelids. Most of all he tried to forget that he was supposed to be responsible for this boy, he was supposed to protect him from things like this. Their neighbour had said that salo absorbed the sickness, so Stefan found all the pigs' lard he could and fed it to his son in mashed chunks, which would dissolve painfully slowly in Bohdan's dry mouth.

Bohdan did not greet his illness with grace and resignation, but raged against it, yelling in pain and crying with frustration. He was no hero. Stefan could no longer explain or express what he thought and felt: he wandered around in a daze which had no end. Indeed, as Stefan saw it there *was* no balm, no reassurance, nowhere he could turn to make his situation easier. He thought about killing his son to end his suffering, but even at the end he could not help himself hoping that Bohdan would somehow recover, as though he believed his own lies. Bohdan wrote a note for his mother and one for Nicholas, and told his father to give the messages to them when he finally found them.

It seemed, during these days, that someone else was looking out through Bohdan's eyes. Stefan spooned soup into his son's crooked mouth and changed his soiled sheets. He had taken to spending all his time on a chair by his son's bed, where he held his hand, careful not to press too hard in case the skin should break and bleed. And as Bohdan got into the habit of sleeping with a hand in his, his father learnt that history happens naturally and quietly, without pomp, parades or crowds.

One spring morning at the end of April, when the cherry trees burst into bloom, Bohdan died. Stefan stopped his watch and the clock in the kitchen: twenty-one minutes past nine. He made his son soup for lunch and left the bowl to cool by the bedside. He talked to him as he had done for months now, telling him about the crops on the farm, about what had survived and what hadn't. Then he made him a cup of tea and mopped his brow delicately so as not to disturb any skin. He sat with him through the night. In the morning he changed the sheets on the bed, cleaned his oldest child and dressed his bruised and crumpled body. Then he unscrewed the door of their room and laid his son out on it, a thick piece of birch painted green on one side and white on the other.

The door was Stefan's family heirloom – it was a fine slab of wood – and his father had been laid out on it and his grandfather before him. On the white side of the door were marked, with a row of neat little indents which cracked the paint, Stefan's height (as measured on his birthdays), beside it Kalyna's height (she had just one notch though it was deep and wide, for Stefan had insisted on measuring her every year they were together), beside that the marks for Bohdan's height (which crowded together like a furry caterpillar) and beside that, evenly spaced and clouded in doubt, were the marks Bohdan had made with the blunt side of his knife to indicate Nicholas's imagined height.

Stefan Beimuk waited for death with a concentrated intensity, as though waiting for a sneeze he could feel in his nose or another bout of vomiting. Bohdan's body, still on the door, flattened like a sheet, the skin turned grey and cool and he stiffened, like ice forming over a lake. Spring turned to summer and Bohdan began to smell – a high, dangerous vapour which brought saliva to Stefan's mouth and a soreness to his throat. Still Stefan did not die. His neighbour, an elderly woman with a swollen neck and bloodshot eyes, whose son had been part of the 340,000-strong clean-up crew, stood in his doorway and said that Bohdan had to be buried in a lead coffin, under fifteen slabs of concrete, for that was what had happened to her son and that was the only way to be truly safe. Stefan buried him in the garden, amongst some potatoes and cabbages which had come back, dragging the door out there too and letting it fall with a thud on the stirred earth. The remaining neighbours had a funeral for their daughter's baby who had been born with liver cirrhosis, a heart defect and a small, third hand flapping, like an ingenious castanet, from her left wrist.

Stefan ate berries and nettles, and when September came, mushrooms, for they were free and easy to find. His apple tree bore fruit but the small neatly formed globes were skin all the way through. Looters came around the houses, taking pieces of furniture, rugs and scrap metal to sell at car boot sales in Minsk and Moscow. Stefan sat through a long winter. When the spring came round again he placed one of his wife's dresses on Bohdan's grave and a towelling bib which Nicholas had used. Then he took Kozak's red leather shoes, tied them around his neck, stole a thin horse and rode away.

With the shoes around his neck and the scar like a map of Chile down the side of his face Stefan rode into Lviv and told everyone he met that his name was Kozak. He had taken nothing else from his room – not his birth certificate, not his miniature bible, not the lavender-scented cotton stocking that his friend's wife had left under his pillow one morning many years ago. He kept nothing to remember who he was and had no trouble believing that he really was the feared Kozak. Chornobyl ran through him like a rich seam of coal, threatening to split him apart. The Ukraine was independent. A dream had been realized and on June 1991 the country had been granted its autonomy. Naturally it floundered, with tales of corruption and extortion within the Government. In a fit of autonomy it decided, for no good reason, to change time zones and become an hour earlier than Moscow. A train leaving Kyiv for Moscow departed at either seven in the morning Kyiv time or seven in the morning Moscow time, depending on the nationality of the driver.

When Kozak returned to Lviv, with his trademark red shoes, the mafia men quaked under thick moustaches and solemn expressions, for never before had anyone other than Jesus returned from the dead. They asked him whether he was going to continue with his work and Stefan said yes, so they told him when and where the next cargo of cigarettes was due to cross the border and off he went to hijack it, with a knife and a gun and best of all, absolutely no fear. Stefan did not care any more. While he was here he thought he might as well live someone else's life. Stefan Beimuk had not yet died. He hoped that Kozak would.

He rode into the mountains, robbing travellers and those foreigners foolish enough to come to visit, overnighting in the small villages along the roads or the remote mountain huts where he would lie awake at night and stare into the darkness above him. Stefan had learnt to think of nothing and he liked it this way. Life was simpler. He did not question the fact that he had robbed a young German couple who were camping in the high mountains by a lake. They both wore good watches and had a good knife, not to mention 350 Deutschmarks bound to the leg of the man. He did not think about the Russian man he had chased through the forest for no reason other than he was Russian and had, in Kozak's eyes, no right to be in the Carpathians to begin with. Over time, and without doing anything particularly gruesome, Kozak became known as one of the most feared bandits.

As well as his crimes in the mountains, he controlled a large area of Lviv, with a team of pensioners who would sell on cigarettes for him through their kiosks and who would never dare take a packet for themselves without pedantically counting out the notes to pay for it. He had two lovers in the mountains in separate villages, and one bore him a girl after a year. He paid her no attention, for he had had enough of children. His way of life eventually bored him and he took to faking his own death, wondering how many times he could fool his dumb colleagues. He would fill up his clothes with rocks and grass and force them over ravines or into ice-cold lakes so that sooner or later someone would spot the 'body' and the good news would flash, like current down a wire, from one village to the next, small explosions of relief erupting like artillery fire until, of course, the real Kozak was sighted again. Kozak saw these dress rehearsals as a way of sending a signal, of courting his real desire, of wooing her, laying his cards on the table, showing his monstrous willingness, but no respite came. Each time he fought, his utter absence of fear led him to a certain victory.

One day in Lviv, while Kozak was checking on the kiosk of a man who said he'd been robbed of his cigarettes, one of Kozak's main rivals in the town, a tall blond man with a cheerful expression, sneaked up behind him and hit him on the head with an eighteenth-century table leg. He then put the body in the back of a van of some of his friends who worked for a company which made transformers and who were about to drive a load of illegal stock to Slough, England. He told them to throw the body out whenever they felt like it, but not until they were at least as far as West Germany.

As it turned out, the men hadn't thought through their trip properly, and heard Kozak awaken and start furiously hammering on the van wall by the time they reached Berlin. They carried on driving until they reached Slough, and there, too terrified to open up the back and face Kozak themselves, they left the van in the factory yard, and explained, as best they could to the security guard, that the transformers were in the back. They left on foot with a series of shrugs and brisk nods at the guard before spurting away in a fit of panic.

Stefan Beimuk, or Kozak as we will call him, had arrived in England, though at this point he didn't know it. When the van door finally came down he was faced with a tall, ape-like man with a shaven head and long red lips. Behind him stretched the low, redbrick building of the factory, new and colourful and entirely alien to Kozak's eyes. It had been a factory which manufactured car parts. Now, in 1989, it was still suffering the effects of the recession and had taken to importing parts and selling them on at a higher price. The components it imported from the Ukraine were of a worse quality than those it had once made itself.

'What are you doing in there?' asked the man with a semi-sneer. Kozak looked briefly at him, decided, from the hang of his T-shirt and trousers, that he probably wasn't armed, and climbed from the back of the van. He was hungry, unshaven, his skin clinging to him like scales. In front of him was the factory and behind that some trees. The air felt damp, the light diffuse and grey.

'You all right?' the man asked, taking a step backwards and resting his fists on his hips. Kozak could work out his environment: there was a row of cars to his left, some metal trolleys to his right, a person, a truck; and yet the details were wrong and threw him. The number plates on the cars were unfamiliar, the metal trolleys sparkled with newness unknown to him, the man spoke a strange, nonsensical tongue. Kozak turned back to the truck – that at least he recognized as being from the Ukraine – but nothing came to him. Was he in America?

'I'm going to unload this lot then,' said the man, and set to work hauling the transformers out of the back of the truck and loading them onto pallets. Kozak watched him, unsure what to do next. 'Is it your truck?' asked the man, but Kozak didn't even turn around to face him. He looked instead at the dirty white English sky above him and wondered how he could discover where he was. He walked off, after a while, out of the factory car park and into the industrial estate which surrounded it, where he puzzled over signs for businesses and an old pile of Yellow Pages which someone had left in a concrete doorway. It was there, sitting on the cold surface with his back to a wall where one of the workmen habitually spat, that he saw many mentions of the word 'London' and he realized, from having seen it written down in its own alphabet on a tub of cream his wife had once owned, that he was in England.

TWELVE

Nicholas rang the doorbell and let his hand fall back by his side. He was nervous, and he suddenly felt conscious of his whole arm, hanging there doing nothing. He had been to his audition the day before and his fingers felt tired, over-used. The audition had passed off without incident: Nicholas had been satisfied with how he had played, a woman with dark hair long enough for her to sit on told him they'd be in touch. The door eased open and revealed a man, not much older than Nicholas, tall and gently rounded.

'Hello there, you must be Nicholas,' he said, speaking as though inhaling through his words. His eyes made him look bored and critical, but the tone of his voice was jocular and slightly hopeless. 'Alistair. Her – you know – husband-to-be,' and he held out his soft hand, a fat signet ring on his little finger glinting in the morning sunlight.

'Hello,' Nicholas replied automatically as a cold panic filled his head. It felt as if his blood had thinned and was racing through him; air was scarce. *Beatrice's*, he thought, shaking the man's hand. He must mean *Beatrice's* husband-to-be, he thought, but he knew that this man was Faye's fiancé. Nicholas stood and looked at him, shocked and feeling betrayed and then embarrassed by his own feelings. She owed me nothing, he told himself. I should not have made any assumptions. Alistair looked kind and friendly. He was probably entertaining, professionally successful, reliable. Nicholas disliked him all the more.

'Come on in then, old chap. I gather you're sitting for a

– you know – what's it – portrait – for her. Well done, old boy. Rather you than me. She's funny about all this painting thing. Don't know why she bothers. And don't expect anything that looks like you, either. She told me she thought your face would be a *challenge*,' and with this he clapped his hands together and, for the first time, looked Nicholas in the eye. Nicholas looked back and saw in there the dull gleam of a threat.

Alistair was in his early thirties, large, untrustworthy and inscrutable. He was neatly dressed in a mid-blue shirt and beige twill trousers, which buckled and threatened to collapse with the bulk they were asked to contain. He had made the laudable decision, early in his career, never to achieve anything on merit alone but rather to ascend the sagging rungs of the ladder to banking seniority by periodically telephoning his uncle, who was a partner in his firm and with whom Alistair had always enjoyed a familiar, jovial relationship. His school had taught him how to dress, speak and sidestep and he himself learnt, in the first couple of years of his career, to disguise the soul-shattering sacrifices required by his profession as tributes to his indispensability and brilliance. He had no soul to shatter any more.

'Hello.' It was Faye, descending the stairs slowly and carefully. She kissed him on the cheek and the cold wetness she left smarted. Nicholas thought he sensed a sheepishness in her manner. He tried to pack up what he had been feeling for her and put it away. I am *a friend*. 'How are you?' she asked. 'Come on then. Come and see my studio,' she said with a neat smile, taking his hand carelessly and leading him up the stairs.

'Happy painting, darling,' Alistair called as he went off. 'Be gentle with the old chap. Give him a few tea breaks, won't you? Remember there's no heating up there. Don't make him freeze his nuts off.'

Her studio was in the attic and it could only be reached by climbing up a ladder and clambering through a square in the ceiling. Apart from the lack of heating it was as comfortable as the rest of the house – it had good light, running water and a stripped wooden floor. Moreover it was spacious: a game of badminton could easily be played under its high roof.

'This is nice,' said Nicholas.

'Yes,' replied Faye, relieved that she had got him up here but still nervous, still worried. She had been nervous all week, feeling a tension just above her eyes whenever she thought of Sunday. 'Cup of tea?' she said.

'So that's your fiancé?' Nicholas said, pacing the room. He stopped by a card table and picked up an aubergine – Faye had put it there especially this morning with the thought that she might paint it. He admired its dark sheen. Like a very small seal, he thought, weighing it in one hand.

'Alistair, yes,' said Faye, crossing the room to turn the kettle on. 'We met at university. He's a banker,' she continued, setting out two mugs and dropping in tea bags. Nicholas was now juggling with the aubergine and two onions he had found.

He had his back to her and juggled to distract himself. He hoped she would notice and be impressed. He put the vegetables down and thought I am twenty-nine and try to impress a woman by juggling.

'You're marrying a banker?' he asked gently.

'Yes,' she replied defensively. Their eyes met for a moment and then she laughed.

'Why?' he asked.

'What do you mean, why?' she asked.

Nicholas didn't reply.

She paused and regarded him. 'Opposites attract,' she said lightly. Nicholas thought of the girls he had been out with and asked himself how different they had been from each other. There had been Victoria at university, who told him one day that he looked 'colourful and appealing'. He had felt like a piece of fruit. Then there was May who had a boyfriend in Sheffield but couldn't afford the train fares. Then there was Véronique, the French girl, and Tabitha, whom he met at a bus stop.

'So,' Nicholas said, arranging the vegetables into a face on a wooden box, 'am I to go there?' and he turned his head and looked to the far end of the room, where a long sofa had been draped in red.

'Yes,' said Faye, 'please. Sit in a position you find comfortable. I need you to face towards that corner to start off with.'

'Okay,' he said and he sat himself down on the couch and looked at her. Faye turned her back on him but there was nothing more for her to do: she had already switched off the kettle, taken the tea bags from the tea, poured in the milk, dissolved half a lump of sugar into her own. Standing in front of her were two mugs of tea, ready for drinking. She felt sick. She had wanted to talk to Nicholas, to get to know him again but at the same time the thought of reminiscing frightened her: she did not want to remember who she once had been.

'You're very – er – relaxed,' she laughed and turned back to the mugs of tea. She had glanced at the side of his face – a stretch of soft, pale skin shining in the mid-morning light – and it enlarged itself in her head until she could see in front of her the tiny hairs that must surely lie on his cheek.

'Well,' he replied and fidgeted a little on the couch. Inside him his heart thumped and thoughts raced. Faye pursed her lips and busied her hands and got on with what she was doing with an impenetrable matter-of-factness.

'I've told Alistair all about you,' she said, picking up the mugs of tea and bringing one over to the end of the sofa. Nicholas listened to the sound of her shoes on the wood.

'Oh,' he said.

'And you should hear all about him,' she replied. She set up her easel and pulled on a painting smock. 'You'll get on really well, I think.'

Nicholas laughed. Faye stood back from her easel and looked at him. As she began this long, narrowed-eyed observation a rosy tinge bloomed on her cheeks. She felt a fraud – she had never painted a proper portrait before – and yet was desperate not to be one. At the same time her eyes scanned his skin and she logged, with a certain amount of satisfaction, that her model had grown into an attractive man.

With a 2B pencil on thick watercolour paper Faye began to make preliminary sketches. She had watched a programme on television earlier in the week about painting and had made notes on the back of a theatre ticket. *Preliminary sketches* had been at the top of her list of notes. Faye watched a lot of television. She also read a lot of magazines. In this way she kept herself informed of fashion trends, running her soft fingertips over dark shiny pages and shuddering with delight at the pictures she found. There was something compulsive about magazines, she found, with everything so finished and perfect and beautiful, and she would spend hours examining the crook of a model's elbow or the supple creases of a pair of leather shorts, believing that her attention to the immaculate creations before her suffused her own life with glamour.

Faye knew that there was nothing to this world, but at the same time it made her happy. It gave her a sense of belonging and identity which she had failed to find in her own family and also, when she recognized the work of a photographer or designer, it gave her a sense of accomplishment which she had rarely experienced in school. Most importantly, the fact that she was able to concern herself with a certain calf-skin handbag or a pair of tasselled loafers was a bold and irrefutable testimony to how much her life had changed.

As she sketched, surprised by the softness of the pencil and the difficulty she had capturing even the most basic lines of Nicholas's form, a silence settled over them. Nicholas couldn't stop himself smiling. He wanted to laugh. Faye frowned at her efforts. She wanted to throw her paper aside and go and sit beside him on the sofa.

'How many portraits have you painted?' asked Nicholas, after a while. He folded his arms loosely across his chest.

'Iffle,' Alistair called up through the trapdoor.

Iffle? thought Nicholas.

'Yes darling?' Faye replied, moving over to it and looking down at her husband-to-be from above. Not a flattering angle, she thought.

'Ingrid's on the telephone. Shall I tell her you'll call later on?'

'Yes please darling,' she shouted down. Then Nicholas heard the secret moving of mouths – tongues clicking against wet palates – but knew that they couldn't be kissing. They must be whispering to each other, he thought. Sweet nothings.

'None,' Faye said, coming back to her easel. 'You're my first.'

'I always hoped I would be,' Nicholas replied. Faye looked up at him with a frown.

'What do you mean?' she asked. She knew what he meant; she was questioning more the fact that he dared say it. He caught her eye for a moment and then smiled.

'It was a joke,' he said, wishing that they could just get along as they used to.

'Oh,' Faye replied.

'Have you painted for a long time?' he asked, shifting in his seat.

'No,' she replied, holding up her pencil in the air and squinting at it. 'Could you unfold your arms please?'

'Iffle,' Alistair called up again. Nicholas tried to see Faye's face from the corner of his eye but she turned away and went back over to the hole in the floor.

'Ye-es.' At the far end of the attic Nicholas closed his eyes.

'Just to remind you that my parents are arriving in just over an hour.'

'No, I hadn't forgotten,' she replied, cheerfully, 'can't wait!' and Nicholas heard her steps approach the easel once again.

'I began painting just recently when I gave up my job,' she said. 'I used to work for *Intrinsic,* I was their features writer but I gave it up. But good things did come of it – I got a lot of experience.' Nicholas had never read *Intrinsic* but he had seen it in the magazine section at work. He had a vague recollection of something quite thick and shiny with ink-soaked paper and a glossed front. 'How's life at the supermarket?' she asked quickly.

'My grandfather was a painter,' Nicholas replied, though he had never seen any of his paintings. He scratched his nose.

'Was he really? Oh, how wonderful!' said Faye. Nicholas could have told her the story of how he had disappeared one night and was never heard from again, taken, everyone supposed, to a gulag for painting when he should have been ploughing the earth, but he said nothing. There was no response she would have been able to give other than the usual sympathetic sighs and head-shakings.

'Was Morgan Lodge really terrible?' asked Nicholas, head off to one side from how she'd positioned him. He bounced his right leg on the ball of its foot.

'What?'

'Morgan Lodge. Was it unpleasant?'

'No, it was a very good school, thank you,' she replied, annoyed with his question. 'I'm doing your mouth now so please stop talking,' and she busied herself again, drawing the line of his jaw which just didn't look right. She rubbed it out and tried again. She gave up and drew a few light strokes in its place, hoping that their cumulative effect would solve her problem. They didn't. She worked for some time without speaking. Nicholas stared at a patch of bricks.

Faye broke the silence.

'Nicholas, you just can't sit still,' she said with a half-smile. He shifted his gaze across to her, surprised by her outburst. Faye was, however, right. As soon as he was required to sit for any period of time he found himself inexplicably itchy and restless. Immobility, for Nicholas, took tremendous effort.

'I don't like not doing anything,' he told her truthfully. 'Shall we go out somewhere?'

'No,' she said with a laugh. 'You are sitting for your portrait. I could be Modigliani for all you know.'

'I hope not,' said Nicholas, thinking of the artist's frenzied demise.

'Why do you say that?' Faye asked him and so he told her of Modigliani's pregnant girlfriend Jeanne, who after his death had returned to her home, kissed her mother and then promptly leapt from the bedroom window.

Despite the tensions between them Faye liked his company, as she'd thought she would. He seemed to have come from a different world. He had a different version of London; a different approach to life. He brought with him verve, and Faye felt awake and alive. She looked at her surroundings with new eyes now that she knew Nicholas saw them too. Scanning the sketches for the portrait, she thought that it actually might turn out to be quite good.

He told her what he did for a living and she smiled.

'You're a teacher. That's nice,' she said. Nicholas imagined that Faye had been to a lot of cocktail parties. He felt out of his depth.

'I enjoy it,' he returned. The bland meets the bland. 'But I had an audition yesterday for the Birmingham Symphony Orchestra,' he went on. He'd said it to impress her and wished straight away that he hadn't.

'Wow! That's amazing. What a fantastic job. You must be a really good musician.' She let her head fall to one side. Quite a few of her friends went to classical music concerts. No-one she knew played in them.

'Well, I'm not so sure.'

'What did you have to do?' she asked, taking a new pencil and sharpening it with a few strokes of a pocket knife.

'I'd prepared a couple of pieces to play. And then a bit of sight-reading.' He wanted to end the conversation. He didn't want her to know about the job or to be impressed by it. He knew that he did not want to play in an orchestra. He did not want to travel or have long empty days to confront. He wanted to work when everyone else worked and spend his evenings at De Vere Gardens, where at least there was a child to bring things to life.

'Oh God!' she exclaimed. 'I used to hate sight-reading. And when do you hear?'

'I'm not sure.' Nicholas shook his head.

'Hold still!' Faye called and she laughed.

He told her that he'd studied at Edinburgh University and she told him that she'd been at Durham. 'I wasn't even that far away,' she said and Nicholas wondered what she meant. When Nicholas got a place at Edinburgh to study music Mr Squirrel kissed him. Nicholas came for his last lesson before the Easter holidays with a letter confirming his place if he got his grades. The grades were low, the place an almost certainty. Mr Squirrel had never before had a pupil go on to study music. At best his pupils carried on playing into their twenties. Most let their instruments gather dust.

'Nicholas! My boy! That's fantastic!' Mr Squirrel had cried, striding across the room and planting a large wet kiss on Nicholas's cheek. Nicholas's instinct had been to pull a face and wipe his cheek with his sleeve. Instead he had stood still and reprimanded himself for his thoughts. Quite suddenly his eyes watered as he thought that it was probably the first time he had been kissed by a man for many years. 'You'll have marvellous tuition. You'll finally realize what a bad teacher I am. I'm happy to teach you over the summer, of course. If you want to have some lessons.' Mr Squirrel had given Nicholas some extra lessons before he went for his interviews and auditions. The lessons had been free because Nicholas couldn't afford to pay for them, a fact which embarrassed and shamed him. Mr Squirrel made light of it: you teach me as much as I teach you, he had said but Nicholas had just tightened his grip on the fingerboard and shifted into the wrong position.

'I can imagine you as a student,' Faye said to him. 'I imagine you had long hair and wore black and smoked dope.'

Nicholas shook his head. 'I did all that before I went,' he replied, and he told her of his mother's feelings about his hair. Despite his adolescent sullenness Kalyna had liked living with her son. He was funny and lively and she felt glad in the evenings when his clipped, concertinaed footsteps would ring out on the stairs. She could usually tell what kind of mood he was in from his first few seconds in the house: a good mood and he would track her down (more often than not in the kitchen) and ask her what was for dinner. He asked with a sense of irony and with an incline of his head, which, when he was in the sixth form, caused his long hair to flop around in his face in a way which Kalyna found unappealing. 'Let me tie it back for you,' she used to plead with him, reaching out to run a hand down his mane.

'No way,' he would reply, ducking her hand 'you'll have me in plaits and everything. Red ribbons. Shish,' and he would shake his head. If Kalyna were honest with herself she would have to admit that she didn't like men with long hair. In her world men's hair should be at the very most curling gently around their earlobes. Short back and sides was best of all. But she was, as we know, a firm believer in liberty and so she held her tongue over her son's hair.

His eighteenth summer was a hot one and he had arranged a job for himself working in a solicitor's office, where he hoped he might learn something about the practice of law. In the event he learnt to keep the piece of paper he had to shred in his left hand and the piece of paper he was reading – usually a magazine – in his right so that he didn't confuse the two and end up shredding his magazine and reading legalese all day. The day before he started his work experience he returned from town with a number two all over. Kalyna couldn't hide her pleasure. She grinned at him like a Cheshire cat and thought how handsome her son looked. Then she noticed his ear.

'What's that?' she asked cautiously. Mothers and fathers ten years in the future would have other types of piercings of their once intact offspring to object to. In the late Eighties in Bradford few had gone beyond the insertion of a plain gold stud in the earlobe. Nicholas put his hand up to his ear. He fingered it gently.

'It's my birthday present to myself,' he told her.

'How much did it cost?'

'Five pounds.' Five pounds, Kalyna thought. A lot of money for a hole in your ear. She thought he looked like a yob. She let her eyes drop down to the floor in front of her and assumed an expression of unappreciated martyrdom.

'I had been thinking of having a tattoo,' Nicholas said.

'Oh, Nicholas, no . . .' Kalyna began, lifting her hands to her cheeks.

'But I settled for this instead. The hole will close up if I decide I don't like it one day.'

One day, thought Kalyna. Hopefully tomorrow. When you wake up and see how you really look. 'I don't like it.'

Nicholas let out a burst of laughter. 'You don't say, Mother.' He had imagined she wouldn't like it. But he had done it anyway. It's about time, he had thought before he went in, that I started making my own decisions about my own life. He was eighteen, after all. His mother, he felt, was too present in his life. He wanted some distance from her.

'Why do you make yourself look like that?' she asked him. 'I would cross the road if I saw you opposite me at night.' Her brow furrowed.

He tutted. 'Well, you shouldn't go around making assumptions about people based on the way they look,' he replied petulantly.

'I can't help it, Nicholas. I can't help it. I see someone like you and I feel scared. I see an old person and I think . . .' and she trailed off, defeated by language, unable to argue with him in English, when she was angry.

'You see an old person and you think, aw, doesn't he look nice: benevolent, friendly, full of old stories. In reality he's probably bigoted, racist scum.'

Kalyna paused and looked him full in the face. 'Racist *what*?' she asked.

Nicholas shook his head gently. 'Scum,' he said. 'It's

what you find in the sink.'

'In the sink?' She peered at him.

'Oh, Mother,' Nicholas exclaimed. He moved to flick his hair off his shoulder and realized only once he turned his head that his hair wasn't there any more. 'Look it up in the dictionary. It's just a word.' He took a deep breath and rested his hands on his hips. He was taller than his mother now, clearly stronger. When she looked at him she saw a softer, mousier Stefan, with dark eyes and a slighter build. At times he looked more beautiful than she could have ever imagined. She could not express how much she loved her son, nor did she want to. For the time being expressions of affection were not appreciated by Nicholas. Perhaps later on, she thought, perhaps one day I will tell him.

'A scum,' Kalyna tried it out. 'I quite like it.'

'It's scum. Just scum,' Nicholas shot back, exasperated. 'I'll let you know next time I have some,' he said. Kalyna picked a knife from the drying rack and then laughed. Nicholas always found it easy to make her laugh. She laughed too easily at his sarcasm and his jokes. She shrugged and reached forward to slide a palm over his thick, bristling hair.

'Aw,' Nicholas complained and scowled at her. Putting the knife down she fiddled with her hands and then held one out to him.

'Here,' she said. Her wedding ring.

Nicholas frowned. His heart skipped a beat. 'Why are you giving me that?' he asked critically. The last thing he wanted was a display of emotion. Kalyna knew her son better than he realized.

'You like jewellery,' she said with a half-hearted shrug. 'You should wear a ring as well as an earring.' She wiped a stray hair from her forehead with the back of her hand. Nicholas took the ring in the palm of his hand and looked at it. He was unsure what do to with it.

'People might think I'm married,' he countered. It was a nice ring: a plain gold band. But why had she given it to him? Did she no longer expect to see his father again one day? Had she met someone else? Did she want to be free?

'You have to give the other men a chance,' she replied with a half-smile. 'Anyway, you shouldn't judge people on their appearances.'

Nicholas ignored her jibe. 'Don't you want it?' he ventured. It was the best he could do to try and understand her act.

'Yes,' she said. 'But I'd like you to wear it,' and she swung open the fridge door and looked inside. She had no idea whether she'd see Stefan again. It seemed unlikely. The most appropriate place for the ring was on the hand of one of their children.

Faye placed her pad of paper on the floor and looked at it from above, pacing backwards and forwards over it. She brushed the palms of her hands on the front of her smock, taking hold, between the finger and thumb of her right hand, of her engagement ring: a twelve-carat diamond set in white gold. Nicholas thought of the week ahead. Tomorrow was Monday so he was back at work. It would be nice, at least, to catch up with Sean again.

'How is your mother?' Faye asked, looking up at him. Nicholas did his best to seem impassive; a flatness overcame his face. He nodded once as he told Faye that his mother had died.

THIRTEEN

It had just started to rain but instead of looking in her bag for an umbrella, which she knew was there nestled beneath a loaf of bread wrapped in fine paper and a bag of three parsnips, Kalyna turned up the collar of her coat and shook out her hair into the Yorkshire dampness. She set out to cross the road, where street lamps glinted in the wet tarmac and a discarded bag of chips began to disintegrate under its celestial pounding. The car, as they say, failed to stop, which meant that it hit her, bang in the middle of the zebra crossing, and she was flung into the air, damp hair and all. The driver of the car, no hero, carried on driving, talking to himself quietly and quickly, astonished by what had happened. After five minutes he turned around and drove back, climbed from his car and sat on the kerb with his head in his hands, the early evening rain falling gently onto his uncovered head. An ambulance arrived and then the police cordoned off the road and began the long and naive process of formulating a thorough and acceptable explanation of the death. Kalyna died in Bradford City Hospital, at half past ten at night, four hours after being hit by a car just outside the town hall.

Nicholas had been at university, his first year in music at Edinburgh, when an urgent message was brought to him in his room by a red-faced faculty secretary that he should telephone Borys Smyck, or Boris Smith as she had written in large loopy letters. Nicholas made the call and Borys, the condescending tones of his pulpit voice having momentarily escaped him, told Nicholas that Kalyna was in hospital in a *very bad way*. Nicholas was sick in his sink and then he packed his bags, leaving a note for the soft Scottish girl with a brace he had met and been out with a few times. On the train to Bradford a girl with purple glasses sat opposite him and tried to chat, but each time after she finished speaking Nicholas nodded a little and resumed his study of the darkness beyond the train window.

A policeman came to see Nicholas, a day before the funeral, at Borys's house.

'She didn't feel much pain,' PC Windward told him, after he had blown his nose loudly and picked up his cup of tea, too-large hands around a too-small bone china cup.

'She was in hospital for four hours,' Nicholas replied quietly. He had arrived too late. When he got there they told him that she was dead.

'Yes,' replied the policeman, realizing that he had confused this case with the death of another woman, a pensioner, on the outskirts of the city three days ago. 'But the doctors told me that she didn't feel much pain,' he repeated in a nasal voice, covering his mistake with a lie. He slid his narrow bottom back on the sofa and crossed one leg over the other. Nicholas nodded and looked down at the inside of his wrist, at the curious intersection of creases in his skin crossed underneath by a train track of tendons.

'Would you like some more tea?' Nicholas asked.

'It was a black man driving the car,' the policeman said self-righteously, as though this piece of information explained everything.

'He stopped though, didn't he?' Nicholas said, but he knew the answer already.

'He wasn't drunk but we think he might have had some wacky baccy,' the policeman whispered at Nicholas, a small fleck of spit jumping like a flea from his lip to teacup as he spoke.

Stupid, stupid man, thought Nicholas to himself, though he wasn't sure whom he was thinking about: the driver, the policeman, himself. The policeman sighed wheezily and put down his cup on the small oak table in front of them. 'Accidents will happen,' he said to Nicholas. He put his hat back on and left.

On the day of Kalyna's funeral the sun shone so brightly that Nicholas thought they couldn't possibly bury her. No-one could go into the earth on a day like this. Reverend Borys Smyck laid a firm, veined hand on Nicholas's shoulder and told him that the good Lord had sent the sun to show his appreciation for Kalyna's soul.

'If it was so good why did he take it?' Nicholas asked.

'Because he wanted it with him,' replied Borys, with a slow, sympathetic half-smile.

'Is that not selfish, when she had two sons and a husband?' Nicholas said, a dart of dark anger lifting his gaze to Borys's. Borys did not like to be reminded of Kalyna's husbands. Although nothing had ever happened between them he had harboured desires for the woman ever since she had arrived in the town.

'I can understand your anger, Nicholas,' he said. He blinked slowly and mournfully and proceeded, with a stately gait, to the front of the church where he climbed into the pulpit and read a passage from Ecclesiastes. The usual church community attended, tilting their heads in sympathy at Nicholas, accepting him, piously and self-consciously forgiving him for his rejection of them all.

Nicholas's clear large eyes narrowed at his mother's funeral. Not because he had tears to fight back – he would not cry in public – but because of the terrible, writhing anger that closed his throat and made his chest burn. His mother's friends were all there: dabbing at tears with cotton handkerchiefs, heads hung and inclined in a display of grief.

'She was a fine woman,' Oksana said to him after the service. The reception was held at Lydia's house; a table laden with sandwiches, gherkins and cakes ran the length of the front room. Oksana's eyes bore a weariness in them; she slouched against the door. Nicholas nodded at her, more furious with these women now than he had been at the start of the service.

'It comes to us all, Nicholas, in the end,' Oksana continued. 'She had a hard life, you know. We all struggle. And then this happens.' Oksana shrugged slowly and raised her eyebrows in saintly resignation.

'My mother had a good life,' Nicholas said calmly. 'And normally this doesn't happen. Most people live until old age.' He couldn't bear to think of his mother like these other women. Their very presence seemed to suck the life out of him, dulling his vision, slurring his speech. 'She was unlucky, and don't say that that's only to be expected.' He could hear a buzzing in his ears and he raised his voice to compensate. Heads turned. 'My mother was not like all of you. She enjoyed herself. She did not think of herself as unlucky. She did not see problems everywhere she turned.' He caught Oksana's eye and saw in it a self-righteous resignation. A hush had descended in the house. Nicholas's skin breathed fury. He felt as though he almost wasn't there. 'The way you go about your lives you might as well be dead already. At least when you're dead nothing else can go wrong,' he said. He placed his glass down carefully on a sideboard and, barely feeling the ground beneath his feet, he left the house.

No-one came to see him. One of his mother's friends and colleagues might have listened to his outburst and under-stood his point, or, at the very least, put any kind of scene down to shock and emotional stress. But they did not understand. Instead they gossiped over his words, took each and every one as directed at themselves, bathed in the insult and the rudeness of it all but paid no attention to the actual content of what he'd said. Oksana phoned Lydia to discuss the outburst. Oksana said she was hurt and upset. Nicholas would have to apologize to her face. Lydia suggested he should have to apologize to all of them, en masse. She also confided that she'd never liked the boy anyway; she found him aloof and cold.

Nicholas stayed in the flat. His mother had left him her belongings and £452.13. His watery eyes bulged as he stared out of the kitchen window for hours on end. His gaze passed over the rooftops opposite, all running into each other like the spine of a giant reptile, the patchy, translucent sky, the playgroup-green leaves of an oak tree streets away. He saw nothing. He was twenty. He had thought that he had grown up, was a man. Able to live alone in a city, to pay his own bills, cook for himself, diffuse his own troubles. He was five foot eleven and had no fat to speak of. He had finally come to a point in his life when he understood what his mother meant by liberty and he had savoured it in a way which made her proud. On a wicker chair in the kitchen he sat and stared, crying from time to time. As he pressed his hands between his thighs in grief he felt that he was six again: lost, hopeless, desperate for reassurance.

He did not feel safe. There was no one specific danger which stalked around his head but rather a general, pervasive fear of the future. He did not know what would become of him and night, when it fell, did little to quieten the terror inside him. He sat in the dark in the kitchen, chewing his lip and rubbing his bony hands together, clicking his joints. He had not touched his cello for two weeks. He wanted to take it to him and feel its fit: his thumb snug in the curve of the bow, the ridges of bodywork resting against his knees. But he was frightened to go near the instrument, too. Mr Squirrel had told him when he learnt his first concerto, 'You feel too much, Nicholas. There is too much feeling. Relax. Detach yourself a little.'

Nicholas tried to imagine his future. He willed his imagination to stretch and contort, to show itself off to him and reveal something – just one glimpse – of a life ahead. His imagination was stubborn. It sat still and cold – a frog playing dead – and refused to budge. He could not even imagine himself the very next day. When he was not at home Kalyna was supposed to be there, wiping down the kitchen surfaces, running herself a bath, humming to herself as she tidied up the living room. She was supposed to be there for him to telephone, for him to think about when he entered a supermarket and stood before the crates of vegetables wondering what to buy. He could think only of what had gone. He had never asked her about their journey, about the parts he couldn't remember. Rarely had he plucked up the courage to mention his father or his brother. He arched a hand across his brow and covered his eyes. His head spun with questions no-one could answer. His heart, soft and impressionable, strained with grief.

After eight days of sitting alone in the flat Nicholas entered his mother's bedroom. His hand on the doorknob felt strong and secure, but when he went into the room the strength seemed to vanish – whisked away by a malevolent goblin – and he stood face to face with Kalyna's assumption that she was going to live. A blue cotton T-shirt lay on the end of the bed, nonchalantly indicating, with its curves and folds, the shape of her body. A cheap paperback lay beside the head of the bed – *Metro* by Alexander Kaletski – the end of a red electricity bill poking out towards him. He looked at it, two thirds of the way through the book, but thought only that his mother would never know how the story ended, and not that the bill explained why the lights had stopped working and that he should pay it. With a thickness rising in his throat he realized now how little he had thought about her. A tube of athlete's foot cream lay on the chest of drawers, half an aspirin beside it, a safety pin and a razor. Had his mother shaved her legs? Nicholas paused, frozen, and in this immobile state it seemed that a muscle tore inside him. He hated the objects he could see.

Resentment bubbled inside him against each and every piece of evidence that his mother had not known she was going to die. He raised a hand to his face and pushed his palm up through his beard. Why had she left the Ukraine? What did she think when she arrived here with her young son? What had she planned? With a tremor of guilt Nicholas tried to imagine himself into her shoes. She had given birth to Bohdan when she was twenty-one, a year older than he was now. Why had he not thought of all this before? His protruding ribs heaving with agitation, he left the room and closed the door behind him.

Nicholas's dark, wiry beard grew. His mouse-brown hair matted and rose off the crown of his head. His still eyes were puffy and small, the whites shot through with red like the meanderings of a delta. The trousers he had worn for the past two weeks fell low around his hips; dirt collected in caked crescents under his fingernails. It was in this state that Borys Smyck found him, one morning when he finally dared to ring the doorbell. He pushed the button and sucked in his stomach. He was ashamed of his neglect of Nicholas and as he stood waiting for the door to open he defended himself in his head: I am busy doing to the Lord's work, Nicholas behaved very badly at the funeral, I have let him go for two whole weeks now without asking for the rent. By the time Nicholas had crept to the door Borys felt self-righteous and strong.

'Hello,' Nicholas said flatly as he swung the door open.

Nicholas started at the sound of his own voice. It was a long time since he had spoken. Borys stared at him. Borys missed Kalyna. He had still hoped that one day she might have agreed to be his wife.

Borys slowly took in Nicholas's dirty clothes, his beard and unkempt hair. He had never liked Nicholas. Seeing him in this state angered him, moreover it made him feel guilty. His eyes flashed.

'You are an embarrassment to your mother,' he told him. He thought Nicholas should be getting on with his life, sorting out the flat, moving out. Nicholas, gazing at the lapel of Borys's jacket, considered, for the first time in days, how he might look, for a moment saw himself with Borys's eyes. He put a hand up to his chin and felt the thick thatch of his beard. He frowned: he did not follow the priest's logic.

'What can I do for you, Borys?' he asked coldly. He felt cut off from these people now, and was astonished that his life could have changed so radically in such a short space of time. Cards, it seemed, had been laid on the table: he didn't like Borys and Borys didn't like him.

'Your mother was very prompt with the rent,' Borys told him, interlacing his fingers underneath his stomach.

'How much is it?'

'You do not know?' Borys asked angrily. 'You have lived here for over ten years and you do not know what the rent is?'

Nicholas seemed to come back to life. He had somewhere to direct his anger.

'How much is it, Borys? I'll pay you now,' he said and he went off to get his mother's savings, which she'd kept in the pocket of her best woollen jacket.

Like a traveller returning from a long trip abroad he started to notice things about Bradford which he had never seen before.

He found it insular, backward, hostile, a collection of communities as separate and incompatible as oil and water. He acknowledged his dislike of Borys, of his mother's friends, of the pitiful attempts they all made to keep alive a country and culture which had never really existed.

He took a year out from university and worked in a super-market, prowling through the city at night and wondering whether he would ever know anyone again. Occasionally he would find himself in the red light district where the young and bawdy Bradford girls would eye him suspiciously and mutter suggestions to him as he passed. It was here that Véronique stopped him one night and asked him if he had a light. He had given up smoking; one day he found himself with no cigarettes and decided not to buy anymore.

He shook his head at her.

'Merde,' she said and looked up and down the street. It was February; the prostitutes paced and no-one could hide their breath. Véronique's plain, clear face and worn beige cords made it clear that she was not here on business.

'You shouldn't ask men for a light around here,' Nicholas told her.

'Why not?' she asked with a dart of pale eyes.

'It's the red light district,' Nicholas replied and he wondered whether she would understand.

'What?' she said.

'They're prostitutes,' Nicholas whispered, with a lift of his head.

'Ah. Elles sont *les filles*,' she said.

Nicholas paused. Of course they were girls. That much was clear. He didn't know whether she understood what he meant.

'Well, so what?' she said with a shrug. 'I don't care,' she fingered her unlit cigarette. 'La vie est terrible. I don't care about anything.' At this time in his life Nicholas felt much the same and he asked her to go for a drink.

She wanted to stay a virgin, that was the first thing she made clear to Nicholas. Véronique the virgin, he heard in his head and it made him laugh because her zeal for every other sex act both in and not in the book remained unsurpassed by all the other girls he had known for many years. Still, if that was what she wanted then it was fine by him.

Her father had been a car-dealer in Aix-en-Provence and her mother had run a cucumber farm until they had both died in a midnight fire in a seaside villa in Spain. It was Véronique of course who first told Nicholas of the magical properties of cucumbers. 'They make you taste good,' she said with her tongue behind her top teeth where she often seemed to leave it, 'down there.' She had demonstrated her interest in the down there tastes right from the start when she would guess – usually correctly – what Nicholas had eaten for his last meal. 'Haricot beans,' she would say after she'd swallowed and wiped her mouth with the back of her hand, watching as his penis slowly softened. Or 'that's easy, asparagus.'

'How many times must you have done this to know all those tastes?' Nicholas once asked her.

'It's not something I've learnt. It's intuition,' she replied, but judging by her sexual appetite and prowess, Nicholas wasn't so sure.

Véronique, of course, ate a lot of cucumbers. She skinned them and pressed them with salt, squeezing out the water and covering them with yoghurt and garlic. Or she just ate them, like some would eat an apple. She objected with a passion to the way they were packaged in England. 'Why do they wrap them like this?' she asked him once as they lapped a supermarket (Nicholas was often to be found in a supermarket), running an open palm along the tight cello-

147

phane cover. 'It is almost as if they are telling you what to do with it. The cover is like a . . . how do you say it . . . *préservatif*' she would cry, suddenly morally outraged – this girl who educated Nicholas – at the packaging of a vegetable.

Nicholas just nodded and said that he supposed it was, imagining that the plastic sheath did help the cucumber keep for longer. 'La vie est terrible,' Véronique would mutter as she filled her basket with vegetables. Nicholas would escort her from the supermarket as quickly as possible and take her home to bed where she would, despite or perhaps because of her gloomy diagnosis, press herself against him as though it was the last request of a condemned man.

The next September, Nicholas returned to university and graduated from Edinburgh with a third-class degree. He had sat over his exam papers as a terror crept up his spine and scrambled what was in his head. His body willed him to flee, to rise from his seat and stride from the room and return to the library, where he had spent the past few months tucked safely away amongst books. When his heart and his head told him that he could not stay in the examination room he willed himself to remain seated. He regulated his breathing and read, for the fifth time, the essay question in front of him. Sweat gathered between his eyebrows, at the back of his neck, behind his knees.

In the run-up to their final exams the other students turned in on themselves. Some had their parents arrive at the weekends with clean clothes and food. Some were taken out for expensive meals. Others even disappeared, returning home to revise in peace. He had worked hard. He had piled up books on his desk in the library and worn his socks two days in a row. He had not particularly enjoyed university, but he did not want it to end. Once he graduated he would have no reason to be anywhere. The thought terrified him.

FOURTEEN

Kozak's first Saturday night in England found him sitting back in his doorway at the industrial estate with one note and a line of coins on the unusually smooth concrete step in front of him. The note was a ten-pound note, soft and supple as cloth and not bad for his first day's work, though he didn't know it. He had stumbled, that afternoon, on a car boot sale. Wandering from the industrial estate towards the edge of town, he happened to walk past a school playground, full of cars and stalls and prowlers. He made his way in and felt instantly at home, for this was not the overbearing West he had been expecting, with shiny cans of Coke and new, tight jeans but the ragbag West, where people flocked together to sell on carburettors, bookends, lighters and lampshades. This was the West being just like the East, and Kozak felt, for a while at least, that he might be able to make a living here.

Once he had discovered the sale he hurried back to the industrial estate, stole four old televisions which had been left by the back entrance to an office block, and sold them, in the space of an hour. He examined the ten-pound note closely, wondering about the man and the woman on its sides and what the pair of them had achieved, or not, for his father had always told him that it should be villains and criminals whose portraits were put on money. He realized, as a damp purple spread across the sky, that his survival depended on money and money alone, and the sooner he familiarized himself with his armoury the better. The numerals on the note and coins were the same as those in his own language, and for this he was grateful.

After a few minutes of deduction he had four different categories of currency: pounds, pound, pence and penny. He put these in his head, reciting them over and over. He reasoned that penny was less than pence, for the former were bronze and the latter silver. But as for pounds, pound, and their relationship to pence, he was stumped. If you had told him that the ten-pound note he had weighted down with his watch was worth a fraction of the twenty-pence piece which he rolled between a grubby finger and thumb, he would have believed you. Once it was properly dark that evening he collected up his money, slipped it into his right sock and went off.

Slough by night. Kozak wandered along the road from the industrial estate and turned off it as soon as he could, into a quiet, narrow road with large, detached houses which stood like lighthouses against the sky at the end of rolling front gardens. He stopped before one and wondered who lived in such places, with two sleek cars in the gravel driveway and a brass knocker on the large front door gleaming flatly in the orange light of the street lamp.

As he stood there a light came on in a downstairs bay window and a cream room sparkled before him, a huge room which ran the depth of the house and ended in a strip of French windows, so that it was possible to see a little of the illuminated garden beyond. Beside a large cream sofa a woman in the room was moving cushions around. She had short dark hair, curled loosely like an abandoned coil of rope, a flat, wide mouth and a nose which would have suited a man more than a woman. Kozak watched her closely as she moved about the room and asked himself whether he could have stumbled upon the house of the woman whose face was on his banknote. Could this be her, he wondered, as his eyes roamed over the opulence of the house and the lushness of the grounds.

He took the note from his sock and examined the face again. Apart from the fact that the woman on the note was wearing a crown, she certainly looked like the woman in the house before him. He did not know enough of England and its systems yet to realize that the Queen could not possibly live in Slough.

At the end of the street was a pub and he sat outside this for a while on an upturned blue bucket, watching the people inside drink and chat. He observed a game of darts, and then a sandwich was placed on the stretch of bar he could see and he felt an empty ache inside him. He moved off, stopping to look over a notice board by the side of the pub. The letters and words of the fluttering notices intrigued him, and, like a child with a tendency to perversity, he tried to spot the similarities in sentences and blocks of text instead of the differences.

Had he been able to read English he would have seen that the Slough Botanical and Biological Society was advertising a talk on the Health and Welfare of Captive Reptiles; the Amateur Operatics announced that they'd raised £5,109 with their sponsored silence; a financial services company informed that last year had been a torrid one for corporate bonds and someone was selling twenty-three square metres of fleur-de-lys patterned lino with hologram effect.

He moved on, walking stealthily along the edges of roads, slowly beginning to panic about where he might get something to eat. Even in the darkness it seemed to Kozak that he had arrived in a land of fairy tales: where the grass was green and the hills rolled and a moisture hung like gold dust in the air. The tarmac beneath his feet glistened like the back of a snake, smooth and safely asleep. Kozak bent and touched the surface: he had never seen such a perfect road, thought perhaps that it might stretch the whole length of the country and then out onto the sea, flowing like errant lava over earth and water alike, proclaiming civilization until there was nothing left to be civilized.

He began, the day after the car boot sale, to collect his wares for the next one. He had hoped, at first, that perhaps it was a daily event, and had gone to the car park the following day, only to be greeted by empty lots and a lone teenage boy who sat with his back against a wide concrete pillar and lit and blew out matches, one by one. Kozak wanted to reprimand him for his wastefulness but instead turned on his heel and went back to his doorway.

He knew little of England and the English. The Englishman who lived in his head was pale and a little overweight; soft and warm like the udder of a cow. Kozak imagined that he ate porridge for breakfast, wore hand-knitted socks, owned three or four large, steaming dogs and ducked apples as a pastime. He wore a bowler hat and carried a briefcase which contained a cake of soap, a small white towel, a cricket almanac from 1955 and a ham sandwich. Kozak had also heard that English people competed over the size of the vegetables they could grow and so he supposed that his bloated, harmless man would diligently care for a fledgling crop of potentially Promethean root vegetables.

He spent his first few weeks in England sleeping in the doorway in the industrial estate. He fed himself from bins, gardens and allotments. It was late April, 1993; warm enough to sleep outside if you could keep from getting wet, although he woke every morning with a damp stiffness in his limbs which made him think of the dead. After three weeks he had saved up fifty-six pounds, and he treated himself to a couple of nights in a bed and breakfast, where he showered until the landlady came to rap on the door and where he slept in his shoes, as he would for the rest of his life. That Friday he passed by a bank which was closing down and which was being stripped of its insides. Kozak stashed the swivel chairs, wall calendars, desks and telephones in the copse by the estate and the following day made £156 at the sale. He was hooked.

It wasn't a woman which kept Kozak in Slough. Nor was it the weather, which ranged from a slow, mouse-grey drizzle which coated everything on his stall with a fine, slippy mist, to a steady, straightforward rain which made people pack up and go home, used to the weather disrupting their plans. What kept Kozak in Slough was the fact that he had no reason to go anywhere else. He knew some people by sight now, did his best to keep clean, and practised counting, addition and subtraction most evenings, until a car could not pass him by without his brain obsessively working out the total of all the digits displayed on the number plate. As well as enjoying the success of his fledgling business, Kozak liked to look at his new country – often he would stand by a field with his hand in the air before him, comparing the vivid wet green with the waxen translucence of his skin.

He was standing in the rain one afternoon, a plastic dust sheet over his stall and another over his head, when a tall woman with dark deep-set eyes came and stood before him. He glanced at her, as he did with all potential customers, and took in the information he needed: her hair, a shoulder-length dark bob, had been cut by a professional; she wore what appeared to be a silver ring on one hand, set with a large green stone; her clothes were manly but tidy and her shoes were good – solid, sturdy walking boots, hand-sewn from thick leather by a craftsman.

'Hello,' she said. She had seen him look up at her and suspected, though she could not see his eyes behind his sunglasses, that he had registered her.

'Hello,' Kozak replied, wondering what it was on his stall that she was after. The plant holders, perhaps. She wore no protection against the weather and drops of rain fell occasionally off the heavy points of her hair.

'Are you trying to give the rain a hint with those glasses?' she asked cheerfully. Her voice was sonorous and sure of itself and though her enunciation was careful Kozak hadn't quite caught what she had said. He had heard the word glasses and thought perhaps that she wanted to buy his sunglasses.

'Not for sale,' he said, using the joint of his forefinger to push the item back up the bridge of his nose.

'Oh I see,' replied the woman, dropping her voice a little. 'I didn't realize you were – well, not a native speaker. Standing there in the rain with all your – well – I'd assumed you could only be English.' She took a step towards him and peered at him, trying to see what was behind the dark lenses, taking in the dull potato colour of his skin and thinking that he was perhaps a refugee from the war in Bosnia.

'I speak English – numbers,' Kozak said. 'You want to buy?' and he indicated with a drop of his head and a sliding of his hand the landscape of plastic before him.

'Oh well, I hadn't even thought – I was just making conversation, I –' and she smiled at him, showing long, toe-like teeth. Kozak surveyed them and took her to be wealthy. 'I can't even see what you have,' she said, lifting the wet plastic happily with bare hands and peering underneath. Kozak watched her, thought her a strange woman with a forthright manner and a lack of femininity. She will choose the plant holders, he thought to himself, screwing up his nose briefly to ease an itch in his moustache.

'How much for the ramekins?' she said as she emerged.

'For the . . . ?' he repeated. He hated not knowing the

names of the things he sold. It put him in a weak negotiating position.

'Ramekins,' the woman said. 'These,' and she pointed out the three pale yellow dishes, like delicate French cakes beneath the polythene.

'One pound for each,' Kozak said. He had found them the week before in some boxes of rubbish outside a church hall.

'Done,' trilled the woman and she dug into her trouser pocket and produced three coins. Kozak wrapped up her dishes and put them in a bag. She handed over the money.

'Excuse me,' Kozak said as she was about to leave. 'The word?' he asked, indicating the plastic bag in her large hand.

'Goodness,' she said, 'did I forget to say thank you?'

'The word,' Kozak repeated, pointing this time and miming the shape of her new dishes as best he could.

'Aah,' she said, sticking her chin out into the wet. 'Ramekin,' she continued, taking a step towards him. 'Ra-me-kin.' He repeated the word after her but struggled with its pronunciation, granting the syllables a magical exoticism, as though perhaps somewhere in the land the weighty door to a secret, damp chamber might slide open. 'It means little dish, I suppose. You can bake all sorts of things in them, one dish per person. Besides, they're terribly handsome,' and she lifted the bag a few inches in the air and tilted her head towards it.

'Ra-me-kin,' Kozak said again.

'Yes,' said the woman. 'Well, good day,' she said and she strode off jauntily into the rain.

'No ramekin today,' Kozak said to the woman when she passed the following week. She had tied her hair back and wore a lilac skirt and looked, Kozak thought, more fluid than she had.

'I'm sorry?' she said with a frown.

'No ramekin today,' Kozak repeated. He examined her through his sunglasses, wondering what it was about her that made her look slightly different. Perhaps just the colour of her clothes.

'Oh,' said the woman. 'Right,' and she came to stand before him, casting her eyes down briefly over his stall before letting them rest on the shiny opaqueness of his lenses. There were indeed no ramekins on his trestle table, nor anything much that interested her, for it was covered this week in a few old tools – a wrench, a bradawl, a hacksaw and a hammer lying on top of a nest of old wires, bolts, sockets, plugs, clothes pegs, hinges and pieces of metal which had a purpose only few would recognize.

'You must be thinking of my sister,' she said, and Kozak, who understood her words, frowned. 'We look the same,' she explained, clasping her hands in front of her, 'there are three of us. Triplets.'

'Triplets,' Kozak repeated in his head, though he had no idea what the word meant. He shrugged at her and thought suddenly of the people in his village, and he wondered where they were now and who had died. He felt like a veteran of a war that never ended, because while he had survived this far, he knew that the repercussions could come at any time. Already occasionally he would find blood in his ears, though he thought nothing of it. For the time being he felt fit. I will know when I have it, he thought.

'Can you speak English?' the woman asked him, a question which Kozak understood. He took a small step to the side and she regarded his size: the thick broad shoulders on which he could surely carry a pregnant sow and the long-fingered hands which reminded her of the hallucinations she had had last summer. She had been struck down by a fever and spent three days in bed believing, in her hot

156

liquid head, that each part of her body had grown large and unwieldy around her.

'No,' Kozak replied, for he felt that this woman posed no threat to his business, found it hard to imagine that a woman could ever pose a threat to his business, and so happily told the truth.

'Oh,' said the woman with a small smile. She fiddled with the leather strap of a small bag which she wore diagonally across her, like a sash at a beauty parade. Miss Slough, perhaps. 'Well, your word for today is triplets. Like twins but there are three of them. Which is why you mistook us,' she said, and she smiled at him again, a slow smile that seemed to sneak across her face like a fox with a hen.

And so Kozak made the acquaintance of Hester, Vicky and, later, Beth, who, as Vicky had explained, were triplets, identical in genes if nothing else. They lived together, still, now thirty-four, in an oversized house in Oxford which had a damp cellar and bells in each room to summon servants who had long since departed. Hester was the oldest by three and a half hours. Then came Vicky, and, fifty-five minutes after her, Beth, who bounced into the world keen not to miss anything. They kept their appearances similar, they always had, but now it served them to be that way. Each had dark shoulder-length hair and a physical energy that came from exercised limbs and busy lives. They lived, so they said, off their inheritances, from their parents and benevolent, childless aunts and uncles.

Hester was an expert in unarmed self-defence; she had learnt judo from the age of eight and had got into the habit, from her early teenage years, of assessing everyone she met in terms of their physical capabilities and comparing them to her own. Kozak, she decided, for it was Hester who had bought the ramekins from him, was stronger than her, but in his movements she saw a slight clumsiness and a physical unsureness which she knew she would be able to take apart if she was quick. She was brusque, Hester, with a tendency towards self-righteousness and arrogance. She wanted only to fight. She trained every day, at a sports centre on the edge of the city, and her sisters were frequently glad of her talents, though they seldom all went out together.

Vicky was a nudist. She enjoyed wearing nothing, for clothes, along with tax returns, supermarkets and death duty she saw as an infringement on her liberty, though how she could exercise that liberty once she was dead, as Beth pointed out to her, she didn't know. She did not practise her nudism at home, since anyone could walk around their own home in a state of undress. Instead she went away, at least once a fortnight, to a utopian community on the border of Wales where she concentrated her thoughts and energies on wearing no clothes. Her sisters mocked her for her interest, which she took seriously, with an earnest concern for social reform. She was a gentle and quiet woman with a startling intellect and a fearsome will, both of which she frequently resisted from inflicting on her peers since she knew it simply wouldn't be fair. She spent much of her time away discussing and debating with her naked friends and when she was home was an active member of the Green party.

Beth preferred to put her thoughts into prose, and would sit up at least two nights a week writing letters to prisoners. She wrote to women and men: murderers, robbers, tax-evaders, fraudsters, anyone who had requested correspondence. She wrote with no particular compassion but with a developed and complex interest in current affairs, explaining her views to many an inmate on the contemporary economic situation or the benefits and drawbacks of intensive farming, and unashamedly depicting of how she spent her days. When she wasn't writing she painted portraits and had stacks and stacks of what she'd called self-portraits, though they were all either of Hester or Vicky. Both sisters had quickly tired of sitting for Beth, but still, occasionally, one would relent and the two of them would spend an afternoon in the north-facing back room.

Beth was also the sister who ran the house: while Hester and Vicky would both notice when the milk carton was empty, it was Beth who went to the shop for a fresh pint, as both Vicky and Hester knew she would, time and time again. She restored domestic harmony not only materially but also spiritually – it was she who made peace between her sisters and who, when Hester slammed the ill-fitting door to the kitchen which bounced straight back out of its frame and Vicky quietly followed her, furiously calm and determined to make her point clear, would raise her eyebrows at them with a resigned shrug and an affectionate shake of her head and make them both a cup of tea while she changed the subject. Beth also had a love of language which turned her towards idiom and phrases when, as Hester would say, plain words would do.

It was Beth, of course, who first invited Kozak to come to the house for dinner. She had warned her sisters that she was thinking of it; was likely to spring the invitation any day now, was prepared to cook and clear up alone if need be. 'I think he lives like a plover,' she said to her sisters over a late breakfast one Sunday morning, 'let's give him a real feast.' And then one Saturday lunchtime, as she stood by his stall and saw that he had nothing much of any value this week, she asked him whether he'd like to come over the following Friday. Kozak accepted; it would be his first experience as a guest in England and he looked forward to seeing the sisters together; a triptych of reflections kaleidoscoping before him.

'Come in, Kozak. You found us then?' It was Hester who answered the door, having just come down from the shower in a blue towelling robe.

'Good evening,' Kozak said, without risking adding a name. He could not tell them apart. He held out a bottle of vodka.

'Oh. Thanks,' said Hester and she took it from him, sensing, as the bottle passed from her hand to his, the strength of his grip. 'Come in,' she said again and she led him to the kitchen where Beth, already washed, dressed and made-up, was mashing potatoes with swift, businesslike plunges of her forearm.

'Hello Kozak,' she said warmly and she tapped her masher on the side of the pan, flinging a few lumps of potato off into the air and over the kitchen surface before turning to him and giving him a kiss on the cheek.

'He brought this,' Hester said and waved the bottle in the air before putting it in the freezer.

'How lovely,' said Beth. 'What will you drink?' she asked kindly, in a clear voice. Kozak noticed that she had coloured her lips. Around their edges ran a deep red line, like a date carefully circled on a calendar. He looked from Beth to Hester and back to Beth again, unable to pinpoint and specify their differences, yet able, somehow, to perceive them, because the women who stood in front of him were two separate beings. And then Vicky arrived to complete the trio, floating in from somewhere upstairs in jeans and a jumper.

'Hi Kozak,' she said with a luxurious blink, and she joined her sisters in the kitchen.

Kozak stood and looked. He found them peculiar, these women, and tonight, as he saw them together for the first time, he felt as though he had entered into a myth. Had a king appeared and demanded that Kozak fulfil three onerous tasks before being allowed to dine with his daughters, Kozak would not have been surprised.

'Would you like a drink?' Beth repeated, stacking some plates on top of the wide gas oven and looking Vicky up and down. Kozak shrugged.

'Water,' he said, because, apart from vodka, it was the only liquid name he knew. Hester laughed out loud, Vicky turned to him with a frown and Beth tripped merrily to the sink and gave him a glass of water.

Since his arrival in England Kozak had become used to keeping his lips pressed together for days on end. His mouth had developed a tightness – a constant, biting pressure in its corners which lent his face an air of disapproval when really none was meant at all. Instead of talking, he watched people. Now, as he stood in their sparsely furnished kitchen, he noticed Beth's tiny glance as Hester took a spoonful of mashed potato and saw that Vicky had seen it too, though she was pretending to be absorbed in sorting out the cutlery.

'Why don't you go and get changed, Hester?' Vicky suggested, polishing a fork. Kozak took a sip of his water and looked blankly at them. He barely understood a word they said.

It was six weeks later that the three sisters decided they would offer Kozak somewhere to stay. Beth had found out what he was paying at his bed and breakfast and said that he could live in their attic room and pay half that. 'Your landlady shall pay for her pleonexia,' Beth announced as she helped Kozak bring his cardboard boxes of belongings into their house. She smiled at him and her cheeks dimpled, and for a second Kozak saw an hourglass on either side of her mouth.

The women did not need the money, nor did any of them feel the need for the presence of a man in the house; they were neither lonely nor bored. They liked his junk business, however, and Beth enjoyed teaching him English, taking it upon herself to haul dictionaries down from shelves and spin through them with small, short-nailed fingers until a word was found and the charades began. Beth taught him her favourite phrases, distilling from the process the pleasure of teaching a parrot to swear.

'Life isn't all beer and skittles,' she taught him to say and laughed when he used it.

Kozak was a slow learner and he knew it. There were times when he would look up at her through his dark lenses and raise his eyebrows a little, implying, she had come to understand, that the exercise was hopeless, that they would be better off trying to teach tricks to a cat. 'A tradesman must know his wares,' Beth would admonish him and he knew she was right, but knew also, given the nature of his trade, that he could sell almost anything at all – from a piggy bank to a thimble to a jump lead – and, lost in a jumble of words, his learning seemed to have no end in sight.

It was Beth with whom Kozak spent the most time; she often cooked for him and he liked to watch her adjust the line of their knives and forks on the table before they sat down together in the evenings. 'You must let me paint your portrait,' she told him one evening while he struggled with modal verbs. She had been eating cherries and was perched on the arm of the sofa, her right hand cupping cherry stones and stalks.

'No,' Kozak shook his head. 'I don't sit still,' he said.

'You can't sit still? Oh, I'm sure you can,' Beth replied, slipping a cherry stalk into her mouth and wondering whether she could knot it with her tongue. She had seen someone do it in a film once.

Kozak remained firm. 'No, I do not like to sit still,' he said.

Every few weeks Beth would ask him to sit for her and every few weeks came the same reply. All three of the sisters took an interest in his business, and since he had moved in they had written him a list of every car boot sale in the area, lent him books on how to date earthenware and porcelain and were more than happy for him to stack his boxes of stuff up on the moulting paisley carpet in the hallway. Kozak told them what he had learnt so far: at one of the markets he always positioned his stall near the home of a family of feral cats. 'I use the best dish I have and put it on the floor with milk on it,' he said. 'When a person walks into a market and I give him something, he doesn't want it. He must find his desire by accident. I always want food on the plate next to me. It's the same.'

FIFTEEN

Alistair had gone to play golf when Nicholas arrived for his next sitting the following Sunday. Nicholas's week had passed quickly. He had gone to work, had tea with Mrs Sten and played his cello. Each activity seemed somehow easier than before; his smile, when Mrs Sten invited him to tea with her, came more readily. The woman from the orchestra had not been in touch, but Nicholas had spent more time thinking about his next sitting with Faye than he had worrying about the silence from Birmingham.

Beatrice, Nicholas learned as he came into Faye's house and shook the rain off his shoulders, was still asleep and Faye raised her eyes at her friend's torpitude as she hung up his coat.

'I'm surprised her eyes don't close up completely,' Nicholas said to Faye and they went up to the attic and embarked on the lengthy and arduous process of creating art.

Faye squinted and asked herself why she didn't seem able to convincingly convey the line of Nicholas's shoulders onto paper. After a few minutes she gave up altogether and decided to begin on her canvas, which she had lovingly stretched and primed the day before. She had also rearranged some of the objects and furniture in her studio. She loved the idea of being a painter more than the actual painting itself and had felt a charming, bohemian thrill pass through her as she had thrown an old drape over the water tank and positioned a fern underneath one of the skylights. She preferred *being* to *doing*.

'Forty days and forty nights,' Nicholas said and he ran a finger over the ridges of his thumbnail.

'I'm sorry?' Faye said.

'This rain,' Nicholas replied. 'And in the twenty-first century came the flood. It's rained for the past two days solid. So much for July.'

Faye turned her attention to the canvas and drew the neat grey line of the neck of Nicholas's T-shirt. She looked up and saw that he wasn't wearing a T-shirt, but had come in a dark red shirt instead. She looked back at the line and wondered what to do.

'How are you?' Nicholas asked. He was twitchy. He had left her house last week feeling bewildered and he didn't want to feel that way again.

'Fine,' Faye smiled.

Downstairs Beatrice opened her eyes and saw the magnolia moulded ceiling of her bedroom. She deduced that it was Sunday morning and that it was raining again. Up and down the street broadsheets were opened and closed over organic orange juice and coffee. She listened to the sounds of the house and remembered that Alistair was out and Faye was, as Beatrice thought of it, playing Georgia. Next thing she would be wearing a headscarf and collecting skulls.

A throb of anxiety passed through Faye as she questioned whether there was any future in painting at all. Painting was dead, surely. Perhaps she should try sculpture?

'Why do you want to paint?' Nicholas asked, seeming to sense what was on her mind. The couple next door climbed up into their loft space, planning for a trip to B&Q and Faye and Nicholas heard some dull thuds from the west side of the house as the husband patted the wall in different places.

'Well . . .' Faye said. She daubed some pale salmon over the line of his T-shirt to see if she could obscure it. The grey line hung now in a pink cloud, resolute and unforgiving. 'I've always just loved painting.'

'Oh,' Nicholas replied. 'Did you paint at Morgan Lodge?'

Faye paused. 'Occasionally,' she said. 'Have you heard from the orchestra?'

'No,' he said clearly. Nor did he particularly want to. If they rejected him he would feel like failure. If they offered him a position he would feel equally useless for having to turn a job down for a reason as silly as his. He could barely acknowledge it. He imagined the sort of question he could never have asked in his interview: *and if I wake up one morning at ten o'clock and rehearsals don't start until five is there anywhere I can go where there will be someone around with whom I can chat?*

'Anyway, I enjoy teaching,' he said.

'Those that can, do. Those that can't, teach,' Faye said with an apologetic expression. Alistair thought of teachers as grubby socialists, imbued with corrupting ideals and a corrosive self-righteousness. Faye did her best to defend the profession in front of him, but parts of his opinions rubbed off on her.

Nicholas raised his eyes. 'And how do you think *those that can* learn how to do what they do in the first place?' he asked with a grin. Faye dropped her brush into a glass of turps and wiped her hands on a tissue.

'Still clever then?' she smiled. She was wondering which of her friends would find Nicholas amusing and whether she should arrange a dinner party.

'So when's the wedding?' Nicholas ventured. He did not want to know but at the same time knew that he had to ask, if only to demonstrate that he too had been socialized, could be polite.

'In three months, one week and four days. There's still so

much to do. I almost have my dress, but my bridesmaids are currently going down the aisle in their birthday suits.'

'That should liven things up.'

'Are you suggesting that my wedding will be boring?' She raised her eyes from the canvas and looked at him.

'Not at all. Joyous, poignant, melancholic, dazzling, tragic, maybe. But not boring,' he replied. *You were my best friend*, he thought.

'You are funny,' Faye replied. 'Still. You're still funny.'

'Why did you stop writing?' Nicholas asked casually. He had not planned to ask the question. If he had planned it he would never have summoned the gall. He caught her off guard and she looked up at him again, her pink-tipped paintbrush suspended in mid-air. She saw in his face the Nicholas she had known as a teenager, the boy who had charmed her with his bold eyes. *Why on earth do you ask questions like that?* she thought. *Where do you get the courage from?* She dropped her eyes and wiped her brush on a sheet of kitchen roll. She felt herself blushing. Thinking of Alistair helped her. *I am an adult*, she thought. *A grown-up.*

'I owe you an apology about that,' she began. 'It wasn't what it looked like.' Nicholas didn't reply.

'It wasn't that I didn't want to stay in touch with you. It was just that I had this whole new life. It seemed simpler to start from scratch. I didn't even open the last letter you sent me.' Faye made every effort *not* to remember those days. She spoke matter-of-factly.

Nicholas watched her as she replied. He did not really hear what she had to say, but instead observed her as she selected a new brush, pushed its bristles over the back of her hand. *What is the matter with her?* he asked himself.

'Can I paint you?' he said suddenly.

'What?' Faye was surprised, relieved.

'Can I paint you instead?'

Faye glanced at her canvas and smiled at Nicholas. It would be a relief to stop painting, she thought. 'I know you can't sit still but that's taking it a bit far.'

'It was just a thought.'

'You always were a trouble-maker,' Faye grinned.

'That's not true,' Nicholas replied and a smile crept into the corners of his mouth.

'Yes it is. I only started smoking because of you,' Faye said as she crossed to the sink to wash her brush.

'Did you?' asked Nicholas.

'I saw you smoking in the street. So I went out and bought a pack, smoked a few and then asked you for a light.'

'Yeah, but you made me skip lessons. In fact it was you made me jig a whole day once.'

'Now that is a lie,' Faye protested.

'No, it isn't,' Nicholas replied.

They had been due to go to the moors, to the place where the Brontë sisters had lived. Nicholas would rather have taken a day trip to the house of the Nolan sisters and Faye would really rather not have gone on a school day trip at all. She had waited for him at the end of his road and whistled casually when he passed, so casually in fact that he carried on walking and she had to resort to calling his name.

'Hi,' she said, once she'd got him to stop.

'Hi,' he said. Nicholas had had an argument with his mother before he left about what he should wear on the trip – in the end he had got his own way, but she had made him take a sweater, kagoul, cap and change of socks with him in his rucksack. Faye, Nicholas could see, had clearly had no such problems: she stood in front of him in a small polka-dot T-shirt, a short green skirt and a pair of pumps. She didn't even have a bag with her.

'Look what I've got,' she said, with a smile in the corner of her mouth. She held up a couple of pieces of cream writing paper with a pink line round their edges, and two envelopes.

He eyed her.

'I'm not going on some shite trip, are you?' she said, and she walked up to a bus stop and sat down.

He followed her and she handed him one of the sheets of paper and a blue biro.

'My mum's called Jenny,' she said, but he knew that already. 'You'll have to tell me how to spell your mum's name. Now, what's the matter with you, Nicholas Beamish?' she asked and she turned to him with a bold grin.

'I'm sick,' replied Nicholas, with a sly smile.

'Lovesick?' asked Faye with a mock innocence.

'Put that I've got tonsillitis,' he said. 'I like it when they know it's an excuse but they can't do anything about it.'

'No, no,' replied Faye, 'I think we should have really rare, scary things,' and she stared off across the road for a few seconds. ' "Dear Mrs Weston," ' she began, reading out her words, ' "I'm afraid to say that Nicholas will have to miss the school trip today because of an auto-associative protoplasm. Yours, Mrs Beamish." '

'They'll never believe that.'

'Yeah they will. Baffle them with science. Go on then, write mine.'

Nicholas spread the small sheet of paper out on the bench to his side and neatly dated it at the top. ' "Dear Mrs Weston, Faye cannot come to school today because of a severe case. It fell on her in the night and she has to see a doctor. Yours in earnest, Mrs J. Peters." '

'Oh, that's so obviously a joke,' wailed Faye.

'No it's not,' protested Nicholas, pleased that he had written something even less believable than the note that

169

was going on his behalf. 'Your mother just has a way with words.'

Faye shook her head and folded the notes in half, one by one. Nicholas watched intently as she stuck out her small pink tongue and licked the envelopes. Her eyes met his. 'Now keep a lookout for Adrian Holmes. He should be passing any minute.' Adrian Holmes was a small, scared child who was always late. He blinked with every word he spoke – tiny pale blue eyes round with fear – and he would do anything anyone asked him, particularly if they threatened him.

'Oi, Adrian,' called out Faye, as a scramble of blazer and undone laces rounded the corner. Adrian glanced up and terror filled his face. He came over. 'You off on the school trip?' asked Faye, looking him up and down.

'Yes,' he said and blinked. He held a large sports bag in one hand which weighed him down. Nicholas thought, looking at him now, that Adrian would easily have fitted into his own bag. 'I'm late.' Two blinks.

'You don't say,' said Faye. Regardless of what she might admit, Faye liked Adrian. She liked to watch the effect she could have on him. 'Don't worry Aid, they'll wait, they have to. Now,' she said, picking the two envelopes off the bench, 'I need you to give these to Mrs Weston as soon as you get there. And Adrian, you haven't seen me or him,' she went on, pointing at Nicholas with an elegant out-stretched index finger.

'I haven't see you what?' he asked, blinking and confused.

'You haven't see us *today*. Your mum got those letters off our mums. All right?'

'I have to go,' he said, his knees buckling with anxiety. He failed to mention that he didn't have a mum and hoisted his bag up onto his shoulder.

'You didn't have to wear uniform today,' Faye said.

'Didn't I? Aw, no,' he said, four blinks, and ran off, hurtling down the hill, completely out of control.

They went to the park and ate Nicholas's packed lunch, though Faye thought his sandwiches were peculiar.

'What kind of weird bread is this?' she said, holding a sandwich in front of her, as though it might answer her back.

'My mum buys it,' replied Nicholas, conscious for the first time of the thin, chewy bread that he had always eaten. Once they had finished all the food Faye had a cigarette and lay back on the grass so that her skirt rose a little up her legs and her T-shirt pulled tight across her front. A man walking a dog stared at the two of them as he passed. It was half past ten on a sunny Wednesday morning. Nicholas lay down beside Faye, pulling a section of his fringe as casually as possible over his forehead to hide a spot. He didn't know what to do and was embarrassed. He wanted to lean over and kiss Faye, and then bury his face in her mane of hair. He shut his eyes and felt the sun on his face. He thought that perhaps he would pretend to go to sleep.

'What are you two doing?' It was the man with the dog again, an old rounded black Labrador which looked at them with weary eyes.

'We're doing fieldwork for our geography projects,' replied Faye, moving only her lips. Nicholas smiled to himself. He admired her bravura.

'Shouldn't you be in school?' he asked gruffly. He was about seventy, with dark beady eyes and bright white hair.

'That's the thing about fieldwork. You do it in a field. Just like housework is done in a house,' Faye said.

'You don't look like you're doing any work to me. What school are you from?'

'Grange Hill,' said Faye.

'Where?' the man said. He looked down at his feet. 'You think lying will get you out of trouble. You're from Moorside, aren't you?'

Faye and Nicholas were quiet. Neither had a clever answer. They didn't want to get caught. Nicholas couldn't let his mother find out, because she had paid for him to go on the trip, and finding the money had been a struggle. He felt terrible already. Faye had been cautioned by the head-mistress that if she missed any more schooltime she would be excluded for the rest of the term, and her mum would kill her.

'That's a nice dog,' said Faye, sitting up. 'What's he called?'

'Skip,' replied the old man.

'Here Skip,' sang Faye, patting the ground beside her with a hand. The dog didn't move. 'We are missing school. But we're not missing lessons, there's a school trip today and we didn't want to go. That's all. We go to our lessons.'

'I don't give two monkeys what you go to and what you don't. I walk in this park every day and we don't have young people in it. It's not right. The two of you. Lying there like that. A girl and a boy.'

'Where should we go then?'

'Well, I don't care. Just not here. Go home and stay indoors. Go on, clear off,' and he put his hand into his pocket and retrieved something which he passed to Skip, a long pink tongue catching the tips of his fingers as he gave it to him. Nicholas and Faye got up, gathered their things and wandered off, sulkily.

'And when you get home change your frock,' the man shouted after them.

'Okay,' Nicholas shouted back, in a high voice. And they ran off laughing.

172

The following day Faye really was ill and didn't come into school for the rest of the week. By the Monday of the following week Nicholas, though he wouldn't allow himself even to think it, was missing her. A teacher told him that Faye had flu and that she probably wouldn't be back for a while. By the first period after lunch on that Monday afternoon it felt as if time too might be ill, for it had slowed terribly.

Nicholas had never been to Faye's house, though he knew all of her family by sight. By Wednesday evening he had had enough and he went round and rang the doorbell. He had wanted to bring her something, but he had nothing to give her, so on his way he had picked some buttercups from a piece of waste land.

'Oh, hello.' It was one of her sisters, the middle one Nicholas thought, and she stood in the door frame in tight stonewashed denim with a nonchalant expression. She had Faye's golden hair, but she had pulled it up into a tight bun on top of her head which seemed to pull the skin on her face tighter, her features jutting out at him, as though unearthed on a dig.

'Hi,' said Nicholas. 'Do you think I could see Faye please?'

'You're the Ukrainian boy, aren't you?' the girl asked, taking a step back from the door and slipping a hand into a back pocket of her jeans. She raised her eyebrows and a small smile formed on her mouth. Nicholas nodded. 'Hang on, I'll just go and see if she's awake,' and she turned and flew up the stairs giggling.

Nicholas looked at the hallway in front of him. The wallpaper was bluey-grey and had been torn from the wall underneath the coat pegs, as though someone had begun to redecorate and then found something more interesting to do. On the coat pegs hung two sports jackets, a worn donkey jacket and a pink umbrella with frills along its edges. The door at the end of the hall was closed – a brown veneer with a golden wave of handle – and Nicholas thought that he could hear shouting behind it, though it could have been the television.

'Nicholas!' It was the girl again, standing at the top of the stairs, swaying her hips. 'Faye says you can come up now,' she sang down in a mocking voice. Nicholas came in and shut the front door behind him, noticing as he did the looseness of the latch and a broken chain, swinging around with no weight on the end. He went up the stairs and held his breath as he pushed past Faye's sister, trying not to let any part of his body touch hers.

'It's the door on the left,' she said to him.

'Thanks,' he said, with a large exhalation of air once he'd reached the top.

Faye's room was perfectly square and the ceiling hung low like the roof of a tent. The walls were covered with posters – thin, badly printed sheets from which stared smiling, made-up young men. The floor was covered in mattresses, three in a row, and Faye lay on the one nearest to him, covered in a baby-blue blanket. At her feet was a pile of boxes. The air was still and thick with the vapours of sugary drinks and menthol lozenges.

'Hi,' he said. He sat down on the floor by her head. He dug around inside his jacket and pulled out the flattened butter-cups. 'I brought you these. Sorry that they're squashed.'

'Oh. Thanks,' she said and she put them in a cup of water by her bed.

'Are you all right?' Nicholas asked, as he took in her glistening brow and flushed cheeks. He felt uncomfortable in her room, at having come at all. It was the first time he'd been alone with a girl in her bedroom. What would she think?

'Yeah,' she said, coolly, 'just desperate to get out of the house. It's such a mess.' He looked at her lips and wondered whether she might have just put some lipstick on. 'And I'm bored,' she said with a sigh. 'I'm so bored I could eat my hands.'

'My grandmother used to bind my mother's hands to her sides when she was a girl, because she kept trying to eat them.' Faye frowned at Nicholas. 'There was a famine. In fact, there were three famines in a row.'

'Oh,' said Faye and nodded her head slowly. There was more noise from downstairs. Sprawled sentences and squashed words, packed with anger, came to them. 'My parents,' she said with a fake smile. 'Shut the door, would you?'

Nicholas got up and did as he was asked, but when he sat down again he saw that it was now even worse. They were enclosed, locked off from the outside world, like mice in a cage.

'Thanks for the flowers.'

'That's okay,' Nicholas said and looked at the yellow stitching on his boot. He ran his finger along it.

'Have you brought me my homework?' she asked.

Nicholas shook his head. 'No. I . . . I just wanted to . . . see you,' he trailed off, hoping that she wouldn't have heard, that she wasn't paying attention, that somehow she wouldn't realize what he had just said.

'Well here I am,' she said, 'this is full face, and this is profile,' and she turned her head against the pillow. Nicholas smiled uncomfortably and looked down at the lino on the floor to his side. A peach line made a recurrent pattern of ornate cubes and circles.

'This your room then,' he asked, looking up at the posters.

'We share it,' she said, 'me and my two sisters. That was George who let you in. Those are their beds.'

'Oh,' said Nicholas. 'Where do you put your stuff?'

'It's here,' she said, sitting up in bed and leaning forward to grab one of the white cardboard boxes. Nicholas saw that she was wearing a kid's nightie, with cartoon animals cavorting across the front. She pulled the blanket back over her.

'This is my stuff,' she said happily and she took the lid off the box. Inside was a clump of colourful objects. She took out a tiger badge and laid it on the bed, then some blue paper clips followed by a key, but she didn't know what it fitted. A pen with a flower on the end and a pack of heart stickers joined the exhibition on the sheets and Nicholas thought that it looked as if she was setting up a stall at a car boot sale.

'This is one of my favourite things,' she said, holding up a green match with a head at both ends, 'and this is my favourite book,' she continued, pulling out a tatty paperback. *My friend Flicka*, Nicholas read. Nicholas hadn't heard of it but judging by the picture of horses on the front, he didn't think he'd like it. The collection of belongings continued: a blue plastic ring, half a packet of mints, some hair slides, a Dinky toy van and a cream candle. 'I'm going to burn that one day when I have my own house,' she said, and then, 'oh, look at this, do you know what this is?' and she held up what looked like a grain of rice in front of her.

'Let's have a look,' and Nicholas held out his hand.

She dropped it into his palm.

'It's a tooth,' he said, for nestling into his lifeline was a small tooth, shiny and pointed at one end, flat and wide at the other.

'It's *my* tooth,' said Faye, with a vivacity in her voice, and she leant over to see into his hand. 'My first tooth that fell out. Isn't it amazing how small it is?' With her head close to his Nicholas could feel the heat she was radiating and the stuffy air that surrounded her. She moved back and rested against the wall. Nicholas collected her prize possessions together and put them back into the box, carefully wrapping the tooth in the ball of cotton wool that it had come in.

'I feel shite,' she said quietly, lying down again. She shut her eyes and turned onto her side. In his mind's eye Nicholas saw himself lean over her and kiss her forehead, feeling the sweat grow cold on his lips as soon as he moved away from her. He didn't move but took a deep breath. A pinkish soft vapour with a brandy-sweet smell filled his nostrils.

'You'll get my germs,' she mumbled with hot breath into the pillow.

'So?' he said and he replaced her box at the foot of the bed. 'Far far away not so long ago –'

'What?'

'Ssh,' Nicholas replied and he looked up to the window. 'Far far away not so long ago there was a girl called Palageya who lived in a cottage in the forest with her mother and sister.'

'Called what?'

'Pala-geya,' Nicholas repeated. 'The cottage was surrounded by pines which moved in the night, so some mornings she woke up right in the thick of trees and other mornings she woke up in the middle of a clearing. Her mother used to tell her that the forest was a kind of sea, with its own creatures and plants, and like a sea it had a tide. So some mornings when they awoke the tide would be out, and others it would be in, but Palageya never saw the trees move. The Ukraine in which she lived was constantly under attack, from each country along its borders and even those farther afield. Turks would attack it, stealing what they could, taking people for slaves. They were followed by the Greeks. One day a messenger came through the forest to Palageya's house to ask for the family's help. A Greek general had been shot with a poisoned arrow and was on his deathbed. There were many people who couldn't help him and many others who could but wouldn't. Palageya wrapped up a bundle of herbs and potions and set off to help the general, because she had heard that he was a man of valour, justice and courage.

'For forty days and forty nights she soothed his wound and mopped his brow. As each day passed he got stronger and healthier, but as each day passed he looked sadder because he had fallen in love with the girl who nursed him, and dreaded having to part from her. Eventually, when the colour had returned to his cheeks and Palageya was packing up ready to return to her home in the forest, he knelt beside her and asked her to marry him. She was really happy and there was a huge celebration to mark their wedding. Then they prepared to leave for Greece but before they left Palageya said farewell to her sister, Kalyna. "Before I leave my land I am going to give the plant which I love the most your name. It has soft white flowers in the summer, which move the nightingale to song. In the autumn it produces deep red berries, filled with the blood of our land. From now on the plant will be called Kalyna." And that is how the most beautiful flower in the Ukraine got its name.'

Faye opened her eyes and raised her eyebrows at Nicholas.

'What?' she said.

'It's a story,' Nicholas shrugged.

'But it doesn't make sense. Why does she help a general who's been attacking her own land? Why does she go back to Greece with him? And how can she just decide to call a flower by her sister's name? Didn't it have a name already?

That's like me deciding I'm going to call those buttercups Nicholas.'

Nicholas shrugged. 'It's a fairy tale,' he said.

'You should read *My Friend Flicka*,' she said. 'It's much better.'

They were together as the day put on its dark cloak and said its farewells and the sky in front of them turned first to purple and then to black. Beneath them in the house a door opened and closed and a television set was turned on. In the cold blue light that came in through the window Nicholas watched her as she slept: her mouth was open slightly and every so often her breath caught on her lips, making a soft, whistling sound, like the wind in the pines. Her eyes moved beneath smooth eyelids – like a hand slipped under a satin skirt – sparring, no doubt, with a feverish Lilith. Her hair, gently matted, framed the picture. She looked peaceful. Nicholas wished that he could capture her stillness and keep it somewhere private for the rest of his life. He wanted to wait for sunrise.

'There's no funny business going on in here, I hope.' Nicholas turned suddenly, and a figure was silhouetted against the door.

'Er, no – no,' replied Nicholas. He had never met Faye's father.

'Why're the lights off then?' the voice asked, and a harsh yellow light filled the room. Nicholas blinked and felt irritated by the interruption of their peace. He saw in front of him a squat man with thick forearms and a round head. The man's nostrils flared and he crossed his arms over his chest.

'She's sleeping,' replied Nicholas, or at least she was, he thought. Faye stirred and sat up a little.

'It's fine, Dad. I was asleep,' she mumbled.

'Right. Well. It's time you were going,' he said to

Nicholas and he stomped down the stairs and slammed a door somewhere beneath them. Nicholas stood up awkwardly, not wanting to let his big boots touch her bed.

'I'll see you later,' he said. He felt a heat touch his cheeks and a wave of light-headedness pass over him. For a brief period he couldn't see.

'Nicholas?' she replied, sleepily.

'Yeah?' he said. She pushed herself up in bed and reached for her box of things. Nicholas saw this time that the right sleeve of her nightdress finished in frays and stray lengths of cotton, just above her elbow. The artificial light made her look shiny and pale, as though she'd been kept underground for her whole life. She handed him the nest of cotton wool with her tooth in it and for a moment her fervid hazel eyes met his.

'Thanks for coming over,' she said, lying back down. Nicholas nodded and closed his hand around the ball of softness. He could only just, by pressing with his little finger, feel the tooth inside it.

'Get better,' he said and he let himself out.

SIXTEEN

It was Hester, Vicky and Beth who taught Kozak that a glass of wine with the evening meal was to be recommended and that sleeping late was a pleasure – like paddling in the sea or tossing pancakes – to be exploited whenever the opportunity arose. During his first few weeks in the house Kozak would often sit at the kitchen table – neatly set for breakfast by Beth the night before, complete with dark green paper napkins curled round into pigs' ears – and quietly salivate for a good hour or so before giving up on them and helping himself.

When they did finally emerge, Hester would be the first. Her thick hair wet from the shower and slicked to her head, she would arrive noiselessly in the kitchen and make the faint-from-hunger Kozak leap from his skin. Hester wouldn't eat anything until she had done her morning exercises and so Kozak would be forced to grasp his white china teacup tightly in a fist while Hester strode into the garden and fought with something that wasn't there. One day, when all four of them were in the garden to help Vicky with a plum tree she wanted to plant, Hester went for Kozak with an almost alien energy. She was not malicious in her attack, but she gave him no warning and tackled him to the ground in a matter of seconds. They fought on for a few more minutes, until it became clear that while Kozak was stronger, Hester was quicker, and technically more adept. After five minutes Kozak was panting. Hester had a mad look in her eyes. Vicky tipped the watering can over her head.

'I am perfectly calm,' was all Hester had to say about it. Kozak hobbled back into the kitchen.

Vicky and Beth were usually the last down for breakfast. They would burst into the kitchen like a circus come to town and while Beth toasted and boiled and grilled, Vicky would sit by the radio and listen avidly to the local news, a look of serene happiness on her face. Finally, by the time they all sat down to eat, Kozak's hands would be trembling so much that he could barely hold his toast and didn't even try his teacup, lovingly filled from a large white teapot by a steady and well-rested Beth.

At weekends Kozak could not partake of these almost lunchtime breakfasts. On Saturdays and Sundays he was gone from the house before seven, his boxes of goods stacked high on the front of his bicycle so that he had to lean out to his right to see the road. He spent the weekends travelling from sale to sale and the weeks scouring the city for junk he could sell. Oxford, as the sisters had assured him with their sly smiles, was full of junk. Whether it was students, landlords or just refurbishing families, there was seldom a time when there was not a chair or some curtains outside a house somewhere, not to mention scraps of carpet, picture frames and rectangular panels of mirror which would lie forlorn, staring blankly at the heavy sky above.

Kozak's business flourished. He redistributed the junk of Oxfordshire as though he'd been born to do it. It seemed as though a sixth sense might tell him when a toby-jug-shaped hole had opened up in the north of the city and that at exactly the same time in Marsden, between a squat, gabled pub and a derelict eighteenth-century cottage, was a house that was being cleared and its belongings sold off for next to nothing. Kozak somehow knew to be there and his fingers twitched when the dresser in the kitchen revealed three monstrous, grinning toby jugs which the bailiff was happy for him to take. He looked upon his business as a ragged, three-dimensional jigsaw puzzle which, regardless how many of his objects he sold on one frenzied Saturday in Beaconsfield, refused to let itself ever be completed.

Beth continued with Kozak's unofficial English lessons. In the same way that she wrote long, rambling narratives to her prisoners she just spoke at him, telling him how the Co-op had run out of 60-watt bayonets so to buy a bulb she had been obliged to visit the corner shop, a place she normally avoided since it was next door to an adult shop and she hated to think of what went on in there. They sell adults, if you see what I mean, she whispered to him, but Kozak just looked at her blankly. Vicky would have taken her to task over her prejudices against the adult shop, but Vicky wasn't there. He listened, though, repeating her phrases to himself as he sat on the loo or laced up his shoes. *Each to his own*, he began to mutter, not quite sure what it meant. *I'd rather not*, he tried. And then the marvellous Bethism *I know*, her daily utterances of which easily reached double figures and which annoyed Hester and Vicky so intensely that often one would leave the room when Beth said it.

After four months of listening to Beth and learning not only to repeat her phrases but also the meaning behind them, Kozak started to talk back to her. He had a different voice for English and mimicked the swaying and stoppings of Beth's words until he spoke it well, with the exception of a thick accent which lay heavily over each syllable.

Whether it was his business which taught Kozak optimism – and it can, like a catechism, be learnt – or whether it was the Twilling sisters, who celebrated Christmas when they felt like it, frequently in the third week of January and with plenty of whisky all round, is difficult to establish. In his day-to-day business he was forced to see the best in things. It becomes impossible for a junk dealer to look at anything but a heap of soil without seeing something potentially saleable. Even soil has worms, and fresh, healthy worms, to the right group of people, can sell like hot cakes.

Kozak changed over his first few years in England. He stopped being alive only in the sense that he wasn't dead. He seemed to loosen; his jaw clenched less in his sleep. He began to think about Bohdan and for the first time in many years let his name sound in his head. He did not think about Nicholas. He had imagined that his own heart was bone dry. He had seen it as stiff and desiccated in his chest, like a crumpled piece of canvas left to dry beneath a burning sun. There were times when he barely believed that it beat. Walking into wind he would clutch frantically at his chest, convinced that his heart would blow away entirely, and get caught in the branches of some tree where it would swing, rigid, for the next few years. Since he had become Kozak he thought that he had a heart only in the literal sense. Once he moved in with Hester, Vicky and Beth he realized that this was not the case. He almost wept with relief.

It was an almighty crash which awoke Kozak, although by the time he had opened his eyes the noise was over and for a second he wondered whether he had dreamt it or not. A second crash made him raise his head from the pillow. It sounded as though vandals had broken in and were destroying the house, starting in the kitchen.

Kozak climbed from his bed and stood, naked but for the shoes on his feet and the shoes round his neck. He slipped on a pair of trousers and crept from his room, stepping slowly down the stairs to the first floor. The noise continued – a stereophonic falling of pans and tearing of wallpaper – and Kozak, fearless as he edged down towards the kitchen, began to simmer with a chest–tightening rage. Who were these people, and why were they doing this? he thought. How could they possibly be making so much noise?

He picked up an umbrella and stalked towards the kitchen, feeling an intense obligation to protect the property of his friends. The noise stopped for a moment and Kozak froze. He listened for breathing, or for organizational whispers, although why the culprits would whisper after having made so much noise smashing the place up he did not know. He heard a steady dripping and a slow creak. He swallowed and swung into the doorway. Before him in the darkness he could make out bits of rubble and plaster all over the place. Water dripped and pooled on every available surface.

When Kozak realized that there was no-one there he reached, in sleepy relief, for the light switch but paused with outstretched hand. He reasoned that the electricity had probably shorted, and if it hadn't it should have. Surveying the damage as best he could in the blue light of the night he was surprised that the kitchen table wasn't already laid for breakfast, since Beth, he'd assumed, did this last thing at night. He climbed the stairs and discovered the cause of the problem: a hot tap, hissing and dribbling in the first-floor bathroom which it had flooded and caused to collapse in on the kitchen below.

When Kozak went to wake the sisters he found that they were not there. He knocked on their doors at first – a sharp, tight rap – and after no answer he had shrugged in his mind and opened their doors, one by one. Each bed was empty, and, as far as he could tell in the darkness, none looked slept in. Kozak was shocked and pictures filled his mind: the three of them lap-dancing; checking greeting cards in a factory; sprouting hairs on their palms and howling at the moon. He lit a honeycomb candle and looked at the electrics in the kitchen. Above him bare wires hung from the ceiling, poised and fatal and from them fell drops of water, like rain falling from forest foliage. He could not mend anything now. Instead he sat down on the stairs and waited.

At half past four he heard Hester's car pull slowly into the drive and the engine die. The skin on his shoulders had goose-pimpled and his eyelids hung heavy. A key slid into the lock and Vicky's silhouette appeared in the doorway. She did not see Kozak but moved on into the house until all three of them were in and the door closed behind them. Beth quietly unbolted the cellar door, Vicky began to unlace her shoes and Hester muttered a brief 'good night' and approached the stairs. Whatever it was they were doing it seemed as though they had done it many times before.

'Hello,' Kozak said. There was a sharp intake of breath from a few metres away and Beth whispered urgently — because in the face of Hester she feared for Kozak's life — 'It's Kozak.'

'You startled me,' Hester said, flexing her hands. Her voice betrayed no indication that what she said was true. For Hester the battle of the sexes meant not equal earnings or life opportunities but an honest and simple hand-fight.

'There was an accident,' Kozak explained. Vicky and Beth gathered behind Hester, though he could see little of any of them. 'A tap was left dripping in your bathroom and the kitchen ceiling collapsed. I imagine the electricity has gone and the kitchen is a real mess.'

'Goodness,' whispered Beth.

'That must have been you, Hester,' Vicky said.

'You were last in the bathroom,' Hester replied, quick as lightning.

'Well, it doesn't really matter anyway. There's no point

186

making shoes for geese. It's happened now,' Beth said.

'Indeed,' Vicky said, 'it has all happened now. Shall we go and sit somewhere? The living room perhaps. We need to talk to you, Kozak.'

'Vicky, I don't think – why don't we –' Beth began.

'No, she's right, Beth,' said Hester and the four of them trooped through to the living room. What Kozak didn't know was that all were relieved that the electrics had blown: they had a rule never to switch the lights on when they left or when they arrived home from their business, and they didn't want to break it now. But that wasn't all Kozak didn't know.

'We rob people's houses,' Hester announced, once they were seated. Silence fell. In the darkness Kozak felt quite awake.

'I'm sorry?' he said.

'Well, it's not a protest against material wealth, if that's what you think,' Vicky said. 'I might believe in a money-free utopia where personal ownership does not exist, but I wouldn't go out stealing to demonstrate my belief. And besides, I don't believe in collectivization, so you don't have to explain to me why *that* doesn't work.'

'We've always done it,' Beth whispered.

'It's how we make our living,' Hester said.

'We only do houses that are empty. We've never hurt anyone. We steal from rich people,' Beth said urgently.

'Oh, Beth. Don't feel you have to justify yourself,' Vicky pleaded. 'Kozak knows us all already. He can imagine how we carry out our business.'

But Kozak couldn't, really. He was shocked by what they had told him. Astonished that he had lived in their house for almost three years without ever realizing, ever even imagining that they had a secret life. He felt himself foolish and obtuse.

'And so the question arises: what do we do now?' Hester said. 'You are the only person on earth who knows what we do. That makes us vulnerable.'

'But I would never—' Kozak began.

'Never use the word never,' Hester replied and she cleared her throat. 'You might be happy to keep our secret today, but who can say what will happen tomorrow? Your knowledge puts us in a position of weakness.'

'Oh Hester, don't be such a drama queen,' Beth burst out. 'It's fine. Probably not what we would have chosen, but it doesn't matter. Don't you even trust your friends?'

'Kozak,' said Vicky, 'why don't you go up to bed? We'll have breakfast together in the morning and we can inform you of our decision.'

Kozak paused. He wanted to say something.

'I have no reason to tell anyone,' he said, wondering whether in the light of day he would feel any *obligation* to tell anyone.

'I dare say you don't,' Hester replied. 'Not this minute. But reasons grow on trees, Kozak. Just ask a writer.'

Kozak rose, dazed by events and by the forced reappraisal of his friends. He went up to his room.

The sisters, in history as on this Thursday morning in the late twentieth century, could not agree. Beth thought that everything should carry on as before. 'I know,' she said, with a twitch of her eyebrows, 'I know that we're in a position of weakness but so what?' Vicky cocked her head at her younger sister and conjured up, in complex, convoluted images the daily fear that would come to reside in all of them now Kozak knew what he knew.

'What happens if one day you see him talking to a policeman in the street?'

'Kozak is not going to talk to a policeman,' Beth replied, 'he's an illegal immigrant.'

'They could offer him a British passport in exchange for information on us,' said Vicky.

'Anyway, there aren't any police on the streets,' Beth countered.

'That's hardly the point,' Vicky replied. 'In any case, does he actually want to stay here? Otherwise threatening him with deportation is pointless.' There was a pause while Hester and Vicky looked to Beth. It was she who was expected to know the answer to Vicky's question.

'Yes,' she said, 'at least I think so. I think he wants to stay.'

'We have to restore equilibrium between him and us,' Hester said. 'Or we silence him somehow.'

'How would you suggest?' Vicky asked.

'I can knock him unconscious,' Hester replied firmly. She sniffed brusquely, as though the thought somehow displeased her, but her sisters knew that exactly the opposite was true. Hester would love nothing more than to be briefed to knock someone unconscious, it made little difference to her who it was.

'No,' said Vicky, 'at least not until we know what to do with him when he wakes.'

'We may have to abandon him somewhere,' Hester suggested.

Beth shook her head. 'But he would still know what he knows,' she said.

'We have no choice,' Vicky announced ominously. 'We have to ask him to join us. That way he has an incentive not to tell anyone.' There was a silence as the women pondered their situation. Hester chewed at her thumbnail and the noise of her gnawing drifted through the dark room.

'He'll get us caught,' she said quietly. 'He's noisy.'

'What would he do, anyway?' Beth asked. She interlaced her tidy fingers and rested them on one knee.

'He could drive. He wouldn't have to come inside,' Hester offered.

'And then we have a lone male sitting in a car in the middle of the night. People will spot that. Men are suspicious,' Beth said. Her sisters were frustrating her. She wanted to trust Kozak, and resented being made to feel a fool for it. 'And why should he join us anyway? *We* told *him*, remember.'

'We had to tell him. We crept into the house in the middle of the night, all dressed in black. Besides, this one will get into the papers. They're back from their holidays tomorrow and that portrait is a Lowry. Unless it's a forgery.'

The women talked some more as dawn rolled in. Eventually Beth gave in, as she knew she would have to and the three of them agreed that in the morning they would ask Kozak to join them. If he refused they would take him to the nearest immigration officer.

An hour later Beth crept up the stairs to the top of the house. She opened the door to Kozak's room and saw that he was lying, wide awake, in his bed, his shod feet hanging over the end of the mattress. He kept his money in his right sock, she knew that. She had seen him pat the ankle unawares, checking it was there. It was something he'd done since he'd arrived in England, and something he would do for many more years. He frowned and she pressed her finger to her lips and Kozak, astonished that she seemed to have arrived in his room making less noise than silence, punched his pillow a few times and then sat up against it. She crossed to the bed.

'I didn't realize I was living with criminals,' Kozak said dryly.

'And that's the way it should have stayed,' replied Beth, and she sat down gently a few feet from him. They had rarely been in each other's rooms and Beth felt strange sitting on his bed, as though she were mid-way through an affair with him that she didn't realize she was having. 'How are you?' She asked, wishing to inject some formality into the scenario.

'Okay,' Kozak shrugged. The sisters' revelation had hurt him; he had thought that he knew them all well. But he was not one to sulk. He appreciated Beth's visit. 'What do you do?' he asked her.

'I'm sorry?'

'When you go out, in the night, what do you do?'

Beth sighed. 'It's a long, complicated process,' she said, glancing up at the skylight above the bed. There was an old patch of bird shit on it and if she squinted it was possible to look up at the sky through it: smoky blue patches through powdery white grey. 'It's not just about the night – like last night – there's a lot of preparation involved. We watch our targets first for one month. Then we plan our access, we plan what to take. We plan for unforeseen events.'

'But what do you actually do?'

'Me?'

'Yes.'

'Well, I drive, for starters. Hester and I cut the phone lines while Vicky deals with the alarm. Usually we do modern houses which are double-glazed so we take the panes of glass out of one of the windows. Either that or we open the front door through the letter box. All of us go in, we carry what we take out in one go and then I drive us home. We can do a large house in one and a half hours. We're really very good.' She raised her eyebrows at him. 'No mess, no noise.'

'I believe you,' Kozak replied.

'We're going to ask you to join us,' Beth said. She was embarrassed at what she'd agreed to. Kozak turned his head to her and tried to read her expression; apart from their smiles, each of these sisters gave little away. 'Over breakfast. Oh, I forgot to set the table,' she added.

'The table almost floated away.'

'Hester and Vicky don't know I'm here.'

'Why are you then?'

'I want you to go. You shouldn't join us. I think you should pack up your things and leave, now, before breakfast. I don't think my sisters will come after you.'

'Oh,' said Kozak. And so he did. Beth helped him carry his things to the door, ensuring that he made as little noise as possible.

'Thank you,' Kozak whispered, in his slow English which Beth had taught him.

'Bye,' she said.

Kozak couldn't, of course, carry everything he owned and he left behind a large part of his business. He went to the coach station, bought a toasted cheese sandwich, put it in his pocket and got on a bus to London. The bus entered the city from the west, coming in through Shepherd's Bush, Notting Hill and Queensway and depositing Kozak just past Marble Arch, at the north-east corner of Hyde Park.

SEVENTEEN

'Four o'clock. Time for high Coca-Cola, I think,' Sean announced. He and Nicholas paced back to their office.

'I actually even quite like this job sometimes, you know,' Sean said. It was Monday and had been quiet all day. Nicholas had arrived late at the supermarket that morning, having run through the park with his cap in his hand as though pursuing a thief. He had arrived covered in a film of sweat.

'Guarding food?' Nicholas asked Sean. 'Of all the things that might need guarding . . .' He bit into an apple.

'Well, okay. But I like looking after the lost property. It's fulfilling. My elder brother had advice from God on his career.'

'Really? I guess He did okay.'

'He says that God spoke to him one day while he was delivering pizza leaflets. Apparently He told him to become a vegetable so he now dresses up as a red pepper when he leaflets. It increased pizza orders by 19 per cent.' Sean raised his eyebrows at Nicholas. 'I have to say, though, this is the same brother that boils milk in his kettle and puts his clothes in the dishwasher.' Sean shrugged. 'Sometimes I think I'd like to join the navy.'

'My uncle was a grave-digger,' Nicholas told him. 'In the Crimea. Spent his nights lifting coffin lids and searching for military buttons.' Nicholas bit his apple core in half and proceeded to eat it.

'Hey, how did it go with Faye?'

Nicholas finished the rest of the core and was left with

only the apple's stalk, poised between his forefinger and thumb.

'She's engaged,' he said, and he flicked the stalk into the bin.

'There's many a slip between cup and lip,' Sean replied.

'Can I take Thursday off this week?' Nicholas asked.

'What for?' Sean demanded with a brazen curiosity.

'Well, I've arranged to see her then.'

'Oh,' Sean said, and he folded his arms. 'Nicholas, in the interests of seeing ladies you can take all the time off in the world, whenever you want. Appointments with doctors and dentists I'm not so keen on, but women – there's no finer reason.'

Faye had already been up in her studio before Nicholas arrived on Thursday, to look over her sketches from the previous sitting and decide which angle she liked best. She had also arranged a few more objects around the place: a chipped blue vase with a dried sunflower in it, an old pair of pale beige shoes, a fresh tomato. Nicholas noticed all of these when he arrived and paced the room, keen to be above and away from the noise and heat of the city. Faye appeared a little distracted this time, absorbed in the task ahead of her, wondering how to transfer the sketch she preferred onto the stretched and primed canvas and, most of all, how to make it good. She wanted to paint Nicholas well.

'Same place as before?' asked Nicholas, standing by the draped and dusty sofa, carefully running a finger across his chin. He couldn't help wondering about the house beneath him and how it all looked. Was it all as pristine and self-conscious as the hallways? He thought that at some point he might be able to slip off and explore without Faye noticing, but today she had pulled up the ladder and noisily shut the trapdoor so they were contained in the room. He would like to see her room, to see what it could tell him about her.

'Er . . . yes, yes please,' said Faye, positioning her easel. She looked beautiful today, Nicholas thought as he sat down on the couch and stared up into the cathedral-like roof above him. He started to imagine himself approaching her, or her approaching him and then stopped himself. He shifted on the sofa and began, instead, to construct their house – the house he and Faye might have one day, a rambling house on the Black Sea, under a wide fan of sky, scorched by the sun.

'How are you?' he asked her.

'I'm well,' she replied and a large pigeon landed with noisy scratches on the Velux.

'Urg!' Faye shrieked and she backed away from it to the far wall.

'It's only a pigeon,' said Nicholas, standing up. 'And it's outside.'

'I hate them,' she said quietly, her eyes staring at the bird and her hand by her throat.

'It's completely harmless. I'll get rid of it.'

'Don't open the window. It might come in.'

'What, for tea? Don't be—' he had been about to call her silly, but as he spoke he turned to her and saw from her cold, pinhole pupils that she really was frightened. 'You don't want me to get rid of it?' he asked her softly.

She stared at the bird. Nicholas crossed to underneath the window and rapped just by the pigeon's feet. The bird looked down at him with small, blank eyes and cocked its head. Nicholas knocked again, harder this time. Instead of flying off the bird shat on the glass and milky droplets ran down the pane. Then it flew off.

'It's gone,' Nicholas said and he turned to her.

'Yes,' she said and took a deep breath. She returned

cautiously to her easel. 'I really can't stand them. The truth of it is that they frighten me. But I tell myself that I dislike them.'

'They're just birds,' Nicholas replied, sitting down.

'But they're not, are they? Birds are just fine, but somehow pigeons don't look like birds. They're like some hideous kind of crossbreed – half bird, half grandma – with sagging knuckles and semi-blind eyes. Sometimes I think that they've probably got tiny little hands hidden under their wings.' Nicholas looked at Faye. She sensed his gaze and looked back. 'What?' she asked.

'You should listen to yourself,' Nicholas said with a smile.

'Why?'

'Well, someone should.'

'Thanks,' she laughed.

She was about to put paint to canvas, staring hard at the line of Nicholas's temple, when a muffled voice called out. It startled her, for no-one was supposed to be in, but she knew, straight away, who it was. 'Iffle?' it called, from somewhere below in the house.

Faye paused and looked at her canvas. She was determined to be a painter. She looked at Nicholas, who continued to stare at the wall, unmoved, deaf as a snake. 'Iff-le?' came the call again. She resented her peace being broken. She tutted and shook her head, but she didn't move. Her feet remained planted to the ground, her brush poised by the blank space. She could hear Nicholas's breathing and he could hear hers. Somewhere above them a magpie called for its partner. She brought her brush to the canvas, dark red marking the porous white and drew, with conviction, the line she could see.

Falling through the air came Alistair's voice again. 'Peachy!' it called out, plump and cheery. 'Peachy, Peachy

Peachy!' Nicholas wondered how Faye had come to be called such a thing. Then there was a woman's squeal, a golden squeal of anticipation and delight which shook the pretty house and its foundations. It rose up into the air like a battle cry, the squeal of a concealed animal, the agitated cry of a religious zealot.

Nicholas looked at Faye. He lowered his eyes. She was listening. There was laughter and more squealing and then a noise as if something had fallen – a dull thud which set a bowl by Nicholas's feet rocking slightly.

A silence fell and Nicholas felt embarrassment descend on him; he froze with uncertainty. His thoughts were interrupted by a groan, followed, like horses after a train, by muttering: words, distinct and meaningful, which had metamorphosed into a dull buzz by the time they reached the attic. More silence and then came muffled puffs and pants. The love-making was gruesomely uninhibited. The woman yodelled with pleasure and Alistair groaned like a bull siring young.

Faye opened the trapdoor and pushed down the ladder, making no effort to soften the noise it made. Nicholas stood up and watched her descend from the room. On his way past the easel he glanced back and took in the one red line on the canvas. He heard a call of 'hello?' and a scuffle. Then the only noise was his feet, as the soles of his shoes carefully tapped against the aluminium steps of the ladder.

There, on the landing, stood Alistair. Red and shiny like a picture-book butcher, his naked body hung over spindly legs. The tip of his penis, disappointed by the discovery of its forbidden joys, was just visible beneath a bower of stomach.

'Faye,' said Alistair and went briefly through to the darkened bedroom. He returned in a mauve dressing gown. Behind him Nicholas could vaguely see a woman lying on

197

her side in bed: Beatrice, dark hair splayed across the pillow beside her like a butterfly displayed in a case.

'Get out of my bed, Beatrice,' Faye said.

'Darling. It's not how it looks,' Alistair began.

'You bastard,' Faye breathed.

'You've every reason to be angry but please, let's sit down and talk about it,' he begged. Nicholas began to creep down the stairs to the front door – this was nothing to do with him, after all – but Faye asked him to wait. He stood there, staring at their authentic nineteenth-century yellow walls.

'Faye, darling,' Beatrice said and she pressed the bedcover to her front, sat up and swung her legs over the side of the bed, exposing, as she did, a large brown nipple on the end of an errant breast. 'Come and sit down here and I'll explain. It's all rather silly, really.'

Faye shook her head and looked down at the ground, seemingly confused by it all.

'Please,' Alistair said.

'I don't think an explanation is what I need,' she said quietly and she started down the stairs, Nicholas leading the way.

Faye walked straight out of the house and turned left at the gate, walking towards the local shops. Nicholas kept pace with her but said nothing. Words had deserted him.

'I don't know where to go,' she said finally, when they had reached the main road and were standing on a corner. She felt foolish in front of Nicholas. Half of her wanted him to go away – she felt ashamed and humiliated – and the other half wanted him to take her in his arms and tell her that everything would be all right. 'Did that all just happen?' she asked and she folded her arms and gazed off over his shoulder, seeming to disappear into a dream world.

Nicholas shook his head. 'Yes, I'm afraid so,' he said

slowly, but she didn't seem to be listening. Someone bumped into him in the street and cursed him for being in the way. He reached out and put his hand on her arm.

'Come on,' he said.

'Mrs Sten,' said Nicholas, 'I wonder if I might talk to you please' and he stood, poised in the kitchen doorway, head on one side.

'Oh Nicholas! You gave me a shock,' Mrs Sten replied, though she had heard him come in. She made a point of looking him up and down, and frowned a little.

'I took the day off work today,' he said. 'I had – well.' Nicholas had asked Faye to wait by the front door, in the dark hallway by the umbrella stand where she was currently listening, as though she hadn't overheard enough today already. She was astonished by the musty age of the house, the darkness of its hall and bumps and dips in its loose wooden floor. The mechanics of survival had kicked in: her adrenalin flowed, masking emotions.

'I need to ask you a favour, Mrs Sten,' Nicholas said in the kitchen, and he looked up at her as he said her name. 'I hope you don't mind that I ask,' and he put his hands behind his back.

'Yes, Nicholas,' said Mrs Sten, her mouth corners curling a little in delight at the way Nicholas spoke to her.

'I have a good friend who is, through distressing circumstances beyond her control, in desperate need of somewhere to live for a few days, just while she finds her feet.' Faye, out in the corridor, recoiled as she heard the word 'desperate'. She had decided, once she had left her large family and council house in Bradford, that she would never be desperate. Mrs Sten lost her charmed smile. She leant back against the sink and pondered on who this female friend of Nicholas's could be.

'I – she's a friend,' continued Nicholas, 'and she is in need of my help,' and he raised his eyebrows at her.

Mrs Sten felt a pulse of anger at this mystery woman, for whom Nicholas was willing to do so much. She supposed she was young and pretty and too foolish to see Nicholas's value. She pressed the palms of her hands together and then let one slide off the other.

'Nicholas,' she said, 'I'm sorry but I cannot break my house rules. I'm sure you understand why and I know that—'

'Please Mrs Sten' broke in Nicholas, 'I really wouldn't ask but she's—'

'I'm perfectly trustworthy,' said a new voice and Faye appeared in the doorway, looking well, Nicholas thought, given what she had just been through. She was fiddling with her hair with one hand, the other tucked away in the pouch of her smock.

'Oh!' said Mrs Sten, taking in the beautiful young blonde woman and feeling something rise inside her, like water in a blocked pipe. 'Well goodness. It isn't that I don't trust you my dear, but rather that—'

'I'm in trouble,' Faye said.

'What kind of trouble?' said Mrs Sten, relishing these few details of Nicholas's life and wondering, at the same time, whether the girl was pregnant and whether Nicholas was the father. The thought made her sick with envy. Faye came into the room and extended her hand to her.

'My name's Faye Peters, Mrs Sten,' she said coldly. 'I've just discovered that my fiancé is having an affair.'

Mrs Sten took her hand, and patted it. 'Well, at least it isn't with your best friend,' she said and Nicholas closed his eyes for a second. There was a silence, as neither of them contradicted the tight-lipped Mrs Sten, as precise and sure of herself as a cat on a fence pole.

'It's nice to meet you, Faye,' Mrs Sten said finally, refolding her arms and surveying Faye's painter's smock and expensive trousers beneath it. 'If you need to stay with Nicholas while you sort out your affairs that will be fine,' she made herself say, feeling a jealous ache rise inside her, 'but only for a few days.'

Mrs Sten had once been beautiful too. Her hair had shone like a deep brown nut oil and curled, affectionately, in semi-circles around the smooth and clear lines of her face. She had worked on the stage, delicately lip-glossed in Cuban heels and pleated skirts as she received news of her fiancé killed in the war, or mini-skirted and geometric as she dabbled in experimental theatre. Offstage she had smoked cigarettes in a mother-of-pearl holder and charmed the men in the cast, so much so that no after-work celebration was complete without the fun-loving Miss Alice Thorn, who would drink champagne from her shoe and offer her naked foot to the perplexed waiter to nibble. She used to laugh heartily, rouged lips wide apart, cigarette held elegantly at a distance, until she had regained her composure and, with a deep breath, could neatly take a drag.

Nicholas took his sheets off the bed and folded them into a pile which he placed on the floor by his wardrobe. He put clean sheets on for Faye and moved his pile of notebooks from the bedside table. Standing back from the bed he thought that it looked mean and saggy. For a moment he saw his whole room through Faye's eyes and recoiled at the sight. A cold shame prickled through him. She sat by the window, staring out into the leaves of the trees that grew in the garden below. Mr Samuels was out in his garden, singing at the top of his voice. Faye peered at him.

'The neighbour,' Nicholas explained. 'He grows a lot of

fruit. I'm going to help him pick it all in a couple of weeks, when the first raspberries are ready.' Faye did not turn to look at him. Nicholas flicked the radio on and tidied up a pile of his clothes.

'At least you hadn't married him,' Nicholas said finally, dropping a pillow onto the bed.

'If I *had* married him when he'd first asked me I would at least be entitled to part of the house,' she said.

Nicholas sat down in his chair and pressed his hands between his thighs. Faye sat on his bed, her feet on the floor, looking down at her knees. Nicholas was nervous; he had not imagined such unease between them. He could not help but think that her comment about entitlement to Alistair's house was an implicit criticism of his room and where he lived, though he told himself that this was surely not the case.

He began to talk, telling her about his job, about Sean, about teaching, his pupils, the pieces he thought the school orchestra could play for the Christmas concert. He told her about his audition for the orchestra, about how he hadn't heard anything yet but didn't really mind. 'I enjoy living here,' he told her. Faye didn't seem to be listening but he continued to talk, standing up and pacing by his window, looking down into the garden below. He hoped that she wouldn't notice the layer of dust on his window sill or the cracks and chips in the paintwork.

If Faye had been honest with herself she would have had to admit that she was horrified by Nicholas's room. Not because she did not know that people lived in such rundown houses or because she did not know that many people had only a few possessions. She was horrified because his room reminded her of her childhood and it astonished her that he had not tried to escape what both of them had known. As she sat down on his bed, the rough wool blanket prickling her through her thin trousers, she pretended not to notice the state of his room. She sat and tried to think about what had happened. Instead her mind focused on the green metal base of Nicholas's bedside lamp, covered in a layer of dust, marked with a few drops of white paint, patterned with fingerprints. The lamp made her feel as if she was living in a trailer park. She began to cry.

EIGHTEEN

The first friend Kozak made in London was a man called David, whom he met early one Saturday morning when they were both heading north to visit a junk market on the outskirts of the city. They boarded a bus at the same stop, had been waiting with others for over ten minutes when the number 316 finally rounded a corner and everyone came to life. Kozak was one of the last to get on the bus. He tripped on the top step and scattered the change he was holding all over the floor.

'Goodness, are you all right?' exclaimed David, who had climbed on after him. He offered him a hand which Kozak could have crushed with one of his own, had he had the inclination.

'Ugh,' Kozak said as he got up, for he had made himself trip rather more forcefully than he'd meant to, and he bent down to collect his coins from the grimy floor. David looked around him, found a two pence piece and he held it patiently while Kozak gathered the rest.

'Seventy pence please,' said Kozak and deposited 30p, in seven coins, on the driver's concave tray. 'I cannot find the rest,' and he shrugged and made a pretence of looking around him on the floor.

'You haven't got enough,' said the driver, vigorously shaking his head, his cold-sored mouth hanging open.

'I dropped it, I cannot find it,' Kozak replied. 'It is somewhere on your bus,' though he knew it wasn't. Usually drivers just shrugged and hit the ticket button. This one, this morning, was not a usual driver.

'Well I don't want it on my bus. I would hazard a guess that there's quite a lotta money on my bus. I wannit on my tray.'

'It is not my fault that I tripped,' Kozak pleaded. On the bus eyes, of which there were plenty, were raised.

'Look, are you gonna pay or are you not gonna pay because if you are not gonna pay then you need to get off this bus, regardless of the fact that it has some of your money on it somewhere supposedly.'

'It's here,' said a voice suddenly, a feeble sing-song voice behind Kozak. David held two twenty pence pieces between finger and thumb. Kozak, behind his sunglasses, turned to look at David nervously, and then let his head fall a little. He wondered what the man's game was.

'Ah! Thank you,' he said and David dropped the neat little coins into the rough palm of his hand.

'Now that is the right fare and so I can now give you a ticket,' the driver said, 'that's how things work in this country because we are civilized,' and he pressed his little red button with satisfaction. By the time David had flashed his travel card at the driver there were only two seats left on the single-decker and David chose the one next to Kozak, sitting down gingerly next to him with just a raise of the eyebrows and a pursing of the lips as recognition. The bus pulled out in front of a new Saab and there was an exchange of horns, both drivers happy to make some noise on a Saturday morning. Kozak began digging in his pockets, fidgeting and wriggling next to David who pretended not to notice and examined instead the curious plastic tartan of a large woman's shopping bag.

'Here,' said a low voice and an elegant, long-fingered hand was placed before him, weightless on its palm two twenty pence pieces. David frowned and turned to his neighbour. The sunglasses were looking right back at him;

the hand, in the air above his knee, steady as the bus rounded a corner.

'You found it then,' David said jovially, 'but there's no need. It doesn't matter.'

'No, you must take it. I had the money anyway,' and Kozak thrust his hand closer to David's chest.

'Oh,' said David. 'Well why did you –?'

Kozak pulled his head back on his neck and watched a young mother with two small children climb from the bus. 'Usually the drivers don't bother. It helps me save money,' he said in a lowered voice.

'Goodness,' replied David, 'that would never have occurred to me.'

'There are many things which do not occur to this land of capitalists,' Kozak mumbled. They rode in silence for a while as a child somewhere behind them told his father over and over again that he didn't want to go to his violin lesson. The bus driver drove punctiliously, stopping self-righteously for some pedestrians at a zebra crossing, pulling away from bus stops only when everyone on the bus was seated and waiting.

'Are you going to Bemley market?' Kozak said after a while.

'Yes, yes I am,' replied David, wondering whether he had done the right thing in telling the truth.

'I too. Come with me and I shall teach you about money,' he said and David, more out of fear than out of curiosity, agreed to accompany him. In the end he was glad that he did, not only because he learnt all sorts of tricks, but also because Kozak, as he found out, approached his vocation with a dark humour which seldom cracked his face into a smile but somehow made the rainy morning more pleasant.

'Look at me,' Kozak said to David, just as they were

about to enter the market through the school gates, and he took a couple of paces away from him. 'How do I look?'

David mentally reprimanded himself for becoming involved with this lunatic and with a brief shrug said, 'Very smart.'

'You lie,' replied Kozak. David would remember this moment more than any others on this particular day, because he felt nothing for this stranger who had accosted him, could have walked into the market without him and let him fall out of his life for ever. In that one moment, when dirty grey rain was beginning to fall, slanting from the checkerboard tweed of Kozak's right shoulder to the same cloth of his left knee, matting down the large man's excited hair, falling occasionally where he wouldn't feel it land – on his scar, the plastic of his sunglasses, the inquisitive bristles of his moustache, David was provoked into honesty: downright, straightforward, curmudgeonly, rude honesty.

'Well actually old chap, you look a bit of a state.'

Kozak frowned and moved closer to David.

'I look poor,' he said, struggling with the pronunciation of the word. 'Old clothes, old sunglasses, long hair,' and he shrugged, his immense shoulders rising into the air like a monster from the sea. 'And very important: *old shoes*. At these markets you should look poor. Always look poor,' he said and pulled David to one side. 'Now, money,' he continued, turning around briefly to sneeze loudly into the rain. 'Keep your money separate. Think of each coin like a magnet, all the same type so they push away from each other. Keep your money all over your body. Look,' he said and he took a battered five-pound note from his breast pocket, some coins from a jacket pocket, a ten-pound note from his trouser pocket and some more coins from the one on the other side.

'Well I say,' said David, 'you must be a pickpocket's

dream. You're a walking lucky dip. By the way, that suit is actually a rather fine suit, or rather once was. It would have been made in Dresden if it's the make I think it is.'

'So you see,' said Kozak sharply, 'money separate. It is good if you have to empty out one pocket to pay for something. It looks like you are spending your life savings.'

'By the way, where are you from?' David asked, agitated by the steady stream of people heading into the market, buying, if his imagination was to be believed, exquisite alpaca drapes and silk chenille curtains.

'The Ukraine,' replied Kozak sullenly.

'Oh my goodness,' said David. 'Happy Independence Day!' because he had read the paper that morning and was the type of man who learnt things from it. It was late August – the 24th to be precise – the day, back in 1991, that the Ukraine had declared itself independent.

David designed costumes for the theatre. He had thinning white hair and a weightless, spindly body which he saw as a burden rather than a blessing. He had been in the navy as a young man but had left after he had been asked to co-ordinate a burial at sea for an old captain. David had forgotten to weigh the coffin down and so when it was lowered into the water it just floated there, in front of the grieving widow and her two voluptuous daughters. In the end they had to usher the family off the ship and shoot at the coffin seven times, until the water around it seeped inside and carried it down to the sea bed. 'Look on the bright side,' David said to his superior, 'if he wasn't dead when they put him in his coffin he will be now,' but his superior was not impressed and David was dismissed.

Ever since his late teens he had experienced terrible bouts of depression which would arrive, one morning, like a giant bird sitting at the end of his bed, and depart just as suddenly, with a clapping of wings and one last screeching call. When the bird visited – when this gruesome creature cracked its beak wide open and forced David to stare into the blackness of its stomach – he could do nothing. He would lie in bed with his eyes closed, unable to open them and look about him, for everything he saw – the bed cover, the paint on the wall, the clock – would assault his senses and serve only to compound his melancholia.

He hated this bird, with its tarred feathers and bulging eyes: it had flown over his whole life, watching his progress, choosing the worst moments to come and sit on his shoulder and empty the milky lassitude of its crop into his ear. But the worst of it was this: David knew that the bird was right. When it visited it would whisper into his ear, *there's no point to this, no point to any of it, whether you live for twenty years or die tomorrow makes no difference to anything. Fry sausages for dinner or don't; stay in bed for three days or don't. None of it matters.* No doubt a different character would have fought with this bird and frightened it away with talk of sunshine and pine trees, but David's make-up was such that he could not argue back. He could never gather together counter-arguments to fling back at it, couldn't bring himself to contradict or impugn, couldn't retort or gainsay. So he would lie there and stare at the blackness of his eyelids, on which was written: *the bird is right*.

David had tried many medicines and cures to rid himself of his illness. He had tried all the NHS drugs, herbal remedies, Chinese antidotes, tables of lunar cycles and pagan calendars, a brass pendulum, a photograph of the sea and nothing else, into which he had been told, by a Native American, to stare for an hour every morning. None of these things worked, but he always had them to hand and respected their rituals, just in case.

He wasn't to know that his fascination with pills came

from the fact that his mother had given him opium as a baby, to pacify him on the nights when the world could do no right. He had, during the course of thirty years, invented his own methods too. One was cocoa. He would drink it bitter and strong every evening, a thick dark liquid which flowed from the pan like lava, and which brought life into his scared green eyes. Another was shoe-polishing. One day, at home one summer from university, he had been polishing a pair of his brother's shoes, laid neatly in the centre of the sports section of the *Daily Telegraph*, and the thought came into his head that if he did this every day for the rest of his life then he would be okay. He wasn't, but he still polished shoes – anyone's shoes – as often as he could.

The last of his self-devised treatments was perhaps the most superstitious. He felt, intuitively, that a way to keep the bird far from him was to let it know, on a regular basis, that he agreed with it, and did not need another of its visits in order to be persuaded of its sagacity. And so, 'there's no point, you know'; 'it's all meaningless'; 'we struggle in vain' came to pepper his speech. Even when he was alone he would make these announcements into the silence of a room, so that the bird would hear and rest assured that David, of all its disciples, was committed to the cause.

It was David's illness that caused the breakdown of his marriage and forced him to leave his wife. She had in those days such a beautiful face and fun-loving nature that he hated to spoil it with talk of a damp, black acedia. When she first experienced it, one spring morning a few months after they were married when he lay in bed unable to move, he told her that it was a particularly vigorous headache which would probably last for a few days. 'I get them sometimes,' he said, 'nothing to worry about.' She cooed over him and pulled the curtains, soundlessly bringing glasses of water and bits of food up to their room throughout the day.

It was a lie which David found difficult to withdraw and for the rest of their time together he went on having these strange bouts of headaches at the most inconvenient periods. She urged him to seek treatment and he did. She was not know that the bottles of pills with which he returned were not painkillers nor sleeping pills but anti-depressants.

It came, the bird, the day before he left the house for good. He awoke that morning and knew instantly, from the pain that consciousness brought him, that it was there, standing motionless by him. He shut his eyes and wanted to die.

'Oh David, not again. Not today. You can't today.' Today they had their first appointment with the adoption agency. They had tried for seven years to have children and failed. They didn't want to know why – they thought it unfair for either one of them to shoulder the responsibility for their failure – and so decided, calmly, democratically, that they would adopt.

'I'll be all right,' he said. He could barely bring himself to speak. What was the point? he thought.

'Can I bring you anything? Any of your pills?' she said, climbing from the bed and placing a hand on her smooth, unfruitful stomach. She had recently begun to learn lace-making and had finished, the week before, her first doily, which lay on her husband's bedside table.

'No,' replied David, 'I'll get up shortly.' Astonishingly he did manage to rouse himself, shower, put on a barely worn suit. The cloth felt strange on his skin, like raw meat hanging against his thighs and back, and he moved uneasily in it, feeling, somehow, that the bird would get him for having the audacity even to climb out of bed.

He came down to the kitchen and told his wife that he was going for a walk to try and clear his head. A greyness had descended over his face, as though he were on the other side of a grubby train window. He'd meet her there, he said. His wife, rereading the booklet on Appropriate Parenting at the kitchen table, an unopened yoghurt in front of her, nodded and told him not to be late.

She arrived ten minutes early and looked immaculate: she wore an aquamarine suit which had pockets in the shape of shells, a deep red blouse and high-heeled suede shoes of the same colour with elegant tassels on the toes. Her hair shone like brass and around her neck – she had toyed with the idea of wearing a crucifix, just in case they should decide that her career on the stage indicated a lack of moral fibre – lay a plain gold chain. Her anxiety about the meeting translated itself into an unconcerned aloofness and she sat in the waiting room arrogantly flicking through the pages of a women's magazine, marvelling at how ghastly the publication had become.

At five past eleven there was no sign of David, and the adoption counsellor – a portly woman with skin, hair and eyebrows all of the same colour – invited his wife into her office. David's wife handed the woman her dark grey appointment card, on which they had printed her name and the time of the meeting, information which his wife thought they probably needed more than she did, since she knew her name and was here on time.

'We can have a little chat while we wait for him to arrive,' the counsellor said and brought in a box of shortbread with two cups of tea. At twenty past eleven David still hadn't appeared. The counsellor ate a fourth shortbread finger, breaking off sections with her teeth as she absentmindedly listened to the noise of the office, and David's wife felt a burning sensation rise in her chest.

'Have you any idea where you husband might be?' enquired the counsellor, pursing her lips. She had been happily able to bring four boys into the world and she felt no pity for this infertile woman – for she assumed that it was the woman who had the problem – indeed she had already, several days ago when she was first required to look over the papers, put her infertility down to a sexually transmitted disease, syphilis probably, which she had contracted sleeping around. It serves her right, the counsellor had thought. David's wife shook her head delicately.

'He's normally extremely—'

'It will have to go on the records,' interrupted the counsellor with a certain satisfaction. She felt her stomach move and wished that she hadn't eaten all those biscuits.

'But really, he's very—'

'He can hardly be charged with the task of looking after the future of this country if he is unable to attend a meeting at the correct time.'

David's wife stood up and picked up her handbag. She looked the counsellor in the face but could not find the right words. Something about the difference between righteousness and being right flashed through her head, but she was no good at speeches. Songs were fine, but not speeches.

'Perhaps we'll forget about this incident,' the counsellor suggested. David's wife turned and saw that she had biscuit crumbs balanced delicately in her downy moustache.

'Oh, do you think we could?' she said. The counsellor looked up at her with large, unseeing eyes.

'Actually, no,' she replied and busied herself with her papers. David's wife left the office, pushing dramatically through laminated swing doors and climbing, furiously, down dusty, rubbish-strewn stairs until she was out in the street. A young man in a suit asked her if she was all right but she just nodded and carried on walking.

David didn't know what he had done. He had left the

house and turned away from town and towards a small stretch of park where he thought he might sit for a few minutes. He didn't get to the park, however, instead he forgot all about it and sat, like a toddler, in the middle of the pavement where he stared at the grey concrete beneath him. He had only a vague recollection of where he was, and an even vaguer realization that he was supposed to be some-where else. The colossal, limp-footed bird had well and truly arrived and a voice in David's head, innocent and singular, called out a tuneful 'why?' to every thought that passed through his head. A man in a Walkman and grey tracksuit squatted down by him and asked him whether he was all right.

'Something terrible's happened,' he said, for he knew that it had. The man asked him what, but David couldn't reply. He just wanted to shut his eyes and lie down and escape from the hellishness which he saw around him. The man – an American – got him to his feet and after many unanswered questions took him home, where David put his coat over his head and curled up into a ball at the bottom of the stairs.

After their first encounter the two men met every week at the market, where Kozak would negotiate deals for David's cloth and David, flushed with excitement over his wonder-ful acquisitions, would buy them both lunch afterwards at a small cafe by the bus stop. They were both dedicated market-goers and they met up through the autumn and winter, in rain and sleet and frost and then through the spring and summer. They came to know each other well.

The café where they ate lunch had round tables and pretty, pearly ashtrays made by a local potter, five of which Kozak had already managed to sell for the tidy sum of £150. There were now only two left in the cafe, the missing ashtrays having been replaced with cheap white plastic ones. Each week when the pair of them went into the small place a peculiar, almost Masonic dance would ensue, as Kozak insisted on sitting at a table with a pottery ashtray and David, unhappy with Kozak's stealing, exploitation and selfishness, tried his hardest to steer him to a table with a plastic one. Their excuses became repetitive and hackneyed:

'I prefer to sit by the window.'

'And I in the corner where it's dark.'

'This table is right in the middle of everything.'

'Which is precisely why we shouldn't sit there.'

One day David, determined that this week he would have his way, approached the cafe and saw their perfect table – towards the back, near the toilets, with a grotty scarred plastic ashtray in its centre.

'I would like to sit by the toilets,' David announced, rather too loudly, as they strode into the cafe. The man who usually served them – a round man with fat hips in a dirty white T-shirt – looked up from unloading the dishwasher and let out a laugh.

'I don't blame you mate, I'm the same,' he yelled across the room, clutching a clean mug to his chest. 'That way, when a bit of skirt walks past you know that she's just two doors and thirty-five seconds away from having her knickers round her ankles,' and he let out a loud laugh which reverberated off the specked glass of the windows and the disintegrating ceiling. David flushed first peach and then plum, and he retreated, defeated and with a polite smile at the large man, to Kozak at his table – a charming, pearly ashtray sitting proudly in the middle of it.

Kozak never sought to defend his actions. A bandit, he wandered along the edge of what was legal and what wasn't, and since he could, after all these years, buy and sell things freely, that was exactly what he did. Besides, David had, for the past eighteen months, been sleeping in a theatre, without the knowledge of the manager or indeed any of the staff, so he was not wholly outside reprehension.

Kozak's criminal background meant that he knew to buy low, sell high, to steal, swindle and cheat whenever possible. He lived in a bed and breakfast in Finchley, then moved to Hackney and then to Golders Green. He saw David every weekend and began to sell his wares at Portobello market, where he found he could charge almost double the amount he asked at car boot sales and no-one would bat an eyelid. He started to make a comfortable living and rented a room in Ladbroke Grove from a bookseller he had met. On his days off he would stroll down Portobello, along Notting Hill and into Hyde Park.

He liked wandering around the park and would spend many hours walking in circles, chewing the inside of his cheek and dodging rollerbladers. When the weather was fine he would spend whole days in the park, stopping off on the way to buy a roll and some fruit from the supermarket nearby before heading first of all for the sunken garden, which he liked to walk around and peer into from each side.

On these walks Kozak often thought of Bohdan. He could not bring him to mind without his stomach falling from him, but he could at least now think of him. He asked himself over and over again whether he had been a good father, whether anything he had done could have caused his son's illness. They had both eaten the mole Kozak had found a few days after the accident. It barely made two mouthfuls each but it was meat. And there then was the washing of the walls and the timber. Kozak and Bohdan had done neither, despite instructions from the clean-up men. Should Kozak have set a good example and followed the orders from the authorities?

Eventually, by the time he had strolled down to the Albert Memorial, he had had enough of these thoughts – beaten and paralysed by their implications – and he would think about something else: whether he should buy a donkey and rent it out for rides across the park, or when he might return to Oxford to pay a visit to the Twilling sisters.

One Saturday Kozak leant to one side and looked underneath the cafe table at David's feet, shod in slippery, pointed brogues which, in the half-light beneath the table, resembled dried, flattened fish staring up at him resentfully. It was mid-afternoon on a summer Saturday and Britain was trying its best to pretend that the sun was shining. David, happy and willing to participate in the pretence, was dressed in a cambric safari shirt, which fluttered around his thin frame like a dim recollection in the brain.

'What?' David said.

'What size are your feet?' Kozak asked and went on to explain that he needed a pair of wellington boots so that he could reach a flooded houseboat on the Thames which a friend had tipped him off about.

'I do have a rather nice pair of wellingtons, as it happens,' David announced, 'they're lined with waxed cotton at the top, a checked pattern I think. By Holland and Holland,' and he joined his forefinger and thumb together in the air. 'But they're at my wife's house.'

'Oh,' said Kozak and he nodded sagely, though he had no idea of the state of relations between David and his wife, of whom David seldom talked. Kozak imagined her as an overbearing woman, with flat, blank eyes and a penchant for all shades of pinks and purples.

'Come on,' said David, draining his cup delicately, 'let's go and get them.'

The sun still wasn't shining by the time the two of them stood on the doorstep of David's wife's house. London's air seemed to have come to a standstill, as though it had run out, all inhaled. The city was left suspended in a vacuum. Kozak eyed the house in front of him and decided that the woman couldn't be badly off, and for a brief moment the life she and David must once have had glimmered in his mind. David, standing before him, had descended into an unnatural calm which betrayed all too clearly the tension that now flickered between him and his wife.

'Oh, hello,' said a voice. Before them stood a small woman, more attractive than Kozak had imagined, though there was something about her – the tuck of the corner of her mouth or the neat, clustered rings on her fingers – which unnerved him. Her hair was neatly curled around her face and her clothes were, for Kozak anyway, a little too tidy.

'Hello,' said David, 'I came to collect my wellingtons.' He wondered what she had been doing when he rang the doorbell. He was actually glad to see her, though he would never have dared say as much.

'Wellingtons in July?' said the woman and she shook her head.

'Gardening,' David replied with a shrug, 'in the garden of Eden.'

'Hah!' exclaimed the woman.

'How are you?' David asked her. Kozak looked down at the tiled path beneath his feet and thought that perhaps he should not have come along. It had started to rain, and he watched as the black and white tiles on the path almost magically sprouted darker circles, like multiplying bacteria.

The woman glanced over her right shoulder, as though someone had appeared on the stairs beside her.

'It's my husband,' she said to the person they couldn't see

218

and a flush came to the knolls of her cheeks. 'Very well,' she said to David and her lips parted a little to reveal a glimpse of teeth. Lord, thought Kozak, and he felt an impulsive urge to see Beth and Vicky and Hester again. Oh, and to fight Hester. Kozak had still not got over being overpowered by a woman, and an English woman at that. England was supposed to breed roses, not gladiators. He put her defeat of him down to surprise – she had taken him unawares – but even now, six years later, he was still surprised.

'Well,' said David, 'you don't happen to know—'

'Beneath the stairs,' she replied.

'Ah, where the monster lives,' David said and he disappeared into the house for a moment, to emerge a few minutes later with one greenish welly in each hand, a sheepish grin on his face. Behind him the woman poked her head around the door and then shut it.

'Here you go, old boy,' David announced and passed the boots to his friend, who turned them upside down to examine, in turn, the sole of each.

'Your wife has a face like a cupboard full of brooms,' Kozak said once they were a few houses away. David paused and looked at him. Then he laughed so much that he had to stop at the end of the road to catch his breath.

NINETEEN

Nicholas did not wake up the next morning and wonder who the strange girl was in his bed. The first night Faye spent in his bed he lay awake with a buzzing in his limbs. He could barely breathe, let alone sleep. He wanted to creep the few feet to her bed and climb in beside her, so that he could kiss every inch of her skin. He wanted her to rise from the bed, take her T-shirt off and stand naked before him, so that he could look at her in all her splendour. He was stifled by desire and teased by possibility. Lying across the room by the wardrobe he stared at the ceiling and felt his penis come to life. He cursed in his head. He fidgeted and knew he would have to lie it out.

Faye too was awake, unnerved by the unfamiliar creaks of her bed and shell-shocked by the events of the day. She sat up in bed, staring at the murky stretch of wall opposite her, and didn't move all night. She slept eventually, sitting up, and dreamt that Nicholas kissed her for hours and hours, a soft, warm mouth pressed to hers.

In the morning Nicholas lay in bed and wondered whether he would ever get any sleep with this girl in his room or whether he fancied her just too much. He left the room to shower and when he got back, a towel round his middle, Faye was awake, staring from the window at a singing Mr Samuels in his garden. This morning he had chosen to sing 'I Got You Under My Skin'.

'He does it most mornings,' Nicholas told her. 'You'll get used to it,' he said, and then hoped that she wouldn't notice his assumption that she'd be staying for a while.

'He's got some voice,' Faye replied. She flicked her eyes over his chest. The sensations from her dream passed through the front of her head but they were gone before she had a chance to recognize them.

'How are you? Did you sleep?' Nicholas asked.

'Not really.'

'Neither did I,' Nicholas said with a grin. 'We should have done something together.'

'Like what?' Faye turned her head to him with a bemused expression.

Nicholas shrugged. 'I don't know. Played cards. I spy. Gone clubbing.'

'Oh,' Faye said and she let a half-smile cross her lips.

'Will you be okay today?' he asked. He picked up his folded shirt, trousers and tie. His pants and socks he hid at the bottom of the pile.

'I don't really know what to do,' she said softly, looking back at Mr Samuels, who was deadheading the geraniums that grew in terracotta pots around his patio.

'Don't do anything,' Nicholas replied. 'Go for a walk in the park. I'll be home around six.' Faye didn't respond. Nicholas looked at her face and thought about the years he hadn't known her. He had changed during that time. She must have too.

For the first few days Faye stayed in Nicholas's room, staring at the wall, trying to persuade herself that all that had happened was real. Nicholas would rise early and dress in the bathroom, returning to his room only to check his appearance in the large, gilt-framed mirror that hung above his rocking chair. Faye would smile at him from her bed as he straightened his tie and, lastly, pressed his cap onto his head.

Nicholas did his best to cheer her up. He told her of the

customers he observed at work: of the man who tied a plastic crate to each foot and glided around the supermarket at a height of eight foot two as elderly ladies cowered by the tills. He recounted the visits of the woman who told him once a week that she had a beehive in her head. And there was a young boy who liked to pretend that he worked there. Having bought an appropriate uniform at a catering outfitters off Regent Street, he turned up early on Thursday mornings and directed customers to the wrong sections of the shop.

'They're a right old bunch of nutters,' Nicholas told her. He watched Faye closely over those first days and would occasionally, unintentionally, copy one of her gestures – the way she held out her hands before her when she shrugged, or the way one corner of her mouth would tuck in neatly when she was teasing him. And he influenced her too. She saw how he approached his days in an easy, cheerful manner. She was startled by how happy he seemed to be.

Gareth took Nicholas to one side the following day by the freezer section, which contained, from north to south, peas, carrots, chips, ready meals, ice cream and cakes. Nicholas knew where everything was in the supermarket. He couldn't help it; somehow the arrangements and configurations of products sat in his brain like a curse. He wished he could remember intricate things instead – elements and their symbols, Shakespeare quotations or cello sonatas – but for some reason these just wouldn't stick. If asked about tinned asparagus or boudoir biscuits he would be able to give directions to whatever section of whatever row, regardless of the constant rearrangement of goods ordered by Gareth, who had been instructed, from way on high, to 'improve the plan of the store at least once a month in the interests of customers and so that store visitors will be exposed to as many of the advantages of the store as possible'. They might as well have instructed their store managers to apply absolutely no logic to the layout of their stores and wilfully disorientate regular customers as often as possible.

'I've been thinking about what Security System of Safety said about you and Sean being a deterrent. You see, the thing is, that if you're a deterrent, then it's inevitable that you'll never catch anyone taking goods because they won't do it while you're there. Do you see? That is the nature of a deterrent. I think we have to lure them out. I decided last night that we are going to pretend that we haven't got any security guards, that no-one's bothered about customers stealing a few products here and there. That way, they'll do it, and then we can pounce.'

'How do we do that?'

'Pounce?'

'Well, how would you like Sean and me to pretend that we're not here?'

'Ah, well,' Gareth said, and smoothly tilted his head sideways, 'Plain clothes. Behind the scenes. None of this striding around in uniforms. We'll never catch them that way. I want you to spend all day in your office, watching like hawks. As soon as you see anything, out here like cheetahs.'

'Right,' Nicholas said, 'but once we've done that once then won't everyone know that you do actually have security guards here?'

Gareth paused and eyed Nicholas. 'You're sharp, aren't you?' he said, shifting his weight. What he really wanted was a woollen uniform and a war to fight in. 'We'll do it outside!' he announced suddenly, a pale excitement passing across his crudely-made face. 'Let them leave with their stolen goods, and apprehend them outside the store! They'll think they've got away with it, and then suddenly bam! Safe Securities strikes.'

'Safe Security Systems,' Nicholas said. 'We have three esses, not two.'

'Yes yes,' Gareth replied.

'So what happened with that au pair?' Nicholas asked Sean, as they picked their way through the chaos of the fresh fruit and vegetables aisle on their way back to the office. Sean had finally arranged a date with the au pair who had come in weeks earlier and had taken her to dinner the previous evening.

'Oh, don't ask,' said Sean 'We had a great evening. Had two bottles of wine over dinner where I practised the old 'listening carefully' routine and concentrated on eye contact, we crept back to her place, past her employers' bedroom and then I looked at her collection of etchings in her room. I was right on the verge of it, about to dock, as it were, when I said "What's a nice place like this doing in a girl like you?" Before I had a chance to blink she was out of the bed and I was copulating with Egyptian cotton. Talk about coitus interruptus. This was just interruptus. Apparently she didn't think that what I'd said was very funny and had had her doubts anyway, so she put her kit back on there and then and kicked me out. I told her that she didn't have to think it was very funny in order to have sex with me but by then it was too late.' Sean sat down in his chair, put his feet on the desk and picked up a magazine.

'Perhaps it wasn't meant to be,' Nicholas said.

'It says here that you have to make sure your circle of friends knows the type of person you are looking for.' Sean had flicked to an article on how to meet the perfect partner. 'Circle of friends, hah. More like triangle of friends. I have two, and you're one of them, Nicholas, so please don't tell me you aren't. Otherwise I'll be left with a line.'

'Don't read that stuff,' Nicholas replied, 'it'll just make you depressed.'

'I'm depressed anyway and besides, it doesn't go into my particular problem.'

'Which is?'

Sean took a deep breath and turned to Nicholas, looking him full in the face. 'Whenever I meet a woman,' he said forcefully, 'I can't help but imagine her naked.'

'So?' said Nicholas, carefully unlacing his shoes and slipping his feet out.

'So? Have you any idea how distracting it is? I can't even buy a newspaper in my corner shop without becoming rooted to the spot because of the . . . the . . . vision in front of me. How could I ever chat anyone up? I look like a fool.' Sean snorted and rubbed at his right eye with the back of his hand. 'Do you know, all the male deathwatch beetle has to do to impress the female is bang its head against some wood. I'd be perfectly happy to bang my head against some wood until kingdom come if it meant I could meet a woman.'

'I imagine you would meet a woman if you did that. But you might have to call her doctor.'

'Well I'm going to take this magazine's advice. According to this I have to make sure that you know I'm on the look-out for a woman.'

'Oh, you are? Well, you should have said. There were four here asking for you half an hour ago,' Nicholas said with a nod of his head. He put his shoes back on and laced them one by one.

'How I'm supposed to find the woman of my dreams in this tin-pot, Podunk, trailer park of a supermarket, I don't know. I was thinking of taking a leaf out of your book and getting in touch with some old girlfriends in the pathetic hope that one of them might be as desperate as me. I called one last night but she couldn't remember who

I was. What women do you know? Can't I go out with one of them?'

'Well,' said Nicholas with a mock reluctance, 'there's Mrs Sten.'

'No,' said Sean, 'not her.'

'Faye?'

'Okay, who else?'

'Martine.'

'Martine,' Sean repeated. 'What kind of men does she like then?'

Nicholas lay back in his office chair and shrugged. 'I have no idea.'

'Oh well. If I can't entertain women themselves at least I can entertain the idea of women. I've got to have some pleasures,' Sean replied.

'Play something,' she said to him on the first evening when he got home from work. It was Friday night.

'Why?'

'I'd like to watch you play.'

'As long as you can't hear anything?' Nicholas asked. He pulled up the chair by the window and unpacked his cello. He warmed up a little, tuning the strings and loosening his fingers and elbow and then began an arrangement of a serenata by Albeniz. His expression became serious while he played: a tension came to his jaw and a ferocity to his eyes.

Faye listened to him and felt her throat close. He had become a good player and she was not surprised. He had always had a concentration which she envied. As a teenager she had wondered whether it was his background which in a strange sort of a way advantaged him: he had something to prove, people to find. One day, when he finally met his father and brother again, he would want to impress them.

'You play well,' she said to him once he had silently lifted his bow from the strings.

'Thank you.'

'How did you get so good?'

Nicholas laughed. 'Practice,' he said and he drummed his fingers once on the body of the instrument.

Nicholas and Faye had never made sweet music together. Faye had played the violin, but had never made sweet music in her whole life. At school Nicholas practised hard and played competently; Faye barely practised and played terribly. She was better at miming and at school orchestra sessions she watched the conductor (she could, since she didn't need to know what notes to play) and made sure her bow was going in the same direction as everyone else's. She looked like an adept and alert violin-player.

When they were fourteen they formed a string quartet: Faye and three boys. They should have formed a band, Nicholas knew, but no-one could play guitar or drums and singing was just too embarrassing to contemplate. To compensate for the tragedy of their ensemble they took to performing in leather jackets and scowls. Their audience – mainly the school and patient parents – fidgeted and mourned the evolutionary oversight which was the ear lid.

Faye, though she shouldn't have, played first violin in the quartet and was initially horrified to learn that she would actually have to play the notes on the page in front of her. A boy called Ranjeet played the second violin part, though he was a better violinist than Faye and he knew it. He had ink-coloured hair which grew like weeds from everywhere his body joined itself. He performed his supporting role as though it was the world premiere of a concerto written especially for him and in rehearsal Faye would often accidentally knock his music from its stand.

It was Ranjeet and Nicholas who held the quartet together and Nicholas often felt grateful to Ranjeet. The role of viola-player was taken, after much coercion on Faye's part, by a candid boy called Anthony Christmas. He had a thick Yorkshire accent and was always being asked to be in string quartets. He only joined theirs when Nicholas and Faye offered to buy him a pie once a week.

'A proper pie though,' he'd said, 'none of this leek and potato rubbish. A proper pie from the butcher's with meat in it.'

'That's fine,' they said, and hoped that his desire for pies would wane once he had discovered the enjoyment of playing with them. It didn't. For the two and a half years that they played together, every Monday lunchtime rehearsal would begin with the loud, indignant voice of Anthony Christmas asking, 'Where's my pie?'

'You'll get fat eating all that stuff,' Ranjeet told him.

'I won't get fat, I'll get big and big is good,' Anthony replied. 'Which of the dinosaurs killed all the others? Tyrannosaurus Rex. Why? Because he was the biggest. Bigness means you can do what you like.'

'I don't think Tyrannosaurus Rex ate pies,' Ranjeet argued.

'Only cos they dint have pie machines,' Anthony replied. 'I'm sure he'd have loved a good pie.'

Anthony didn't just tell the quartet about pies. He rarely held back a view on anything, and soon they all knew what Anthony thought. Worst of all, he could not stop himself commenting on their individual and combined sound.

'That was shite,' he'd announce after he'd rested his voila on his knee. 'I could have farted it better.' And he'd take a bite of his pie, picking up his bow again with greasy pastry flakes sticking to his fingertips. Anthony Christmas was so frank that he could not even stop himself from commenting on their performance when they had an audience present. Often, as soon as he'd rested his viola gently on his left thigh, he would sneer and shake his head. 'Monkeys could have played that better,' he'd say, and Nicholas would cough loudly to try to mask his words.

In their last year of playing together the quartet actually received money for performing. At one do, with the Lord Mayor of Bradford in attendance and after they had scraped their way through their entire classical repertoire, a lady in a long black dress and a flower in her hair approached them. Each regarded her with sore fingers and a sinking heart. By the look of her she was going to ask them if they could play Ravel's string quartet in F major. Only if you can dance *en pointe* to it, Nicholas was ready to reply.

'Excyooose me,' she said, addressing Faye. 'Do you know "The Bear Necessities"?'

Faye was chewing the piece of gum which she stored between her teeth and her cheek when she was playing. She regarded the woman, her jaw working away, and nodded slowly. And so that was what they played. Followed by 'My Favourite Things', 'Chitty Chitty Bang Bang' and a couple of songs from 'The Wizard of Oz'. It was, in the end, these songs which went down best with everyone. As the Lord Mayor said in his broad Yorkshire accent when he thanked them for their efforts at the end of the evening, 'I like a good tune.'

As darkness fell that night Nicholas and Faye laughed about their string quartet and the damage they did to the old classical favourites.

Eventually Nicholas went off to make dinner and Faye was left again with the empty unfamiliarity of the room. He cooked farfalle and spinach and ricotta, the only meal he could cook without a book. Faye had brought nothing much with her – only herself, the clothes she was wearing, her wallet and house keys, which she had piled neatly on top of his chest of drawers. She felt like a nun, living austerely, having vowed to spend her life alone. In the morning she would go and look for a job, she decided, but the thought of leaving the house made her shudder. I can't do it, she thought. Nicholas burst in carrying a plate in each hand and bottle of water under his arm. He hoped that Faye would like the food.

'Mum, Mum, am I a werewolf?' he said.

'What?' Faye asked.

'Ssh now dear while I comb your face.'

Faye looked at him for a moment and then laughed.

'Did you find that on the back of a cereal packet downstairs?'

'No, it just came to me,' he replied and set the plates on the chest of drawers, pressing the cutlery down on the surface after them. 'All that reminiscing is going to bring back a whole load of terrible jokes.' As they started to eat they discussed their plans for the next few days and Faye told Nicholas that she would go and see some old friends in the hope of getting some work. When she told him about it the prospect didn't seem that bad. She would spend the weekend planning the week ahead.

The plates lay on the floor between them as they chatted. To Nicholas's relief, Faye had eaten all her food. Nicholas's grey-soled feet fidgeted and twitched. He knew it and she knew it and their eyes flickered together, eager to catch a glimpse of something – anything – which would confirm what the other felt.

TWENTY

'Goodness Nicholas, you scared me!' It was Mrs Sten, standing in a summer dressing gown with her hands pressed to her chest. Her appearance startled Nicholas too and his heart skipped a beat as he put down his disintegrating copy of *The Heart is a Lonely Hunter.*

'I'm sorry Mrs Sten – I was just – er – reading.' In the darkness Nicholas was sitting beside the open fridge in the kitchen, leaning against the cupboard under the sink. He was clothed in a T-shirt and trousers but there were signs that he had been to bed once already and failed to sleep: his long feet were bare and his hair stood up on his head like a tidal wave frozen in motion.

'By the light of the fridge?' she said, letting her hands fall to her sides and her dressing gown flutter open to reveal a fine lace nightgown hanging somewhat exhausted over a flat chest.

'Faye is asleep upstairs,' Nicholas whispered. 'I thought if I put the room light on down here I might wake you. But it seems that I woke you anyway. I do apologize.' It was Faye's second night in the house and since she had barely slept through her first Nicholas had left the room as soon as she had fallen asleep, pulling the door to behind him with the stealth of a burglar.

'No matter,' said Mrs Sten. 'I hadn't got off to sleep yet anyway. I heard a noise and thought I should just check. One can never be too careful with a London property. I once had a bedsit on the ground floor and woke up from a nap in the middle of the afternoon to find someone climbing out of the window with my television. Mind you, then as now there was nothing very good on television so it was barely worth having.'

'Mm.' Nicholas nodded up at her, feeling the cupboard hard against his back and the first tingle of pins and needles in his foot.

'It's amazing, isn't it, at night? It's so very different. Like another planet. I love the sunset and the sunrise, but I sometimes wish that it wasn't so dark in between.'

Nicholas cleared his throat softly.

'Oh, Nicholas,' Mrs Sten sighed with a smile. She leant back against the cupboards and let herself slide to the floor until she was sitting beside him, a rummaged-through pile of lace and satin and marabou-trimmed slippers. 'Nicholas, Nicholas, Nicholas, what are we going to do with you?' she whispered into the dark kitchen. Beside them the fridge made a couple of banging noises and then revved up to a breezy hum, as though waiting for a passenger to jump in.

'What do you mean, Mrs Sten?' asked Nicholas tentatively.

'You can call me Alice, Nicholas,' she said and her voice seemed right beside his ear.

Nicholas sat up against the cupboards, picked up his book and moved his bookmark to the page where he'd stopped reading. Then he shuffled round slightly and sat cross-legged, his back to the fridge so that the yellow light glowed around the edges of his hair and along the sloping horizon of his shoulders, like a miniature florescent sunset.

'Alice,' said Nicholas, as though talking to a toddler.

'You know, I used to be in the the-a-tre,' she said, giving the word three separate syllables as it came, delicately, from her throat. She crossed one feathered foot over the other.

'Yes, I know,' replied Nicholas, for she had told him many of her stage tales over their early evening teas.

'I was an attractive woman, then, Nicholas.'

'I don't doubt that, Mrs Sten.'

'I could have had anyone I wanted. Anyone. All the best actors wanted me to play their leading ladies,' she said, without arrogance or pride, but matter-of-factly, as though explaining to him how to preheat the oven or defrost the fridge.

'I wish I could have seen you act,' said Nicholas. 'It must have been quite something.'

'I used to rouge my cheeks, curl my hair and carry my trademark cigarette holder. I was Alice Thorn, The Girl with Rose-Petal Lips. I used to get stockings and flowers and chocolates from men I'd never met, not to mention photographs and love letters and perfume. I slept with one hundred and seventy-three men, during that time. Have I shocked you, Nicholas?'

Nicholas shook his head.

'There's no need to lie,' she said. 'I wasn't ashamed of it then and I'm not ashamed of it now. I had a great time. There were all sorts. Lots of actors, of course. They were the funny ones. They always wanted loving, and to be loved. I used to kick them out the very next morning, thank you very much, you can be on your way now. "I have no capacity for love," that's what I used to tell them. I think they thought I was possessed,' and she laughed, a brief note issuing from her throat.

'I used to get all sorts of notes and letters from them afterwards. One sent me a hamper of jellied eels and rollmops from Fortnums with a card that said "You have the limbs of Venus and the heart of Fish." I took the hamper into the theatre and one of my girlfriends went on stage with a pair of rollmops in her brassiere. You should have seen the leading man's face during the love scene. One man, a soldier I think he was, left me his shoes. "The pain of not wearing shoes will be nothing compared with the pain of not having you, regardless of where I go on earth," he said when he telephoned the next day. I still have them. They might fit you,' she said.

Nicholas nodded and thought of Faye asleep in his bed upstairs.

'Have you any idea how boring being beautiful becomes?' Mrs Sten said suddenly, pulling her dressing gown around her and releasing a sweet scent of talcum powder and old roses. 'There was one man, though. You know, Nicholas, it's very important to be able to recognize moments. There are times when you must take action – tiny, fragments of time which cry out for something to happen – and if you aren't able to recognize them and do something then you're lost, you really are.' Nicholas blinked at her.

'His name was Frank and I waited a whole year for him to ask me. He did the lights in the theatre and we used to drink together after the shows. I could see in his eyes that he wanted me and I wanted him too, but he never *did* anything.'

Apart from Frank, Mrs Sten had spent a youth becoming bored with proclamations of love and had, in the end, married not in the interests of love but in the interests of harmony: David seemed a decent enough fellow and was evidently unmoved by her grace or beauty, which she liked. Pledges of eternal love were not for him, her beauty would not drive him to song, but he would look at her with glinting green eyes and laugh occasionally when she said something peculiar. Moreover she found it almost impossible to fight with him, perhaps because neither of them cared that much, which for her was just perfect.

Mr Sten had been a costume designer who pinned Mrs Sten's dresses and selected her shoes. Once they decided to marry he made her wedding dress for her, a cheongsam of heavy ivory silk with an embroidered rose which climbed from the top of one of the side splits to her shoulder and bloomed there, subtly catching the colour in her cheek. When Wednesday September 1st 1963 dawned and the photographers from the newspapers gathered by the small Anglo-Saxon church in Oxfordshire, Mrs Sten looked so magnificent that Eve, had she seen her, would have at least felt some respite from her guilt.

'Frank's behaviour must have been frustrating,' said Nicholas with a brief shrug.

'I could put on my lipstick and have whomever I wanted in bed within an hour. I would tell them how attractive they were, how wonderful, how funny . . . For some reason it didn't work with Frank. After I'd been on stage for three years I took all the cosmetics out of my make-up bag and replaced them with a game of travel solitaire which it took me sixteen months to crack. Oh, Nicholas,' she said again, 'where did you learn such beautiful manners? You remind me of the men I knew when I was sixteen. Such propriety,' and she turned her face towards him, pressing her cheek against the cold plastic of the cupboard behind her and smoothed the satin of her gown down over her legs with the palms of her hands. Her feet, in their decorative slippers, stretched.

Mrs Sten's thin neat fingers were constantly in search of nice-feeling things. She loved to dip her whole body into steaming, fragrant water and then to drape herself with silks and satins. She liked to reach out and explore textures: the brittle lino on the floor beneath her, the disintegrating strip of rubber on the fridge door, a lock of hair sitting on her shoulder. Often, if she could, she would lift these things to her nose, completely unaware that she was doing it, and inhale their scent through her finely powdered nostrils.

She resisted the temptation, great as it was, to stretch out to feel the weave of Nicholas's T-shirt or the thatch of his hair. There was a silence and the two of them listened to the night noises about them: somewhere a clock ticked, the fridge rumbled, a car passed.

'You do need to do something for yourself though, Nicholas. You spend all your time looking after others. Look at you now, sitting talking with a lonely old woman in the middle of the night,' and Mrs Sten forced a laugh out of her tired and slightly sore throat.

'Don't be silly, Mrs Sten. I enjoy talking with you,' said Nicholas. He picked up his paperback in both hands and let it fall, spine first and with a clunk, onto the lino.

'Sometimes, when I come in here at night by myself, I press my face up against the keyhole of that door, to see what's on the other side,' and she indicated, with a lift of her chin, the door opposite them which led into the garden. 'I used to do the same with my bedroom door when I was a child, terrified that one day when I bent down another eye would be on the other side, staring at me.' She laughed a little and turned to him. 'Now if I saw an eye I'd probably open the door and invite them in for a cup of cocoa and cheese on toast.'

Nicholas felt a slowness fill him and stifled a yawn. 'I'm awfully sorry, Mrs Sten, but I think that I –'

'You're quite right,' she replied, 'we should turn in,' and she got up, brushing her front and back with chilled hands. Nicholas closed the fridge door and turned to her. He offered her his arm and she took it. Together they walked along the hallway until they reached her bedroom, where Nicholas bade her goodnight and she slipped through her door. Upstairs in his room, Nicholas silently took off his trousers and crawled into the pile of blankets on the floor.

It was late on a Saturday afternoon. Nicholas was carrying his laundry upstairs when the doorbell went. He turned about on the spot on the stairs, about to drop his pants and socks on the floor when Mrs Sten came dashing from the kitchen. He stood and waited to see who it was. He couldn't see the doorway itself, but could glimpse a strip of the visitor through the crack of the door and was left with a sliver of person: a stationary zoetrope. It was a man and Mrs Sten was put out, that much he could tell.

He leant over the banister to get a better look. The man had short white hair and pale green eyes and a lightness of carriage which reminded Nicholas of the men in black and white musicals. They exchanged a few words, but Nicholas could not really follow what was being said. He saw a flicker of something in the background, and a large man came into view, wearing sunglasses and dressed in a tweed suit. He looked like trouble.

Martine appeared from the room opposite Nicholas's. She came neatly down the stairs and leant over the banister to see who was at the door.

'It's Mr Sten,' she said in a hushed voice when she reached Nicholas, enunciating carefully. Nicholas had never met Mr Sten. He had never even heard mention of the man. Mrs Sten had heard them.

'It is my husband,' she said, turning to them. Her face was flushed. Nicholas and Martine were both cowed by the piqued tone to her words. They retreated guiltily upstairs, where they stood together on the landing. Downstairs they heard their landlady telling her husband they were in the cupboard beneath the stairs. They heard him come in and root around.

'He's looking for wellingtons,' Martine whispered to Nicholas and then she raised her hands to her shoulders and shrugged. A few minutes later the door shut and Mrs Sten returned to the kitchen.

★

Faye had met up with an old friend for lunch on Saturday to see if he could get her any work. The friend, at least that was what Faye had thought he was, found that her desperate circumstances gave him indigestion and noticed that she wasn't looking as good as he'd remembered her. He knew, as he talked with her, that he had no intention of trying to get her work. Instead he gave her a couple of tickets to a charity dinner which his company had organized. He would not attend himself since he had to be in LA.

When it was time to leave he kissed her on the cheek with his fat lips and promised her, with a laugh, that he'd be in touch, which he had no intention of being. Faye, disenchanted and hurt, wandered around the city for the afternoon, peering into office windows and boring herself in shops until finally, when her feet hurt and she no longer felt sorry for herself, she returned home.

As she approached De Vere Gardens she saw Nicholas on a stepladder in front of the house, arms stretched around a prolific climbing rose above the front door. Faye stopped on the pavement and looked up with a smile on her face. It seemed funny, there was no other word for it, that Nicholas – the Nicholas she thought of as fourteen – was up there doing something as domesticated and considerate as tying up a rose. She could see only his teenage self, leather bomber jacket and dark scowl.

'Hanging around on your own doorstep like a vulgar Continental?' she said and leant against the gatepost. Without moving his arms Nicholas looked over his shoulder. He held a reel of twine between his teeth.

'Eo.' Faye just laughed at him.

'Do you need a hand?' she asked, but he shook his head and brought his arms together, pulling the rose into a trunk and tying the fraying string together in a few knots. Faye, gazing up at his profile, the back of his head and bent neck, was suddenly struck by how handsome he looked as his fingers weaved around each other and he frowned with concentration. He finished his job and took the twine from his mouth.

'How was lunch?' he asked, leaning back on the step-ladder and surveying the rose. The tops of a few branches were falling over the front door, bobbing their weighty heads against the shiny red paint.

'Pah,' Faye said, 'not very good.' She was determined not to become depressed. She wanted to follow Nicholas's example, to learn from his cheer. She reached for the secateurs beside her on the wall, and handed them up to him.

'How did you know I wanted those?' he asked with a grin.

'I control your mind,' she replied.

'I'm glad someone does,' said Nicholas. He took them from her and then paused. 'Cutting off those bits isn't going to do any good though, is it?' he said, indicating the swoop of rose in front of him, like the handle of an umbrella. 'They'll just grow again.'

'Can't you get them to go up the house?' Faye asked, peering up at the yellowish brick stretching into the sky.

'Easier said than done. I can't quite reach,' Nicholas replied and they began to ponder how to train the rose upwards, Nicholas sitting on the platform of the stepladder and Faye with her foot resting on the bottom rung. Nicholas saw now that what he felt for Faye today, eighteen years after he'd first met her, was a kind of distillation of his adolescent feelings. Faye, laughing at something he'd said, felt, for the first time in her life, at home in this city. As they discussed their plans for the rose with an inexplicable levity, anyone passing by could have been forgiven for thinking they were newly-weds, setting their house in order.

TWENTY-ONE

The next day, Sunday, was a bad day for Kozak. It was the last Sunday in July; thin cloud spread across the sky and the sun glowed like a bulb behind tracing paper. He woke early, sweating on his narrow foam mattress and knew instantly that something was wrong. Around him, Golders Green was resisting life; traffic came and went in sporadic bursts outside his window and the grocers beneath his room had not yet opened its doors. The door to his room was slightly ajar. Kozak rubbed his hand along his leg and deep down into his sock. His money was gone. He removed both shoes and socks, just in case he'd put it in the wrong one. There was nothing there. He examined the door, looked for signs and clues, astonished that someone could take something from his sock while he slept. I sleep too deeply, he thought. Only dog-owners should sleep that deeply.

Four hundred and twenty-four pounds. A hundred of it from the furniture he'd found on the boat last week. He had planned to pass some of it on to David, as repayment for the loan of the wellingtons. Kozak sat on the edge of his bed and stared at the wall. Then he stood, wounds licked, and went off to the market.

David too looked gloomy when they met for lunch that afternoon.

'The theatre shut yesterday. It's been sold to a Japanese bank for office space. The architects arrived this morning and asked me to move on.'

'Ah,' Kozak said and he took a bite of his sandwich. 'I was robbed last night,' he said with his mouth full.

'It's dark in heaven and it's cold in hell,' David replied. 'How much?'

Kozak told him about the burglary. At the next table a new wife explained to her mother-in-law why it was that she objected to airing cupboards. Kozak had sold a few bits and pieces at the market that morning and had sixty pounds and a few pence to his name. He paid for lunch and the pair of them wandered the streets of Stoke Newington, past an old barber's shop and a bookmakers, two men in their fifties with no homes to go to.

David carried his boots in a see-through carrier bag. A redness filled the sky which turned, drop by drop, to an inky blue. The streets began to fill with people. Kozak and David found themselves in Islington. At least it was mild, Kozak thought, as he prepared himself for a night out in the open. When they passed the tube station David headed in.

'Where are you going?' Kozak asked, holding out his hand.

'You and I are going to get ourselves a bed,' David said.

It was late that evening when the doorbell rang, and Mrs Sten, in a long purple dress with a sash tied at the back, hesitated before setting off to answer it. Nicholas is upstairs, she thought to herself, as she slipped the chain on with veined hands, a shade lighter than her frock. She opened the door and peered out.

'Hello again,' said the man standing there. He wore a long grey coat, expensive-looking and neat, and as she regarded him he opened the front of it and slipped his hands into his trouser pockets, revealing a soft mustard jumper on top of a checked shirt. He wore no tie. He never had.

'I brought my wellingtons back,' said the man, with a pleading smile. 'Thought their presence might restore order in the house.'

Mrs Sten felt a sinking inside, a flash of anger, her throat swelling. She shut the door, thinking perhaps that she should just go to her room and hide. Then she took the chain off and opened the door again.

'Come in,' she said, in her theatre voice, ignoring his joviality. She hoped that she looked good, thought that she must look good. Better than him, surely. He stepped towards her, thinking that it would be the decent thing to plant a kiss on her powdered cheek, but she took a simultaneous step backwards and he walked on through, as though a hasty and direct approach to the kitchen was what he'd had in mind all along.

The house, he knew, would not have changed. The same old problems plus some new ones. 'You're going to die one day,' she used to say to him, 'repainting the front room doesn't mean you've changed the world or been in any way significant. Don't use it as an excuse for real contribution to the world.' That was her outlook on home improvements. In the kitchen, he removed his coat and put the kettle on to boil.

You can't just do this, she thought. You can't just walk back in one day.

'Who've you got here at the moment, then?' he said as he flicked through the cupboards looking for tea.

'Top left,' she said, 'on the bottom shelf. There's Martine.'

'I'm surprised she's not off running a spot com company or something. She's very together, isn't she? Tea *bags*?' He turned to her with a surprised expression. In his hand he held an economy box of tea bags. She felt embarrassed and annoyed. 'You *have* let yourself go,' he said with a cheeky smile. He hoped that a bit of teasing might defrost her. He had buoyed his spirits before arriving. David knew how best to handle his wife.

'There's loose tea behind them,' she said, 'in a tin somewhere.'

'Ah,' he said softly. She noticed that he stooped a little, as though now, at the start of his old age, he was turning in on himself.

'And then there's her son, Harvey,' she continued. She wanted to tell him how much had changed since he'd last gone. How much had happened in her life of which he was no longer a part. 'He's eight.'

'You'll have Orphan Annie here tomorrow. Tomorrow,' he sang lightly, 'tomorrow, she'll be here, tomorrow,' and he executed a neat turn on the lino, which was the same as when he left. His trousers seemed to dent and crumple around his legs and she thought he looked thinner than before. Perhaps he hadn't been eating.

'And then there's—' she had been about to tell him of Nicholas, but something stopped her. She would keep the story of Nicholas to herself. Nicholas was her saviour. She smiled to herself.

He shook out some tea leaves into a strainer and dropped it into a shiny brown teapot.

'Who?' he asked. Mrs Sten didn't reply.

'I suppose I should make your bed up then,' she said, quickly, to get the question of where and with whom he would be sleeping out of the way. Outside in the street Kozak paced up and down, wondering how negotiations were going inside.

'Hum. I suppose. You haven't anything to eat, have you?' David asked.

'There's some corn on the cob, I think. In the fridge.'

'Actually I feel like cake. Tea and cake. Have you any cake?'

'No,' she said, feeling irritated by his whims. He started

243

opening the cupboards once again, taking out flour and sugar and an out-of-date bag of almonds.

'You know, Alice, there's no point to all this.' He turned to her and looked right through her, as though he could see miles away to the end of land and the sea beyond. Pale green eyes seeking out the water from which they had once crept.

'Well, why did you come back then? I didn't ask you to. You know how it is, every time—'

'Oh, no, not that. That's just how it always is. I mean *everything*. There's no point to any of it.' And for the second time that evening Mrs Sten thought how old he'd become.

'Oh don't talk nonsense. You'll be in a home before you know it at this rate,' she said sharply and promptly regretted it.

He raised his eyebrows and pursed his lips. Turning, he made the tea: unplugging the kettle, pouring carefully and slowly to wet all the tea leaves, placing it back on its dark green tile. He moved with a neatness that reminded her of Nicholas – and that it should be that way round, that her nomad, useless husband should remind her of a lodger of eighteen months, piqued her.

He took the corn out of the fridge and settled himself at the kitchen table with his pot of tea. The bags of cake ingredients stood on the counter. Sometimes he wished that he would be welcomed home with a feast: cocoa and pancakes perhaps, or steak and kidney pie and cider. He bit into the cold corn.

'Alice,' he said, using a finger to wipe a corner of his mouth, 'I was wondering whether I might invite a friend to stay.' It didn't really sound like a question at all, more like the statement of a decision he had already made. 'Are there any rooms free?'

Mrs Sten paused. There were rooms free, he knew that.

244

She always kept rooms free, just in case one day she would wake up and discover, joyously, that she had actually had children after all, and here they were, wanting somewhere to stay. She tried to tell herself that not having had children was probably a good thing – she would have worshipped a son and become jealous of a daughter – but she remained unconvinced.

She wondered what kind of friend David would want to bring? A man would be fine, but a mistress, certainly not. Mrs Sten had many weaknesses, the confusion of affection and sex being just one of them, but she would not (at least this was what she told herself) have David's mistress under her roof.

'It's a chap,' said Mr Sten. 'A friend, that's all. Needs a place to stay.'

'Oh,' said Mrs Sten, who in her head had seen a woman younger than herself, with large grey eyes and a soft, supple body which uncannily resembled Faye's. Who could it be? she thought. Perhaps it was the mistress's husband, whom David wanted to house here to be out of the way?

'Well,' said Mrs Sten, 'you can change his sheets and clean his room. But otherwise . . . What's one more?' She didn't go as far as to enquire whether he would be paying rent or not.

'Good,' said Mr Sten and he got up and went to let Kozak in.

'Come and meet Alice,' David said and he showed Kozak into the kitchen, where Mrs Sten was about to wipe her hands on a dishcloth which, she noticed with some puzzlement, had shoe polish on it. David had taken the liberty of giving his shoes a wipe over when he'd arrived. She put it down and hoped her hands would dry.

'Hello,' Kozak said to Mrs Sten and reached out to shake her hand. He kissed her three times on her cheeks and then said, 'You are a kind woman,' and he wondered whether she had very sweaty hands.

'This is Kozak. Kozak, this is Alice,' said Mr Sten as he shepherded Kozak towards a chair and poured him a cup of tea.

'It's lovely to meet you,' said Mrs Sten graciously. 'Where are you from?' She wasn't sure she liked the look of this man. He was solemn-faced and large with a jagged scar down the side of his cheek which demanded a narrative. A long moustache and dark sunglasses dominated his face, and his mouth, tucked beneath the hair like an animal burrow beneath grass, barely seemed to move when he spoke.

He nodded his head at her as she looked at him, so that the inverted V of his moustache bobbed up and down once. He wore an old tweed suit, green-grey with pale blue stripes. In the kitchen his hands grasped his teacup with a compelling certainty of purpose. His hair, she noticed, curled around his ears and the back of his neck like the hedge in Sleeping Beauty, large zealous curls brushing the back of his collar. Why, she wondered, had he hung a pair of child's shoes around his neck?

'The Ukraine.'

'Goodness,' replied Mrs Sten, surprised. She took a seat at the table with them, thinking, as she did so, that she must replace the pale linen tablecloth. Mr Sten winked at her, with a twist of his head. She turned to Kozak.

'Yes,' said Kozak with a nod, assuming that she must know the history of his country. He took a gulp of the hot tea and then added four spoonfuls of sugar. It felt good to be in a family house and he thought of Hester, Vicky and Beth.

'Nicholas is from the Ukraine as well. Originally,' she said to him.

'Who's Nicholas?' said Mr Sten. Mrs Sten continued to

look at Kozak. He had a patch of broken veins on one cheek which showed the redness of his blood just beneath his skin and his hair was a dark brown. The colours reminded her of chocolate and cherries.

'Well,' she said, sensing anticipation from Mr Sten at the other end of the table. 'Nicholas is Nicholas,' she said with a serene smile. She wanted to deceive him. It was about time, she thought. 'He lives here too. I shall introduce the two of you. You can talk about your . . . homeland,' she said slowly, wondering whether she had chosen the right word to describe their country.

'Perhaps,' said Kozak, who rarely talked about where he had come from and why, or rather how. He had told Beth, one Wednesday morning as they walked into town together, but no-one else. The story brought with it a different Kozak. He was no longer that man. Besides, he barely thought of it as a story. It was what happened to me, he thought. It's not a story to entertain England.

He looked around the kitchen, wondering what here he could sell and for how much. 'But first of all will you tell me about you?' he asked and Mr Sten met his eyes across the table and nodded, almost imperceptibly. Kozak had been told that Mrs Sten liked to talk about herself.

It wasn't until lunchtime the next day that the two men brought their belongings into the house. No announcements were made, no permission sought, but just as Mrs Sten had put a pan of baked beans on the stove, the front door swung open and Mr Sten and Kozak began piling boxes in the hall. Mrs Sten stood in the kitchen doorway in a pink twill skirt and cream blouse and watched Kozak carry two boxes for every one of Mr Sten's. In amongst the columns of boxes were some familiar items: Mr Sten's accordion in its tattered black box, a painting of four ducks which he took everywhere he lived, a large yucca which had once stood in the front room. Kozak appeared in the doorway carrying a tuba for which he had not yet been offered the right price.

'Don't worry Mrs Sten, I only play in the evenings,' he said and he began to laugh like cracking earth heralding a natural disaster.

'A tuba,' she said, 'how super.'

'I need to put this one somewhere safe,' Mr Sten said as he appeared behind Kozak, a smallish cardboard box in his hands. His brow furrowed as he surveyed the pile of their belongings. 'I do apologize, Alice. It seems that we have rather a lot,' he said and smiled carefully at her. 'Could I just put this in there?' he said, indicating the kitchen behind her with a thrust of his chin.

'What is it?' she asked, as she moved aside to let him through.

'Oh . . . you know,' he murmured, placing it on one of the kitchen chairs.

Mrs Sten opened one of the flaps and peered inside. She saw a collection of small bottles and tubs, white cardboard boxes and flashes of silver paper. His medicines: there was still a problem to treat. She tutted.

'Every time you come I . . .' she said, and moved her hand so that the flap fell softly back in place. Mr Sten avoided her eyes.

'Yes. Well,' he said and went back to unloading the borrowed car.

TWENTY-TWO

'Hello there!' Mrs Sten called, for she had listened to them leave their room and come down the stairs, step by step. 'The champagne's just the right temperature,' she added and took a bottle from the fridge as Nicholas and Faye came through into the kitchen, ready for the charity dinner. It was Tuesday night. Faye tried to remember what she would have been doing at the same time the previous week. Cooking Alistair dinner probably, she thought sourly. Tomorrow was her birthday and Nicholas had told Mrs Sten. As the two of them walked into the kitchen the sight of them swelled Mrs Sten's chest with a sad admiration. Faye looked as though she had been carved in marble and decorated in silk by the loving hands and delicate tools of a master craftsman. And she knew it too. In her face shone the bright light of self-worth and contentment.

Nicholas's hired tuxedo suited him: it matched his careful manners and formality and lent his body an agility and slickness which stopped Mrs Sten's breath in her throat. His thickly lashed eyes, like furry moths against his pale skin, followed the brightness of Faye's face wherever it went. Mrs Sten had never seen him look so proud and happy.

'Well then, happy birthday darling,' she announced, once she had poured the champagne and handed out the glasses. 'You don't look a day over thirty,' she said and smiled her theatre smile at Faye.

'I'm twenty-nine,' Faye replied.

'Goodness,' said Mrs Sten, 'time for a family,' and she sat

249

down again quietly as the barb in her words took effect. She couldn't help it: she was sick with envy.

'Madonna's had her second baby at forty-two,' Faye replied coolly.

'Well, I imagine it's difficult to control immaculate conception,' said Mrs Sten lightly.

'We're a little late,' Nicholas said kindly to Mrs Sten, keen to separate the two of them. What he wanted, in his heart, was to take Faye back upstairs to his room and undress her. He thought about what Mrs Sten had told him about moments. Now clearly wasn't the time. Instead he gulped his champagne and stood up. He took his glass over to the sink where he washed and dried it, flinging the thick white tea towel over his shoulder when he'd finished. He had wondered, once they'd finished dressing, what his mother would have thought if she had seen them.

'Won't you have another glass?' pleaded Mrs Sten. She didn't want him to leave but she put a smile at the end of her question and appeared not desperate but generous, a welcoming and able hostess. Nicholas was used to so much female attention. Kalyna's love for him had often been overwhelming. Her friends and colleagues had many children, a husband, some brothers perhaps, or sisters-in-law. They were surrounded by family. Kalyna had Nicholas and that was it. Just one boy. When he was late home she stared out of the front window for hours. When he slept at night she crept to his room and watched. She had to let him go, she knew that. And she did: not once did she stop him doing anything because of her own anxiety. But when he was not there she thought of him constantly. He filled her head – had filled her head since he was born – and the habit of not thinking of him was a hard one to kick.

She missed Bohdan. Once or twice, when Nicholas had thrown his dirty clothes in a heap on the bathroom floor or had stayed out until two without phoning to say where he was, she would clench her jaw and say, 'Bohdan wouldn't dream of doing such a thing.' She tried to stop herself from making such comments, but there were times when she couldn't help it. Nicholas grew up with an older, better, more considerate brother. And the brother had one other attribute with which Nicholas could never compete: he was absent.

'I really think we should be going, I'm afraid,' Nicholas said.

'But what shall I do with half a bottle of champagne?' She had not yet mentioned the arrival of two extra people in the house. Both Nicholas and Faye had noticed a few peculiar objects lying around and heard footsteps on the landing outside their room, but neither of them had actually seen anyone.

'Perhaps we could all have it later, when we get in?'

'Do you know when you'll be back?'

Nicholas turned to Faye. 'Midnight?' he suggested.

'We'd really better go,' Faye said lightly and the two of them floated from the house.

The dinner was held in the ballroom of the hotel: a large and long room, evenly dotted with prettily laid tables. Faye and Nicholas took their seats against a background of chatter and beneath it, barely audible, the sound of a string quartet from the corner of the room. Nicholas glanced over at the musicians and caught Faye's eye. He looked down at the linen-covered table in front of him, and took a rough silver fork in his hand, lifting it slightly to feel its weight and then rocking it backwards and forwards, using his middle finger as a pivot.

The rest of the table was beginning to fill up: a delicate dark-haired woman sat on Nicholas's left and next to her a large beefsteak of a man, with a broad red neck and hands that seemed too big to do anything useful, except perhaps clap loudly or hold cigars. Beside him was a blonde woman with a ski-jump nose and curly hair and by her side, and Faye's, was a dark man with strong bones and a troubled expression. Nicholas knew none of them and he looked down at the fork balancing on his hand, observing the reflections of the ceiling fixtures in the back of the polished surface.

'Do you come often?' Nicholas leant over to Faye.

'I'm sorry?'

'Do you come here often?'

'That's not what you said,' Faye grinned at him.

'It isn't?'

'No. You asked me if I came often.'

'And do you?'

'Do you?'

'I would if I was with you.'

She just laughed. 'Have you been to the Sheffield school of seduction?'

'You like my patter?'

'I don't know about like it. It's different at least.'

'Get bored of getting chatted up then?'

'Er, yes.'

'Get chatted up a lot then?'

'That's not what I meant,' she said and shook her head, turning briefly to the man on her right. She leant back to Nicholas and whispered, 'What *are* we doing here?' coming so close that Nicholas could hear not only her words, but also the minute workings of her mouth – the clicks and creaks formed by her lips and tongue that came at the beginning and ends of words. In a second she was gone again and he was left to inhale the soft diffusion of her scent.

'It was your idea to come,' Nicholas replied with a smile,

looking at the shiny folds of her dress, which seemed to fall loosely around her body in a way that suggested to him only one thing: how easy it would be to remove. She turned back to him.

'Well I thought we might as well, but now we're here . . .' she said, and took a sip of her wine. Waiters appeared with the first course and began to place it in front of the diners – a dark brown disc decorated with a deep red sauce, poured over the top to form a mysterious hieroglyph. Faye leaned into Nicholas again and this time he thought he might not be able to bear it – he breathed in while she was close and looked at her soft cheek and the line of her lips, which moved a few inches from his face.

'I don't know anyone on this table,' she said with a light in her eyes which made Nicholas think of a firefly showing off in the darkness. She turned back to her plate and took a mouthful of food. Nicholas felt a terrible compulsion to watch her every move – as though she had, somehow, hypnotized him and for the rest of the evening he would have no choice but to sit and stare. He forced himself to turn to the strange compacted deposit on his plate and prod at it with his fork, but he couldn't help noticing out of the corner of his eye that Faye was holding her hand to her chin and gazing at him.

'What I don't understand is what this has to do with charity. A load of people sit around eating fancy food *in aid of charity*?' He frowned hard, a short groove appearing between his eyebrows.

Faye shrugged. 'How is your food?' she asked him with an expectant expression.

Nicholas paused. 'I don't know yet,' he murmured.

'Probably best to keep it that way.'

He picked up the wine and refilled their glasses. 'We should introduce ourselves,' he said and he took in a montage of polite nods, waning smiles and hesitant mouthfuls of food as he scanned the table. And so they did, each turning to opposite sides and capitulating to the inertia of small talk.

'I have lived my life vicariously through fruit-flies,' Nicholas heard the man on Faye's right tell her. He bit his tongue and reached for his wine.

After the main course Faye excused herself and headed off in the direction of the toilets. Nicholas followed, his heart racing. As she passed into the corridor he reached out and took hold of her hand, brushing as he did so the inside of his wrist on the sheen of her dress. He felt unsteady, surprised by a sudden dizziness. He must have drunk more than he'd thought.

She turned to him with a glint in her eyes. How many times had he seen that glint before? Her mouth eased into a hook of a smile. She took a step towards him. He breathed in, feeling taller, lighter, as though he might float off. She took in the lapels of his jacket, the breadth of his shoulders. Nicholas was suddenly aware of his own attractiveness in a way that he had never been as a teenager. He would like to ask Faye: did you fancy me then? I have wanted you for a very long time. She came close to him. He could smell her hair. Lightly, quickly, she placed a kiss on his lips. He tasted wine. And then she paced away, backwards down the corridor, a look of rapt determination on her face.

Nicholas followed, breaking into a jog, as she laughed at the unfairness of the situation: her in heels, going backwards, him gaining ground on her in seconds. She stumbled on a step and he collided with her, her flesh firm beneath the sheen of the white satin dress which fell about her as though desperate to part and reveal her skin. He stopped her falling over. They stood, too close together, at the bottom of a short flight of stairs.

'I have no underwear on,' Faye whispered in his ear. She too had drunk more than she'd imagined.

'You're knicker-less?'

'No, I'm Faye,' she replied and her bottom lip brushed against his neck.

'You mean you aren't even wearing those things which you leave to dry on my radiator?'

'I'm glad you noticed.'

'The devil takes girls who wear no knickers,' Nicholas said. His hands tingled with desire. 'He looks up from below and picks them out. Just like Jesus coming down and taking the tonsured monks.'

'Well, the devil will just have to wait,' Faye replied. He watched her lips with an intense fascination. She turned then and began to run, up the stairs, along the corridor which turned to the right. She lost both of her shoes on another set of steps, like Cinderella's carefree, drunken cousin. The corridor came to an end ahead of her. There were doors on either side, each marked Private. Nicholas jogged after her and when he reached the dead end Faye grinned at him.

'We're stuck,' she said, leaning heavily against a cold papered wall.

Nicholas tried a doorhandle. It opened to reveal a cupboard, a teepee of mops in one corner, buckets on the floor. He put his hand on Faye's side and pulled her in with him. He pressed his weight against her, hearing laughter come from her throat and tasting the wine on her breath. He placed his hands on her body, their steadiness giving no clue to the convection current of feelings inside him. Faye lifted her dress, sliding up the watery satin to the tops of her thighs, and Nicholas unzipped his trousers. Within seconds he was inside her.

As they moved against a stretch of wall that was surely not built and plastered and painted for this purpose it seemed to be over far too quickly – within minutes her eyelids had fluttered and her throat emitted a low murmur, while Nicholas pulled out and came over the peeling blue paint of the wall behind her. She felt a shocking alertness, as though her senses had been doubled in a split second.

'Wait here,' he whispered, running his index finger along her jaw. With his other hand he zipped up his trousers. 'On no account move. Not even a centimetre.' He slipped from the cupboard and made his way back down the corridor.

Nicholas slipped off to the loo but did not find what he was looking for. Instead he found a doorman – or at least a man in a brass-buttoned suit – and stopped him. Nicholas noted the soft skin on his jaw. The man was barely in his twenties.

'Excuse me.'

'Yes sir?'

'I was looking for – well.' Nicholas paused. How did one ask for condoms in the Grosvenor House Hotel? He was aware of the pounding of his heart and a wetness at his groin.

'Sir?'

He tried to think of a brand name, but could only come up with Dulux. Then he tried to think of a suitably English word for them. There must be one he knew, a Jermyn Street phrase: Special Zeppelins, Jelly-bag Geronimos, Third Socks. The word johnny came to mind.

'Do you have any johnnies?' Nicholas asked in his most delicate accent. Faye, had she heard him, would have laughed out loud. 'Do you always just say the first thing that comes to mind?' she would have asked.

'I'm sorry, sir?' the young man asked. Nicholas supposed they didn't call them that any more.

'My nephew,' Nicholas began, trying his best to sound authoritative. 'I'm looking after him this evening and he's got a rather nice young lady with him and they're about to head off into the moonlight and before he goes I would like to –' The young man looked blank. 'Talk to him about the birds and the bees.'

'Oh,' the man replied and Nicholas wondered at the phrase he had just used. Was the implication that birds and bees made love to each other? And if so why wasn't the sky black with stripy, stinging starlings?

'I've just got to fetch some limes for the bar, sir, if you'll –' said the young man.

'Do you have any condoms?' Nicholas blurted out.

'Of course sir,' the young man murmured, straightening up, and he reached into his waistcoat pocket and discreetly passed Nicholas a small foil square.

'Thank you,' Nicholas said, wondering whether to trust the equipment he'd received.

'My pleasure,' replied the boy and he dashed off to see to the limes.

The pleasure, Nicholas thought, is all mine.

'Come on,' he said and he took her hand and pulled her after him. Touching only her hand was barely enough for him and he gripped it too tightly. She left the cupboard, startled to be back out in public again.

'Where to?' she asked. He didn't reply but took the first flight of stairs they found and then ran down a corridor trying doorhandles.

'We can't do this,' Faye whispered to him. A few beads of perspiration had broken out between her eyebrows.

'Oh yes we can,' he said and swapped over to the other side of the corridor and carried on with his frantic twisting of doorknobs. One gave. 'Aha!' he whispered and he poked his head around the door before flicking on the lights and leading her in.

'But this is someone's room,' Faye protested. Nicholas pulled her to him and took her mouth in his.

'It'll belong to some rich American tourists,' he told her, running his hands down her dress. 'They won't even know we were here,' he said and sat on the bed. It was a square room with a large four-poster bed and a view of the park. Its inhabitants had left a few items of clothing on a chair and their toiletries in the bathroom. On the dressing table lay a newspaper.

'What if they come back?' Faye asked him. She knelt astride him, sinking deep into the bed. He met her eyes and shrugged. She raised her arms high above her as he lifted her dress from her, raising it over her face so that the white cloth covered her hair.

'You look like a nun,' he told her with an ironic smile before letting his eyes drop to take in her naked body. She was soft and white. Her nipples were the pink of roses, her hair the colour of wet straw. He placed his hands on her knees and ran them slowly up to the tops of her thighs, resting his thumbs in the dips on the inside of her legs.

'How come I'm the only one with no clothes on?' she asked, unbuttoning his shirt and then unzipping his trousers. He threw his pants on the floor and Faye regarded him. He barely seems to hesitate, she thought. She put her finger to his forehead and let it drop down the side of his face, passing gently over the dip of his temple and then the rise of his cheekbone and letting it fall away before she reached his jaw. She repeated the movement, feeling a familiar tingling in her finger as it made contact with his skin.

He fixed his gaze on her, dark brown eyes zipping over her face, sparking as they changed direction. Her finger made its journey again, pausing this time at his jaw. Nicholas was transfixed: his inhibition deliquesced in the alcoholic vapours. Faye moved her finger down his neck, feeling the ridges of his throat and the vulnerability of his skin, and then rested it, finally, snug in the cool dip of his super sternal notch.

'Do we trust the bellboy?' Nicholas whispered as he put on the condom. His skin had an almost metallic sheen to it. Faye coiled a finger in one of the hairs on his thigh and brought one of his hands to her mouth.

'Always trust the bellboy,' she replied as she nipped the top of his forefinger. As she lay back on the bed the frog-call of the springs filled the room. Nicholas ran his hands up her legs and slid inside her.

They had one condom: they made love once. Afterwards Nicholas lay on the bed dozing. Faye ran her hand up and down the downy crest of hair in the middle of his stomach. She had surprised even herself. She tried to remember if she had always felt such an attraction for Nicholas and whether she had ignored it for all these years. A noise from the corridor made her lift her head.

'Nicholas! They're coming back!' she whispered, climbing from the bed and gathering his shoes and their clothes in armfuls.

'Nicholas!' she hissed. He opened his eyes to see her dumping their things on the bathroom floor; the sight of her naked back and bottom and legs aroused him again. He leapt from the bed and joined her in the bathroom just as the hotel-room door opened. Faye closed the bathroom door with a gentle click.

'Fuck,' she whispered, turning to him. He looked at her through one eye and smiled. 'What are you going to do?'

'Oh, I have to do something do I?' he laughed. He sat down on the side of the bath and leant over to kiss her on her stomach.

'It was your idea,' Faye replied with a giggle. 'It's all your fault.' She held a finger to her lips.

'Were you nervous?' a female voice said in the room outside. It sounded like a young voice, with a foreign accent, muffled only by the thin pine door that separated them.

'About this morning?' came the reply. The man was closer to them. Reluctantly Faye and Nicholas began to dress. They watched each other as though they might never see each other naked again.

'Yes.'

'Were you?'

'Hell yes.'

'Since when did you swear?'

'I swear all the time. You must remember that.' she replied. There was a pause and then she laughed. 'It is strange to see you again.'

'It's strange for me to see anyone again. Walking through Leicester Square earlier on I thought I was hallucinating. I haven't seen that many people since, well, since I left.' There was more silence and Nicholas and Faye wondered whether they might get away with it, whether the occupants might have fallen asleep.

'Come on then,' The man's voice broke the silence. 'Let's make the most of this room.'

'I'm just going to brush my teeth,' she replied. Nicholas and Faye froze. They were fully dressed and felt suddenly too sober. Faye looked around the room in desperation. There was nowhere to go. To her surprise Nicholas reached out and opened the door.

'Oh my God!' the woman breathed. She had a hand to her throat and stood there staring at him. She was slight with mousy hair which she'd tied back in a ponytail. She was wearing a T-shirt which fell to mid-thigh. The man leapt from the bed. He had blue eyes, black hair and a ruddy face which looked strange against his pale body. Nicholas was relieved to see that he still had his pants on.

'I'm terribly sorry,' Nicholas said. 'We got trapped in here. By accident. We didn't realize this was your room.' He let Faye walk out first and then followed her, placing his arm around her waist. Two light pink patches glowed just by her nostrils.

'What on earth were you doing in our bathroom?' the woman asked. Nicholas wished he could place her accent. It could have almost been Ukrainian but he did not dare ask.

'Well the thing is, we got lost . . . and –' Nicholas paused and looked down at his front. He had misbuttoned his shirt, he noticed, and a whitish stain had appeared on the top of his trousers. 'We had sex on your bed,' he said.

'Nicholas!' Faye said, turning to him. The man looked over to the crumpled bedspread where he had just been sitting. The woman eyed Nicholas for a moment. There was something tough in her expression and he wondered for a moment whether she was famous or prominent in some way. She stared at him.

'Was it good sex?' she asked finally.

Nicholas blinked at her and looked to the man. He was watching his partner with an amused, detached expression.

'Yes,' Nicholas replied.

'Yes,' echoed Faye. 'It happened *on* your bed, not *in* it, so if you'd like us to take away the bedspread I'm sure the hotel would replace it,' she said softly.

'I see,' said the man. He had a squareness to him which Faye liked. He probably has square fingertips, she thought.

'Goodnight then,' ventured Nicholas and he started towards the door.

'I am sorry,' Faye said. The woman walked behind them.

'It doesn't matter,' she said with a laugh. 'It really doesn't matter at all,' and she shut the door firmly behind them.

They finally left the hotel at just after two in the morning. It was the end of July and the dark seemed to have brought with it a soft, sticky air which sat over the city, robbing thousands of their sleep.

'Come on,' Nicholas said, once they were outside, and he took Faye's hand.

'No,' she said.

He turned to her. 'What do you mean?'

'I lost my shoes.'

'There's only one thing for it then.'

'Will you carry me?'

'I only carry women on Mondays and Wednesdays. As it's Tuesday the best I can offer is a piggyback.'

For the second time that night she lifted her dress up and for the first time regretted that she hadn't worn underwear: she could have tucked the sides of her dress up into her pants. As it was she climbed onto him and crossed her legs over his stomach, crushing his Adam's apple with a forearm. A passing car tooted at them.

They made it to the lake in Hyde Park, where Faye climbed down and put her arms around his neck. Nicholas could smell sand on her skin. For that moment they seemed inseparable, built for each other, like one impenetrable unit. He pressed his face against her warm neck, feeling her hair against his forehead, and he took a breath of their shared air, feeling his ribcage shudder as he exhaled. 'I still have your tooth,' he said.

'The one I –'

'Yes,' he said, grinning. 'It's in my room. A portion of your childhood smile.'

She laughed. 'You don't even know which tooth it was,' she replied.

'Oh, I do,' Nicholas said. 'It was that one right there,' he said, stretching out his index finger. Then he took her chin in his hand and kissed her.

He looked at her with the admiration and ardour with which an explorer sights land or a botanist an unknown orchid, ripe and swollen, the dampness of the forest oozing from its iridescent petals. He wanted to announce his discovery to the world: he had found the secret of the universe, the meaning of life, the magic flower of the fern, the veiled woman's face with its enigmatic smile – it was right here, beside him, sitting with a golden dove beneath a pear tree. She gave to him what walking on the beach gave to him: a primal, silent, reassurance.

As the night passed he was gripped by a dark corrosive compulsion to build an ark and lead her onto it, followed by a procession of white panthers, elephants, monkeys and bears. Or search for a Tardis for her to travel in, cryogenically freeze her or send her out into space in a multicoloured capsule, in search of eternity. The impulse to capture her essence grew inside him, but he knew that any attempt to preserve her would necessarily fail: she would fall from his hands like water.

They lay down away from the path and fell asleep on the grass. Two hours later the blue light of dawn intruded and woke Faye. She rolled over onto her front, where an angular pebble dug into her breast and left a secret indentation which would still be there when she eventually climbed into the shower. Nicholas lay beside her, his right hand lolling in the small of her back. She watched a park cleaner push his ragbag trolley dolefully along, stopping to empty a bin. She felt the suggestion of a tremor in her lower limbs, realizing seconds later that it was not an echo of the pleasure she had felt the night before but rather the onset of a peristaltic impatience which crept up on her in times of inactivity.

She wanted now to get on with her life. She wanted a house with three floors and a garden in which she would plant narcissi and an apple tree. She wanted to have it decorated and invite her friends over for dinner. And she needed to get a job. And she wanted to paint. She did not admit it to most people she knew: she burned with a white-hot ambition which blanched her hazel eyes and left her hair brittle.

While Faye lay thinking about fulfilling her aims a peal of bells sounded through Nicholas's head beside her. When he had closed his eyes – temporarily, he had thought – a parade had marched through him. His mouth fell open and he emitted a startled snore. Faye turned to him. Stubble was beginning to appear on his jaw and she reached out to feel its roughness. She shivered with cold.

'Enough of this horseplay,' she said softly, knowing that her words wouldn't wake him. 'Come on, let's go home.'

TWENTY-THREE

It was a number of days before anyone in the household, apart from Mrs Sten, had the chance to meet Mr Sten and Kozak. Everyone knew that someone new had moved in, not only because of the piles of things which had sprung up in the hallways but because when Martine came home from work, followed by an exhausted Nicholas, on Thursday afternoon, neither of them had to stride over the stair with no top. There, concealing the gap, was a new piece of pine, sanded and varnished but not yet painted the same powder blue as the rest of the stairs. The hole in the bathroom had gone too: plastered into oblivion. The cellar doorhandle worked and the toilet had stopped its incessant flushing. The only thing that didn't change was the cupboard in the kitchen that opened onto bricks. For that Kozak would have to knock a wall down. Besides, he quite liked it.

Mrs Sten had not been able to fathom Kozak. He seemed aloof and brusque. In truth he had taken a dislike to Mrs Sten and felt unwelcome and uneasy. His first night in the house was spent with a pencil and paper working out how long it might be until he could afford to pay rent again.

It was Martine who encountered Mr Sten and Kozak first and she shook their hands with an apologetic smile and a suspicious mind. Harvey was shy and stood behind her leg staring at Kozak's scar, wondering whether he had been born like that. Martine told them that it was very nice to meet them and then dashed upstairs with her son and knocked on Nicholas's door. Faye answered and showed her in, and Martine proceeded to describe the two peculiar characters who were currently in the hallway.

'Is Nicholas not here?' Martine asked. It was clear that he wasn't. He had gone out to look for the sheet music for Schumann's concerto in A minor.

'I have to go down and meet them!' trilled Faye, her eyes made bright by Martine's animation.

'You can't do that. It'll be obvious that I've told you about them.' Harvey watched Faye's breasts move beneath her pale blue shirt.

'Nonsense,' Faye replied and ushered the two of them back to their own room, then swayed down the stairs like a cat with a mouse.

'Oh, hello,' she said, feigning surprise. David and Kozak were examining a large straw vase in the hall, muttering between themselves. From the very first instant Mr Sten liked Faye. With her carefree curls and easy smile she reminded him of the younger Mrs Sten and as she swung down the stairs to shake hands he admired the way her clothes fell about her body, knowing straight away what dress he would make for her, if he ever had the opportunity. He imagined himself grabbing her and waltzing with her in the hallway as she shook her curls over her shoulders and exclaimed, 'Oh, Mr Sten!' At this point he imagined he would press his foot lightly over hers and reply, 'My dear, your shoes are a little scuffed. Let me clean them for you.' As she arrived opposite them at the bottom of the stairs he marvelled at her, as one might regard a pink sheep.

'Hello, my dear,' he said in a deep voice. 'I'm David.' He neglected to tell her his surname.

'Hello,' she said and smiled back at him. She liked his manner and the colour of his jumper.

'I am Kozak,' Kozak said stiffly and he leant in to kiss her on each cheek and then once again, but on the third stroke

266

he took the lobe of her ear between his teeth and nipped it ferociously. She gasped and her hand shot up, too late, to protect her flesh. He took a step back and looked at her, his sunglasses obscured his eyes and the rest of his features fell away in a relentless neutrality from those two shiny dark ovals. Faye nursed her ear and looked to his lips for a sign, a clue to the meaning of his startling gesture, but his mouth lay like a crack in the granite of a mountain: straight and still, its line interrupted occasionally by an errant strand of his thick, water-resistant moustache.

'Goodness, what did he do to you?' Mr Sten enquired, glancing from Faye to Kozak.

'He bit my ear,' she said with a frown.

'Now Kozak –'

'I apologize,' Kozak said. He could not explain his actions. He did not feel at home in this house.

'Did you tell us your name?' Mr Sten asked.

'I'm Faye,' she replied, still massaging her reddened lobe.

'Can I make you a cup of cocoa?' Mr Sten asked.

'Oh,' Faye replied, 'Okay,' and they went off to the kitchen. Kozak went out.

Nicholas passed his days in a dream-like state, walking through the park with the grin of a lunatic sitting on his face. He became as good as useless. He no longer listened to what people said to him. The idea of listening at all, of having any attention to devote to anything, struck him as ludicrous. He smiled at Mrs Sten when she explained to him that she had sprained her wrist trying to open a jar of marinated asparagus. He smiled as Sean tried to make him understand the current economic problems facing Bangladesh, so much so that Sean accused him of being on drugs. And Nicholas did, during these days, look drugged: a bright flatness came to his eyes, which no longer seemed to comprehend what they saw, his mouth could not help but smile. His head was filled with nothingness. It was a beautiful, blissful nothingness. He behaved as though he had smoked sixteen spliffs in a row.

When he unpacked his cello and played he paid less attention to the notes and their interpretation. He stopped struggling with them, stopped regarding them as problems to be overcome. Instead he just played. Sitting on her straw-stuffed sofa in the living room Mrs Sten could hear the difference in his music. She pursed her lips as she recognized that his sense of timing had gained an elasticity. He took liberties with the notes before him without even noticing that he was doing it. Mrs Sten paused in her lace-making as she heard, distinctly, the melody swing its way down the stairs, taunting her with its lyrical ease. Nicholas played sweetly and with a renewed vigour. He did not need to suffer to create art, nor did he need to be unhappy to push himself. His cello sounded as though it had been liberated.

He stopped turning on his television. His radio too remained untouched. The door to his room he would kick shut with a flick of his foot when he came home to Faye. He tidied up less, enjoying the heaps of clothes and newspapers which built up around his room, the piles of coppers which Faye stacked on his chest of drawers by the pot of coconut lip balm with its chipped lid and a mug of day-old coffee. Faye's life, her daily routines, seemed almost to have overwhelmed him. He noticed how her shoes were always left apart, often on the floor on either side of the bed. He would, returning from work, catch sight of them and wonder just how they came to be where they were. He found her taste for mayonnaise sandwiches surprising. He could not think of himself as an individual any longer; any projection of self immediately became a vision of a man and a woman. Most of the time he just lived, living in a way he had never lived before.

He turned his alarm off and slept late in the mornings. None of it matters, he thought, as he strode to work in the mornings. It was all rubbish, all details, compared to Faye's arrival in his life. It seemed that Nicholas had a finite capacity for care. Once Faye became part of his life he cared for her and her alone. He stopped questioning himself at every turn. He stopped wondering. His dream had been deferred long enough. He felt cherished and beautiful.

Faye cooked pork chops for him one night and covered them in mushroom soup. She ringed the chops with the tinned soup, once round and once again until the whole plate looked like a ship ready to set sail. Nicholas laughed as he sat down at the table. But the chops tasted good and he went on smiling as he chewed. After dinner he washed up their plates, noticing how prettily the ceiling light was reflected in the rainbow sheen of the washing up bubbles. Then, hands still wet and a dirty knife left in the sink, he embraced Faye and kissed her, pushing his face into her neck and a hand down her skirt. She laughed and together, like participants in a three-legged race, they tumbled up the stairs to their room.

Faye's body was well-proportioned and round. When Nicholas first set eyes on it he could not see it enough. As she had moved around the hotel room gathering up their clothes he watched her like a hawk, hypnotized by each curve and line. When she climbed into his bed the following night he found himself spellbound, fascinated by the straightness of her shoulders, the soft skin of her breasts, the seamless slope from waist to hip to thigh. She smelt English to him, of Pears soap and warm, white towels. He reached out to touch her whenever he could.

'Did you fancy me when we were fifteen?' Nicholas asked. They were sitting opposite each other in an Indian restaurant in Olympia, their menus splayed out on the table in front of them, a picture of the Taj Mahal hanging in a gold frame on the wall beside them. Nicholas had been aware, since their first kiss two days earlier, of an imbalance between them. He could not imagine that she had thought of him as much as he had of her. His life, finally, seemed to make sense.

'I can't believe you have to even ask that question,' Faye replied with a grin.

'Oh, you know me,' Nicholas said, 'I misconstrue the slightest sign.'

'I used to really fancy you.'

'Used to?'

She laughed. 'Well, obviously I still do. I wouldn't be here now if I didn't.'

'Oh, so you go to bed with people you don't fancy but you'll only go out for a curry with people you do,' Nicholas smiled at her. But you have no idea about the years I spent thinking of you, he thought. How could she?

'You know what I mean,' she said with a shake of her head. The waiter approached them and asked them what they wanted. Neither had thought of food, or even looked down at the menus and admired their imaginative use of the skyline of the domes of the Taj Mahal. They ordered between them, choosing the words on the menu that were familiar to them.

Nicholas watched her carefully as he talked, enthralled by how her hair curled loosely around the bottom of her neck. She was wearing the T-shirt he'd lent her to sleep in and no bra. He thought she looked astonishing. She hoped that she wouldn't bump into anyone she knew.

'Can you cook?' he asked her.

'Of course,' she replied. Alistair had sent her on a course when she had given up her job, and she'd spent a week in East Anglia learning how to create soufflés and sauces from a pinched-faced man with long teeth and trembling fingers. 'I'll cook you a meal,' she said. It seemed that there was a lot ahead of them, waiting to be discovered.

Nicholas had imagined taking Faye to bed on many, many occasions. He had, he had believed, imagined the scene accurately. He knew Faye, he knew her hands, her gaze. She had, in the past, kissed him on the cheek. In his head he had transferred that kiss just a few centimetres around to his mouth: the pressure of her lips, their wetness, their shape. He could not, perhaps, be blamed for thinking that he knew her well, that he could predict her behaviour. He had controlled her in his imagination for a long time. Her imaginary hands were soft and firm, her imaginary tongue fast and warm, her imaginary body a poem of curves.

Reality did not disappoint Nicholas. It was rather his fantasies which suddenly paled as he realised their short-comings. Faye's hands were careful and slow but they were real. They touched him. He could not have imagined that she would press her palms down heavily on his shoulders as she moved on top of him. Nor could he have guessed that she preferred to fall asleep with her hands clasped behind her head, like a cartoon character, napping in the afternoon. Often, as he turned over in bed, he would encounter an elbow in his temple. Once, bruised the second time in one night, he had moved her hands gently from beneath her head and laid them by her sides, feeling like an undertaker moving the dead. Her knees were so round they looked like moons, bobbing around in space as she climbed on and off the bed. She lay on her stomach across his bed and painted her nails, her mind wandering as she stared down at the drying varnish. At night she switched off all the sockets in the room before she went to sleep.

He had imagined that she would be exuberant in bed. She was, in fact, quiet and careful, gathering her hair neatly with one hand at the back of her head before she took him in her mouth. She did not, as he had imagined she might, turn her head to him and meet his eyes with her own. She focused her attention on the task in hand.

'Why are you single?' Faye asked slyly.

Nicholas paused. They had not discussed whether they were a couple or not. There had not been an appropriate time. He wondered whether she had meant what she'd just said.

'I didn't realize I was,' Nicholas replied carefully.

She laughed. 'Okay, why *were* you single?' She reached out for his hand and began to play with each finger, pressing his knuckles up and down, stroking the few pale hairs on the back of each finger and twirling his mother's ring which he wore on the little finger of his left hand.

'Because I was waiting for you,' Nicholas said. It was as close as he could come to telling her what she had meant to him. Even now, sitting opposite her, he could almost believe that he was dreaming. They ate bits of different dishes. Their eyes, the waiter happily told them as he collected the silver plates still laden with food, were bigger than their bellies. As they walked home together Nicholas draped his arms around her. It's her, he told himself as they wandered slowly along the late-night London pavements. It really is her.

It was the following evening that the last member of the household was introduced to the new guests. Mr Sten and Kozak were sitting in the living room when Mrs Sten heard Nicholas's familiar jingling of keys outside the front door. Colour rose to her cheeks. She had been dying to show Nicholas off, to present her lovely, pretty boy to Mr Sten and let him see the quality of her tenants. Nicholas had been dying to get home, to climb into bed with Faye. Mrs Sten stood up quickly and smoothed the front of her green wool skirt, noticing as she did a chipped nail on her right index finger. She curled her hand into a fist.

'Nicholas,' she said as he came into the hallway. Nicholas looked up and saw that tonight she had no tea tray.

'Are you all right?' he asked straight away.

'Yes, I'm fine, thank you. Nicholas, we − I − we, well, we have some guests in the house. I'd like you to come and meet them,' and she inclined her head as she watched acquiescence spread slowly over his face.

'Oh, okay,' he replied. Once Nicholas had accepted Mrs Sten's invitation and followed her into the sitting room to find two strangers, he was politely curious and interested, surprised by a large man with a lightning-flash scar, coarse features and red shoes around his neck.

'This is David Sten,' Mrs Sten said. She motioned recklessly in the direction of the thin man with a long face and a chartreuse jumper, who stood up gracefully and stretched out a fine, limp hand for him to shake.

Nicholas looked into his face and wondered whether he was husband or brother-in-law, or indeed any of Mrs Sten's in-laws. He decided, from her casual unease, that he must be her husband. They seemed a couple whose exchange of ideas and bodily fluids had been replaced by information: by what time dinner would be ready and where the car keys were. Nicholas looked at him and imagined that he didn't particularly enjoy being married to Mrs Sten. He seemed like a man who wanted a quiet life.

'And this is Kozak,' said Mrs Sten proudly, anglicizing the

273

vowel so that it rhymed with Prozac. 'You won't believe this, Nicholas,' as though she were on children's television, 'but he's from the Ukraine as well.' Kozak lifted his chin to the boy and then stood.

'Hello,' said Nicholas, in English to be polite and Kozak kissed him on his cheeks, three times.

'Hello,' said Kozak, heavily taking his seat.

'Where are you from?' asked Nicholas kindly. He was the centre of attention. He had been taught by his mother to welcome foreigners with open arms, to listen patiently to their broken English, to give them food and a bed.

'Lviv,' said Kozak. Nicholas nodded.

'I was born in a small village outside Kyiv,' Nicholas replied, 'but I came to England when I was young,' he explained.

Kozak didn't respond. He seemed private and unin-terested, like a animal born in a cage. The two of them talked a little more, observed by Mrs Sten, who was pleased as a mother hen, while Mr Sten took sips of his tea and pondered a scratch in the leather of his shoe. Nicholas asked Kozak what he was doing in England. 'Business,' came the reply and after a few more questions Nicholas, wondering whether it was the language barrier which could account for Kozak's laconism, flipped into a stiff and creaking Ukrainian, thinking helplessly of his mother. Kozak raised his head a little as he listened to this strange language, neat and old-fashioned from the young man's lips.

'Please excuse me,' Kozak said, rising. Without realizing it he lifted a hand to the shoes around his neck and fiddled with the thong that held them, causing the shoes to perform a ghostly jig in mid-air. 'I have to wash my hands,' and he strode from the room, making a white china candlestick rattle on its base.

Nicholas sat back in his chair and wondered what he had

said that could have caused offence. His questions sounded over in his head and he asked himself whether he had intruded on the guest's privacy. He wondered, as Mrs and Mr Sten exchanged a glance, whether Kozak actually was from Lviv, for his accent sounded intimately familiar, could have almost overlapped with his mother's. Perhaps he is a Chornobylite, said a voice in his head. Nicholas knew the problems Chornobylites faced: floors were bleached when they left shops, reproduction for them was a sin. He could understand people fleeing such a fate, escaping abroad with a bitter mind and an irradiated body.

Kozak had not gone to wash his hands. After twenty minutes in Nicholas's company he needed to leave the room. He climbed the stairs slowly and heavily until he reached his door, which he pushed open and closed tightly behind him, breathing hard. The encounter had shocked him. He should not have been surprised to meet a man called Nicholas from his own country, but he was. He sat on the bed and wept silently, tears rolling down the rough skin of his cheeks, navigating the coarse hairs of his moustache and falling, finally, onto the backs of his hands, which he had clasped in his lap. He didn't know how or why, but Nicholas reminded him of Bohdan so vigorously that every time he looked at him sitting on Mrs Sten's floral sofa he saw instead Bohdan, vital and strong, and he wanted to stand up and embrace him. Nicholas did not look like Bohdan. Kozak could have made a long list of the differences. But somehow he also didn't not look like him: a similar age, a similar build (if not height), a similar combination of dark hair and shiny, sandy skin.

He did not blame Nicholas for his feelings – the young man could not be expected to know that he triggered this avalanche of smells and memories and sights, bringing back everything from that life. Instead he cursed London and its ethnic diversity: I will go back to somewhere where there are no other Ukrainians, he thought. But he sat on the edge of his bed, salt water tightening the skin as it dried on the backs of his hands, and finally, after all these years, remembered.

He sat completely still for an hour. Then he moved to scratch at a nostril, shot through with small, deep pink veins. The gargantuan impotence he had felt on Bohdan's death returned, spreading across the ceiling above him like debilitating ink on a blotter. He did not know how to honour his son's memory, he could think of no way of making sense of his death; he sat instead alone and hopeless, dwarfed by his solitude and loss, by the ricocheting randomness of events.

Finally, after he had ignored Mr Sten's polite taps on his door and once the sky outside had begun to close in for the night, he knew that he must move or be lost for ever. He roused himself in the same way that he had for the last thirteen years: by telling himself that there was now no Stefan Beimuk, there was only Kozak who had no surname and no clan and therefore no reason to cry like a child.

'He's a friend of mine,' Mr Sten had explained to Nicholas, eyeing the boy with sympathy. Mr Sten thought Nicholas most likeable and appreciated his self-sacrifice in offering himself up as a focus for Mrs Sten's affections. It had happened before with other lodgers. It would give Mr Sten valuable time to pick through his medicines and explore the various side effects of each, some of which were so enjoyable that he wondered why they were only the side effects and not the main effects of the bogus remedies. Nicholas nodded at Mr Sten and took a sip of his tea.

'So you're from the Ukraine as well?' Mr Sten asked needlessly, a pained expression crossing his face.

'Yes,' Nicholas replied, 'though I have lived in England for most of my life.'

'And at De Vere Gardens for the last two years,' Mrs Sten said smugly to her husband, and, stroking her hands down her thighs, she bounced a little in her seat. 'Nicholas is a cello teacher,' she explained to Mr Sten. 'He plays beautifully.'

Nicholas opened his mouth to contradict her but Mr Sten spoke instead.

'And is Faye a friend of yours?' he asked, pointedly looking at his wife.

'Ah,' Nicholas replied. 'Yes. She's – we –' He had not been explicit with Mrs Sten about the change in their relationship.

'She seemed like a lovely girl. Quite extraordinary.'

Mrs Sten frowned at her husband. She couldn't help herself.

'Yes,' said Nicholas, 'yes, she is.'

'The house is very full,' Mrs Sten said faintly.

'Oh, I don't know,' Nicholas replied. 'I'm sure we could fit a few Australians in here still.' She looked at him blankly.

'Was it you who mended the stair?' Nicholas said to Mr Sten.

'Goodness, no. You have Kozak to thank for that. And for all the other home improvements. He's a junk dealer. Awfully good with things,' Mr Sten told him.

'Oh, I see,' Nicholas said. 'Well, it's great not to have to worry about falling into the understairs cupboard every time I go to my room,' he remarked, realizing too late the criticism inherent in his words.

'If you'll excuse me,' Mrs Sten said suddenly. 'I have a headache,' and she went off to her room.

TWENTY-FOUR

Alistair, standing in the doorway of his large house, sighed. He looked tired now, his rotund smugness replaced by a worn look in his eyes and a slackness in his skin.

'Perhaps we should just get our solicitors to do this?' he said. It was Saturday morning and Faye had come to collect her things. She had, of course, brought Nicholas with her. Since Tuesday night they had spent all their free time together, in bed. The bed in Nicholas's room was an old cast-iron affair, with railings along the headboard and a pole along the bottom, against which Nicholas frequently banged his feet. It was a small double bed, but it was still too big for the room and its dark, spindly presence loomed over the space. Nicholas did not worry that he would wake up and find himself turned into an insect, but rather that his bed might suddenly overnight become a giant, shining beetle.

Once Nicholas and Faye had got together the bed in his room took on a significant role. It was not that they made love all the time, but rather that when the two of them were together in the room the most practical place for them to be was on the bed, and as long as they were on the bed they might as well be in it. When Nicholas got home from work he would make his excuses to Mrs Sten and then promptly go upstairs and make love to Faye. Towards the end of the evening, Faye, with flushed cheeks and loose limbs, would trip casually down the stairs to fetch something for them to eat. The peculiar thing about spending so much time in bed, Nicholas had found, was that he felt more tired than ever.

'You're so important that you no longer do your own

arguing?' asked Faye, dragging a black bin bag out into the street to stand with the crowd of others, filled with her clothes, a few books, some records, a picture. Nicholas stood by them, evening out the contents so that he could pretend he couldn't hear.

'Is that all?' Alistair asked quietly.

'No,' said Faye indignantly, turning to face him. 'Of course it's not all.'

Alistair sighed again, his large torso falling half an inch as he exhaled. 'What I meant was, is that the last of your belongings?' Nicholas squatted down by a bag, his back to the couple, and patted it needlessly.

'For the time being,' said Faye slowly.

'You have a set of keys, don't you?' asked Alistair, hopefully. There was a pause. A car roared by a few streets away and at the bottom of the road someone was calling an animal in for its lunch.

'Yes,' said Faye.

'Good,' he replied. Suddenly there was a movement from their comfortable kitchen and Beatrice appeared in the bay window, slow and content, in a red blouse embroidered with a passion flower. She passed by, glancing out the way an old cat might look at a bird, and then turned her back and began to open and shut cupboards.

'Come by. Whenever you want to,' Alistair invited.

'The pair of you seem very cosy,' Faye said.

'She's moving out. I asked her to,' Alistair said, jerking his head back towards the house.

Faye shrugged as though she didn't really care.

'Faye?' Alistair asked.

Faye shook her head and turned her back on him.

Alistair, after a brief pause, shut the door.

Nicholas heard its expensive, smooth click and turned around. Faye hadn't moved. It was half past twelve on

Saturday afternoon. The August sun blazed. Nicholas thought it would be nice to be in the park, by the Italian fountains where they could nip over to the drinking fountain of the embracing bears. He looked up at the house and saw Alistair now in the kitchen window, his mouth moving soundlessly while he watched his ex-fiancée in his front garden.

Faye pulled her engagement ring off her left hand and dropped it onto the path, where it bounced once, then rolled around its weighty jewel like a loaded die. Nicholas heard a faint tinkle, as though a bike had been unchained. Alistair thought that Faye had performed some strange gesture – a meeting of the hands and then a parting – which he failed to understand. He frowned and shook his head, staring intensely at where she had stood in the hope of understanding what she meant.

Beatrice leant into the fridge, hoping that the sight of her soft round bottom would distract him. Alistair watched Faye in the street. She walked up to Nicholas and dropped her arms around his neck. He kissed her, sliding his hands around the small of her back. From time to time Nicholas caught himself thinking that he might have imagined his relationship with Faye. As he interlinked his fingers behind her back he felt an urgent need to take off her clothes and stare at her, to look at the pale skin of the back he touched. It seemed to him, when he held her, that her beauty still escaped him. Alistair, watching them, felt sick. They might as well just have sex right there in the street, he thought. He found he could barely breathe.

'Faye! Hello! How are you?' A small woman with an inundation of hair came down the garden path next door and out into the street. A child followed her in a miniature designer dress. Faye and Nicholas broke from their embrace moments before, and Faye waved over at the child who was hovering by the path to Alistair's house.

'Hi, Tania, very well.' Faye forced a smile and folded her arms. 'How about you?'

'Yeah, I'm really well,' said Tania with a smile to match Faye's. 'I've just had my hair done,' she said, ripe and thrilled, and she tossed her head to one side, her dark locks, as if taken by surprise, following. She had features made of a few lines – a delicate curve of nose, an arch of eyebrow and a Botoxed expression of content. She wore a dark green dress, embroidered down one side with jasmine flowers, from shoulder to ankle.

'Mummy,' called the child, 'I've found a ring!'

'Oh, it looks lovely,' replied Faye tensely, 'really . . . big.'

'It's the autumn look,' beamed Tania. 'Paolo was just this minute saying. Big hair and patchwork.' And a red nose, thought Nicholas. 'Darling, *don't* pick things up off the pavement. They're *dirty*,' she called over her shoulder at her daughter and then turned back to Faye. 'Having a good sort-out, are we?' she asked, brushing her hair off one shoulder and turning to the bags. A vague flicker of horror passed through her eyes.

'Oh that, yes,' replied Faye, 'just old jumble. This is Nicholas,' she said. 'Nicholas, this is Tania.'

Tania eyed him quickly, seeing a pale face and uninteresting clothes. He disappeared from her vision.

'But I can be a princess, Mummy. It shines.'

'You already are a princess, sweetheart.' Tania's voice took on an impatient firmness. 'Now put it down and come over here. Other people *wee* on the pavement, darling. You're looking a little run-down, dear,' she said to Faye.

'One could be forgiven for wishing you were,' Nicholas mumbled to himself. Faye suppressed a smile.

'I hope Alistair isn't tiring you out with all the wedding preparations?'

'Oh no, no,' Faye laughed a little with her reply. 'It's

almost like it isn't happening,' she said and Nicholas dropped his head.

'It'll all just fly by,' replied Tania. Her daughter had wandered over to join her, sulking at having been denied the chance to possess a £10,000 ring. 'Before you know it, you'll be having kids,' and she absent-mindedly dropped her hand to her child's head.

Faye took a step back and shook her head. 'Oh no, I don't think so.'

'I'll tell you what,' said Tania, 'my father always said to me – and he was right – that the best contraceptive was just two words,' and she paused to let Faye guess. *The father*, thought Faye.

'School fees,' Tania announced triumphantly. 'He was right, I can tell you. Once you get it all down on paper, Alistair will realize that he'll have to spend the rest of his life working,' and she raised her eyes to the radiant sky. 'Anyway, I have a facial to get to,' and she bent to reach her daughter's hand. 'You're not going to leave those bags there, are you?' she asked, as she walked over, with a neat clipping sound, to her Land Rover. Faye and Nicholas stood by the sacks, in the middle of the pavement, as though they had no plans.

'No,' called Faye cheerily, 'Nicholas is bringing a van for them. It's ever such fun,' and she turned away to hide her face.

Nicholas went up to the top of the road and hailed a cab to take them back to De Vere Gardens. When the vehicle pulled-up outside the house, Nicholas felt reluctant to go inside, to expose Faye to the thin mauve carpet outside his room, worn in a strip up the centre, to the sparseness of his room, the yellow edges of his bed linen, the mealed mirror, the wilted curtains. He went to open the front door and then began the job of relaying the bags upstairs and stacking them, as neatly as possible, by the chest of drawers, in which he had cleared some space earlier that morning, feeling, all the while, as though his skin had shrunk and he was bent double inside his own body. He wished he had his own place to take her back to. At the same time he was trying to avoid Mrs Sten. She would, by now, have surely noticed that he and Faye were together. Faye, sensing Nicholas's unease, dropped a sack on the floor in the bedroom and sat down on the bed, wiping a hand across her face.

'It feels a lot better being here with my things,' she said brightly.

'Well, compared to living in that house it must be . . .'

'I'm grateful for what I have,' she said with a pleading look in her eyes. 'You know where I used to live, it's not like . . . Besides, I did yoga once and they taught us to manufacture a room in our heads, to go to for peace and quiet. So I have a room in my head.'

'Better than a head in your room,' Nicholas said and he pulled open the drawers he had emptied to let Faye fill them. He crossed to her and dropped his arms around her neck.

'That woman we met,' she began, scanning his face with her eyes.

'Tania.'

'She used to come to me for cooking tips,' Faye said. 'I did a cooking course once. Do you know what she did one night?'

Nicholas shook his head.

'She put suncream on her chicken because she didn't want it to burn.'

'Suncream on her chicken . . .?'

'Uh-huh. Those were the kind of neighbours we had. One roast chicken, basted with suncream.'

'Did she eat it?'

'They fed it to their dog.'

'You should have called the RSPCA. Come on, we can unpack tonight. Let's go out,' he said, breaking away from her and tying a jumper around his waist. He wanted to cheer her up.

On their way out they found Harvey moping at the bottom of the stairs because Martine had work to do and had banished him to the garden. They took him with them, meandering up the road. At the top of De Vere Gardens stood a large, ramshackle house with blue shutters and cracked panes and a green fire extinguisher which had stood on the step outside the front door for as long as Nicholas had lived there. The house had once been a hotel called The Majestic, but the M had fallen off and the letters that spread across its peeling front now spelled out The ajestic. Nicholas liked this house, admired the way it stood out in the street in its brash state of disrepair and idiosyncrasy. He had never seen anyone go in or out, but it seemed that someone lived there, for the bins were often full and shutters opened and closed in a ghostly fashion. The three of them crossed the road by the gleaming Albert Memorial and headed into the park.

'This place was first opened to the public in 1635,' Nicholas told Harvey as they entered the park, 'by Charles I. He put a cow in the park and you could buy milk to drink straight from it.'

'Ugh,' Harvey said. 'I hate milk.'

'During the plague people camped out here, to try and escape the illness.'

'Do you think it's still here?' Harvey asked.

'The plague?' They were walking through the wide stretches of grass, criss-crossed with paths, heading for the lake. 'I imagine that, in the dead of night, the earth opens up and breathes a little contagion back into the world.'

'What?' said Harvey.

'Probably. Deep down in the earth, there's probably some plague somewhere.'

'Down with old bones and skulls and stuff?' Harvey asked.

'Yep. And there used to be duels here when dawn broke, and public hangings up near Marble Arch, at Speakers' Corner.'

'Excuse me please.' A Chinese man stood in front of them, inclining his head. Small steely eyes met Nicholas's. 'Photo, please?' and he turned through forty-five degrees to indicate, with a lift of his hand, a well-dressed woman and a child, standing together, smiling. The man brought a black compact camera over to Nicholas and pointed, with small, bouncing finger movements, at a silver button. The man bounded over to his wife and son, placing his arms around them stiffly as though posing with goods from a shop. Nicholas duly took their photograph and the man thanked him, still wreathed in smiles, as he checked that the film had wound on.

'Now you!' he said. 'You!' and he shepherded them together on the opposite side of the path despite their protests.

'Oh, Jesus,' mumbled Harvey.

'We're not –' said Nicholas, as the man looped Nicholas's arm around Faye's waist. He wanted to explain that they weren't a family.

'Oh, come on Nicholas,' said Faye as she put her hands on Harvey's shoulders. 'Smile, Harvey,' she told him. And the three of them were frozen in time: Nicholas with an amused smile, Faye with a large grin and Harvey looking up at her. In the picture he looks like an adoring son; in reality he had raised his head to tell her that he wasn't going to smile. The picture would be stuck to a peach kitchen wall in Beijing for many years to come and the father of the family would tell visitors of the lovely English family they met in the park.

They sat by the lake for a while as Harvey wandered about finding things to try and skim into the water. A twig didn't work, nor did an acorn.

Nicholas held Faye's hand and kept an eye on Harvey. He held her hand tightly, quite without realizing it. When he finally disentangled his hand Faye was left with four temporarily bloodless patches of skin beneath her knuckles. Faye thought that he must be anxious about something, and imagined that he was thinking about his career. She too watched Harvey. He kicked at something in the grass.

'He seems like a nice kid,' Faye said.

'He is,' Nicholas replied. For a moment he imagined that Harvey was their own child, that they were already a family. With the idea of children came a whole collection of dizzying associations: pots of pastel paint, mortgage forms, Peugeot hatchbacks. *Faye and I*, he thought, *will have a different sort of a family*. They would sell up after a year and take their children around the world. Or they would live in a boat or a lighthouse.

'Do you want to have children?' he dared to ask her.

She looked across at him and caught his eye for a moment. She wanted to see whether he felt the question significant. She looked away.

'Well, yes,' she began, cautiously. 'Eventually.'

'I meant just . . . in general,' Nicholas added.

Faye giggled. 'You're funny,' she said. She squeezed his hand and Nicholas, suddenly aware of his own, let go of hers and scratched his temple.

'Why?' he asked, looking at her with a smile.

'You just are,' Faye replied, poking him in the stomach. 'If we had kids I'd hope our children would get your sense of humour. I'd just laugh at them all the time.'

286

'I'd hope they'd get your hair,' Nicholas replied. 'Then they could do shampoo commercials to pay for our retirement yacht.' The hair on her head was the colour of straw. Her pubic hair, Nicholas had been surprised to discover, was signifcantly darker. This knowledge was information that Nicholas prized. It felt as though he had been admitted into a secret room, which few would ever enter. The intimacy, the secretness of it all, nearly overwhelmed him. In the face of such intensity, not knowing what else to do, he smiled. Faye seemed, at the same time, both magical and undeniably real.

'They can have my hair if they get your eyes,' Faye said. She leant across and kissed him. Nicholas, for a moment, tried to imagine their offspring and found it impossible. *How was it that two separate beings could combine?* he asked himself. Harvey was squatting at the water's edge, peering at his own reflection.

'It's called the Serpentine because of its snake-like curves,' Nicholas said.

'Is that so?' Faye said with a grin.

'Queen Caroline had it built. George II's wife.'

'How do you know all this stuff?' she laughed.

'There's a guidebook in lost property at work with a big section on the park. I read it when I'm bored.'

'Which must be all the time.'

'Well,' Nicholas shrugged. 'Not *all* the time.'

'Why are you doing it, Nicholas?' Faye asked quietly. An old woman in a brown nylon cardigan walked slowly past, each step an effort.

'The story of supermarket security is, as ever, tantalizing, dazzling, mesmerizing, titillating, but, above all, a story of hope.'

Faye turned her head towards him and shot him a harsh look.

'There are no Monday afternoon drinking sessions, social lives start and end at home and worst of all femininity's hand has barely brushed the aisles of the supermarket.'

'I'm serious, Nicholas,' Faye replied. He had hoped to cheer her up but in order to succeed he needed her co-operation. It didn't appear that he was going to get it.

'You really should think about your career. It's some-thing to take seriously. You should think about when you work well and what you want to do.'

'I work well under constant supervision and when cornered like a rat,' he replied. Still no smile.

'Can we possibly have a serious conversation about this?' she asked.

'Did you hear about the hide-and-seek champion who was found dead in a cupboard? You see, there are downsides to taking your job too seriously.'

Faye laughed. Finally.

'Careers are important though, Nicholas. Have you heard from the orchestra?' she asked him.

'Well, I'm a teacher. And no, I haven't heard anything. I don't imagine they want me.'

'You could always try for other orchestras,' she replied.

'Look, even if they offer it to me, I'm not sure that I'll take it,' he told her softly. He decided, as he said it, that he wouldn't take the job. He liked Hyde Park too much. He wanted to stay in London. Bradford had not been his home. He saw it as a city that he and his mother had borrowed, against its will. He had come from a place where the land was flat. Field followed field followed field until, at the end of the earth, the sun went down. Bradford's concertinaed roofs had crowded him. It was a place of terraced terraces, with a low, imposing centre, towards which the lime-free water from the hills rushed. Nicholas was not from Yorkshire. Its rivers did not move him. The air always seemed too damp. Nicholas had known that he would have to claim a home. London, he felt, could be claimed by him.

'Why on earth not?'

'Because it's a very different life,' he tried to explain. 'There's touring, for a start. Working in the evenings. When you teach someone to play you necessarily work quite closely with them. I'm happy as I am. Playing in an orchestra is not like that,' he said.

'You'd be a fool to turn it down, Nicholas. It would be a better life.' That phrase again, Nicholas thought. The phrase his mother often used. *A better life.*

'Hey,' he said. She turned to him. He kissed her. Faye looked into his eyes and wondered whether she had ever been able to understand him. Nicholas had always been a bit of a mystery. But that was what attracted her to him. She smiled at him.

He stood up. 'Come on, Harvey,' Nicholas called, standing up.' 'Let's go and find Peter Pan.'

'I'm too old for Peter Pan,' Harvey replied, jogging over to the bench.

'Proud and insolent youth, prepare to meet thy doom!' Nicholas lunged at Harvey. The boy shrieked with delight and ran off. Nicholas chased after him.

TWENTY-FIVE

Kozak sat down heavily at the kitchen table and exhaled loudly, interweaving a 'hello' into his sigh.

'Hi,' said Nicholas brightly.

'This city,' said Kozak and shook his head. He took a sausage from the side pocket of his jacket and a small Swiss army knife from an inside pocket. Lifting the end of the sausage to his nose he casually flicked open the blade of the knife and, with a fierce concentration, sliced off a piece and ate it.

'What's the matter with this city?' Nicholas asked.

'Hah! What isn't the matter with it?' Kozak exclaimed, opening his hands wide, the knife blade pointing at Nicholas. 'The air is like the inside of a Hoover bag, you can get shot dead by the police for carrying a table leg around and sooner or later they'll be putting roofracks on the tube trains.'

'But,' Nicholas said, holding up a forefinger like a bishop's blessing, 'the people make it all worth it.' Kozak chewed and considered Nicholas's point. He supposed that the boy was right. When he thought back to the months he had spent in Slough he decided that the place had suffered a social version of heat death of the universe. Differences between people had ended, diversity had been kicked out of the door and told not to come back. Energy transfer was over. A homogenous equilibrium had been reached. The place was dead.

'The man next door,' Kozak began between mouthfuls, 'does he grow his fruit to sell it?' Nicholas shook his head and went on to detail Mr Samuels' night-time vigils.

'I'm due to help him pick it all, any day now,' Nicholas told Kozak.

'Let me know when you go,' Kozak said flatly, 'I should be glad to help,' and Nicholas glanced over to him, surprised by the offer.

Not only did Kozak make his presence felt in the house by quickly and painlessly mending all that was broken, but he made a lot of noise too, happily letting his weight fall onto each step of the stairs as he jogged up and down the two flights that led to his room. He sang as well, in Ukrainian, the same song over and over again, with a sliding, sneaking melody that seemed to come from the back of his throat. As Nicholas began to get dinner ready Kozak began to hum to himself while he sliced the salami. After a while Faye came downstairs. It was Sunday evening and the two of them had decided to cook together. Nicholas turned to her and gave her a shy, dolphin smile. Kozak, underneath his sunglasses, looked at her for longer than was polite.

'What does it mean, that song you sing?' she asked him idly.

'This song?' Kozak asked, as though he hadn't been aware that he had been singing.

'Yeah,' Faye said, lifting her gaze from the tomatoes she was chopping.

'Well.' Kozak paused.

Nicholas looked to him, an oven glove on his right hand.

'It's Shevchenko, isn't it?' Nicholas asked and he bent down to open the oven. Through the grey cloth of his T-shirt Faye could see the outline of his ribs at the back.

'Yes,' Kozak replied. He had known the poem for many years, but had only learnt a tune to go with it when he had lived in the Carpathians. An elderly woman used to play it in the evenings on a bandura.

'Don't wed a wealthy woman, friend,' Nicholas began, placing a baking tray of bread on the top of the oven.

> 'She'll drive you from the house
> Don't wed a poor one either, friend,
> Dull care will be your spouse
> Get hitched to a carefree Cossack life
> And share a Cossack fate:
> If it be rags, let it be rags –
> What comes, that's what you take
> Then you'll have nobody to nag
> Or try to cheer you up
> To fuss and fret and question you
> What ails you and what's up
> When two misfortune share, they say,
> It's easier to weep
> Not so: it's easier to cry . . .

. . . When there's no-one there to see,' Nicholas finished and tore a corner off the bread.

'But that's terrible,' Faye remarked. She held a tomato in her right hand, rubbing her thumb over its skin. 'Do you really believe that?' she asked.

Kozak shrugged and took a seat at the table. Nicholas placed the bread in front of him.

'Help yourself,' he said with a quick lift of his eyebrows.

'I think that's a horrible song,' Faye insisted.

'It has a point,' Kozak said. Nicholas glanced at him and wondered what Kozak really thought about the words.

'Where did you learn the melody?' Nicholas asked him. He did not know it himself.

'Do you like mules?' Faye turned to Nicholas suddenly.

'Mules?' Nicholas frowned at her.

'I saw these mules last week. A little heel, with a sort of

green-gold band across the front. They're lovely. Some people hate backless shoes, that's all,' she said, meaning that Alistair had hated backless shoes, but unwilling to mention his name.

'Shoes?' Nicholas said.

'Shoes,' said Kozak.

'Mules, Nicholas,' Faye began, with the small smile of a schoolmistress, 'are shoes with no backs. That you just slip your feet into. They were in Dickins and Jones. Just lovely,' she added absent-mindedly.

'Well,' said Nicholas, but he could not think of anything more to say.

'Right!' Gareth burst into the office on Monday morning, took a couple of strides towards the far wall and then turned, feet neatly tucked together, to Sean and Nicholas. They were sitting watching the screens with their backs to him. They had just been admiring Sean's new trainers, but as they heard sounds in the corridor they turned to the screens and assumed expressions of deep concentration.

'Well, boys, some attention might be appreciated,' Gareth said in a peeved voice. He sounded like a school-teacher, asking them whether they'd do that at home.

'Forgive us if we don't turn around, but you see thefts have tripled in the last six weeks. We are listening,' Sean said casually to the screens.

'And I am giving you special permission to turn and listen to me with your eyes. This is an exceptional case,' Gareth retorted.

'Camera seven,' Sean said to Nicholas and his eyes flashed to the rough image of a light-haired woman in a long dark dress who was advancing towards the camera, pixel by pixel, smiling up at it. Reluctantly they turned to Gareth.

'I wouldn't trust my daughter with you lot, if I had one,

let alone a supermarket full of produce,' Gareth announced.

'How old would your daughter be, if you had one?' Sean asked

'What?' Gareth said, a splodge of crimson on his face creeping to his hairline. He frowned at Sean and clasped his hands together. 'We are going to revolutionize store security,' he proclaimed, clearing his throat and tightening his tie-knot. 'Other stores up and down the country will be coming to us to ask what we did to achieve such a low rate of product-theft. We might even be asked to present a case study at the AGM.' He pursed his lips and looked down at the floor. Excitement scampered across his features like a frightened mouse.

'I realized last night that what we are in need of in this department is . . . *adrenalin*. Look at you both now, slumped on your chairs like sacks of potatoes and it's only quarter past nine in the morning. You get used to your jobs too easily, there are people out there actually stealing and the pair of you sit in here like old women at a beetle drive. Well, it falls to people like me to liven you up a bit,' and he lifted himself briefly on his toes and let his heels drop, with a satisfying click, back onto the lino.

'I am going to pit you against each other,' he announced. 'Nicholas, today is your day to steal. Sean, today is your day to catch him. Nicholas, at the end of today I will count up how many products you have managed to steal. Sean, at the end of today I will count up how many products you have managed to remove from Nicholas.' He rubbed his hands together. 'The last thing: Nicholas, you will need to be in mufti, so I brought in my tracksuit for you. It's in my office. I shall see you both at six to tally up,' he finished and briskly left the room, shoes clicking down the corridor.

*

'Have you ever noticed the similarity between the words fiancé and finance?'

Alistair stood in front of Nicholas with a red carrier bag in one hand. He looked Nicholas up and down, his face a tired sneer. Nicholas was in Gareth's tracksuit: the ribbed cuffs of its bottoms finished an inch before his socks started. He felt his exposed bits of leg anew and a pulse of annoyance passed through him. So far he had done quite well, having managed to steal a bulb and some wrapping paper, but he had been dreading an incident like this: meeting someone he knew.

'No,' said Nicholas, 'I can't say I have.'

'No. Well. Have you noticed that Faye, whenever she relieves her bladder, hums "Rhapsody in Blue" to herself? Used to drive me mad. Now it's the thing I miss the most.' Alistair looked puffy and red-eyed, suffering, no doubt, for his money. Nicholas noticed the stiff points of his collar, which seemed to push away from him as though they had a life of their own. They were standing by the in-store bakery where Nicholas, in a private homage to Igor in Budapest, had been stealing cakes and eating them, much to Sean's annoyance since the evidence would be safely digested by the time six o'clock came around. He put his hand to his mouth to check for flakes of pastry.

'How is Faye?' Alistair asked suddenly, brushing his jacket to one side and putting his fist on his hip beneath it.

'She's well.' Nicholas noticed the fine silk weave of Alistair's tie. It looked as though it had been made from the thread of exhibitionist worms. He found it hard to imagine what Faye had seen in Alistair. And harder still to work out what would have taken place had she not discovered his infidelity.

'Where do you live, Nicholas?' he asked, putting his hands behind his back and bouncing now on his feet.

Nicholas hesitated. In his stomach four Danish pastries settled.

'I think that perhaps Faye herself should disclose her address to you. I would rather not do it for her.'

Alistair lifted his chin in the air. 'I just want to see her. I need to talk to her. You can understand that, can't you?' Without waiting for an answer he brought the red bag around in front of him and folded the top of it over whatever was inside. 'Will you give her this from me? It's a mobile phone. I'm paying all the bills,' and he put the package into Nicholas's hands. 'Just tell her that I'd really like to speak to her,' and he strode out of the supermarket, overcome by a need to get out of this strange, depressing environment.

'I've got something for you,' Nicholas said when he came into his room and saw Faye sitting on the bed, 'from Alistair.' She put down her book and looked up.

'Oh. What is it?'

'A mobile phone,' Nicholas said and handed her the red bag. 'He said that he'd be paying the bills and that he'd like to talk to you.' Faye unpacked the phone. It looked like a laptop for a Barbie doll.

'Oh, cool,' said Faye. 'Where shall we call then? Know anyone abroad? Do you have anyone's number in the Ukraine?'

'No,' Nicholas replied with a brief smile and he sat down on the side of the bed.

'Oh,' said Faye, surprised by the answer to a question which she hadn't really meant to ask.

'What are you going to do about your family, Nicholas?' she said.

Nicholas shrugged.

'Do you want to see them?'

'I don't know,' he replied. 'If I knew that it would work out then yes, I'd like to meet them and get to know them. But it might not. My brother and I might be totally different sorts of people. I've had a life here, he hasn't. It would be terrible to finally find him and not like him.' Nicholas turned his doll-eyes to her and looked at the texture of her skin: matt and pale with tiny hairs, like a huge petal of a shy tropical flower. 'It's all adventures in the land of conjecture.'

'I see what you mean.'

'But I can't help but hope that I'd find him and my father alive and well, that they'd be happy to see me and we'd all actually like each other.'

'How often do you think about them?' she asked, stretching out her legs in front of her.

'Less often than I think about you,' he said and he leant over and kissed her.

'No, tell me,' she said. He looked into her eyes for a moment, examining the threads of green which ran through the hazel, like pondweed in a muddy stream.

'At least once a day,' he said.

'Oh,' she replied and she laid a hand on his cheek. They sat in silence for a few minutes, Nicholas quietly unlacing his shoes, Faye beginning to assemble her telephone. Nicholas did not want to talk about his family. When he was with Faye it often seemed as though his mother might still be alive. Faye's presence was enough to transport Nicholas back to the cramped streets of Bradford and to a time when he had not been alone, when he had thought less about his father and brother because he had had, at least, a mother to live with. As long as he was with Faye his feeling of dislocation eased. He did not want that to change.

'Why did you give it to me?' Faye asked.

'What?'

'The phone. I mean, if your ex-girlfriend gave me something to give to you I'd probably throw it away.'

Nicholas smiled. 'The thought did cross my mind,' he told her, lifting the hair from her forehead and kissing her there. Every bin he had passed in the park had made him reappraise his decision. 'I realized that my not giving you a phone wouldn't change your feelings for him. If you wanted to be with him, you would be, presumably.'

Faye looked at him for a moment. The look in her eyes made him feel he was the most attractive man ever conceived, let alone created. He felt her gaze roam over him, full of anticipation and delight. Her appreciation of him loosened his joints and made his insides hum. She peeled off the sticker that covered the phone's screen and pressed at the tiny buttons beneath it.

'However,' Nicholas began, 'it's one thing me passing on the phone to you. It's entirely another you playing with it as soon as I get home,' and he unzipped her trousers.

The next day at work Nicholas was watching a group of schoolkids when his radio crackled. 'Aisle four northbound, brown T-shirt,' Sean said over it and Nicholas half-turned on the spot and headed toward the designated area, side-stepping a middle-aged woman with copper hair who was just at that moment slipping a packet of chocolate buttons into the front pocket of her apron. His radio crackled again and Sean's voice returned as Nicholas rounded the corner and almost walked straight into her: a slight woman with skin the colour of clotted cream and hair like a jet waterfall flowing down her back. Her small red lips pouted a little, like the bottom of a red pepper, and she said 'Sorry,' quietly, and glanced at him with large, sculpted eyes.

'What fantastic creatures conspired to make her?' demanded Sean through the black box. 'What was the moon doing on that amazing night that her parents decided to mate? And what noises did they make when she was conceived?'

'Aisle six, southbound,' Nicholas replied, for indeed the object of their attentions, oblivious to her admirers, had spurned aisle five – canned fruit, vegetables, tea and coffee – and headed straight for aisle six.

'Can you make her drop something?' Sean asked over the radio.

'What, like her trousers? How am I supposed to do that?'

'I don't know,' he replied. 'But I have to talk to her.'

'Well, take something from the shelves and ask her if she dropped it.'

'But she'll see that I've just taken it off myself.'

'Well, take it from another aisle then,' Nicholas replied. 'She has a packet of Buitoni spaghetti in her basket. Get another one and ask her if it's hers.' Nicholas moved off, casually sauntering down to the other end of the store where Sean, tongue-tied, was watching his woman transfer her choice purchases into a red leather satchel at the checkout, seemingly unaware of his scrutiny.

'Another tragic and sublime love interest lost from under my nose. Why couldn't she have just forgotten *something*?' Sean said, shaking his head as she turned on her heel and glided out. 'Just one tiny thing?' he asked, looking at Nicholas. 'Why can't beautiful women be more forgetful? I mean you see them walking around the aisles with their handbag and their umbrella and perhaps a paper and when they get to the checkout what do they have along with their basket of upmarket I'm-so-single groceries? Their handbag, their umbrella and their paper. Why can't they just sometimes leave something behind? *Why?* How is it that they manage to have everything: looks and a good memory. I can't hold onto an umbrella for more than a few days and

I'm pig-ugly.' Sean stretched out his arms in frustration, letting his shoulders fall in a heavy shrug.

'Well, I wouldn't agree with that,' Nicholas said with a smile. He took off his cap and scratched the dent it made in his head. Behind them, in the wines, beers and spirits aisle, a nineteen-year-old man slipped two cans of Stella into his wellington boots and two into each pocket of his Barbour.

'What then? Gnu-ugly? Warthog-ugly? Eel-ugly?' Sean idly scanned the queues at the tills.

Nicholas laughed. 'Well, male gnus aren't ugly to female gnus, are they?' he said, pulling his cap back onto his head.

'What, so I have to go out with a gnu? Asian male, twenty-nine, GSOH, seeks cordon bleu, nudist female gnu for friendship, laughter, reckless marriage and tragic divorce?'

'There's no-one up there matching up the beautiful and the damned,' Nicholas replied.

'Tell me about it,' said Sean.

TWENTY-SIX

'I buy and sell things. Not junk nor antiques. The things in the middle. I am asking everyone in the house whether they have anything old they would like to sell to me?' Kozak stood in Nicholas's doorway, his hand resting on the handle of the door. He had dared himself to face this boy and now that he was here found himself spotting the differences between Nicholas and Bohdan. There were many. Nicholas was almost a foot taller. His features were finer, there was something fragile about his eyes. He moved quickly and often seemed not to be listening, becoming easily distracted by noise from the garden below or the sound of the doorbell. Bohdan had given things his full attention. Kozak felt reassured.

'Oh,' said Nicholas and he stood up and put his book to one side. 'Come in,' he said 'please.' Kozak took a few steps into the room and sat down on the bed. 'So you have a stall?'

'In a manner of speaking,' Kozak replied. 'Is that painting yours?' he asked, eyeing a picture of a woman in a bonnet which hung by the window. Nicholas hated it, found its thick Renoiresque brush strokes crude and cack-handed. It was the kind of image, he knew, that would come into his head when he was drugged to his eyeballs in an old people's home somewhere. It would probably be the image he would see at the exact moment of death. If he did it would certainly help him die more quickly.

'No,' Nicholas said, 'it belongs to Mrs Sten. I considered asking whether I could reframe it once upon a time, but I decided against it.'

'Like putting lipstick on a pig,' Kozak said. Nicholas threw him a glance and then laughed. 'You don't like it then?' Kozak asked.

'No, I don't,' Nicholas replied.

'I'll take it. I know someone who'll like it.'

'But it's Mrs Sten's.'

'Pff,' said Kozak, batting away an imaginary fly. 'I'll replace it, don't worry. Do you have anything of your own?'

'I don't think so,' Nicholas replied.

'The chair?' Kozak nodded his head.

'It's Mrs Sten's.'

'The cello?'

'Oh no, I need that.' Nicholas laughed. 'I teach music in a school. And give cello lessons.'

'So you play it?'

'I practise about three or four times a week at the moment. You'll probably hear me. I'm not very good.'

'I always wanted to play a musical instrument. But I have no natural talent.' Kozak held his hands up in the air.

'You don't need natural talent. You just need to practise.'

'I have a violin,' Kozak said suddenly. 'I bought it last month. You'll probably hear me. Would you look at it for me?'

'Sure,' Nicholas said.

Kozak returned to the room with an old wooden case shaped like a child's coffin and opened it to reveal a violin the colour of a brindled Staffordshire bull terrier. It had no E string and resin dust covered the wide end of its finger-board. Nicholas picked it up and looked inside: *Nicolaus Amatus fecit in Cremona 1651. Made in Czechoslovakia.* The date was fake.

'It looks all right,' Nicholas said, plucking the D string with a swipe of his thumb. 'But I don't really know about these things.'

'Hello,' Faye came in, carrying a bunch of anemones. She had bought them to cheer herself up. 'Oh, hello,' she said to Kozak.

'Just the woman we need,' Nicholas said and he kissed her. 'Faye used to play the violin,' he explained to Kozak.

'Barely,' Faye replied. 'In the end my teacher refused to teach me,' she laughed.

Kozak rubbed at his eye, beneath his sunglasses.

'It's a nice colour, that one. The bow needs to be rehaired.'

'Can you do such a job?' Kozak asked her.

'Goodness no. You'd need to take it to a specialist.'

'I think I might just sell it as it is,' Kozak replied, packing the instrument away again. Nicholas glanced across at Faye. She winked at him.

'I've been offered a job with the orchestra,' he said to her. That evening when he had got home from work a letter had been waiting for him.

'That's fantastic!' Faye exclaimed and still with the flowers in one hand she embraced him. Kozak wanted to congratulate Nicholas on what appeared to be good news, but as he stood there waiting it became clear that the two of them were not going to separate. He made his excuses and left.

Mrs Sten thought the house was too full. As she bustled around its corridors she would tut if she found objects not in their usual places – if someone had put the oven glove in a drawer and not on its hook, or if the telephone pencil wasn't happily in the hole of the telephone pad. She felt suddenly out of control – she couldn't possibly keep tabs on this many people – and every coming and going made this more apparent.

Faye, on the other hand, was pleased by the arrival of the

two old men. At least it gives this place some life, she thought, and then laughed at the idea that two old men, one in a ragbag suit and the other with a weakness for cocoa, *could* liven up the place.

Of everyone in the house Kozak would wake the earliest, get dressed hurriedly in his suit and head straight into the garden below, where he would begin the simple and lengthy routine of his morning exercises, bending at the knees, waist and neck and whistling sadly into the dawn. Some mornings Martine would curse and stagger from her bed when she heard his melancholic whistling, only to rest the tip of her nose against the cool glass and watch this large man bend and stretch with wonder. Nicholas too would creep across his room and admire the strong, determined movements of the mysterious man.

On Friday morning Nicholas watched him with his usual curiosity and with a touch of envy, for it was a fine morning and he too wanted to be outside. He sat up in bed and looked at Faye, asleep beside him and he bent over her to smell her skin. He left the room as quietly as he could, changed into his work clothes in the bathroom and headed out of the door before anyone could stop him.

The early morning sky was still white with moisture and the low angle of the sun cast long shadows across the stretches of grass. The park was almost empty apart from a few dog-walkers and joggers, the dogs chasing the joggers and the dog-owners chasing the dogs, so that, in the end, they all returned home with heaving chests and trembling legs.

Nicholas paced, his thoughts silenced by the brilliance of the light. He had no idea that his appreciation of this wide park came from his memory of the Ukrainian steppe, which he had last seen when he was four years of age and used to stick the ends of his shoulder-length hair together with handfuls of mud gouged from the side of the stream. There was no way for him to know that his eyes intuitively sought a far, low horizon because his genes had flattened his eye-balls and given him a tendency towards long-sightedness. The image of his own hand would form crystal clear some-where behind his retina, but he could see every notch and corner of the outline of a figure in the distance. He lifted his face automatically to the wind, because the skin on his cheeks was thick and felt no chill and, were he ever to climb onto a horse, he would feel instantly at home. When he walked through the park in London, gazing far ahead of him, he knew nothing of what he had inherited.

A figure approaching Nicholas in the park caught his eye.

'Good morning,' Kozak said, and he stopped in the middle of the path and regarded Nicholas with his blank, sunglassed eyes. This morning, at least, it was appropriate to wear sunglasses.

'Good morning,' Nicholas replied. 'You were exercising in the garden just now.' Kozak stood tall and straight, the sun's glare on his glasses occasionally blinding Nicholas.

'I stretch and then walk. Every morning. Particularly in London. Otherwise this city makes you ill.'

'Oh,' said Nicholas.

'Well,' he began and they started to walk. 'I am ready to leave the city now.'

'And go . . .?'

'I spent some time in Oxford. I might go back there. I need to get in touch with some old friends. Congratulations on your job, by the way.'

'Ah,' Nicholas said. 'Thank you. I don't know whether I shall accept it.'

'Oh,' Kozak replied.

'It's a job with an orchestra. It's very prestigious but you see, at the moment I teach and I enjoy that and—'

'I thought you worked in a supermarket.'

'Well yes, for the summer,' Nicholas began. His professional situation confused almost everyone he knew. Let it, he thought. 'But during the school year I work in a primary school.'

'Young children?'

'Eleven and under.'

Kozak gave a brief nod and paced in silence.

'I don't like children,' he said after a while.

'They make much better students than adults,' Nicholas replied. 'They're happy to make mistakes. They're quick. They have no guilt about having fun. They're affectionate. From time to time I get a good student who plays well,' Nicholas said. His hands moved in front of him as he told Kozak about his pupils. One day I shall have some young children of my own, he thought. At least four.

'It sounds like you enjoy your job very much,' Kozak said.

'Does it?' Nicholas asked.

Kozak nodded as he walked.

'Are you having a nice time at De Vere Gardens?' Nicholas asked him. David had told Kozak that he was welcome to stay for free and for as long as he liked. David hadn't told his wife this.

Kozak shrugged. 'It has quite a family atmosphere,' he said sardonically. 'What with Mrs Sten and Mr Sten; Martine and her child; you and Faye. But I don't want to outstay my welcome,' he said and he pushed his sunglasses up the bridge of his nose with the heel of his hand.

'Normally it's just Martine and Harvey and me. I mean that's how we've been for the past eighteen months now.'

'And no Faye?'

'Faye and I only just got together. And she's looking for her own flat anyway.'

306

'You seem very – well – what's the word – relaxed with each other.'

'We knew each other once before,' Nicholas said and so he told Kozak about his history with Faye.

'It was funny,' Nicholas said, 'because I was really unsure about getting in touch with her again after all those years – I mean I almost didn't do it – and look what happened.'

Kozak wondered whom he could return to, and he thought straight away of Beth. Not for romance, but it would be good to see her again.

'Do you have a –?'

Kozak shook his head. 'No,' he said. 'But I had a wife once.' He shrugged and looked down at the yellowing dust of the path. Over a patch of grass Nicholas watched a mother hide a beach ball behind her back from her small son. The boy looked from his right to his left to his right again.

'When I was young I knew a pretty girl too,' Kozak said, 'she had dark eyes and soft white hands and a fine character. When she was a teenager her father asked her to tie his tie for him one Sunday morning. She tied it into a bow tie which she knotted so hard he couldn't undo it. The village laughed for days over it. He had to bath himself in his bow tie. I didn't know her that well, but each year in spring there was a swimming race across a river near the village. The winner's prize was to ask one of the villagers for their hand in marriage and since the winner had always been a boy, the girls had almost all given up competing. I was the favourite that year – I was sixteen. Just before the race the girl approached me and said that she'd bet that she would win the race. She didn't smile easily, this girl, or not as easily as the others, but still I thought her bet a joke and willingly shook her hand.

'"The forfeit is to be decided," she said and took her place on the bank.'

'She won, didn't she?' Nicholas asked, rubbing his thumb over his chin.

'Hah,' Kozak said sharply. 'By over three strokes. I was second, but by the time my fingers touched the bank she was out of the water and standing over me, while the villagers stood around with puzzled expressions.' Nicholas smiled. 'She was quite something, this girl. I knew then that I wanted to marry her. She would keep me on my toes.'

'What happened?' Nicholas asked. He was going to be late for work. He hoped Sean wouldn't mind.

'As a forfeit I had to push a walnut with my nose from our farm to her farm. About two and a half miles in all, hands behind my back. My knees were raw at the end of it. I think you can still see the dent today that the walnut left,' he said and ran a forefinger down the bridge of his large nose. 'There was quite a crowd gathered at the other end to watch me nudge the nut up to the front gate. She was there too, standing with her weight on one hip, looking sceptical. Since I was already on my knees, I asked her.'

'Asked her what?'

'To marry me.'

'Oh,' said Nicholas, 'what did she say?'

'She waited before she said anything. It almost seemed like the sun could have gone down in the time it took her to reply. "Okay," she said finally. Not "yes," but "okay." And then she smiled.'

'And so you married her?' Nicholas asked.

Kozak nodded. 'Yes, I did,' he said. 'When we'd arranged to meet up somewhere I used to turn up early and stand across the road so that I could watch her and think who is that beautiful woman waiting for me?' Nicholas glanced over at a child on a bike. He didn't want to ask what had happened to Kozak's wife.

308

'She died when I was thirty-two,' Kozak volunteered. 'She did something that I wish she hadn't,' he said.

'Would you ever go back to the Ukraine now?' Nicholas asked him.

'No,' Kozak said, 'I won't go back.' They crossed a road and carried on, covering ground which Nicholas had walked hundreds of times before.

'What about you? Have you been back?'

'Not since I left,' said Nicholas with a shrug.

Kozak began to delve around in his pockets, brow furrowed with concentration, using his other hand to hold his jacket still. He found what he was looking for and unfolded it, a soft piece of paper, almost cloth-like in its creases, a severe and stern face staring out on one side: a five-Hryvnia note.

'Oh,' said Nicholas and took it from him, to feel it between his own fingers so that he could try, just through touching it, to understand its value. 'So what would this buy me?'

'Nothing,' Kozak replied, 'everyone trades in dollars. I can't remember why I've kept it. For posterity, perhaps.'

'Right,' Nicholas said, taking the note from him. It barely seemed real. He handed it back to Kozak.

'Keep it,' Kozak said. 'Have you ever seen the Dnipro river?'

Nicholas shook his head. He had no real memories of the Ukraine. His mind, however, had been filled with its fairy tales, with his mother's intricate tapestry of its interminable deprivation of how it was and the broad, flat Eden it could one day become, with its fertile earth, orchards and sweet, melancholy songs.

'It's a nice river,' Kozak said. 'Broad. My mother,' Kozak said, 'she lived through two world wars, a revolution, a civil war, three famines, violent occupation by four armies and ten years' imprisonment in Siberian work camps.' Nicholas nodded. 'The invading Nazis were greeted with salt and bread and seen as liberators because people thought that nothing could be worse than what they had.' Nicholas nodded again. As he talked Kozak's face had taken on a colour – a rosiness which lay over his cheeks like the fine web of a spider, wet with dew. Somehow, with this sheen on his face and an urgency in his voice, he looked like a different man, more ordinary, jovial and friendly. 'And Babi Yar?' Kozak asked, his voice dropping a little. 'Do you know about that?'

'Yes,' Nicholas replied. When he was a teenager his mother had shown him photographs in a book of the ravine where, in 1942, 33,000 Jewish people were killed in the space of two days. 'The Nazis were helped of course, that kind of killing is not easy to organize. We helped them organize the Jewish people, the gypsies and homosexuals, helped line them up, helped shoot them,' his mother had explained gently, for she wanted to give her son an education, but not nightmares. And what had Nicholas thought? He wondered why, given that his homeland's soil was so fruitful, new people hadn't been able to spring up where the bodies of others had fallen, bushes and trees of new life, a paradise of individuals, undeterred by guns and bullets.

'Okay, good,' Kozak said and he fell silent for a moment. 'Your parents told you that?' he asked.

'Yes,' Nicholas replied, not bothering to explain that his father had stayed behind.

'That's good,' Kozak said, 'they are good parents.'

'There is one thing,' Nicholas said, staring out in front of him at the mournful branches of a willow falling down to the lake's edge. If this man was leaving in a few days this might be Nicholas's only chance. He did not seek out the company of other Ukrainians. In the end living in the community in Bradford had got too much for him. 'If I were a sheep I'd live with the cows,' he remembered saying to his mother, who could not understand his objections. 'I don't really know about Chornobyl,' he said to Kozak.

Behind his sunglasses Kozak blinked. Nicholas, his head half-turned towards him, looked at the shiny, pulled skin of his scar and at the ridge it made where it joined the ordinary skin on his cheek. Made uneasy by his own question, Nicholas felt anxious to fill the silence which had met it. 'My family are from near there. Some of them were still there when it happened.' He said.

Kozak turned his head a little and caught sight of the boy beside him. He liked Nicholas. Of everyone he had met in London, Nicholas was one of his favourites. His friendliness seemed genuine, seemed as though there was nothing masquerading beneath. Nicholas was unlike Mrs Sten, who welcomed him into her home with pursed lips and a suspicious glance. Kozak felt, as he clamped his teeth together, a responsibility settle on him, an obligation. Chornobyl was a disaster which would not tax the imagination of future generations. Its effects would last for ever. It was a disaster for the entertainment age; had considerately constructed its own museum. Kozak could not honour the obligation he felt. Those who know no history get along, he thought.

'Neither do I,' he said with a brief shake of his head.

TWENTY-SEVEN

The first weekend Nicholas and Faye spent together they stayed in their room, unsure of what to say to each other. The second weekend they spent mostly in bed. On their third weekend together they went to visit Anthony Christmas. Neither had seen him for thirteen years. Anthony had gone to a technical college and then moved away, but he and Nicholas still exchanged Christmas cards. Yet it was Faye who brought his name up, one day when she had come into the supermarket and she tracked Nicholas down in the pet-food aisle.

'Do you remember Anthony Christmas?' she asked him.

Nicholas nodded and explained about the Christmas cards.

'I often think about him,' Faye said, letting her eyes scan the tins of dog food in front of her. It had been their secret at the time and both had kept it for many years. It involved, of course, the pies. Since neither Nicholas nor Faye could have afforded to buy a pie for Anthony Christmas once a week, Faye had hit upon the idea of asking her grandmother to make them. Her grannie would have baked cakes, flans or pies for all of England if she could. 'There's a war on,' she would say to Faye as she busied herself in the kitchen. Each Thursday evening Faye would pop over with a can of Butcher's Tripe and Stomach chunks in jelly ('For Pedigree Prowess') because it was the cheapest meat she could buy. Her grandmother would happily cut out some pastry, put it in a tin and Faye would drop in the meat before it went into the oven for half an hour. The dog food cost 43p. Everything else was free.

'I feel guilty about that to this day,' Faye said.

'He didn't die,' Nicholas said and shrugged.

'We fed him dog food, Nicholas,' she replied.

'He deserved it. He was such a bad viola player.'

That evening Nicholas telephoned Anthony Christmas. He ran a chicken farm in Oxfordshire.

'Anthony. It's Nicholas Beamish.'

There was a pause at the end of the line. 'Nicholas Beamish. Well I never. How are you?'

'Fine,' Nicholas told him. 'I thought I might come and visit you for the day. Bring a friend.'

'Who would that be?' Anthony asked.

'Do you remember Faye Peters?'

'Oh for God's sake. You're not bringing your instruments, are you?'

'No, no we're not. How about Saturday?'

Another pause. 'Aye. Saturday would be grand. I'll get a pie. We can have a bit of lunch.'

Nicholas almost laughed but realized just in time that Anthony Christmas wasn't joking.

'See you then.'

'He's not really going to feed us pie?' Faye asked on the train there.

'He is,' Nicholas replied.

'Well I won't be able to eat it,' Faye said.

'Well don't then. That's okay. Say you're vegetarian.'

'I bet he's planning on revenge. It'll be a pie with something horrific in it.'

'Maybe,' Nicholas said.

'What do you mean, maybe?'

Nicholas grinned and shrugged.

'Nicholas, what?'

'Do you know what he told me on the phone?' Nicholas said.

'No.'

'He has a farm.'

'You don't say.'

'And yesterday the vet came to visit, because Anthony's got a new calf and it needed to be castrated.'

'So?'

'Do you want to know what they did with the testicles afterwards?'

Faye didn't say anything. She stared at Nicholas.

'Thinly sliced, fried in butter with a bit of sage on a nice bit of toast. Delicious, he said they were.'

'You are joking.'

Nicholas shook his head.

'But what about the calf?'

'What about it?'

'Did it just stand by as someone ate its bollocks?'

'I suppose so.' Nicholas shrugged.

'I feel sick,' Faye said. They travelled in silence for a few minutes as Faye tried not to imagine what might be awaiting them in Anthony's kitchen. 'I thought you said he had a chicken farm?' She said eventually. Nicholas started to giggle. Faye leant towards him with her book and hit him squarely on the head. Nicholas grabbed the book from her hands and dived at her, slipping his hands underneath her top, tickling her. She shrieked and an elderly man across the aisle looked over at the two of them.

'We're too old to be doing this,' Faye giggled, pushing his hands away from her. Nicholas pushed back and they remained, for a moment, locked together, partners in a static dance.

The train passed through neatly cultivated green fields and small level crossings. Nicholas, after a while, took a drink from a bottle of water. He wiped his mouth on his hand.

'I've decided not to take that job with the Birmingham Symphony Orchestra,' he said. Faye stopped reading and looked up from her book. She frowned slightly.

'Are you mad?' she asked sharply, slipping her index finger into the book and closing it.

'It's not really what I want to do,' Nicholas said, dropping his voice. 'I prefer teaching.'

'Well I prefer staying at home, Nicholas, but we all have to earn a living. Why do you think I'm going to three job interviews next week?' Nicholas swallowed and did not reply. He did not follow her.

'What about banking?' she said. Her expression told him that she was serious.

'Faye,' he said gently. He did not want to argue with her. 'I'm a cellist. I play the cello. That's what I do.'

'You could play the cello in the evenings,' she muttered. He stared at her.

'I do not find money interesting,' he ventured.

'What?' Faye said. 'It's about a lot more than just money,' she said. 'Mergers and takeovers. What stocks to buy and in what form, what's happening to markets. It's very complicated, Nicholas. It's a worthwhile job. Or politics? You could go into politics. You've never done anything bad,' Faye said. She wished that she could explain to Nicholas what she felt, that he was throwing away an opportunity, but ended up instead sounding silly.

'I would have thought that would disqualify me,' he replied quietly. He wished now that they were not going to see Anthony but were at home, where he could at least roll her onto the bed and make love with her. When they made love they were good together.

'Cynicism is pernicious and immoral. It's the problem

with the world today, the world's biggest vice.' Faye gathered her hair behind her head and pulled, gently, at its ends. 'You could always go travelling?' she suggested. Nicholas shook his head. He had done enough travelling to last a lifetime. Not for him the materialism-dressed-up-as-spiritual-enlightenment trips to Asia and South America. He did not, nor would he ever, see travel as a leisure activity. Travel was leaving Calais on a child's plastic lilo one evening, hoping, like the first mammal, to climb unnoticed from the sea at Dover the next day. His was a self-righteous attitude, that much he would admit, but he could not shake it.

'I'm happy playing the cello,' he said to her. 'School's due to start again in two weeks. I can't just leave all my pupils. Even if most of them don't do any practice.'

'Well, I think you should take the job with the orchestra. At least you might become famous and successful and get on television. At least that way you're a *musician*.'

'I don't really want to go on television,' he replied stonily, angered by her implication that he wasn't, currently, a musician.

Faye met his eyes and shook her head.

'That is bullshit, Nicholas. Everyone wants to go on television.' She was angry with him for what she saw as a superiority complex. Nicholas did not think himself better than others, but he found it hard to tell the truth – that he didn't want to go on television – without a note of aloofness creeping into his voice. 'You mean you wouldn't want to be famous?' Faye continued.

'No, not really. Would you?'

'Yes.'

'What for?'

Faye shrugged. 'For the money. For all that fun, going clubbing, just having a good time.'

'No, I mean what would you want to be famous for?' he asked.

'Well, I mean, nothing bad. I wouldn't want to be famous like Fred West was famous.'

'Well, if you don't murder anyone I don't think you will be,' he replied. He was angry and upset. Forgive her, he told himself, but his soft heart was easily hurt.

'Wouldn't you want to be a famous cellist?' she asked.

Nicholas paused. 'I'd like to be a better musician. But anyway, I really don't think this has anything to do with you,' he added. He said it to hurt her.

'Really,' was all Faye said in reply.

They were silent for a while. Nicholas counted the fields that sped past. He did not want to dwell on what Faye had said to him.

'Nicholas.' She turned to him after a few minutes. 'I think it's really important that you take the orchestra job,' she said firmly.

'Why?' Nicholas asked. Their eyes locked: Nicholas's deep brown with Faye's pale hazel. He was waiting for an answer, though he had already decided that he knew what she would say. He would not like it and his face was already locked into an expression of stubborn disapproval. Faye was looking at him angrily, annoyed by the position he'd forced her into. She was convinced she was right, thought that the sooner Nicholas got a new job, moved out, bought some new clothes and had his hair cut, the better. *A musician* as a boyfriend sounded better than *a music teacher*. Nicholas, she decided, had not changed. His peculiarities had become exaggerated with age.

'Because,' she muttered, 'just because.'

The farm was a collection of modern-looking sheds around a small pale bungalow. A red Nissan Cherry propped up on bricks stood in the driveway and two large dogs were chained up beside it. They barked as Faye and Nicholas arrived, rising on their hind legs so their chains pulled taut. A small Jack Russell ran out to meet them too, leaping up at Faye's hand to lick it.

The big dogs were chained right by the front door so Nicholas and Faye decided to stay where they were – twenty-odd metres from the house – and wait for Anthony to show his face. Nicholas looked at the windows of the house, wondering whether Anthony would sneak a glance before coming out. One window was covered with a dust sheet. On the other side of it, in the living room, was a 22-inch flat-screen television, a video recorder and a DVD player, but Nicholas couldn't see them. The other window had what looked like furniture piled up against it.

'I see you made it,' a voice greeted them from round the side of a shed. It was followed by the man himself: longish gingery hair framed a plump freckled face. As he loped towards them his shirt tails danced about him from beneath a distended, geometrically-patterned jumper. The Jack Russell ran to him, tiny legs a blur beneath its body. Anthony sent it away.

'Hello,' Nicholas said. He smiled. Anthony Christmas seemed to have become almost twice himself; apart from that he looked the same. Nicholas felt glad to see him. He'd got as far as they had.

'Hello,' Anthony replied, looking at Faye.

'It's a beautiful area here,' Faye said to him.

''S all right,' Anthony replied. 'You two together then?' he asked straight out.

'Yeah,' Nicholas said and he told him what had happened.

'God, you took your time.' It was all Anthony had to say on the matter. And then, 'I'll show you round before lunch.'

Each of the sheds had chickens in it. Rows and rows of beakless hens sat in cages, weak-winged and blank-eyed. A few had lost their feathers, others slumped against the grills of their cages like deflated balloons. Anthony showed how he fed them, how he collected the eggs and chose those for slaughter.

'That one looks a bit sick,' Faye said as they got to the end of a row and a hen in the bottom cage half-opened its eyes.

'Don't talk to me about that bird,' Anthony said, shaking his head at the cage, 'she's laid a quarter as many eggs as all the other birds since I've had her. If she hasn't copped it by tonight I'm going to kill her myself.'

'What, and eat her?'

'You shouldn't really eat sick birds,' Anthony replied. 'I might sell her though. We'll see.' Faye looked pale when they finally got outside.

His pride and joy he kept until last.

'Behind the bungalow was a large, chicken-wire structure with a wooden house inside it. Anthony unlocked the large padlock on the wire door, sent the Jack Russell flying with a hefty kick and let them in quickly. A pigeon poked its head from a hole in the house and squeezed itself through, emerging with a shiver and a head tilt in their direction. Racing pigeons. The reason Anthony Christmas was put on earth. Faye covered her mouth with a hand.

'I hate pigeons,' she said, without thinking. Having journeyed to a farm in the middle of the countryside the last thing she expected to meet was pigeons.

'These aren't just any old pigeons,' Anthony Christmas replied, opening the door to the house and emitting a ghostly whistle. 'Just you wait and see.'

'I really think I should wait outside,' Faye said, backing away to the door.

'But you don't understand,' Anthony said as a bird came

319

to land on the back of his hand. He took a step towards her. 'He's as tame as a lamb. He won't hurt you.'

'Honestly Anthony,' Nicholas said, 'I think Faye is better off outside,' and she swiftly let herself out.

Anthony seemed disappointed. He showed his birds to Nicholas while Faye stood a few feet back from the enclosure and tried to stop her skin crawling. Most animals, she thought, were all right. Pigeons were a disaster from thrusting beak to mangled foot. And doves were just pigeons in overalls.

'This one is the son of Silverhill Zoro,' Anthony explained to Nicholas, indicating with a light raise of his hand, the bird that stood on it. 'He's my main racing bird. He's won six trophies in the past two years, haven't you, boy?' Nicholas looked at the bird. The bird tilted its head and returned Nicholas's gaze from the corner of its eye.

'Perry's Lagoon. Paid £32,000 cash for him when he was just a young un.'

Nicholas's jaw dropped. He looked over to Faye but she clearly had not been listening.

'Surprised you, have I?' Anthony asked.

'You paid £32,000 for a pigeon?'

'He's already earned it back,' Anthony replied. 'Besides, Dante's Comet was auctioned last month for £118,000. I haven't even got into the big game yet. But I'm getting there.'

'You should come down to Trafalgar Square. Get you a couple for free.'

'You don't get it, Nicholas. It's all about the genes. Look at his broad chest and nicely rounded flights. It's about the eyesign. You can't just make any old pigeon a racing pigeon. It's got to be in the blood,' Anthony replied. He shook the bird from his hand and they let themselves out.

'Do you still play the viola?' Faye asked as they sat down for lunch. She looked pale. They were eating in Anthony's kitchen, a square room with a window which overlooked the pigeon house. Everywhere was filthy: the surface below the window was piled high with dirty pots and plates; beside it on the top of the cooker stood a wilted pot plant and a collection of half-empty cans of dog food. Faye eyed them warily.

'No, do I hell as like,' Anthony said, pulling his sleeve over his hand and reaching into the oven. 'I was crap at it.' He told how after he'd left school he had gone to do a course in rural economy. 'I found it really hard,' he said, filling the kettle and lining up cups (he drank a cup of tea with every meal). 'I thought I might be ill in the end, I just couldn't work at all, so I went to the doctor's. They did a few tests and sat me down in a room by myself. Then they told me.' Nicholas met Faye's eyes without moving his head. 'It was the big C,' Anthony said quietly. 'Dyslexia,' and he roared with laughter. 'But seriously though, I had it all the way through school and no-one ever noticed. They just thought I was thick. Which I am. But I'm thick and dyslexic, and that they didn't know. So, anyway, after that I dropped out of studying and decided to cycle round the world.'

'You didn't,' Nicholas said.

'Down through Africa and up the Americas,' Anthony said and Nicholas puzzled over the route.

'I got as far as Morocco and decided it was a bit hard.'

'Just a bit hard?' Faye asked with heavy sarcasm. Nicholas glanced over at her, surprised by the bitterness in her voice.

'Well, you know. Came back and started working on farms.'

He produced, as promised, a pie and he placed it quickly on the table where the dish promptly burnt a perfect circle into the wood. 'There you are,' he said. His cheeks were pink and his eyes shone. 'Pie.'

Faye cleared her throat softly. 'What kind of pie is it?' she asked.

'Chicken,' Anthony said and he slipped a fork into his mouth, wiped it on the back of his trousers and set it down by Faye's plate. Nicholas thought of the sad creatures who lined the sheds around him and found that he had no appetite. Anthony passed him a plate with a huge hunk of steaming pie on it.

'Do you live here alone?' Nicholas asked.

'Aye,' Anthony said.

'No women in your life?' Faye asked. She had mustered the courage to split her piece of pie in two and was examining the filling.

'No,' said Anthony. 'I don't have time for women,' he said, with a mouthful of food. 'And not for men neither. No. I have my pigeons. And the pleasures of the palm,' and he wiped his hand over his mouth.

'I still play the cello,' Nicholas told him.

'Get away,' Anthony said.

'He teaches it,' Faye told him, speaking carefully. She had taken one forkful of pie and had turned it over in her mouth slowly, unable to swallow. Now it sat at the side of her mouth. 'Though he's going to join the Birmingham Symphony Orchestra in September,' she finished. Nicholas shot her a puzzled glance. She didn't seem to notice.

'Good for you, Nicholas. You and Ranjeet were the only ones who played anything that resembled music.'

'Or muzak, perhaps,' Faye said.

'I don't think we even got that far,' Nicholas replied, 'we played musuck, with the emphasis on suck.' Faye coughed loudly and put her hands to her mouth, rising from her chair.

'Excuse me,' she croaked and left the room by the first door she could find. Anthony looked at Nicholas.

'She doesn't like the food, does she?' Anthony asked. His eyes were sad.

'No, no, I'm sure she does,' Nicholas protested.

'Do you like it?'

'It's very nice,' Nicholas replied. And it was. Anthony Christmas might have been tactless, dirty and pigeon-obsessed, but he had a feeling for food, pies in particular. He usually kept a few chickens free range, but the newly acquired Jack Russell had taken to killing them all, as well as all the local cats, rats and mice. Anthony had just managed to salvage the last free-range chicken from the dog the previous night. He had put it out of its misery and plucked it himself; simmering it with a bay leaf, peppercorns, onion, carrots and potatoes for half an hour before carefully removing the meat from the bones. The pie pastry he had made the day before.

Once he'd strained the meat and the vegetables and put them into the pie base he went about making a sauce with butter, the stock, flour, sherry, lemon juice and pepper. To this he added just a few drops of the juice and chunks of jelly from one of the tins of dog-food meat, not as some half-hearted act of revenge, for he never did realize what was in those pies, but because he thought this secret ingredient of his made his chicken pie taste just that bit better. And he was right: it did. He could not be expected to know that Faye was choking on her own conscience.

'Is it really?' Anthony asked. 'I mean, I like it, but I don't normally cook for guests. Women, I mean.'

'No, it really is very good,' Nicholas said. 'I'd tell you if it wasn't.'

'I believe you would,' Anthony replied. He put his fork

down on his empty plate and sat back in his chair, as though eating was difficult and he was pleased with himself for having finished. 'I'm glad you came,' he said. 'I don't really see anyone from school. It makes you think.'

'I'm glad we came too,' Nicholas replied. He ate in silence for a while and wondered whether he should go and look for Faye. Somewhere a dog began to bark.

'That bloody Jack Russell,' Anthony murmured, 'if he's not killing something he's yapping away.' Nicholas nodded and chewed. 'He's desperate to get at the pigeons. I've told him, if he does any harm to any of those birds I'll shoot him.'

'Do you think he understands?' asked Nicholas, hoping he might make a point.

'He'll understand once he gets a bullet in his head,' Anthony said casually. 'Anything that threatens my pigeons is a goner. I shoot about one owl every two weeks at the moment.'

'The owls eat your pigeons?' Nicholas asked.

'Oh yeah. And kites too, when they're around. They breed them up in London – red kites – and then bring 'em here to let them go. Puh. I shoot them as soon as I can. I've lost a lot of racers to other birds.'

'Aren't red kites endangered?' Nicholas asked.

'Round here they certainly are,' Anthony replied and he laughed heartily. 'I shoot the foxes too. Never seen one take a pigeon but I know they would. Shoot them just in case. Badgers too. Poison works well with them. They'll eat anything.'

'Is there anything that you let live?' Nicholas asked.

'Aye,' smiled Anthony, 'me.'

Faye returned to the table with a pinched expression.

'Anthony, I've been meaning to tell you something for a very long time. It's—'

'– about the weather,' Nicholas interrupted.

'About the weather?' Faye said to Nicholas.

'About the weather?' Anthony said to Faye.

'About the weather,' Nicholas repeated. 'I thought you said you wanted to tell him that on the way here it seemed as though his farm had its very own weather, because all around it was rain but we had a patch of sun.'

'Yes,' said Faye weakly.

'You've been wanting to tell me that for a very long time?' Anthony looked at Faye.

'Well, since we got here,' she replied apologetically. 'It seems like a long time ago. You know what they say – time flies . . .' She stopped suddenly.

'Your pie's cold,' Anthony said.

'I'm sorry, but I'm really not hungry.'

'You don't like it, do you?'

'It's very good, really. I'm just not hungry.'

'Oh well,' Anthony said, rising from the table, 'Bo'sun and the Major can share it,' and he took Faye's plate away, cut the remains in two and disappeared out of the front door. Faye raised her eyes at Nicholas.

Faye sat in the minicab as it pulled away from the farm and closed her eyes.

'That,' she began, 'was awful. Did you see the state of his house? And his clothes? How you could eat that sorry excuse for a meal he served us I'll never know,' she said. Nicholas turned towards her, surprised by the vehemence of her outburst. Perhaps she feels unwell, he thought, or tired. Or perhaps the events of the past few weeks are finally beginning to sink in. He did not imagine he might be patronizing her. He was reluctant to believe that she could be so entirely heartless.

'I liked seeing him,' Nicholas said softly. He shrugged. 'He lives how he lives. He—'

'Oh Nicholas, how can you say such a thing? He lives like a pig, no, worse than a pig. He's fat, he's filthy, he's . . . just a brute.' Like a social Houdini, Faye had spent her life escaping her situation: a justifiable, understandable escape. There was nothing pleasant about poverty. She learnt that it was not noble to go without food, nor was it saintly to be cold in bed at night. Faye had had no choice over these things when she was growing up. Now, as an adult, she revelled in choice. The simple word *or* brought her a deep content. Excess and variety reassured her. She had seen how the rich lived and copied them, a master counterfeiter. She felt uneasy around people for whom this was not the case.

'Anthony's nice,' Nicholas replied. 'It's interesting to see what people do with their lives. To talk to them.'

'But the pigeons. The pie. Did you see how he cleaned my fork?'

'It was good to see him. He seemed happy. He does interesting things. I'm glad about that. Aren't you?'

Faye did not reply.

TWENTY-EIGHT

'Nicholas, come on. We've got to do it tonight.' Someone had left a set of car keys at till number eight and Sean had spent the whole of his lunch hour scouring the car parks and streets for BMWs, into the doors of which he would nonchalantly try the keys. He had, in the end, found it: a 3-series convertible in peacock blue parked round the back of the supermarket on a street of tall white buildings with pillars and sash windows. Nicholas looked up at the keys dangling in the air and then to Sean. 'Where do you want to go?' he asked.

'The seaside.'

And so they found themselves filling a bag with some food and a few bottles of wine and heading off to their temporary car after work. They had agreed to take two precautions: Sean had promised that he would drive carefully – 'I'll drive like Delia Smith cooks' he'd said; 'Oh, Jesus,' Nicholas groaned – and they had agreed to wear gloves inside the car so that if, for whatever reason, the BMW was fingerprinted, it would not be traceable to them. Since it was summer the only gloves they could get hold of in the supermarket were rubber ones, and so it was with garish pink hands that Sean took hold of the wheel and fiddled with the buttons on the radio. Once they'd settled themselves into the front and admired the moulded dashboard Sean slipped the key into the ignition.

'Ba-by,' he said, revving the engine.

'It's very clean,' said Nicholas, for indeed it was. The leather of the seats seemed never to have been touched and

327

the silver outlines of the dashboard features gleamed proudly in the evening sunlight.

'Company car, I think,' said Sean, 'so with whose company shall we fill it?'

'Whose do you think?' asked Nicholas.

'Well, let's see. Given that you've talked about Faye solidly for about the last week I would say hers, possibly?'

'Right first time.'

'Weren't you just. You've beaten all my records. Leaves her folder in Lost Property and you're in the sack with her four weeks later. Not only that, she's moved in.'

'She didn't have anywhere else to go,' Nicholas told him.

'She could have stayed with me,' said Sean with a smile. He manoeuvred the car out into the road and tooted the horn at nothing in particular. 'De Vere Gardens then to pick up Faye? I'm looking forward to meeting her.'

Nicholas looked over at Sean's profile. He had a peculiarly delicate retroussé nose, which didn't sit with his Yorkshire accent and straightforward ways. Beneath it his jaw sat heavy and almost too square, as though he might have filled his dusky cheeks with nuts and bolts. 'Don't worry friend, I shall behave myself.'

'Who would you put money on if you and I had to fight?' Nicholas asked Sean suddenly. They were driving along by the park and the pink summer sunshine fell down, through the trees, and caught, like the bullets of a sniper, odd sections of the car.

'Who do you think, you silly bastard? Me,' he replied and laughed out loud. He tooted the horn again, bouncing the rubbered palm of his hand lightly in the centre of the wheel. 'Now, who shall I take?'

'Who's in the running?'

'Let me see,' Sean said and accelerated out of a bend. They drove in silence for a little while, halted every so often

328

by the rush-hour jams. Nicholas looked out of his window and caught the expressions of people as he and Sean glided past in their fancy car: a few raised eyebrows, a few quarter-turns of heads. One woman stared directly at him and then frowned. It was then Nicholas became aware not only of the rubber gloves, but also that they were both still in their uniforms.

'My mother,' Sean announced at last. 'But she's in Hull.' Sean's mother was a Bangladeshi woman who had married a Yorkshire fisherman because that way, she thought, she would never go hungry.

'I see,' replied Nicholas. 'I can see if Martine's free. She's usually around in the evening. But she'd come with Harvey.'

'Dog, boyfriend or father?'

'Son,' said Nicholas, 'he's eight.'

'Marvellous,' replied Sean, 'the beach isn't the beach without kids. Yeah, ask them along.'

The sun gleamed in front of them like a siren, drawing them near, as they drove down to Brighton. Once they'd arrived they lay beneath it – Nicholas, Sean, Faye, Martine and Harvey – rejoicing in the small miracle of being able to get to the coast on a summer evening and in the singular brashness of the English sun. The beach was almost empty except for three men in suits standing nervously by the shore. Martine glared at them from underneath a furrowed brow – in her view corporate culture and the seaside didn't match.

She had a long, pale face out of which protruded her cheekbones, forehead and chin as though rising from the sea. Her hair hung limp and loose from her head and one eyelid hung slightly lower than the other, lending her face a curious asymmetry. She was, in the end, unremittingly plain and she knew it, but she had been saved by a brain which more than worked and an urgent desire to have a better life than her mother, who had never sat an exam in her life because no-one got paid to sit exams. Her mother ended up by herself with five children on a council estate, which dissatisfied her only because she rightly felt that most of the people making decisions about her life were less competent than she was.

Martine was old enough to have got herself a good education for free. When Nicholas had first moved in she had knocked on his door late one evening. 'Does my sleeping in the next room interfere with your radio?' she had asked with a lopsided smile. Nicholas had liked her ever since, though he didn't see that much of her.

'It was a hive of scum and villainy,' she said, talking of the large consulting firm for which she'd worked a couple of summers ago. She rolled onto her front and reached for a stick of celery. 'And you should have *seen* some of my colleagues. Never have I witnessed such a gruesome procession of verminous infamy. And of course, I managed to work for the worst ones. The last boss I had, the one who accelerated my departure faster than physics allows, was the worst of a woman and the worst of a man – a bitch and a bully all rolled into one.' Martine sat up and gesticulated with the celery. Harvey, beside her, was enthralled by a copy of *Viz* Sean had bought for him on the way down, fascinated by the swear words and the fat women whose nipples stuck out of their dresses. Martine, pleased by her son's sudden studiousness, hadn't noticed what it was he was reading.

'I thought you were going to say that they had stretch marks *and* a moustache,' said Faye.

'I swear, I can no longer comprehend how anyone works for any of those companies,' Martine said, eyes flashing, waving the celery in the warm sea air. 'I can barely even bring myself to pass their building any more.'

'And relax,' said Sean from somewhere on the ground, in a deep voice.

'No, but it's true, Sean. Being a halfway decent person and trying to work in a large company is like expecting a lot of deskwork when you join the circus. It's a faceless chrome vortex. Work is a stallion, and you're only ever a little rusty clasp on the bridle.'

'No, *I'm* the stallion,' replied Sean, 'but I do like the sound of a bridle. Did you ever do any teaching then when you were doing your PhD?' he asked suddenly, propping himself up on his elbows and peering out at the horizon.

Faye sat up and brushed the sand off the palms of her hands. She looked a little disgruntled, seemed to mutter something to herself. On the way down in the car Nicholas had told her that he'd turned down the job with the orchestra. He told her in front of Sean on purpose. He did not like conflict. Faye had shaken her head slowly and looked out of the window. She was furious

'No, not really,' Martine replied.

'I sometimes think I'd like to teach,' Sean said, squeezing an olive between finger and thumb. He dropped it on the sand and buried it quickly.

'What for?' asked Nicholas.

'Wooing women, what else?' he replied and dropped another olive into the sand. 'I don't know what I'd teach, though. The only things I know are how to spend ten hours a day in a supermarket and how to make up formulas for things.'

'Like what?' Faye asked idly. She was sitting up, facing towards the sea, throwing misshapen pebbles distractedly in the direction of the water. Out of the corner of her eye she could see Nicholas's square hand, palm down on the sand.

Just to look at it made her angry. She wanted to talk to Nicholas by himself.

'Well,' said Sean, 'take the formula for establishing the probability of bumping into someone where you live – a town, say. I suppose town population would be in there somewhere, along with number of acquaintances in the town and then I suppose a number of assumptions along the lines of the entire population moving around the town at a constant pace and in random directions.'

'Oh. I see,' said Faye.

'I have formulae for almost everything I do,' Sean continued, 'the number of months I should go out with someone, the number of times to raise a bid, the number of minutes I should wait for a bus, who to talk to at work parties. I count up how many drinks I've had. Then I subtract that number from five, and the number I'm left with is the number of years seniority that person should have on me in order for it still to be safe for me to talk to them.'

'So what's your formula for number of hours to sit on the beach in the sunset?' Nicholas asked, his head cocked on one side.

'Well,' said Sean with a half-smile, 'sundown minus current time divided by number of people times the tog factor of their combined clothing.'

'What's a double en-tend-re?' Harvey asked everyone. Sean jumped up from where he was sitting and crossed over to the boy.

'Let's have a look,' he said, squatting down. He began his explanations to Harvey in a lowered voice and then the two of them went to skim pebbles.

'Harvey's lovely. How old is he?' Faye asked, watching the little boy straddle a patch of stones and bend over it, looking for things to throw.

'Eight,' Martine replied.

'You must have had him when you were very young,' she sniffed. Nicholas glanced across at her, unsure whether the sniff was an intentional sign of disapproval. Her expression gave nothing away.

'I was twenty-three,' Martine replied, raising her eyebrows so that her brow formed into grooves.

'What happened to his dad?' Nicholas asked, all too aware of the possible mercurial landslides in family life.

'He was an artist,' Martine replied. 'Obsessed with death and mortality,' she said, shaking her head a little to emphasize her point. 'He did an installation in which he faked his own death. That was when I left him. He hadn't told me that he was going to do it and I thought he'd actually died. I spent four solid days in our flat, quenching my thirst with a bottle of vodka and holding onto my head with my hands, sick at the touch of my own tedious flesh. Apart from his obsession he had good genes. Strong, good-looking, healthy. You can see it in Harvey.'

'What happened to him?' Nicholas asked.

'He didn't die, if that's what you mean. He gave it all up and went into life insurance.'

Nicholas laughed. 'You are joking,' he said.

'Nope,' Martine said, shaking her head and sitting up. She gathered her hair behind her head and fastened it in a loose ponytail. 'Descending deep into the regions of thought where the monstrous vegetations of the sick mind flourish, there's some sort of justice in that, I think.'

'Does Harvey ever see him?' Faye said. 'It's important, isn't it, for children to have two parents.'

'No,' Martine replied. 'The judge refused to grant his dad access on the grounds that he was insane and recommended he seek the advice of a psychiatrist. Then, after the case, he went and bought up all his work.'

'Who? The judge?' Nicholas said.

'Yeah. And Marcus refused to go for treatment so hasn't seen Harvey since. Though I suppose he must be all right now. He married again, a woman called Sumatra who I believe is responsible for his proselytism.'

Faye frowned and shot a sideways glance at Martine. She looked down at the palm of one hand. 'Well, you know what they say. Behind every successful man –'

'Is a surprised woman.' Martine finished her sentence for her.

'Does it bother you that he doesn't see his dad?' Nicholas asked her.

Martine paused. She looked out at her son, whose mouth hung open as Sean's pebble bounced and bounced and bounced again, against the sheet of water.

'Yes and no. Two people bringing him up would be better than one, but only if the second person is, well, stable. His dad wasn't when I knew him.'

'Will Harvey ever meet him?' Nicholas asked, pulling his knees up to his chest and wrapping his arms around them.

'Yeah, I hope so. I don't really know how to prepare Harvey for that, though.'

The sun set behind a comic-book cloud and a chill crept around the group, who sat marooned like Bedouins in the long stretch of sand. Everyone else on the beach had gone home and Sean and Harvey, back from returning things to the sea, were sitting down talking about bicycles.

'I have more rural fantasies than sexual ones now. A sure sign of being over thirty,' Martine said quietly to Faye. The evening seemed to have slowed. Faye was becoming bored with waiting to talk to Nicholas about his decision. Her anger simmered and bubbled inside her. It would not go away.

'Hmm,' said Martine, taking a sip of wine from a plastic

cup. 'So you split up with that guy Ian?'

'Well, there's the thing,' said Faye, breathing out as she lay down on her back next to Nicholas. He turned his face to her so that he could peek at her familiar profile and imagined it as a city skyline, with minarets, forts and concert halls looming over dark, even earth.

'Well I *did* split up with him, yes on my twenty-first birthday. But I think that I forgot to tell him. You know when you've had a conversation so many times in your head that you're not sure whether you actually had it in life or not? Well, that's how it was with him.' Nicholas thought he heard a slurredness to her words and wondered how much she had had to drink.

'But can't you remember anything he said, I mean, if you had the conversation?'

She rolled her head slowly from side to side on the blanket. 'No,' she said.

'Perhaps you're going mad?' suggested Sean.

'I don't think so,' she replied. She rolled onto her front and tipped some strawberries into a Tupperware dish, placing one between her lips and tugging at the green starfish with her forefinger and thumb. They lay in silence for a while, as the sea rumbled and the buzz of traffic carried from the town behind them. The bottles they had arrived with now lay strewn around the blanket like defeated skittles. Sean was wandering around the three of them picking up these bottles, shaking them a little, holding them up against the sun.

'Right, there's one glass of champagne left for whoever wants it,' he announced as he sat down again.

'All of us, I think,' replied Martine.

'I thought you were asleep,' said Sean with a slow smile.

'I'll fight you for it,' Nicholas mumbled.

'What, you versus me and Martine?' asked Sean, 'sounds like you've had enough already. Let's have a quiz,' he continued. 'Martine, you're clever, ask a question.'

'Always tell a beautiful person they're clever, and a clever person they're beautiful, my mother used to say to me,' Martine replied.

'And what if they're beautiful and clever?' Sean asked, zipping up his brown jacket of his uniform. A breeze had begun to blow, curling the waves to a crest of white which stood out against the deep blue of the sky. Martine chewed the side of her cheek and looked to the sea.

'What,' she began, 'is the last sentence of *Ulysses*?'

'A manly trap, finely laid,' murmured Nicholas.

'If I remember rightly, it's about eight pages long,' said Sean.

'And the champagne goes to the beige man,' announced Martine.

'I'm in beige too,' Nicholas mumbled. 'And that's not actually the answer to the question though, is it?'

'No, no it's not. But does it matter?' replied Martine with a laugh and she tossed a handful of sand up into the air.

'Nicholas?' Faye wrapped her arms around his neck, breathing heavily into his ear. She clenched her jaw. He put his arm around her and rested his hand on her soft hip. He wanted to reach out for more of her. His hand tingled. If only he could touch her all at once. He could smell the alcohol on her breath.

'Let's go home, darling,' she said, unaware of the volume of her voice, 'your friends are a bunch of losers.' Nicholas raised his eyes. Sean was looking back at him.

TWENTY-NINE

'I've got it this time, boys!' shouted Gareth as he burst into the room and thrust his two hands down onto the back of the nearest chair. It was Tuesday morning, the day after Nicholas's and Sean's trip to Brighton. Nicholas was hungover, Sean was disappointed – the owner of the BMW had come in to collect the keys early that morning. Sean had been planning a trip to Epping Forest. When Nicholas got to work he apologized to Sean for Faye's words.

'It doesn't matter,' Sean said with a wave of his hand. A blankness in his eyes showed that he had been hurt.

'She was drunk,' Nicholas explained.

'Don't worry about it,' Sean insisted, 'really.' Nicholas had not known what else to say.

Once they had left the beach the previous night Nicholas had wanted to ask Faye about her comment. He had been unsure how to broach the topic. He had sat down on the low wall which ran along the seafront and dusted the sand from his foot with a sock. Sean and Martine had already begun to walk to the car, Harvey trailing behind them. My friends are not losers, was all Nicholas could think to say. He knew it wasn't right.

'Have you had a good time?' he said, slipping his foot into his sock and then into his shoe. Faye sat down on the wall beside him. She was slowly beginning to realize that she and Alistair had actually split up, that the life she had known, the beautiful, cared-for house in which she had lived, were no longer hers. At first being away from these things was something new. She had congratulated herself on her open-mindedness, on her flexibility. For the first time this evening she had an inkling that her new way of life was all she had.

'It'll be nice to get back to your room,' was all she said. In Nicholas's room she felt insulated from her concerns.

'Sean and Martine are not losers,' Nicholas said softly. He was embarrassed to be so literal, so unimaginative in his objection.

Faye sighed. 'You really haven't changed, have you?' she said. '*At school* your friends were losers, *now* your friends are losers. *You'd* be a loser, for fuck's sake, if you weren't so . . .' she trailed off.

Nicholas stopped lacing up his shoe and looked up at her. 'And why would I be a loser?'

'Because, Nicholas,' she began, 'you're working as a fucking security guard, you've turned down possibly the best opportunity of your life, you live in a fucking boarding house. And you're almost thirty.'

Nicholas stared at her. She stared back. He did not tell her that he'd taken the summer job to fill up his days, that if he took the job with the orchestra he would have the same problem facing him: long, empty days; that he lived in a boarding house because he liked to be around other people in the evenings. He was, though he did not realize it, in some ways jealous of Faye. She seemed to have managed to have left everything behind. No trace of her past remained.

'Do you really think that?' he asked her, brushing sand from the palms of his hands.

She looked down at the pavement and shook her head. She was ashamed at what she'd said and wished that she could take it back. It had come out of her mouth before she'd even realized what she was saying.

'No,' she said. And then 'I'm sorry. It's just that at times

I find you hard to understand. Will you ring the people from the orchestra and tell them that you are actually interested?'

Nicholas paused. No, he thought, I won't. He didn't say anything.

He stood up and held out his hand to her. She took it and they walked along the seafront in silence as the lights on the pier lit up. Nicholas told himself not to compare her to how he'd remembered her. He did it all the time.

'It came to me,' Gareth hissed, eyes bulging, 'at quarter to six this morning. My mind went white and I felt that I could see myself, lying in my bed as dawn broke. Like a flash the answer came – if I hadn't been awake I would never have caught it.' He was wearing a pinkish shirt today and his hair looked unusually bouffant, a good inch of space separating the top of his scalp and the ends of his loose mousey-grey curls. When his blue eyes circled and spun like loads of washing between blow-dried hair and skin-coloured shirt he looked like an aggravated banshee, wildly cogitating the mysteries of the universe. Sean yawned. Nicholas hummed to himself.

'Self-service!' Gareth announced, making a chopping motion with first his right hand and then his left, in time with the words. He brought his palms together and opened them like a book. Looking down at Sean and Nicholas he pretended to read. 'And in the beginning there were shop assistants,' he said. 'You see, so long as people can serve themselves, they can steal for themselves. Self-service is the cause of our problems. It's the bane of our lives. It's the pea under our mattress. Do you remember those old shops, where you would go in and all the goods would be lined up behind a large counter? And also behind the counter there would be an old man with creased skin and shaking hands? What would the criminals say to him then, eh, men? Ask him to pass them something so they can steal it?' Gareth snorted at his scenario, enchanted by his brainwave, by his personal revelation that he was probably one of the best store managers the supermarket would ever have. Suddenly he sagged a little and moved around to sit in the chair in front of him, where he pushed a palm across his forehead, taking care not to touch his hair.

'It's hard, you know, boys,' he said quietly to them. 'It takes its toll on me, this pressure,' he added.

'You do an amazing job,' Sean said flatly.

'Do you really think so?' Gareth asked, looking at Sean with a pleading expression.

'You're an amazing store manager,' added Nicholas gently.

'A-maz-ing,' echoed Sean, and he wasn't lying.

Gareth exhaled and let his head fall back against the green nylon headrest of the chair. He pursed his lips and patted his fleshy belly with a hand. 'Right,' he said, emerging from the tailspin of manufactured confession, 'how do we turn this store into an old-fashioned shop where every single item is handled first by an assistant?'

'Three hundred and fifty-three people use this shop on average every day,' Sean said. 'A lot of them young, attractive women,' he added for his own satisfaction.

'There are fourteen aisles and three counters, not to mention the kiosk at the front and the separate little wine shop,' Nicholas said.

'Exactly,' Gareth replied, raising a hand back in the air. 'I have two methods so far. One is to cordon off all the aisles and have an assistant at the end who goes and gets the goods consumers ask for, one by one. Consumers can see, but they can't touch,' he said and a lock of hair, tired of performing gymnastics on his scalp, lowered itself gently onto his forehead. Gareth flicked his head backwards.

'Method two, and this is my preferred strategy, is not to

let the shoppers in the building at all.' His blue eyes widened and he looked from Sean's face to Nicholas's and back to Sean's, searching for the rapturous recognition his idea deserved. 'We'd have some windows at the front and shoppers would submit their lists and then assistants would relieve their unsatisfied and unfulfilled needstates.' Gareth laced his hands together and laid them on his thigh, leaning back in his chair. He had done it, he knew. By this time next month he would have no shoplifting at all, would have stamped it all out and his store would be set apart as an example of how to run a supermarket.

'You won't be a store manager for long,' Sean said, adjusting his thick-rimmed glasses.

'No,' said Nicholas.

Gareth glowed with pride. 'Do you really think so?' he asked, seeing himself, as he formulated the question, in a navy pinstripe suit behind a large desk. He would have an accommodating, red-headed secretary and cups of tea and never have to deal with the public. Every part of his body yearned for the life behind that desk. Lord Gareth Mitchell, he heard in his head.

'Have you mentioned anything to head office?' Nicholas enquired, fiddling with the SSS patch on his breast pocket. It was coming loose.

'No!' said Gareth, 'we mustn't! They'll pinch the idea and say it was theirs all along. I think it's best to get on with it and show them what we can do!'

Sean became red in the face and coughed, covering his mouth with his hands and barking into them, with small forward rocks. Nicholas took the opportunity to hit him hard on the back.

'Aha!' exclaimed Gareth, 'I know why you two look so glum! Don't worry boys, there'll still be a role for SS Securities in all of this. Oh yes.'

'SS Systems,' Sean corrected him.

'That's what I said,' Gareth replied. 'Now, not a word to anyone!' he said and marched out of the room.

'So you look after lost property in the supermarket, is that right?' Kozak opened the cupboard in the kitchen that gave onto a brick wall and stared at it.

'Yeah, that's right.' Nicholas poured himself a glass of water and leant against the sink while he drank it. He had just escaped from tea with Mrs Sten, but since Faye was out he was in no particular hurry to get to his room.

'And how long do you keep it for?'

'The lost property?' Nicholas asked. Kozak, examining the hinges of the cupboard, nodded. Nicholas shrugged. 'For ever, it seems.'

'For ever?' Kozak turned to face him.

'Well, I think so. Apparently some of those things have been there for quite a few years – lost for ever, merged with the infinite, consigned to oblivion.'

'For ever?' Kozak could hardly believe his ears. In his world things – objects – belongings – were in a constant state of flux. They reflected, he believed, the fundamental physical laws of the universe, although were someone to ask him exactly what these were he would be at a loss to provide an answer. 'Who on earth would return to collect something they'd lost there four years earlier?' he said, although it seemed that he asked the question of the wall and not of Nicholas.

'Well . . .' Nicholas began.

'I have an offer for you,' Kozak interrupted. He shut the cupboard and gave Nicholas his full attention. Nicholas felt suddenly daunted by Kozak, with his sunglasses, moustache and suit. The thought occurred to him that perhaps the man was in disguise. Perhaps, thought

Nicholas, he is on the run.

'My offer is this: I will relieve the supermarket of its excess lost property free of charge.'

Nicholas smiled. 'How kind of you,' he muttered. 'You mean you'd like to sell our old lost property?' Kozak paused. Then he smiled. The movement cracked his face like a fork in hard earth. Nicholas found himself extraordinarily moved that Kozak had smiled. He did not know why he felt that way.

'Yes, that's exactly what I mean,' Kozak replied. Nicholas rinsed his glass in the sink and placed it on the draining board.

'I'll ask the guy I work with,' Nicholas said.

'Thank you,' Kozak replied. 'I'd appreciate it.'

Nicholas headed for the doorway and then stopped. 'I turned down that job with the orchestra,' he said. His face filled with colour for a moment and Kozak thought how pretty the two colours – the dark brown of his hair and the red of his cheeks – looked together.

'Ah,' was all Kozak said. Nicholas turned to go. 'And is Faye happy about it?' Kozak asked.

Nicholas stopped again. He turned back and shrugged. 'Well, I . . .'

'But you're happy?'

Nicholas was surprised by the frankness of the question. It seemed, coming from Kozak's tight mouth, to refer to the general rather than the specific. It was a spare and elegant question. Nicholas took a step backwards and then one forwards. His hands, restless and fidgeting, he slipped into his pockets.

'Well, yes,' he replied. 'Yes, I am.'

It was on this day that Beatrice turned into the top of De Vere Gardens, coming, she told herself, to try and talk to

Faye. She wanted to make it up with her friend. Besides, she hadn't seen Alistair for four days and she wanted to check that Faye hadn't seen him either. He had been going missing rather a lot lately and while Beatrice was usually too lethargic to worry about him, she did, on occasions, feel enough curiosity to get her out of her friend's flat.

A few yards down the street the De Vere Gardens cat, Hamlet, spotted her and ran up to her, weaving between her legs with a motorized purr and then, in a grand finale, shouldered himself onto the ground where he rolled from side to side and showed her his parsnip-coloured belly. Beatrice bent down to stroke him and just at that moment Kozak emerged from the house, on his way to Paddington to meet a colleague bringing some ex-army equipment in from Reading.

'Good evening,' Kozak said, with a lift of his chin. He looked at her, finding her luxuriously attractive, though slow to respond.

She lifted her head and gave him a brief, false smile. She was too good to talk to him. Another woman might have been frightened by Kozak, with his peculiar suit, sunglasses, dramatic scar. Beatrice had a lazy confidence which left her happy to ignore the strange man in front of her. She could not actually have defended herself had she needed to – she couldn't run or fight or even scream particularly well – but her peace of mind was maintained by a thorough misunderstanding of the nature of the crime: she thought that someone like this would not dare to accost someone like her.

'He is mine,' Kozak said in his two-dimensional voice. 'His name is Hamlet, he is two and a half years old and I love him very much,' and he clasped his hands behind his back and inclined his head. 'Unfortunately I have to go away, to go back home to my sick mother-in-law and I cannot take him with me. I have to sell everything I own. I am very sad.' Hamlet, revelling in his role, purred loudly and scratched his face against Beatrice's outstretched hand.

'That is sad,' Beatrice said, warming to this fellow and his mournful voice.

Kozak squatted too and ran his hand gingerly between Hamlet's ears.

'I don't know what to do with him,' he whispered, his face like granite, his balance impeccable. 'Sometimes I think maybe it is kinder to take a sack and some bricks . . . or else I turn him loose.'

'You couldn't do that,' Beatrice said suddenly, outraged.

'But is it kinder than turning him onto the streets? I love him very much, I want to do what's best.'

'Well, I'll have him,' Beatrice announced. Her life so far had been a slow and idle accumulation of possessions.

'Maybe I will try to take him back with me.'

'No, honestly, I really like him. I'd love to have him, wouldn't I, darling,' she said, addressing her last few words to Hamlet himself.

'But he is a rare cat. Maybe the courier company will let me travel with him.'

'Oh no, please let me have him. I'm staying in a large house and a garden, he'll be very happy.'

'But I think he is a lucky cat. Maybe he will be able to help my mother-in-law.'

'I'll pay you!' threatened Beatrice.

'Money in exchange for him, no,' said Kozak and shook his head sadly.

'How much do you want?'

'But he has such luck. My wife and I, we have been very happy together when he is around. Since we have had him our love is like a jewel.'

'Twenty pounds,' Beatrice announced, 'it's all I have in

my purse. Take it. I will look after him. I promise,' and she pressed the money at Kozak's chest, feeling the rough cloth of his suit and the hardness of his body beneath it. Then she scooped up Hamlet, who sat, purring and still in her arms, and continued down the road. Kozak pocketed the money and went off to Paddington.

Fortunately it was Nicholas, made restless by Faye's absence and on his way to the kitchen to fetch a glass of water, who answered Beatrice's ring, failing to hide his surprise at seeing her on the doorstep. He was less surprised, given the cat's nature, to see Hamlet in her arms.

'I've just acquired a cat, Nicholas,' Beatrice drooled at him with a slow blink of her large eyes. She had a look of cow-eyed privilege and a pronunciation and intonation which bestowed on her words a gloss of intelligence and reasonableness where there was none at all.

'Yes,' said Nicholas, about to explain that Hamlet was indiscriminately affectionate, a feline gigolo. 'Many a widow around the world would have died intestate if it hadn't been for cats.'

'I bought him from a very strange man. Actually I think he was Russian, now that I think about it, so you must know him. He wore sunglasses and an old suit,' she said, as though explaining that he'd been smeared with earwax.

'Ah,' replied Nicholas, 'Kozak. He's not Russian, he's Ukrainian.'

'Whatever,' said Beatrice and she bent over Hamlet, shaking her head from side to side and cooing. Nicholas paused. He didn't really want her to see the room he was sharing with Faye. He looked at her.

'Aren't you going to invite me in?' she asked childishly.

'No,' said Nicholas.

'I'd like to sit down,' Beatrice replied. Mrs Sten, who had been listening for woodworm in the living-room door,

346

crossed over now to the window, from where she might get a glimpse of this woman.

'The step's clean,' Nicholas replied.

'You rude bastard,' she said indignantly. Nicholas looked amused. 'I came to see Faye.'

'She's not here,' he told her.

'You know, I don't mean to be nasty, Nicholas, but Alistair said that Faye had never mentioned you ever to him. *Ever.*'

'No,' Nicholas said. 'Well.'

'Is that all you have to say?' Beatrice asked. She let herself lean against the door frame, inclining her head. 'You're entertaining,' she said. Sincerity, in this century, Nicholas thought, was like obesity: its proponents seen as indulgent and lazy, slow and self-deceiving. Satire was called for. 'Besides, she likes money, our Faye,' Beatrice murmured.

'People have to live on something,' Nicholas replied.

'She won't want to live in Borehamwood.'

'She won't have to.'

'Do you have ambitions?'

'Oh yes,' Nicholas replied cheerily. 'Being a wild, impoverished child from the Northern wastes I aspire to a good pair of shoes and a good bed,' he said. 'I spend most of my life in one or the other.'

Beatrice frowned at him, unsure whether he was joking.

'Can I come in and wait for her?' she asked. 'I would like to see her.'

'No,' Nicholas said. 'I'll tell her you called.'

'You're so polite,' she said.

'That should go on my tombstone,' he said with a faint smile. 'Or tin, for that matter.'

Beatrice leant towards him, Hamlet clutched to her once again, and kissed him just to the side of his mouth, so their lips overlapped by a fraction.

'Bye then,' she said.

'Goodbye,' Nicholas said and watched her as she made her way down the path and out of the gate, pulling it to with a slow bang behind her.

It was that night, as Nicholas and Faye made love, that Nicholas felt something slip. It was as simple as that: a joint out of place, the tooth of a zip misaligned. He lay beside her and tried to work out what had happened and how it could be fixed. It seemed that he had been watching a display of intricate shadow puppets, engrossed in the story, but suddenly he had realized how it was all done and could no longer enjoy it. He did not dare turn his head to look at Faye in the darkness of the room. He was terrified that if he looked at her he would feel nothing at all.

A fascination, perhaps, had been exhausted. Faye had returned towards the end of the evening and Nicholas had no longer felt he had enough energy to make up for their argument in Brighton. They had talked little, relieved when they could make love to hide their silence. In the morning he rolled over towards her and made love to her with renewed vigour, in an attempt to deny what he'd felt the night before.

'Good morning,' Faye said to him afterwards with a smile. She leant over him looking for a glass of water and as her breasts pressed against his bare chest and her hair fell about his face he felt the same peculiar dullness fill him as he had the night before. He resisted it. I am tired, he told himself. A lot has happened in a few weeks. Just because I am finally with Faye Peters does not mean that I have to feel ecstatic every minute of the day.

He climbed from bed and, naked and hungry, began to unpack his cello.

'What on earth are you doing?' Faye said, sitting up in

bed. She leant back carefully against the metal rail and watched him. He tightened his bow and sat on the side of the bed, drumming his fingers on the body of the instrument and plucking each string lightly with his right hand. A frown settled on his forehead. He began to play.

'Nicholas?' Faye shuffled her feet beneath the bedclothes in the hope that the movement might distract him. 'Nicholas?' she said again. He stopped playing, lifting his bow from the string and turning his head towards her. The blood in his fingers throbbed.

'What *are* you doing?' she said. 'There's something a little bit too determined about you sometimes.'

He looked at her. How could he tell her that he was trying to see if he was still human, if he still had anything inside him? How could he say: I currently don't feel for you what I did feel for you and so something's wrong with me and I'm trying to work out what it is?

Faye stared back at him and for the first time wondered if he was as sane as she'd thought he was. Wasn't there something just a little bit odd about him?

'I have another audition,' Nicholas lied. He had the day off work today. He was unsure what to do with it. He wished he could have taken it back as soon as he'd said it. It was the worst kind of lie. The kind that involved more lying.

'Oh, Nicholas. You mean you rang them like I told you to? That's great!' she said. She crawled across the bed and planted a kiss on the back of his neck.

Faye left to have a shower and Nicholas put his instrument down on its side, the bow resting neatly on top. He hung his head. His eyes wandered over his bare flesh and he stared, without seeing, at the dark hairs against the pale skin of his thigh.

Voices from outside woke him from his daydream. He

crossed to the window and saw Martine and Kozak chatting by the pear tree at the bottom of the garden. Martine had stretched her arms out wide and was laughing, Kozak was leaning against the trunk of the tree, his arms folded across his chest. Nicholas put on a pair of jeans and a shirt and headed downstairs.

He walked over towards Kozak and Martine and greeted them. As they replied he examined himself, as though watching a caged rat, for signs of abnormality. Could he still laugh? Does fantasy necessarily wither if it touches reality?

'I am explaining to Kozak the difference between public and state schools,' Martine said to him.

'Oh, I see,' said Nicholas. 'Well, they're not called state schools for nothing.'

'I'm sorry?' Kozak said but Nicholas gave up and listened to the pair of them instead. Martine talked well. Her explanations were clear and precise. Nicholas watched her as she pressed her palms together and moved them up and down to indicate how children were put into different sets. Nicholas liked Martine a lot but he did not fancy her. He could see, however, how someone could. Why then, he asked himself, do I feel more affection for Martine at this moment than for the woman with whom I currently share my bed?

'Nicholas?'

'Um?' He turned his head towards Martine.

'Faye's up there,' Martine said, bouncing her head up towards his bedroom window. 'Looks like she's looking for you.'

'Oh. Thanks.' Nicholas did not look up at the window. He paced around on the spot and thought how nice it was to be outside on a sunny morning.

'Well, aren't you going to go up and see her?' Martine said. She and Kozak were looking at him.

'Oh. Yes,' Nicholas replied. He cleared his throat.

'You could take her breakfast,' Martine suggested. Nicholas scanned her bony face for any sign of irony or bitterness but could find none. Martine, it seemed, had forgiven Faye for calling her a loser.

'And this.' Kozak held out a flower to him – a single marigold – though Nicholas did not know its name.

'Thanks,' Nicholas mumbled and took the flower from him. He would rather have stayed with the two of them and chatted about anything: how to remove limescale from kettles, the intricacies of railway timetables across Europe, the diagrams and labelling of self-assembly furniture. When he felt that he wanted to stay in the garden he realized that he was at least still human. He turned on his heel.

'Good morning, Nicholas!' Mrs Sten had been watching them from the kitchen window. She stood in a shaft of sunlight, a reddish sheen to her hair, the golden light turning the pale blue of her dress into an aquamarine. For a brief moment she could have been in her twenties again. Nicholas wondered who would look after her when she became old.

'Good morning,' he replied. He handed her the flower. 'This is for you,' he said. Come on, he thought, flirt with me so that I can feel uncomfortable. I need to check that everything is as it once was.

'Well thank you, Nicholas. You killed it for its beauty. How poignant,' she said. Nicholas stopped in the kitchen doorway and did not know where to turn. He felt trapped and thought briefly of the days when he had first come to live here, and he and Mrs Sten had sat awkwardly over a tray of tea in the evenings. He had never imagined that he might look back fondly on those days.

★

That evening Nicholas and Faye made dinner together in the kitchen. Nicholas was quiet. He peeled and sliced an onion, frowning as he rinsed the knife under the cold tap.

'Are you all right?' Faye asked him for the second time that day. She had been shopping that afternoon and bought a black and white dress with tiny straps and geometric stripes. Nicholas admired it on her. The colours made her skin look pink and soft.

'You eat too much pasta,' she said, placing her hand absentmindedly on a packet of penne which lay on the surface.

'You shouldn't walk with bare feet in the kitchen,' Nicholas replied. He had noticed when she had walked into the room that her feet were naked.

She blinked. 'You'll get fat,' she replied, and she picked up the kettle. He moved out of the way so that she could fill it from the tap.

'You'll cut your feet,' he said in response.

'Some women are like black holes. Once you meet them and get to know them it's impossible to ever escape them. Their influence hangs over everything you do.' Kozak brushed down his moustache and pushed a raspberry into his mouth at the same time. He and Nicholas were in Mr Samuels' garden, that evening, on fruit-picking duty. Faye had declined to join them. 'Then there are those creatures of the fairer sex who resemble the Milky Way. Creamy beauties whose presence reassures whenever you manage to catch a glimpse of them. And then there are white dwarves.'

'I don't know what white dwarves are,' Nicholas replied, exasperated. His fingers, working tirelessly in a pizzicato of fruit-gathering, were stained a deep pink.

'White-dwarf women,' Kozak mused, 'are women who are . . . well, white and very short.' He burst into laughter, a smile violently creasing his face, his torso bouncing and jiggling like a cork on water. Nicholas put his saucepan down on the ground and muttered 'oh, man' under his breath.

'And what about Faye?' Kozak asked into the soft evening air. 'Is she a shooting star? The moon? A whole spiral galaxy?'

Nicholas paused, resting his forefinger on a thorn, pushing against it gently until it snapped. He pushed the prick of it into his fingertip. 'Do stars explode?' he asked casually.

'Oh,' said Kozak, rotating his hand and letting a palmful of raspberries fall into the pan. 'Faye is a supernova,' he said quietly.

'Lemonade for the workers.' Mr Samuels appeared on his terrace, a tray pressed into his chest and sloping dangerously to the left, so that the two long glasses on it peered over its edge and eyed the resolute concrete feet below them.

'Thanks,' Nicholas said and rescued the glasses from their fate.

'You two talking about your homeland?' Mr Samuels asked with a smile.

Nicholas shook his head and handed a glass to Kozak.

'If you don't mind me saying so, you should capitalize on this opportunity, Nicholas. If you don't have no history, you don't have no future. Dead men made our laws. Dead men brought us to the land where we are,' Mr Samuels announced with a low shake of his head.

The three of them stood in the evening sunshine in silence. Mr Samuels was wondering what containers he had in the kitchen for the raspberries. Kozak was thinking of Mars, waiting patiently all these years for some visitors. As the lemonade hit his mouth he frowned briefly and licked his lips. In Mr Samuels' house lemonade came laced with a good two fingers' worth of Jamaican rum. Nicholas barely noticed and gulped his drink as the mongrel song lyric tenaciously circled his mind: Faye is a supernova, Faye is a supernova, Faye is a supernova.

Nicholas did nothing with the lie he had told Faye about a second audition. He did not mention it and nor did she. On Sunday, they went to the park, where Nicholas pretended to sleep in the sun and Faye watched other people in London and tried to imagine what they were up to. When early evening came they wandered back home, past the queues gathering outside the Royal Albert Hall, past the Ajestic. They bumped into Mr Sten in the hallway and Faye began to ask him about metallic organza, since she had recently heard that it could rust and her seamstress hadn't mentioned that to her when she had been working out her wedding dress. Nicholas excused himself and went next door.

'You need to tell her. It is unfair to turn a person into a dream,' Kozak lectured Nicholas, once he had established that Faye's star was waning and that, more to the point, she didn't know it. That evening Mr Samuels had deemed the currants ready for harvest and so the two of them were hunched over a sprawling bush, covered in outstretched tight clusters of red fruit.

'I know that,' Nicholas said. He felt that he had revealed too much to Kozak. Why had he told him about his feelings for Faye, when Faye herself didn't know?

'So you will tell her?' Kozak asked. Nicholas frowned and threw a bad berry over his shoulder.

'You have to see it from her point of view,' he said.

'From her point of view it's better that she knows,' Kozak replied.

'She had just found out that her fiancé was having an

affair with her best friend. Then I came along and distracted her, gave her somewhere to stay. Made it a bit easier for her, I would hope. Now I'm going to tell her that she isn't right for me either? It's a terrible thing to do. I've done a terrible thing,' Nicholas said. His anger came from himself and the situation he had got himself into, but he couldn't help it: he directed it at Kozak. They worked on in silence. Above them a child's helium balloon floated over London towards Kew.

'You can make it easier for her,' Kozak said after a while. Nicholas took a deep breath and unknotted his brow.

'How?' he asked quietly.

'Well,' Kozak began, 'you could find her somewhere to stay. Or better still ask Mrs Sten for another room that she can have once she knows. Then we could introduce her to other men. We could have a whole evening with lots of men for her. And we could get her a dog. A small dog. I think she could like it.'

If Bohdan had been alive and had met Nicholas, he could have told him. Our dad, he could have said, gives terrible advice. With a sharp chisel and a strong hammer he can remove a piece of skirting board in a matter of seconds. He can fix a lawnmower in a matter of minutes. He can tell a joke. But his advice is terrible. Had Bohdan been there he would have raised his eyes and laughed at his father.

'She might not want another man or a dog,' Nicholas replied.

'No, she might not,' Kozak admitted grudgingly. 'But at least you have tried!' he sang, standing upright and holding out his hands on either side of the bush, which cowered beneath him.

THIRTY

'She hasn't called,' Alistair said, glancing off down the aisle. He was in his dark suit again, which hung as tailored and sculpted as possible around his misshapen body. Beneath it was a pale yellow shirt and a gleaming grey tie, which was strangely foreshortened as it climbed the crest of his stomach. Nicholas thought he could smell alcohol. Suddenly the smell surrounded him and almost overwhelmed him, making him take a step to the side and inhale quickly.

'Inor?' Sean asked over the radio. It stood for In Need Of Reinforcements and made the pair of them feel like cops.

'No, no thanks,' replied Nicholas into it. He looked up at Alistair, a good half a foot taller than him. Alistair's lids hung heavy over his eyes and he blinked at Nicholas – a slow, uninterested blink which brought a slight frown to Nicholas's forehead because he didn't know what it meant. 'I gave her the phone,' Nicholas said blankly. Alistair didn't move.

'It's always switched off,' Alistair said. Still he stared at Nicholas, seeming to perpend his next move. Suddenly, like a weary and awkward horse, he sat down on the floor, body part by body part. His head bobbed up and down and he muttered to himself, interspersing his rambling whispers with musical groans and gasps. Nicholas summoned Sean and together they walked him to their office where they dropped him on a chair. He began to cry, peculiar half-sobs echoing from his mouth which he tried to stop by plastering a hand over his perspiring face. He was pathetic, pitiful, ashamed, lonely, desperate and drunk.

'I can't stand it any more,' he slurred, 'I just can't stand it.'

'Perhaps she doesn't want to see you,' Nicholas said calmly, dialling the number of the house, the number he had kept in his wallet, copied down furtively from Faye's CV all those weeks ago. There was no reply. Alistair laid his head on the table and rested a hand over his eyes.

'If you put your ear to our desk you can hear the sounds of the forest,' said Sean, idly scanning the screens in front of him. 'JCBs, small animals screaming, the crash of trees.'

'I miss her,' Alistair mumbled.

'I'm going to call a cab for you now. I hope you have some money,' Nicholas told him.

'Have you felt it, Nicholas? In bed, she's so loving,' Alistair murmured. 'I didn't want to hurt her. It wasn't supposed to . . . I've been tricked. He tricked me, the bastard.'

'We'll have Ricki Lake in here in a minute,' Sean said with a raise of his eyes. 'Late afternoon confessions of a drunken banker, the pros and cons of claret therapy.'

'A cab's coming to pick him up,' Nicholas said. He felt uncomfortable about what Alistair had said.

'I didn't mean it,' Alistair drawled, 'I thought she'd . . .'

'It seems that life's novelty helium balloon has floated limply back down to earth,' Sean said.

'Oh, that's what it was he kept reminding me of,' Nicholas replied.

'I've been a fool,' Alistair said and he opened his mouth like a fish. For one horrible moment Nicholas thought that he was going to be sick, but he shut it again and took a deep breath. 'Joggy told me that she was having an affair and I believed him. I wanted to get back at her. Joggy told me last night that he'd got his facts wrong.'

'Ah,' said Nicholas.

'Please, Nicholas, you have to tell her to call me.'

'Leave her alone, Alistair. She doesn't want to be with you,' Nicholas replied. He sat and listened to Alistair's groans and snorts, as underneath the fluorescent lights Alistair's skin slowly sweated.

It was Wednesday night. Faye had gone out to meet up with a friend from university who was about to go off travelling around Asia. Nicholas had returned to his room and played his cello, relieved to see that Hamlet, the cat, was back in residence at De Vere Gardens when he got home from work. Towards nine o'clock hunger drove him down to the kitchen where Kozak was cooking buckwheat. Nicholas had recognized the smell and guessed that only Kozak would cook buckwheat.

'Good evening sir!' Kozak announced when Nicholas came in.

'Hi,' Nicholas smiled. He opened the fridge and tried to remember which carton of milk belonged to him.

'Are you hungry? You're welcome to share this with me,' Kozak said, and Nicholas was surprised by the friendliness of a man who had once seemed so aloof. Kozak dished out the food onto two plates and placed them on the table. Nicholas was intrigued that Kozak added nothing to the buckwheat. It steamed alone on the plate like a pile of rubble. They sat down to eat together.

'And how is Faye?' Kozak asked through a mouthful of food. Nicholas turned his fork between his finger and thumb.

'It's not getting any better,' he mumbled. His face reddened slightly; he dropped his eyes. 'But I don't like to be alone.'

Kozak was startled by such an admission. He sat back from the table and placed his hands on his thighs. It seemed that this boy had a softness to him, a tender vulnerability which he was willing to let others see. Kozak did not look upon this characteristic as a weakness. On the contrary, he looked over at Nicholas's hand, lying loosely curled on the tablecloth, and thought: where does he get the courage to say such a thing?

'Sometimes it is easier to be alone,' he said quietly. He had spent many years alone. Watching his son die had taught him that companionship and attachment came at a price. He was not prepared to pay that price ever again. The only people in his life for whom he told himself he cared were Beth and David, and even then, not that much.

'In what way?' Nicholas asked, raising his large eyes to meet the lenses of Kozak's sunglasses. He was grateful now for the man's eccentricities. He did not want to see his eyes. Kozak inhaled and exhaled. Each breath seemed to take a long time as his large chest rose and fell. His mouth twitched.

'Life is simpler by yourself,' he began. He pressed his teeth together. He did not like to hear himself say such things. He believed what he said, and to share his outlook on life was also to violate it. He reached for the red shoes and wondered whether Nicholas had been teased as a boy because of his eyes. They were so delicate and brown, it seemed at times as though he was unable to hide anything: fear, anxiety, affection, laughter – all glinted in there like gold in a riverbed. Kozak often thought when he looked at Nicholas's eyes that he must be imagining things: they are just eyes, he told himself, he uses them to see.

'I can understand that,' Nicholas replied. 'I can understand that it might be simpler. But is it better? Is it actually better by yourself?' he asked in a low voice. He picked up a teaspoon from the table and pressed it into the palm of his left hand, looking at the distorted reflection of his head and the kitchen cupboards behind it.

Kozak pressed his lips together and put his hands palm down on the table.

'You do not have to care for anyone, and they do not have to care for you. When there are reports of train crashes on the news and they put up emergency numbers to call, you don't have to worry. There is no-one for you to hurt. And no-one to hurt you,' he said. 'Have you seen Mr Samuels today?' he asked.

Nicholas sat back in his chair and replaced the spoon on the table. 'No, no I haven't,' he replied. He wondered whether he had said something to upset Kozak.

'He's probably out there now sowing seeds. And by the time it is the morning there will be fruit everywhere. He could plant a pig's ear and a fruit tree would grow,' Kozak said and let out a brief laugh, old air pushed from the back of his throat.

'I hope I didn't say anything wrong,' Nicholas said. Kozak looked up at him in surprise and caught him looking straight back. There it was, that softness again. That crazy, strange, almost kamikaze courage.

'No,' he said instinctively. 'No, you haven't,' he answered properly. He felt exposed by Nicholas, wrong-footed. How could a bandit from the mountains be thrown off balance by a young Englishman?

'I don't understand how what you say can be true,' Nicholas continued. 'How can you live without people? Do you keep them away from you so you can control them?' he asked gently, almost breathlessly.

Please stop, Kozak thought. He is like a bird tugging a worm from the earth. The intensity of Nicholas made him think back to when he had first met his wife and she would turn to him from time to time and ask him, with an alarmed look in her eyes, what he thought life would be like in the desert. I don't know, he'd reply. But can you imagine? she'd ask. He would try, he really would but he couldn't imagine life in a desert. He'd never been to a desert, knew nothing about them. His wife would look at him with wild eyes as she willed him to imagine what she could see. At times it became too much for him.

'People have different reasons for being alone. I have my reasons,' he said, brushing down the side of his moustache with a knuckle. 'In an ideal world I wouldn't have that reason. What I am telling you is that it is not as bad as you might imagine. It's like being scared of the dark. The fear is of the *idea* and not of the actual thing itself.'

'I would like,' Nicholas began, clasping his hands together in front of him, 'to have ten sisters.' He shifted a little in his chair and folded his arms to hide his trembling hands. 'I would like ten sisters and ten brothers. I would like two parents and four grandparents to talk with. Three nieces and three nephews to crawl all over me. Some aunts and uncles. A rude, mad aunt who might offend everyone in the family. I want sisters who are younger than me and older than me. Some who can tell me how it is to have children and others who are still children themselves and who can remind me how it was to have an exam at school in the morning. I want all these people,' he said, his eyes glinting like gin, 'around me in a large kitchen where we will cook and laugh.'

He looked fiercely at Kozak and instantly regretted what he had said. The man wouldn't understand it, Nicholas knew. He would not realize what it was that he had heard, what it was that Nicholas had laid out before him. He would shrug, pulse his eyebrows, toss Nicholas's dream aside like the day's newspaper.

Kozak regarded Nicholas. He didn't say anything. While Nicholas had been speaking Kozak had seen his vision more clearly than Nicholas had ever seen it himself. Now, in the silence, the animated group lingered in his head, unwilling to disperse. Still he didn't speak.

What have I said this time, Nicholas thought and realized, like a blow to the stomach, that it could have been anything he'd mentioned. Sisters, brothers, parents, children, Kozak could have lost any of them. He cursed himself for his insensitivity and felt ashamed for his indulgence. He frowned.

'Being alone is not so bad,' Kozak said finally.

'It's not as bad as I might imagine,' Nicholas said. Kozak waited for another attack on his argument. This time it did not come. They were silent. Nicholas pressed the thumb of his left hand against a finger, feeling the rough skin on his fingertip. Kozak listened to the traffic noise from the street. A noise which, in London, was hard to escape.

'And so!' Kozak said after a few minutes, clapping his hands together. 'I am going to track down Mr Samuels and find out what is in store for tomorrow evening. I am going to a market in Edgware at the weekend and could sell some of his fruit for him.' He rose from his chair and paused, unsure whether to make some reference to their conversation. He cleared up the dishes, washing them briskly, almost flinging them into the drying rack. The large chopping knife – a six-inch steel blade – he stabbed into the chopping board which lay on the side. Nicholas took it as a sign of aggression. Kozak stored his knives in this way because he thought it was practical.

'Bye then,' he said, clenching a hand into a fist and unclenching it again.

'Yeah,' Nicholas replied. 'Bye.' Kozak turned his back and headed for the kitchen door.

'I'll see you tomorrow for the fruit picking then,' Nicholas called. Kozak raised his hand in the air but didn't turn around.

'For sure,' he called. He really doesn't like being left alone, he thought to himself. Nicholas watched the man walk to the door and close it heavily behind him. He picked the spoon up from the table and slipped his thumb into its dip. He had been aware of the fact that he lacked a role model when he was growing up. Now, in his late twenties, he thought himself too old for such things. He did not watch Kozak leave and think the man his hero.

He had not dared to ask Kozak what it was that had made him live his life alone. As he sat there fiddling with the spoon he imagined a heavy grey cloud which hung over Kozak's past: departures, illness, murder, addiction. Nicholas would not ask him. But despite whatever it was that he had been through he still lived, and if he was to be believed, lived well. Nicholas replaced the spoon on the table and stood up. He looked to the window, at his ghostly reflection in the dark glass. I shall live how he lives, he thought to himself. It will not be as bad as I imagine it to be.

By the time Faye came back that night Nicholas was already in bed, the lights out. Faye tried her best to be quiet but she had drunk rather a lot of gin and stumbled, halfway across the room, over the leg of the chair. Nicholas opened his eyes and did not move. His feeling of unease did not develop gradually. He was impulsive when it came to people, feeling his way around them until he found an area that gave, like a loose brick in a wall, against which he could push and see things that might otherwise remain hidden.

Tonight, as he lay in bed, he realized that he did not particularly like Faye. She was not the woman he dreamed of or imagined her to be and this conclusion chilled his insides with a slow-moving, heavy disappointment. Had he been mistaken all those years ago? Or had what he looked for changed? With the disappointment came an accusatory guilt. How can you lie here and think these things? he asked himself. You should get out of this bed and declare what you feel. You are a fraud, a snake, a coward. You are lying to her, screamed a voice in his head.

He listened to her creep to the window and drop her bag on the floor. It was followed by her jacket, her top, the rest of her clothes. Nicholas watched her in the half-light, a shadowy form defined more by the noises she made than by what he could see. She climbed into bed and he smelt alcohol and smoke, felt a coldness to her body. He did not move.

THIRTY-ONE

When Nicholas crossed the park that Friday evening, a grey cloud hanging above him, he made his decision about Faye. It was not, in the words of competition judges the world over, an easy decision. His instinct deserted him; left him lost. Permutations and possibilities filled his brain and yet he was none the wiser. When he sat down for tea with Mrs Sten that evening he asked her whether he could rent the remaining spare room in the house. She blinked at him and pursed her lips.

'Instead of your current room? You should have told me, Nicholas, if you didn't like your room. You've been in it for such a long time.'

'No, no. As well as. I – er – I would like to rent it, on a short-term basis, for Faye.'

'Oh,' said Mrs Sten and frowned. She gazed down at the cream teapot in front of her and pretended to consider his words. In truth she was prodding and prying with her mind, looking for an explanation for Nicholas's request. She pushed her eyebrows upwards in sympathy.

'Are you not getting along as well as you might?' she asked. Satisfaction spread across her face.

'I don't mean to be rude, Mrs Sten, but I'd rather not answer that question. Can we get back to the room? Can I rent it?'

'I'm not entirely sure that I want Faye as a lodger,' she replied.

'Just for one week. Can I rent it for a week?' Nicholas put his teacup down onto the coffee table with a clatter. He was losing his patience. In his head he had already begun to dress the room for Faye: a vase of flowers (he didn't know which kind but thought they should last as long as possible. Nothing to remind her that beautiful things die. Perhaps plastic ones?). A few pictures on the walls which Kozak could lend him. Some books and a television set for company. And of course the cat, curled up asleep on her bed.

'I shall let you know in due course,' Mrs Sten replied primly. While Nicholas's violent replacement of his cup had, in her eyes, reinforced his masculinity she objected to her Worcester china being treated in such a way.

'Plain English would be better,' Nicholas replied. 'Is it a yes or a no?'

Mrs Sten met his eyes but she looked through him. She tried to see the renting of a room to Faye in terms of a chess move: tried to imagine far-reaching, unforeseeable consequences. In the pressure of making a decision she gave in to Nicholas in the hope that it would make him like her more.

'Okay,' she breathed. 'That's fine. For one week.'

'Thank you,' Nicholas replied.

Nicholas crept up the stairs and slowly opened the door to the room he was renting for Faye. It smelt musty and made Nicholas think of old people. He opened the window and, hands on hips, looked around, wondering how to improve it. What am I doing? he asked himself, but did not have time to answer the question. He slipped back through the door and down the stairs. He went out.

When Nicholas got back he went to his room. Faye was sitting on his bed. He suddenly thought that she must be able to see from his face what was going through his mind. He took in the chaos of his room and felt a hopeless sadness descend. A roll of Sellotape lay on the floor in front of him, beside it the day's newspaper, next to that a light bulb, a pair of scissors and tub of vitamins. Nicholas had encouraged Faye to make a mess and take over his room. Few things cheered him more than to return from work and find her there, a book face down on the bed, her wallet and old bus tickets on the chest of drawers, sheets of newspaper stepping-stoned across the floor. Had he grown up with a brother other people's mess would probably have annoyed him. Instead it thrilled him.

'Hi,' he said nervously. He smiled too much.

'Hello,' Faye replied. She did not ask him about his day. She did not want to know about his days as a security guard. Regardless of Nicholas's attitude to his job it depressed her.

Nicholas suggested they go for a walk. It was a Friday night in August. He imagined that Faye would, in the long term, take what he had to tell her in her stride. He did not flatter himself. Still he had to fight to keep the words in his mouth until they reached a suitable place for a discussion. They left the house and walked up De Vere Gardens and on to the park. As they approached the lake he began.

'Look, Faye, I've done a terrible thing.' His breath seemed hot in his mouth. He trembled.

'Had sex with Mrs Sten?'

He paused. 'This isn't right. I'm not right. You're not right. I was confused. We can't be sixteen again.'

Faye stopped in her tracks and looked at him. Nicholas wished he could look away. He saw only one thing in her face: hurt. Her irises glinted like pebbles at the sea's edge, smarting and bright from salt water. He wanted to cry, for her and for himself, because of the exile that awaited him.

'I'm sorry,' he murmured. *I have to listen to my heart. I have to learn that my mother will not come back.* She frowned.

'I love you,' she said. She didn't, but she imagined that

367

she did. She liked the idea of Nicholas. She liked him in theory. In practice, she would have often found him irritating and embarrassing. His fingers were too active, his eyes too large, his sense of self, his convictions too much for her.

'I love you too,' he duplicated, 'but not . . .'

'Platonically. You love me *platonically*,' she whispered.

'I'm sorry,' he said again. If she made him explain why, he would have to clutch at straws; each and every one of them would hurt her.

Don't leave me to this, Faye thought. Please don't leave me to face what has happened. To accept that my ex-fiancé had an affair with my best friend and I currently have no home and no job.

'I've got a room ready for you,' Nicholas gabbled, feeling his skin tighten as he heard himself in his head. He sounded, he realized, like the proprietor of an unpopular hotel. 'It's just – you're welcome to stay in my room but I thought you might not want to, so the room across the hall, you can stay there as long as you need to,' he said. The silence that followed his announcement felt as though it was being injected into him: at first he felt nothing much but as the seconds passed something inside him began to hurt and hurt. 'I'd like to stay friends with you,' he said quietly. 'You're important to me.'

'But not that important,' Faye replied.

If Nicholas had been honest with her he would have opened his soft mouth and told her: they have made a monster of you, Faye. You care for nothing but trifles, your attention, your emotions, your energies, your *very being* concerns itself with nothing but a deadly sheen. Can you not see that? You live in a house with a man full of stories and you talk to him of the shoes you hope to buy in the summer sales.

Nicholas called an abrupt halt to his internal tirade.

'You're a mess, aren't you?' Faye said.

They began to walk back to the house; someone approaching from the other direction could have passed between them.

'You know, an old boyfriend once told me that you should always have something in reserve. He said I should tell someone they look nice when they look beautiful, just in case they look even better the next day. That's what you always were, Nicholas. You were my reserve.'

Nicholas didn't reply. He gazed up the road at a bus approaching them and imagined, for a moment, that the pair of them might throw themselves under it.

'You've got me out of your system, is that it? It's not the catch, it's the thrill of the chase,' Faye continued. The bus passed and they crossed the road in the dirty air it left behind. For a moment Nicholas briefly lost her among the crowds outside the Albert Hall, but as soon as he'd realised she'd gone she was there again, a few paces ahead of him, her blonde curls bouncing before him.

'Do you feel anything, Nicholas? Sometimes I think you've been inoculated against feeling anything at all, hardened to everything,' she said as they turned into De Vere Gardens.

Nicholas frowned at the pavement, surprised by her words. What she said was not true, and he struggled to believe she said it sincerely. Perhaps she was trying to provoke an outburst. She turned to him and saw his frown.

'What?' she asked.

He shrugged.

'Don't shrug at me, Nicholas. For fuck's sake, don't shrug. Sometimes I think you could really benefit from doing an office job for a while. You can't sit in meetings and shrug when people ask you questions.'

'Don't get angry,' he muttered.

'You'd also learn to deal with confrontation,' she replied, an icy edge to her words.

'Do you know, I didn't expect to like you as much as I did,' Faye began. 'If someone had asked me, two months ago, whether I'd want to meet up with you again after all these years I would have hesitated. Just because I liked you once doesn't mean that I was destined to like you again. People change, Nicholas. Well, some people do.'

'What do you mean by that?'

'I don't know,' Faye shrugged and looked up ahead of her. 'You seem kind of naive.'

'For thinking that you and I could work?' Nicholas asked. Had he not just ended their relationship he would have resented her suggestion. As it was he gave it no consideration, attributing any attack from her as motivated by revenge and therefore not to be trusted. She would say anything to hurt him. At least he would have, in her position.

'Naivete isn't very practical,' Faye continued.

'What's practicality got to do with anything?' he ventured.

'Why did you come and find me then?' She asked. She stopped walking and faced him. Behind her stood The Ajestic, deserted and watchful.

'Well . . .' Nicholas began 'I'd spent a lot of time thinking about you.' He paused. 'Years,' he continued. He did not meet her eyes.

'So why are you ending it?' she asked. He had not imagined that he would be able to get away without addressing the question of why. He had prepared many answers; none of them was right. He took a breath and looked into the sky above him, as though a justification or explanation might fall on him.

'Because we don't get on,' he said. He looked at her and felt duplicitious. They had had fun together.

'I thought we did,' Faye replied. She folded her arms. 'I thought we got along fine.'

'We don't agree on many things,' he replied.

'And we should?' she asked, taking a step backwards and raising her eyebrows at him.

'Fundamental things, yes,' Nicholas said.

'Since when did we have a discussion about our fundamental beliefs? Which of my fundamental beliefs exactly is it that bothers you so much?'

Nicholas did not reply. He knew that he owed her an answer but he could not find one. A maroon Vauxhall drove past them. Nicholas focussed on its number plate and added up the digits, one after the other. Fifteen.

'Is this about revenge, Nicholas?' Faye asked.

'What do you mean?'

'I stopped writing to you when we were sixteen, fourteen years later you end our . . . well . . relationship.'

'No,' Nicholas said coldly. 'This is not about revenge.'

'But it feels good?' she said, scanning his face with her eyes. She wanted to understand his actions. She wanted to be able to ascribe his decision to a psychological failing on his part. It was how she defended herself.

'No, Faye, it does not feel good,' Nicholas snapped. She had angered him.

Faye felt, when his eyes flashed with his reply, a certain satisfaction. At least she could still hurt him. 'It does not feel good at all,' he said, more quietly.

'You're quite a confused man, aren't you? Faye said boldly. She looked directly at him. He looked back. In those few seconds communication between the two of them ended. Faye had chosen to see him in a particular way: as unstable, hopeless, lost. She would, regardless of what he went on to do with his life, always think of think this way. Nicholas, in those few moments, gave up on Faye.

He showed her the room he had prepared for her and she glanced around it, noticing little of what he had done.

'I'll stay tonight,' she said. 'Tomorrow I'll find somewhere else.'

'Stay as long as you like,' Nicholas replied. Do not judge her, he told himself silently. When he judged others the softness in his eyes was replaced by a pane of glass: clear and brittle and hard. He did not like himself for it. He knew that the hurt she felt was just as real as his own. She cleared her things from his room, he helped her transfer them across the hall.

'I'd never imagined this might happen.' She turned to him and looked him dead in the eye. Her right eyebrow flickered. 'You're a bastard,' she said. 'All men are bastards.'

'No, they're not,' Nicholas replied quietly.

'But I'd be forgiven for thinking they were?' Faye asked him.

'I don't think you're the one who needs to be forgiven for anything,' Nicholas told her.

Faye sat on the bed in her new room and remembered reading an article about Getting Dumped. It had advised readers to make themselves as attractive as possible in the shortest possible time, advocating exercise, a trip to a beauty salon, shopping and meeting up with friends. Hurt pulsed inside her and she hung onto these activities, planning the next day as intricately as she could. She would go jogging in the morning, round the park. She would leave when he left so that he could see she was fine without him. Then she would go to Celia for a massage and a facial, have her legs waxed and nails painted. Through her tears she hoped that she'd be able to get an appointment. She would return to the house looking gorgeous, she vowed, thinking for the first time that perhaps such an effort would only go to show exactly how hurt she was.

As she deliberately concocted detailed plans she looked around the room. The wallpaper was plain cream, with a blue line which ran along the skirting board and around the door frame. It had torn in places and, she noticed, become shiny and slightly grey in an oval patch just above the bed. A bureau stood beside a chest of drawers, on which one of the handles was missing. The bed beneath her seemed to squeak with each breath she took. The room was hideous. It was awful and it provoked in her a deep, resentful anger which tightened her jaw and furrowed her brow. How could she have let herself get into this situation in the first place? Why did she agree to stay one more night in this tragic, ramshackle boarding house?

She stood up and the bed let out a mighty creak. Nicholas has not changed, she thought to herself. He is the same old weird boy he used to be, who does not see what's important in life. She could not believe that she had let herself be taken in by him, that somehow she had not realized that while she had moved on in the world he had stayed exactly where he'd started. She crossed to the window and pulled aside the net curtain, which felt damp and lifeless in her hand. She wanted to tear it from its rail and tightened her fist around it, pulling it towards her, testing its strength. The street below was empty. This is all your fault, Nicholas Beamish, she thought.

Nicholas returned to his room and shut the door. He turned the radio on and then turned it off again. He did not look to his cello. This is it. Here I am, he thought. He sat down on his bed and the moment when he had shut the door to his room replayed in his head, like the climax of a feverish

373

dream. At least he couldn't die here and not be discovered for days. Mrs Sten was sure to come nosing around sooner or later.

He felt agitated by himself and wanted to go out or seek company in the house but he shrouded his needs in his head, deciding that he needed a glass of water or should really go for a run, anything to take him from the abrupt reality of his room. A stifling confusion descended on him. It seemed that his childhood was leaving him, to be replaced by nothing. He had been so certain, felt so clearly that he knew what he wanted. He knew his desire intimately. Like pieces of cliff crashing into the sea, a large part of his identity had fallen from him. *I have always loved Faye. And now?* I am Nicholas Beamish, he told himself. But he was not. Nicholas Beamish loved Faye.

Immigrant, orphan, musician: he knew no longer who he was. He looked to his surroundings for help. The bedspread was the same yellow blanket that had been there since he'd moved in. Feeling its roughess against his palms he told himself: when I first sat down on this bed I knew who I was. When I first sat down on this bed this blanket felt the same as it does to me now. The pale pink wallpaper was as it has always been. The stripped wood floor was the same: there was a knot by the leg of the bed, a dark, deer-eye, ringed with anxiety. He stared at it. It looked neither familiar nor real. He did not understand why not. With the mannered ease of an obsessive compulsive he took his cello to him. His fingers moved carefully, his right arm sawed and crossed strings.

He did not get into bed that night. He cried as he had never cried before. Then he stood and watched the motion-less, illuminated gardens below while the house gradually fell silent. The moon moved around in the sky and Nicholas tried not to think of Faye sleeping alone in the room across the hall. At one point he saw the cat cross the lawn and snake through the fence into next door's garden, dragging something which looked like a large mouse.

A slow heaviness came over him. It was the same feeling, which his uncle Myron had felt when he realized he had shot his own cousin who had joined up with the Germans, through the shoulder and the gut, in 1944; that his great-grandmother Lesia felt when she stood for four months in a row in front of a pan of water on the stove and wondered what she should put in it; that his half-brother Oleh in the Carpathians felt when, aged six, his dog lay down on the wooden floor and closed his eyes for the last time, a spider's web of saliva stretching from his mouth down his fur.

Worst of all, it would be Nicholas's son, Stefan, who would feel this thick black velvet curtain descend when, aged seventeen, he painted his first proper canvas and saw, with his own eyes and honed judgement, that it was of no merit whatsoever. He would sit by the window in his room overlooking the North Sea and stare, painfully trying to understand why his mind and heart told him to become a painter when he clearly couldn't paint. It was a difficult time for the boy – perhaps the most difficult of his life. If he could have known what his forefathers had faced, that they had once felt similarly despairing, he would have been able to raise his chin and wash his brush more easily.

Towards dawn Nicholas lay down on his bed, watching the sky lighten. He saw himself from far away, up above the world, lying by himself in a large city. He thought of hermits and prisoners, castaways and shepherds and then of the number of orphans in London. I am no longer soft, he thought. I have only myself and that must be enough.

THIRTY-TWO

Kozak, waking just after six o'clock on Saturday morning, climbed from his bed and looked with horror at the pile of clothes he had carried late the night before from the shower. On top of it, when he had gone to bed, had lain the red shoes. This morning they were gone.

'Gone!' he shouted, pulling on a pair of tracksuit bottoms. He put on his sunglasses and dashed from his room. 'They've gone!' he yelled and he banged on David's door. From there he ran down through the whole house, hammering indiscriminately on every door he encountered, shouting at the top of his voice until he reached the ground floor and found himself at a loss for what action to take. He jumped up the stairs in twos and started his hammering all over again. Martine's was the first door to open.

'What on earth's the matter?' she asked him.

'My shoes. They've gone!' Kozak announced breathlessly. He was bare-chested and tousle-haired. He looked as though he had have spent the night in a cave.

'Oh,' said Martine. Mr Sten emerged, followed shortly by Faye. From across the hall came Nicholas, alarmed and tight-eyed. David tripped down the stairs in his pyjamas. Nicholas saw Faye and she saw him. She didn't want to look at his face and yet couldn't stop herself. She was conscious of her tired eyes. Mrs Sten joined the crowd, hair brushed, wearing a lilac dressing gown.

'Whatever's the matter?' she asked Kozak. Nicholas looked back at Faye and she averted her eyes.

'My shoes! My red shoes!' Kozak said, appealing to

everyone around him. 'They've gone. I have to find them.'

And so the house began to look. Nicholas muttered that he'd look upstairs on the second floor and went off. Faye said she'd check *the room she was staying in* and she returned to her room. Kozak didn't know what to do: he couldn't understand why anyone would steal his necklace. In his bewildered state he started to search: turning over cushions, opening cupboards, gazing around rooms unsure where to begin.

Mrs Sten, back in her bedroom, covered her mouth with her hand. A thrill passed through her: she had seen, with her own eyes, Nicholas and Faye emerge from separate rooms. He is mine, she thought. At last. She flung open the doors to her cedar wardrobe and began the long process of deciding what she should wear that day.

Nicholas put on the previous day's clothes and left the house. Mrs Sten, peering from her bedroom window, saw him go next door and ring Mr Samuels' doorbell.

'Nicholas!' Mr Samuels opened the door. Nicholas had clearly woken him.

'I'm sorry to call so early,' Nicholas said.

'No problem. Come on in. Let's have breakfast.'

Mr Samuels, always ate outside, even in the winter, when he would cook porridge and then pace along his patio blowing enthusiastically on the steaming spoonfuls. This morning he laid out some bananas and muesli.

'Do you think I could just have a look round your garden? I think our cat might have brought something in here last night.'

'Help yourself,' Mr Samuels replied with a broad grin. 'And if you see any bugs scare them away, won't you?'

Nicholas found what he was looking for without much trouble: Kozak's two red shoes lay under a cannabis plant towards the back of the garden. He picked them up and carried them over to the patio table. They were light, these funny small shoes, and the thong was shiny with wear. Nicholas looked at them, at how their short laces had been tightly tied onto the thong. It was hard to believe that anyone had ever had such small feet.

'How are you, boy?' Mr Samuels asked.

'Well,' Nicholas replied. He didn't mention Faye. That she had once crept into his soul and pierced every part with an invisible thread, drawing it together into a scrunched-up ball, now seemed hard to believe.

'She's a lovely-looking girl,' Mr Samuels said. He winked at Nicholas.

'Yes,' Nicholas replied, faintly, and he thought of the single people he knew and the lives they had. He would pay another visit to Anthony Christmas. 'How's the garden doing?' he asked.

David, glancing from his window, saw Nicholas sitting with Mr Samuels, the red shoes lying on the table between them. He raced downstairs to tell Kozak.

'Good,' Mr Samuels replied, taking a mouthful of banana. 'I am awaiting my gooseberries. All year round I've been putting my potato peelings around that bush, so I'm hoping the fruit will come up good.'

Nicholas, fiddling with the worn thong, tilted one of the shoes so that the raw leather of its inside faced him.

'God alone knows why I grow them,' Mr Samuels continued, 'I cannot abide gooseberries. I wouldn't even want to stand on a gooseberry, let alone eat one.'

Nicholas saw his own name.

'An eyeball full of pips, that's how I think of it. A blind eyeball full of pips. A bitter, blind eyeball full of pips.' Mr Samuels laughed out loud.

*

It was like being hit by a bullet: he felt it inside before he actually understood what he read. The information, which should surely have preceded his emotional response, seemed instead to have come after it, and it took some seconds before Nicholas's brain made sense of what he had seen.

'Nicholas!' It was Kozak, striding into the garden. Nicholas stared into his lap, but he saw nothing in front of him because he was looking instead at a scene in the front of his mind.

'You've found them!' Kozak cheered, seeing his prized necklace safe under Nicholas's hands. 'I could kiss you!' he announced and he walked across the lawn to the boy and, bending over him, kissed him once on each cheek and once again. Nicholas's thoughts were invaded and disappeared; he awoke to the bristles of a moustache on his cheek and a soft smell of carbolic soap and vegetables. Kozak had thrown on a shirt before coming round.

'Good morning, Mr Samuels,' Kozak said. Mr Samuels raised his chin and smiled. The doorbell rang and he went off to answer it.

'I knew these people,' Nicholas said, with a frown. In his head he tried his best to remember the mother and daughter to whom they had given his shoes, but he did not know whether what he saw was how it had actually been, or whether it was a memory he had created, from picture books and television, tea towels, cereal packets, album sleeves.

'Where *were* they?' Kozak said. He sat down at the table and began to help himself to some breakfast.

'Well, they were in the mountains with us. The Carpathians. That's where we met them,' Nicholas said. 'The woman and the child.' He wondered how Kozak had met them, where they had got to.

'What are you talking about? Where were my shoes?'

The sun was rising behind the trees. Nicholas had to squint to look across at the big man.

'I knew the people who wore these shoes,' Nicholas said again, more emphatically.

Kozak paused. He closed his mouth and lifted his chin. He felt suddenly quite small. A ripple seemed to pass through him: a defensive, armadillo hardening. 'The woman and the child,' Kozak repeated.

'Yes.' Nicholas stood up and moved out of the sun. Kozak stood up too. 'What happened to them?' Nicholas asked. His voice seemed to have structure but no sound. A truck in the street began to reverse and its nursery call rang through the morning.

'They were killed,' Kozak whispered.

'How did you know them?'

Kozak took a breath and looked up at the sky above him. He was puzzled, a little lost suddenly. 'They were my family. My wife and our child.' Nicholas struggled to imagine Kozak as the father of the small girl with blonde hair who had taken on, in the years she had spent in Nicholas's mind, a ghostly, insubstantial quality. She seemed so small and delicate. How she could have sprung from Kozak's heavy limbs Nicholas did not know.

'You met them in the mountains?'

'I met them once,' Nicholas replied. 'Near Slavsko.'

'Is that where you lived?'

Nicholas shook his head. 'I was crossing the mountains with my mother. We walked out of the Ukraine into Hungary and then Austria. Then we made our way to England.'

Kozak blinked behind his glasses and put his hands in his pockets.

'I think that's what my wife had intended to do.'

Nicholas didn't know what to say. He felt uncomfortable at having survived. There was a sound from the house and Mrs Sten emerged with Mr Samuels. Kozak stood in silence, befuddled.

'Coo-ee, Nicholas! I just came to apologize for our *misunderstanding* about the room. I hope you'll forgive me.' Nicholas frowned. 'Oh, Kozak,' said Mrs Sten as she reached them. 'I see you found your shoes.'

'Yes, yes, they're here,' Nicholas said and he came to his senses. He shivered, and he held out the shoes to Kozak. Kozak took them. He ducked under the thong, guiding it over his sunglasses, slipping the shoes beneath his shirt.

'Well,' said Nicholas.

'Well,' breathed Kozak. He lifted his hand and patted the shoes. 'Where were they, anyway?' he asked.

'Over here,' Nicholas said and paced towards the back of the garden. Kozak followed, ducking under the branches of an apple tree. 'Just by this plant,' Nicholas said. 'The cat left them here last night. I saw him drag them through our garden.'

Kozak looked at the patch of earth.

'Well, thank you,' he said. 'I am very grateful. I hate losing things.'

'Don't mention it,' Nicholas replied. 'Reuniting people with their lost possessions is one of the things I do for a living at the moment.' Kozak scratched at his moustache and turned to go.

'You know what's amazing?' Nicholas said. The lost family of the big man seemed to make sense.

Kozak shook his head.

'Originally these shoes were mine,' Nicholas said quietly. 'I gave them to— well, my mother gave them to your daughter when our paths crossed. They have my name in them. If you look inside there's a name in blue ink. Beimuk, that's my family name.'

Kozak stared at Nicholas. Possibilities swirled in his head as he wondered whether there was any way he could be mistaken. His breathing was hard, stertorous. *You*, he thought.

'What?' said Nicholas.

'I did not have a daughter,' Kozak said quietly. His voice seemed barely there, fragments of what had been. 'I am Stefan Beimuk. I had a son.'

Nicholas stared. He watched Kozak's face for any sign that what he had said was untrue. What he said to Nicholas was hard to believe. How does he know? Nicholas asked himself. How does he know my father's name? How does he know about me? I have never told him. The garden around him seemed to take on a new identity; he felt he could be in a green sea which was carrying him, gently, away from what he knew. This man is not my family. He is Kozak. He is a friend, but look how large he is, look at his big sharp nose. He cannot be my family.

'I am Nicholas Beimuk,' Nicholas whispered. 'My mother was called Kalyna Beimuk. In 1975 we left our village of Dytyatky and came to England.' He let the words drum out of him like fast, determined rain. He would clear up the misunderstanding.

'You had a brother called Bohdan,' Kozak said quietly. Nicholas could hear Mrs Sten chatting with Mr Samuels at the other end of the garden. 'You need to keep the roots in the shade,' he heard Mr Samuels say in his deep voice.

'I *had* a brother?' Nicholas asked. He could not understand what was happening.

Kozak did not reply immediately. He raised his hand and removed his sunglasses, revealing to Nicholas for the first time his grey eyes. Nicholas was startled. He had expected

Kozak's eyes to be a strong brown: fearless, unforgiving, sure of themselves. He had expected warrior eyes from this man, toughened by the sun and wind, panned with nonchalance. Not pale grey, watery eyes which held in them a look of hesitation, the recalcitrant culpability of his immigrant status.

'Bohdan died when he was twenty-one,' Kozak said.

THIRTY-THREE

'He's your father?' A touch of horror crept into Mrs Sten's voice. She worshipped Nicholas and thought of Kozak as nothing better than a vagrant. She found him aloof and ill-mannered and peculiarly resistant to her charms, which annoyed her intensely. Moreover, Kozak was of a similar age to her and the revelation of their relationship brought home to her that she could be Nicholas's mother. She was far too old to be mooning around over a boy his age.

'Yes,' said Nicholas. He was still dazed, astonished that his father was so imposing. If Nicholas had seen him coming towards him on a dark street he would have crossed the road.

'Well,' and Mrs Sten sat down. She looked out of the kitchen window at a small acacia tree. 'Are you sure?' she said.

'Yes,' Nicholas replied.

She stared off into space for a little while longer. A bird flew into the foliage of the tree and she came back to life.

'Well!' she said. 'I always thought this house was lucky and now we see it is. We must have a celebration. Go and tell everyone: I invite you all to have dinner this evening. In the dining room!' she trilled.

Nicholas stood for a moment and tried to understand the events of the past few days. He felt like an old man; he had had enough coincidences to last him a lifetime. He shut his eyes for a moment as Mrs Sten busied herself in the kitchen. He had come to understand the potency of expectations.

★

Nicholas had never seen the dining room. It had sat, quiet and empty, between the kitchen and the front room, ever since he had moved in. The door had always been shut. He had not been curious enough to try the door, but if he had he would have found it locked. The key lay in a bone-china tray on Mrs Sten's dressing table in her bedroom. She didn't like the dining room. When she and Mr Sten had first moved into the house they had used it all the time: for breakfast and lunch and supper. When he left she stopped using it altogether. Eating at a long table only made her more aware that she was eating alone. Besides, it was a dark room, full of the furniture she'd inherited from her family but hadn't wanted. She preferred to pretend that it didn't exist.

But that day Mrs Sten opened up the dining room and aired it thoroughly, leaving its windows wide open while she went to the supermarket so that any passing burglar could have easily climbed in and stolen the silver samovar which stood in the far corner. She had decided to cook salmon. It was 24th August and too hot for meat so she stood at the fish counter asking the young man behind it to press the eyes of the four fishes on offer. She pondered her clothes, then the lighting, the food and the seating plan. She took a bottle of lavender water and dabbed the perfume onto the light bulbs in the dining room and hallway. It was a long time since she'd given a dinner party.

'So I woke up at four in the morning,' Sean told Nicholas, 'in bed, by myself, with my trousers and trainers on.' Nicholas nodded. He found that he could barely keep his eyes open, as though in an advanced state of desiccation they would crumble shut. Kozak had told him that morning that he had a couple of commitments during the day, so they had arranged to meet for lunch.

'But get this,' Sean continued. 'The T-shirt in which I had sweated copiously and then spilt curry down, I had gone to the trouble of hanging up on a coat hanger.' Nicholas laughed. 'Sleeping in my shoes having hung up my T-shirt. And then when I woke up I found that I'd made a call on my mobile on the way home. To a company called Manganese Bronze Holdings. I called them this morning but since it's Saturday there was no-one there. The phone company told me I'd made forty-three calls to them. What can they expect if they advertise their number in the back of black cabs? I think Kenos Doddos, the god of wit, was with me last night.'

Nicholas stared off down the drinks aisle and saw a beautiful, black-haired woman disappear by the Spirits section.

'Nicholas?' Sean said. Nicholas was still looking down the aisle, hoping for a reappearance. 'Nicholas?'

'Yeah?'

'And a probe discovers life on planet Beamish after all. What are you doing this afternoon?' Nicholas had asked Sean whether he could take the afternoon off work.

'I'm having lunch with my dad,' Nicholas replied.

'Oh,' said Sean. Nicholas had not told Sean about his family. It had never come up.

'Anywhere nice?'

'Don't know yet.'

'Will Martine be there?'

'Sean,' Nicholas smiled at him.

'What?' he asked, in mock innocence.

The woman in the drinks aisle appeared again. Nicholas stared at her. She was one beauteous vision. Sean hadn't clocked her and as she walked around a new gondola-end display of cheese strings Nicholas saw something fall from her bag. Her wallet. He almost called out but stopped himself just in time. He waited until she had disappeared into the next aisle and went off to retrieve it. As he bent down to pick it up he imagined the gratitude the woman would show when she got it back. Perhaps she was the kissing sort?

'There's a lost wallet here, Sean,' he said, returning to where they were standing and handing over the neat brown pouch. 'Happy Christmas. I'll see you on Monday,' and he went home.

Nicholas took Kozak for fish and chips in Hammersmith. They sat opposite each other at a lime-checked table, decorated with sepia vinegar rings and a scattering of salt. Nicholas liked how Kozak looked and imagined that an observer, seeing them seated together, would never guess that they were father and son. Kozak didn't really look like anyone's father, caught up in the business of fathering. He looked like a man with his own life, his own moustache, his own women.

Nicholas took a seat and splayed his hands out on the table, as though waiting to talk business. He looked down at his hands – long, even fingers with nails pinkish and ridged like skinned almonds – and pretended that he was at ease. Kozak sat down opposite him, dropping his bulk into the plastic chair and emitting, as he parted his legs and pulled his chair beneath him with one hand, a friendly, low grunt. He dropped his arms onto the table before him and as he did so the knuckle of his thumb caught the tip of Nicholas's index finger. Before he could even think about it Nicholas made his hands into fists and then brought them to his body where he let them rest on his knees. He looked up at Kozak and smiled, but it was more an exercise of muscles than it was a signal of happiness. He had seen, in a brief moment, that his father's hands were the same as his.

Kozak had Nicholas's long, elegant fingers. They were the hands of a scribe or a prince and looked out of place on such a large man.

'You and I have very similar hands,' Nicholas said, holding one of his own out in front of him and looking at it. He could not, he realized, hold it still.

'You have put yours to better use,' Kozak replied, with a half smile.

Nicholas felt uneasy. He didn't know what to say. Kozak had such a strong physical presence that Nicholas sometimes imagined him to be a whole planet, with his own gravitational field. He didn't know what to do with this man.

The waitress arrived and they ordered their food. Nicholas scanned his menu and asked for haddock and chips, with mushy peas and scrapings. Kozak looked up at the young girl and asked her what she'd recommend. She flushed and lifted the top of her pen to her lips, where she pressed it into the corner of her mouth.

'I like sausage and chips,' she said quietly, glancing across at Nicholas.

'But I should eat *fish* and chips, shouldn't I?' Kozak asked her with a grin. Nicholas wondered whether his father was trying to make him feel more at ease. In reality Kozak was feeling even more agitated than Nicholas was. A slow, boggy sickness had filled his chest and his vision had become blurred. I cannot lose another son, he thought to himself. The waitress shrugged in answer to his question.

'I like sausage,' she said to him. 'I don't like fish.'

'Okay,' announced Kozak, his mind racing and failing to think of another question to ask her, 'I'll have sausage and chips.' She nodded at him and didn't even wait to write it down before escaping back to the kitchen. Kozak and Nicholas were left to each other.

Kozak asked how Kalyna and Nicholas had managed to stay in England. Nicholas scalded his throat on his mushy peas as he swallowed them too quickly.

'My mother remarried. I mean, she married in order to stay here. So that we could get passports. Eventually.'

Each word sounded over in Nicholas's head. Each word badly chosen, each thought badly phrased. He felt that he had put his foot in it.

'I see,' Kozak said. He added some salt to his chips with a few bold shakes of the cellar.

'She had to,' Nicholas continued, 'we wouldn't have been able to stay otherwise.'

And the man?' Kozak asked.

'He was called Ray,' Nicholas replied.

Kozak did not want to know what Ray was like, but he could not help himself imagining. He assumed that Ray slept with Kalyna, assumed also that Ray became, in effect, Nicholas's father.

'Where does he live?' Kozak asked. He did not want to meet this man.

'Sweden. I think,' Nicholas said.

'Oh. Do you see him?'

Nicholas shook his head and took a gulp of his water. 'But he was good, he was a good man,' he said quickly, because he did not want Kozak to think that Ray had hurt his mother in any way.

'Good,' Kozak murmured. He was not used to feeling so much. It made him uncomfortable.

Nicholas dared to ask about Bohdan. He was told the outline facts, bereft of details. He gave his father a version of his mother's death. And he told him how he had anglicized his surname, from Beimuk to Beamish, when he was twelve.

'You have an education?' Kozak asked Nicholas, sawing his way through a sausage the length of his foot.

'I have a degree in music,' Nicholas told him, but he neglected to mention the class of his degree.

'That is marvellous,' Kozak said. He had to wait to put food into his mouth. Their conversation became a blind-date conversation, a foreign-language oral-exam conversation.

'Can you play tennis?' Nicholas asked his father, chewing on a mouthful of food.

'No,' Kozak replied. 'Can you?'

'Not really. D'you like Indian food?'

'Don't know.'

'Chinese?'

'No. Not dim sum. Did you learn Latin at school?'

'No. French and German. And then only in the let's-go-camping sense. I can't understand one sentence of French literature but I know the word for jump leads.'

'Ah.'

'There's more to life than jump-starting your car, though I don't think our teachers saw it that way.'

'And you think in English?'

'Yes.'

'And dream in English?'

'I dream in gobbledygook. Would you like to go for a curry tonight?'

'I thought Mrs Sten was making dinner?' Kozak frowned.

'Oh, that's right. The *dinner*.'

THIRTY-FOUR

When they returned home Nicholas got into the shower and let the warm water fall down his back. He stood for a few moments extricating real events from dream ones in his head. The night before he had had a few hours of deep sleep punctuated with some semi-conscious moments when he had opened his eyes and become thoroughly confused. He dreamt that he had met Scheherazade, that she had seduced him and then told him story after story after story: an uncle who returned to his wife; a man who cut out his belly button and became immortal; a goat herder whose children rejected him.

He showered slowly, carefully soaping between each toe and vigorously scrubbing at his fingertips with the nail brush. He thanked someone in his head that he no longer worked on the meat counter because the cold, flat smell of uncooked fat and flesh used to take him hours to remove each evening. His thoughts were on Kozak as he shaved, slowly navigating the profile of his chin. He stared at himself in the mirror, searching for some indication of what he'd been through. He almost expected his hair to have gone grey. There was a knock at the door and Martine asked him how long he would be.

'I'm just coming,' he called and gathered up his clothes. He wrapped his towel around his waist and opened the door, steam billowing out into the landing as he did so. Martine was leaning against the wall holding towels and a toiletries bag to her chest.

'Hi,' Nicholas said. 'Sorry.'

'Thanks,' Martine said, embarrassed by the sight of his naked chest.

'Nicholas,' she said suddenly.

'Yes?' he replied.

'How's Sean?' Martine asked.

Nicholas looked at her, subjecting her to the strange atmosphere of his open, doll-eyed stare.

'What's the matter?' she asked, her milky brow curdling into a frown.

Nicholas shook his head, pretending to wake himself from a daydream, 'Nothing.' he said with a smile. 'I think he's fine. I'll tell him you asked,' he grinned.

'Yes, well,' she said and smiled briefly at him. 'Harvey!' she called, 'bath-time!' and Nicholas slunk off to his room.

Mr Sten went around the house cleaning everyone's shoes in anticipation. He rubbed Harvey's black leather lace-ups until they shone like glass even though Martine told him that Harvey never wore them. He polished his own and Kozak's shoes, inserting his hand into each one, a brush whirring over the leather. Mrs Sten was planning on wearing silk slippers, Martine a pair of espadrilles. 'The women are a bit of a let-down on the shoe front,' he muttered to himself as he pottered around the house.

Once he was dressed Nicholas went downstairs and called Sean to invite him to the dinner. Returning upstairs he crossed the landing and knocked on Faye's door. He had not seen her all day and felt, as he stood there, that she would instantly see his visit for what it was: a visit of the guilty, an indulgence of conscience.

'Yes?' She opened the door and looked straight at him. She stood straight, a look of defensive disapproval in her face.

'Hi,' Nicholas said softly. He reached with his left hand

up to his left shoulder and scratched at the back of his head. It seemed hard to imagine that only a few days ago they had climbed into bed together.

'I was just wondering whether you were going to come to the dinner this evening?'

'If you'd wanted to have dinner with me you wouldn't have ended the relationship,' she replied, fast and sharp. Nicholas dropped his hands to his sides and leant against the door frame. Faye took a step backwards.

'I— did you hear about Kozak?' he asked. She nodded. She did not like Kozak. The fact that he wore the same suit every single day perturbed her; his sunglasses made her suspicious. That Nicholas had such an eccentric father suddenly made sense to her. She mentally pushed Nicholas further away from herself, remembering the odd things he did and ascribing them all to an indelible genetic perversity.

'Look,' Nicholas began. He wanted to ask her to stay for the dinner, he wanted to ask her to stay in touch. The words would not come. Behind her he saw that she had packed up her things: a couple of carrier bags rested against each other on the bed, on the floor beneath them stood two cardboard boxes.

'You've packed up,' he said.

'Alistair's coming to collect me,' she replied, meeting his eyes, waiting for criticism. It didn't come. Nicholas felt sad. He could no longer see the point.

'I know what you think of me,' she said.

He raised his head. 'You don't—' he began.

'You've always been superior. You and your mother. Because you were immigrants, you thought you were better than everyone else. You thought we owed you something,' she said. Nicholas watched her face and saw that she was wearing make-up: darkish lines around her eyes, an unnatural sheen to her lips. Do not meet anger

393

with anger, he thought. He could not bring himself to speak.

'My mother did not think she was better than anyone,' he replied eventually. 'You seem to have forgotten where you came from,' he said, angry with her and with himself.

'And you seem unable to forget, Nicholas. Unable to fucking forget.' She raised her voice. 'You and your stories. Your family back in the Ukraine. How you walked here. You really think you're something special, don't you? Did you think you were doing me a favour going out with me? Did you think you were rescuing me? In case you don't remember, you had no fucking friends when you joined Moorside. Everyone thought you were the weird kid.'

Nicholas sensed that something was being dismantled inside him, pieces carried off one by one. At the end there would be nothing left.

'I remember,' he said. The admission startled Faye. She wanted something with which she could disagree. She breathed out angrily.

'You and I are different,' Nicholas tried. Of course they were different. He was different from all his friends. Difference was what he liked about other people. Difference, he felt, was where life began.

'You're telling me,' she said.

'I really am sorry.'

'You've done me a favour,' she replied. 'You can't even row properly,' and she laughed, briefly. 'I'll be gone in about an hour.'

'Can we stay in touch?' Nicholas asked. You are my oldest friend, he thought, even if I don't like you. Why, when I become friends with someone, do I want to remain friends with them for life? he wondered.

Faye shrugged. 'If you want,' she said.

'Goodbye then,' he said. He kissed her on the cheek and

smelt her perfume. It brought back images from the night when they had first had sex in the hotel and Nicholas had believed that he might have finally found the mother of his children.

'Bye,' she said.

And then they were all there: Mrs Sten looked astonishing in a purple trouser suit and gold blouse. Martine had put on a black velvet tunic and wore beneath it a long black velvet skirt which hung around her like a cardboard tube, making her look like a glove puppet, controlled by an unseen, subterranean hand. Harvey had bathed and brushed both his hair and his teeth. Mr Sten remained in his cashmere sweater which smelt of barley sugar and shoe polish. The dining room was aired and the table set. Sean arrived with a bottle of wine and scanned the room with a bemused expression. He nodded and smiled at Martine, and Harvey, emboldened by his mother's high spirits, came right over and asked him if he had any more magazines.

'Is this your family then, Nicholas?' Sean asked, looking over to Mrs and Mr Sten.

'Not exactly,' Nicholas said.

'Nicholas, could I have a word?' Mrs Sten whispered into his ear. Nicholas's heart sank. He asked himself what sort of invitations he might have to fend off during the course of the evening. He followed her out into the hallway and, steeling himself, looked into her flushed, flustered face. She had been cooking all afternoon and cooking made her nervous. Champagne, on the other hand, calmed her nerves. The more she cooked, the more she drank.

'Nicholas,' she began with a haughty air .'I – I – owe you an apology,' she said. Nicholas watched her. Her manner had changed, it had become contrite and flat, lacking the grace notes of raised eyebrows, the cadences of her smile.

She clasped her hands together in front of her and avoided meeting his eyes. 'I'm sure you're aware what I think of you, Nicholas.' The corner of her mouth twitched. 'And I wanted to say that if my . . . *attention* . . . has caused you any distress then I am sorry.'

Nicholas began to protest. A dishonest, merciful protestation. He shook his head and furrowed his brow.

'I have come to my senses, Nicholas,' Mrs Sten added, raising her eyes to meet his. 'Now, shall we go and enjoy the evening?' she asked, with an almost professional charm. Nicholas nodded, too astonished for words. He followed her back into the dining room.

Kozak returned with a pair of plaster Airedale terrier bookends, a Lloyd Loom bathroom cabinet, a silk chenille throw, a stack of four-inch-square art deco tiles and Beth. He stacked his hoard in the hallway and called out to the crowd in the dining room. 'Hello! I'm back. Everyone, this is Beth. Beth, this is Nicholas.'

Nicholas saw a woman in her late thirties, tall and lean, with longish dark hair. Her features had been created with an enthusiasm for each: big dark eyes, a large bold nose, a wide mouth. Apart from a shrewdness in her eyes which it would be difficult to capture, she would be easy to sketch, could be summed up by the practised, carefree strokes of a street artist.

'Hello,' she said.

'Hello,' Nicholas said and he stretched out a hand. She frowned and smiled at the same time, taking his hand with a firm grip. When Nicholas demonstrated that he was happy to introduce himself, Kozak was proud of his son. Nicholas wondered who this woman was, and what she meant to his father.

'Nicholas is my son,' he said.

'I know,' Beth smiled. 'You've told me that many times already,' and she laughed.

'Well, it's good to meet you, Nicholas. Your father is a living legend, in our house at least,' she said, looking from one of them to the other. Kozak and Nicholas had an equilibrium about them, though they could not see it themselves. Pointing out their affinities to them would be like painting with water on glass.

'And hopefully Beth *won't* go down in history,' Kozak said, and behind his sunglasses he winked at her.

Beth was introduced to the rest of the house and champagne was poured for everyone. Nicholas wished that Kozak would take his sunglasses off so that he could see how his father looked again.

If Kalyna had been asked, the day before she was run over, whether she would have left her family and home again, if she had the chance, she would have replied with a calm but unequivocal yes. Not because she was a woman who could not admit a mistake but because she believed, that a child needed the freedom of political and religious beliefs more than it needed a father and a brother. Kozak shepherded Nicholas over towards the window and leant towards him.

'I told Mrs Sten that if she laid a finger on my son I'd take the house to pieces, bit by bit,' Kozak said dryly. Nicholas stared at him.

'You did not,' he said. He glanced over at Mrs Sten, who was chatting to Martine in the doorway, a pile of white linen napkins in one hand.

'She is a succubus,' Kozak replied. 'I had had enough of all her girlishness.'

Nicholas laughed. 'I can't believe you did that,' he said.

'I have some uses,' Kozak replied.

Nicholas talked to Beth about where she had met his

397

father and was surprised to learn of all the places Kozak knew in Oxfordshire. She told him that Kozak had lived with her and her sisters. It seemed that she and he were just friends.

'You must know Britain better than I do,' Nicholas said to Kozak. 'Were people friendly in those places?' he asked.

Kozak shrugged. 'No-one's a foreigner for ever,' he said and he took a gulp of his drink. 'You get used to it. Besides, I had a very good English teacher,' and he smiled over at Beth. They talked about his business for a while and he described the day's purchases to the group. Martine asked him whether he would like to open a shop one day.

'A junk shop?' Kozak asked.

'Well, yes,' Martine replied, 'what other kind of shop would you have?'

'Well, what kind of shop would you expect an optimist to run?' Kozak said. He had never drunk champagne before and found that it turned him into a lighter, more golden version of himself. Spirits he knew to avoid.

'A cake shop?' suggested Mr Sten.

'With cherry trifles and Victorian sponges and meringues. I love meringues!' Kozak replied.

'Victorian sponges?' laughed Martine. 'I think they might be rather stale.'

'No, no,' replied Kozak, not realizing his mistake, 'all fresh, made every day, served by children in red skirts and flowers in their hair.'

'Dinner is served,' Mr Sten announced but he couldn't be heard. He said it again, the effort bringing two patches of red to his cheeks.

'Before we sit down I would like to propose a toast,' Kozak declared. Nicholas saw that the champagne glass in his hand was shaking a little, the glistening bubbles of liquid, obedient to gravity, still and calm in the centre. He stood and examined the liquid, staring off into its middle, imagining that he was upstairs lying on his bed, having got home from work and changed out of his uniform. An early Saturday evening before any of this had happened.

'Firstly thank you to Mrs Sten. You are a hostess in heaven,' Kozak began, cursing the drink for his lie. He rocked slightly forward on his feet and held his glass against his chest. 'To David and to Beth, for friendship,' he continued, questioning himself suddenly. He swayed a little on his feet. 'And to Nicholas,' he said quickly as he lifted his glass and took a mouthful of liquid. He sat down abruptly.

He liked Nicholas, had liked him from the very first meeting. He was proud of him and the pride sat in his throat like a noxious gas. Now, as the guests began to take their seats, he looked down at the linen tablecloth in front of him and ground his teeth. His son reminded him of his own father; he felt at once old and young in his presence. When he looked into his eyes he saw his wife – the boyish, broad-shouldered girl who had challenged him at the swimming race and the woman whose hand he used to hold. It was as though Nicholas took in decades, centuries and compacted them, distilled his ancestry in the curve of his features with the ease and unknowingness of youth.

Kozak found that he could just watch him, observing how he scratched his cheek with the back of his thumbnail. Like the lens of a camera he took in time and focused it. Nicholas, it seemed, could have lived through the Russian Revolution, the invention of the gramophone, the rise of Hitler, the moon landing, the famine in Ethiopia, the birth of telecommunications. It was hard to believe that the man sitting next to him had once had small enough feet to wear the shoes around his neck.

Mrs Sten began to carry in dishes of food. With a

couscous salad in one hand, she surveyed the table and felt that she might be young again.

'You sit down, dear. I'll bring in the rest,' said Mr Sten, pulling out a chair with both hands. Nicholas sat between Kozak and Harvey, who was looking at himself in his spoon. Sean manoeuvred himself next to Martine. Both Kozak and Nicholas smiled as they sat at the table. Not particularly out of happiness, it was both too early and too late for that. They smiled because they were embarrassed, thrown by their discovery, wrong-footed by a relationship that was too important to fathom. Mrs Sten clucked around everyone like a mother hen, dishing out food, refilling glasses, passing around napkins.

It was nine o'clock on the last Saturday evening in August and Nicholas was sitting in a room filled with family and friends. He sat back from the table and watched the commotion. His hair curled loosely around the back of his head and his eyes had taken on a darkness which made them appear almost black. He gripped his left hand with his right and felt his fingers tap up and down his thumb, beating time to a song that only he could hear.

THIRTY-FIVE

The house slept late on Sunday morning. Nicholas was hungover. He lay in his bed and stared at the ceiling, remembering the events of the day before. He began the long, slow process of convincing himself that everything which he thought had happened had actually happened. He was looking forward to playing his cello today. As he lay in bed and thought about it he turned his head to the right, so that he could listen to his imaginary notes, scrutinizing their quality.

When he finally got out of bed it was half past ten. He pulled on a pair of jeans to go to the loo. On the floor outside his room he found an envelope with his name on it. He did not recognize the slanted loops of handwriting. Inside was a small sheet of white paper. It contained only thirty-five words but it had taken over two hours to write.

Dear Nicholas
I have left you with nothing. Forgive me. It is not because I have nothing to say to you. On the contrary. It is because I do not know where to begin.

Kozak

Nicholas let his eyes roam over the words a few times. He did not understand. Climbing the stairs to Kozak's room he found the door ajar and the room empty, not only of its occupant but also of things. Nicholas went into the room, scanning the surfaces of the bed, sideboard and chair for something, proof that this man had been here. Was this some kind of joke? he asked himself, feeling faint.

Kozak had got up at six and left the house by six thirty, climbing stealthily down the stairs, one by one. He had, as his wife had before him, walked away from one of their sons. He had walked away with a tight throat and a frown. Kozak did not now want a family. He did not want to hide parts of himself, to think about the example he set, to lie. He did not want to feel obliged to visit someone, to worry about someone else, to remember to telephone. He was not used to it.

The dinner the night before had been too much for him. He did not want another son to care for. He already cared too much for Nicholas, had enjoyed his company too much before he knew who he was. Now, in the light of the revelation, Kozak felt that his ribs had been prised from him and his heart was exposed to everyone. He had kept people away from him for too long; had deliberately primed himself to be disappointed and let down by everyone he met. Leave him, said a voice in his head as he lay in bed on Saturday night, leave him before he too dies. Nicholas looked so vigorous and vital that it was hard to believe that he would ever die. But Bohdan had once looked that way too. Bathe in paraffin and roll across hot coals, Kozak thought. Do not run this risk.

He had grieved once for Nicholas and Kalyna. To learn that his wife had lived all those years, that she had been warm flesh on this earth while he had wept for her, hurt him. That she had then died, before he could see her again, hurt him even more, like scar tissue torn apart. Kozak's behaviour was learned. He had taught himself to deflect and dodge. He did it well, without even realizing he was doing it. It was brief and effective, a blow to the back of the head of anything that

402

threatened to make him feel. He had made a promise to himself when he had lived in the Carpathians that he had done enough weeping for the lifetime of one man.

Nicholas stood on the top step of the stairs and waited. He did not know for what. His body barely seemed with him any longer. His heart broke. I need something to do, he thought, panicking, a fine sweat gathering on the tips of his fingers which held the letter. He had wanted a family. He put on a T-shirt and shirt, raced up to the second floor of the house and knocked on David's door.

It was half past eleven, late for David still to be in bed, though Nicholas didn't know this. Nor did he know about David's problem, about the black gull, the devil-faced bird, which came in from the sea to roost on his shoulders. David had woken up that morning unable to climb from his bed. It felt to him as if a heavy and tarred piece of timber had landed across his forehead in the night. Opening his eyes seemed like inflicting a wound on himself. When he heard a knock on the door he groaned. Nicholas walked in.

'Oh, I'm sorry,' Nicholas began. David lay in bed, a sheet up to his chest, one hand over his eyes. 'David, are you all right? I wanted to ask you something.'

David groaned again. 'I'm –' he started. His hand moved from over his eyes to his forehead, where his three middle fingers rested at the top of his nose. His eyes remained shut. Nicholas took a step closer to the bed. He thought David must be hungover.

'Kozak's gone,' Nicholas whispered. He felt ashamed by his own announcement. 'I need you to tell me where he goes. Where he might be,' he blurted.

'Nicholas,' David croaked. He had not really listened, found the effort it required just too much. 'I – I wouldn't bother,' he managed.

Nicholas stared. David looked old this morning. His skin had taken on a sickly colour, his hair looked sparse and dull. Nicholas sat down on the edge of the bed but did not let his weight rest there, barely making a dip in the mattress.

'What do you mean?' he asked. David covered his face with both hands. He had meant to send the boy away, not bring him closer, make him ask more questions. Nicholas looked at the backs of David's hands, where the skin shone and sagged.

'I cannot help,' David murmured. The bird inside him was screeching, dive-bombing, tearing at his organs. Nicholas looked at the man and did not understand. The room was small and stuffy, the bed almost filling it.

'Please,' said Nicholas. He looked at David's neck. The skin hung over tendons and collarbone like rolled-out dough, heavy and powdery. The dip at the bottom of his neck seemed to go so deep that it must somehow penetrate into the space of his chest. Nicholas felt as though a droplet of heavy metal – platinum, lead, mercury perhaps – had been placed at the back of his throat and was slowly making its way down to his stomach. He knew the feeling well and wanted to escape it if he could, to kick himself free from its slick creeping torpor and the coagulated fog which it would inevitably cast over his internal landscape. Along with an anger which seemed to fill every cell in his being he felt a terrible hurt.

'The markets. He goes to markets,' David murmured. Nicholas's jaw dropped open and then shut again.

'I know that,' he said, exasperated with this man. He got up and headed for the door. If he were to say thank you it would issue from his mouth stained with sarcasm. He said nothing and left.

The light was cold that afternoon and a sharp wind blew

from the west, chasing summer out of the capital. Nicholas crossed the road by the Albert Memorial and jogged up its steps, without stopping to glance up at it. Tourists walked through Hyde Park in large groups, cameras hanging, guidebooks in hand. Rollerbladers avoided dogs. Nicholas broke into a run, an almost straight line from south to north. His shoes slipped on the sandy paths, the cold air burnt in his chest. He was shocked by Kozak's betrayal. He was going to Portobello, the most obvious market, the market for tourists. Kozak would not be there, he knew that, but he did not know where else to start.

Just as he was approaching the end of the park he had to slow his pace for a crowd of people who blocked the path: a rollerblader had hit not a dog, but a dog's leash, and was sitting on the ground shouting obscenities at the owner. Nicholas slowed to a walk, panting. Sweat trickled from his armpit down his ribcage and into the cloth of his T-shirt. He had to hurry. Then he glanced off up a path to his right to check for cyclists and stopped on the spot. He breathed hard and stared. He closed his eyes and, between gasps of breath, began to curse.

There, on a bench with his back to him, sat Kozak. Nicholas glared at him, unable to believe what he saw. It was an outline which had been burnt onto his retina: bushy shoulder-length hair, big shoulders, even sitting down it was clear the man was tall. He sat with his arms by his sides on the bench, in his tweed suit. He seemed to be staring straight ahead.

You fuck, Nicholas thought. You leave me this morning and then come and sit in my park, as though nothing has happened? You spend four weeks getting to know someone and then when they turn out to be your son you leg it. Have you any idea? His thoughts collapsed in on themselves. His breathing was still hard from his running. Now his chest

405

shuddered and creaked, like a ship trapped in ice, waiting to be crushed to nothing. He found himself feeling an anger rise to his eyes, felt the sharp release that meant tears. I will not cry, he willed himself. I have done enough. I am too soft.

Nicholas stood and regarded his father. His breathing slowed but his heart continued to pound. He stood less than a hundred yards from the exit he used every morning to get to work. He was only two paths away from the ground where he had slept with Faye and yet he did not feel that he knew this park at all. His surroundings seemed unfamiliar.

Kozak could not have known just how soft Nicholas's heart was. He could not have known the hurt he caused him by leaving the house that morning. He sat on the bench and thought about Bohdan, about his life as Stefan. He knew how Daedalus must have felt when he saw Icarus fall away from him. He thought about Stefan as though he were a character in a book he had read many years ago. He saw Nicholas as a strong, wilful man, full of vigour and courage. Kozak told himself that he was taking no risks whatsoever. In fact he was taking the biggest risk of them all. Somewhere deep inside him, where he would not acknowledge it, he hoped that Nicholas would come and look for him. He willed it, as a gambler might will a horse to win a race: with narrowed eyes and acid in his stomach. He had already seen that Nicholas could turn the other cheek. It was a characteristic which Kozak envied in his son. He did not understand how Nicholas could have been through what he had and still have any mercy in him. Like a child run away from a good home, Kozak was waiting to be found. He was determined, with the patience of a submariner, to wait. He wanted someone to come to him, but as each minute passed it seemed less likely that they would. Perhaps Nicholas had brushed the events aside and was playing his cello?

Nicholas looked at the outline of his father and tried to control his anger. How can you do that? he heard in his head. How can you meet me and then leave me? How can you leave your own child? I will never leave my children, he thought, but the idea of his own offspring served only to increase his sense of isolation. He was single; he could not imagine his children.

A middle-aged woman jogged past him, creases of consternation on her forehead, a black ponytail bouncing behind her. Nicholas watched her feet ahead of him as she ran, rhythmic alternations of trainers in shades of blue. He saw in his head himself following her, pulling himself together, moving on, walking off. He did not want to expose himself to any more pain. My mother walked away from him once too, he thought. I have followed my mother: I practised my cello when she told me to; I understand the liberties I have; I have her silly, vulnerable eyes. She walked away from him once, now I must do the same.

I shall just pretend I have not seen him. He raised a hand to his face and wiped sweat from his chin. His legs trembled. He didn't move. Who are you? Who are you to walk into my life and do this to me? He did not know that when he was thirteen months old, one late summer afternoon, Kozak lay back in a field by the farm and held Nicholas up in the air above him. Nicholas gurgled and smiled, a bubble of saliva rose to his lips and popped, showering Kozak with tiny droplets of spittle. Kozak bent his arms and lowered the baby onto his large chest. Nicholas lay on his round baby stomach, arms bouncing beside him, his pure gaze on Kozak's face. Kozak rested his hand on Nicholas's back. He could feel his own heart beating inside him, slow and steady like the heart of an elephant. Superimposed over his pulse he could feel Nicholas's, a quaver to his minim. A tiny heartbeat, the heartbeat of a cat: weak and fast. Between the two of them they beat time to many dances: a polka came and went between their oscillations, a hopak, a hutsul dance, a mazurka, as their pulses coincided and diverged like a pair of birds in the air.

Nicholas took a deep breath and put his hands on his hips. What he cherished most about Kozak was that he did not fit; he would not fit, Nicholas was sure, anywhere. He seemed impervious to pressures, incorruptible in the face of sidelong glances. Nicholas celebrated in Kozak precisely what Faye had found offensive about him: she was hurt that he did not care for her opinion, Nicholas was thrilled. Even now, on a bench in Hyde Park on a Sunday afternoon Kozak looked out of place.

Nicholas took a step away. He paced around in a small circle, his head bowed. It was a collection of steps that he had developed at work in the supermarket; at the end of each aisle he turned a circle and then continued. His cellist's hands twitched at his sides: he did not know what to do with them. I cannot forgive him for this, Nicholas thought. Now I understand what he meant when he said that life was simpler when it was lived alone.

Nicholas looked down on the ground and noticed that he had no socks on. He frowned. I have a new life to begin, he thought. A breeze blew from the west. Nicholas buttoned up his shirt with graceful fingers and began to walk towards his father.